C000089012

JAMES CORBETT is an author an[...]
all over the world for the BBC, *Gu*[...]
numerous other publications. His no[...]
with the legendary goalkeeper Neville Southall, *The Binman Chronicles*,
named by TalkSport as one of the ten best sports books of all time, and
Faith of our Families, longlisted in the 2018 British Sports Book of the
Year awards. *The Outsiders* is his first novel. He lives and works between
his home in Ireland and his home city of Liverpool.

Praise for *The Outsiders*

'A gripping debut novel with surprising twists that is part love story, part
mystery and part love letter to a city, and also asks profound questions
about the very nature of identity'
Nick Harris, *Mail on Sunday*

'A masterful tangle of the domestic and the epochal, a novel which flows
from decade to decade with Liverpool as both backdrop and beating,
tumultuous core'
Portico Prize judges

'It's fabulous. A great read and a great story, by one of our own'
Sean Styles, BBC Radio Merseyside

'A novel full of intrigue, where the past is weaved with the present,
forms the basis to this superb debut. Liverpool – its history, culture and
atmosphere – shines brightly within the pages. This has leapt into my
list of favourite reads'
Buzz Magazine

'An evocative paean to a city and its people. A fantastically crafted debut'
James Montague, author of *1312: Among the Ultras*

THE
OUTSIDERS

JAMES CORBETT

First published in 2021
by Lightning Books
Imprint of Eye Books Ltd
29A Barrow Street
Much Wenlock
Shropshire
TF13 6EN

www.lightning-books.com

First paperback edition, published in 2022

ISBN: 9781785633041

Cover by Ifan Bates
Typeset in Adobe Jenson Pro

British Library Cataloguing in Publication Data
A catalogue record for this book is available from the British Library.

For Catherine

Prologue: Liverpool, 2021

Paul couldn't find it at first.

This secret garden lay hidden in one of the city's best loved public spaces, amidst the cool shadows cast by the largest Anglican cathedral in the world. He had been here many times, but until a few moments earlier had never known of this little enclave within it.

The cemetery was an oasis in the middle of the city. Gravestones lined its walls, freeing the ancient burial grounds to serve as gardens that existed in a man-made valley between the street above and the cathedral's Gothic magnificence. The sound of children playing in puddles after a recent downpour sang in the humid air.

Yet, in this corner, municipal order gave way to decay and neglect. Nature had taken over. Trees shot up from every free space of dirt they could find, wreaking chaos amidst the memorial stones. One grave-bed was uprooted by a tree, the roots pushing the headstone out of its resting place.

As he wandered deeper into the garden, the path began to get more cluttered as the fighting between trees for soil – and, ultimately, light – grew fiercer. The earth which wasn't taken by the trees was claimed by bracken, fallen branches, dead saplings and browned leaves. All of it lay coated by moss or snared by ivy. Ivy crawled all over the back of one headstone and hung over its front like a wispy fringe.

Paul momentarily lost his balance, tripping on some low railings forged a century or more ago in a vain attempt to protect its crypt from invaders. All ownership had long since been ceded to nature, the inscription washed off its sandstone page by years of wind and rain. The next place along, a headless statue lay on a bed of rotting leaves. She looked peaceful in the brown mulch with her bedfellows: unripe horse chestnuts, a juvenile fern and a couple of snails. An open marble book sat over an accompanying tomb, its original inscription lost under the scrawl of faded graffiti.

In another spot, a clearing, poppies and other wild flowers lived, awoken from their seedlings by the sun which earlier had shone so intensely.

He read the inscriptions, looking for the name imprinted on his consciousness for four decades. Madeleine Reichwald: *Sadly Missed, Lovingly Remembered.* Robert Darwin: *In Memory of My Father, His Daughter Sarah.* Maurice Jones: *Deeply Mourned.* Samuel Cornish. Joseph Bellefied. David Andrews. Hannah Jones. Suzanne Pontremoli. Each one was sadly missed, lovingly remembered, deeply mourned. Each had the briefest epigraph. There were no pebbles left by visiting friends or family adorning the tops of headstones, no flowers. None had died after 1939. It was as if life itself had ended that year.

Then, at last, he saw what he had come for: a small white stone, more recent than the other memorials but nevertheless stained by decades of moss and lichen. The inscription, still bearing gold leaf, was modest for someone who assumed such importance, barely hinting at the many lives she had lived. He had thought of her so often over the years, but in the pursuit of her past had come to consider her almost solely as a foreign being, when this city which they once both called home – where she now rested – had formed such a central part of her existence.

He thought of her fate, of her end and how its mysteries consumed so much of his life. And then he started to cry. Barely suppressed tears at first, and then more sustained weeping. He stood there alone, crying until the rain came.

Part 1: Liverpool, 1981

1

You didn't become a Liverpudlian simply by living there. You could be from the city, but not of it; call it home, but never really belong. Other cities chewed you up then spat you out, but Liverpool was different: it would turn up its nose and shrug you off with an ambivalence so damning that it made it feel as though you had never even fallen under its contemptuous glare. Everybody spoke of the sense of community, but once away from the vicinity of family, friends and neighbours, and out into the wider city, you were nobody. Because of the intra-city apartheid that seemed to rear its head in every loose encounter – the whole *I'm more local than you* swagger – everybody was, in their way, an outsider.

These things kept coming back to Paul as he made the journey from the suburban outlands and into the heart of the city where he was meeting his friends for a night out. In a vapid summer, the chance to see Echo and the Bunnymen at the university was one of the few fixtures in Paul's calendar.

It was early evening and men in suits were disembarking from the Southport train to go home to their wives and children, their squares of garden and the last of the day's sun. Liverpool had broiled again under clear skies and a high sun. Beyond the city the expanse of the Irish Sea lay flat, brown and benevolent, the coastal breeze which usually cooled it on such days conspicuous by its very absence. The air was still and dense.

Liverpool also sweated under the gaze of a hundred television cameras as a media frenzy descended upon the city. Liverpool 8, the inner-city district that incorporated Toxteth, had exploded into violence after local residents took an aggressive stand against police brutality. Overnight it became a latter-day Saigon as journalists filled its streets and ran with the rioters. Buildings burned, vehicles were overturned and set alight, while youths hacked away at the wreckages, creating a makeshift arsenal of bricks and masonry. Social commentators lined up to condemn the moral degradation that bred the violence, while police deflected accusations of brutality by inviting camera crews into local hospitals, where entire wards were handed over to bruised bobbies. One man was dead, hundreds of others injured. Bishops appealed for calm; community leaders claimed the battles were over.

For the rest of the city, however, life carried on as normal. People went to work, women shopped, and children played. Concerned relatives telephoned from afar to check up on family, but in a city of suburbs Toxteth's riots were a TV phenomenon for most people: remote, somewhere else.

With his parents, Paul watched the previous evening's nine o'clock news with a rising sense of bewilderment as the sombre voice of Richard Whitmore spoke over footage of burning buildings: 'Liverpool burns as its inner cities rampage.' As the picture cut to a line of policemen forming across the top of a Victorian street, Paul's father leant over and turned up the volume. The police held plastic riot shields in one hand, while in the other metal batons glistened menacingly. 'One hundred and fifty injured as police battle rioters,' said Whitmore and the picture cut to Margaret Thatcher climbing from a ministerial Jaguar and up the steps of 10 Downing Street. The Prime Minister convenes an emergency meeting of the cabinet as tensions rise and police anticipate more trouble this evening.'

'It's the darkies,' Paul's father pronounced. 'On the rampage because one of their lot got pulled over by the police.'

Paul winced at his father's easy distillation of the report. His mother walked urgently towards the netted curtains and looked out anxiously onto their darkened cul-de-sac. There was a sudden nervousness about her, as if a mob might also come rampaging down their little street several miles away.

But the riots, although just eight miles away, may as well have existed on another planet.

∽

'Have you ever heard of Nadezhda Semilinski?' Paul's best friend Christopher had asked him three weeks earlier. It was late, and they were sat out in the sand dunes after a night drinking at their local pub, The Swan. They were accompanied by a half-bottle of whisky, which they passed between themselves, swigging the burning liquid as marram grass flicked in their ears and sand filled their shoes.

'No, I don't think so. Why?'

'She's a poet. She was big in the Sixties and won all sorts of awards. She's local, like.'

'She doesn't sound very local.'

'I mean she lives in the city. I think she was a Jewish immigrant from after the war.'

He changed the subject and they started talking about football. It was close season, a time of wheeler-dealing and expectation.

Previous disappointments palled in the hope that new signings and fresh momentum made for a successful new campaign. To them, football and all its possibilities offered unending topics for conversation, but by the time the whisky bottle had less than an inch of liquid in its bottom, the boys, drunk and tired, had run out of talk. They lay in the sand, their eyes glazed with fatigue, silently looking up at the stars.

Christopher was a handsome green-eyed boy; his black hair was matted with Brylcreem and brushed artfully into a quiff that was incongruous to any prevailing fashion, but which he somehow managed to pull off. He possessed a silent charisma, an intensity that gave him presence among his suburban friends. He and Paul had been friends, best friends, for as long as either could remember. There was a bond between them that made each to the other like the brother they had never had. But like all brothers they were at once friends and adversaries, and this unspoken rivalry, which seemed to heighten as they grew older, seeped beneath their kinship.

Paul knew Christopher had no interest in poetry, no interest in anything, really; but sometimes he dropped the name of an avant-garde or cult figure to create the impression that he was cultured, that he knew more than he actually did.

Christopher took a swig from the whisky bottle. 'Here, you finish this,' he said, passing the dregs to Paul. He took a mouthful and looked up at the stars, the whisky burning his throat. After a minute's silence, Christopher spoke. 'You know I mentioned the poet,' he said, 'There was a reason.' He sat up. 'I pulled her daughter earlier today, at the beach.'

'Yeah, right.'

'What's it to you?' he said, sullenly. 'You've never even heard of this esteemed poet anyway.' He was quite drunk now, slurring 'esteemed' so that he sounded as if he were mocking the poet's credentials.

His womanising was at once a self-created myth and a reality. Amongst a circle of friends that coveted girls, but outside school rarely came into contact with them, no one quite knew how to unpick the truth from his idle boasting. Christopher claimed to have lost his virginity when he was thirteen, though no one believed him. And yet for years he was seen again and again with one or other of his twin sister Helen's friends on his arm before he cast them away, as though it were his inviolable duty to work his way through them all. Rarely did he bring his two worlds into contact, friends and girlfriends, as though one might test the limits of the other. At the same time he used this purported prowess as a stick to beat his other friends, particularly Paul. Nothing was more wounding to a teenager than to be tarred with the truth: *you're a virgin.*

But Paul had learned not to rise to him, and so merely shrugged his shoulders.

'It's true,' said Christopher. 'I got off with her and I'm seeing her again tomorrow.'

It was nearly one am now, and as they ambled drunkenly home the streets were entirely empty. 'She's called Julia,' Christopher told him, slurring her name. He was so drunk now that Paul knew he was incapable of lying coherently. 'She's dark and pretty – like me!' Paul joined him in laughing at his own joke. 'She's from out Aigburth way. And she's a Jew, man! She's a Jew!' This seemed an impossibly exotic notion, for neither knew any Jews. Indeed they knew very few non-Catholics whatsoever. 'She's lovely, Paul!' he said. 'Very lovely indeed!' And then he added caustically, 'When are you going to get a lovely girl, Paul?'

But Paul was too tired and drunk to respond to his taunt, or even be upset by it. He was intrigued by this new girl: he knew nobody like that. Everyone in his world was Catholic and they were the sons of doctors, social workers, teachers, taxi drivers, civil servants, or, like him, a tax inspector. If there was foreign blood in their veins it was Irish or Welsh. They were workers, not creators or artists. He had never met anybody who had published a word. For Paul, such people existed only on the pages of newspapers, books or on film. To be a writer was something exotic, alluring and entirely foreign.

Indeed this notion of a Jewish poet's daughter would not leave his head. Even when he entered his home, climbed the stairs, and sat on the edge of his bed, emptying sand from the inside of his shoes, the poet's name sang in his drunken mind:

Nadezhda Semilinski, Nadezhda Semilinski.

ᔐ

In snatched conversations over the next few weeks, in between Christopher's forays 'shagging around the city', his friend gave updates on his new girlfriend.

'She's different to all the rest,' he said, lowering his voice and smiling. 'There's something about her; she's smart and sensual and worldly. She's something else. She's not just easy. Quite the opposite. I get the sense that she's always testing me, seeing what I'm like.'

'But she still puts out only a few days after meeting you.'

Christopher gave him a delighted smile and shrugged his shoulders. 'Jewish girls, eh?'

Had he met her mother yet, the poet?

Christopher lit another cigarette and blew out a small cloud of smoke. He shook his head. 'It's very strange,' he said. 'They live in this huge dilapidated house, but she stayed in her room the whole time. "Her rooms" is how Julia describes them, like they're a separate part of the house. It's a bit weird. She's spoken about in the past tense, as if she's dead.'

'I'd never even heard about her before last week,' Paul admitted.

'Nor had I,' Christopher said. 'I think she was quite famous. Faber published her – I saw her books.' He pulled himself even nearer to Paul and said in a low, conspiratorial tone, 'I think there was some sort of great scandal, some sort of disgrace that turned her into a recluse.'

§

A few days later, Paul was introduced to the new girlfriend. They gathered in the Caernarfon Castle, a city centre pub that was dark and cool and smoky.

Like Liverpool itself, the pub seemed to carry equal measures of faded elegance and seediness. It had ornate tiled floors, and an intricately carved balustrade around the top of the mirrored bar, showcasing the landlord's collection of Dinky cars. A barman arranged ashtrays on the mahogany counter. Sitting around it, old men idled on their own, reading copies of the *Liverpool Echo* and drinking mild. It was an eccentric place: a mix of office workers, male pensioners waiting for their wives to finish shopping, a couple of purple-faced ex-dockers stuck to the bar as permanently as the brass rail, and curious onlookers like himself, hopelessly out of place.

He ordered a pint of bitter and sat at an empty table, overlooking the pub. In the pit of his stomach there was a hint of nervousness, as if he were about to be examined or judged.

And then, quite abruptly, the poet's daughter was sat opposite him, shaking his hand, telling him how pleased she was to meet him. She was rakishly thin and as tall as him, taller than Christopher by several inches, which surprised Paul. Her long black hair curled around in a demi-fringe and flicked on her white, flawless face. Her cheeks arced elegantly over high, strong bones and she had intent brown eyes. It was a strange face, certainly beautiful, but in a way that was different to other girls he'd met – although he couldn't quite decide why. Maybe it was because she looked like she belonged on a film set and not some backstreet Liverpool pub. She seemed to exude a confidence that came with knowing she was beautiful.

'It's a proper old man's pub, isn't it?' she said, gesturing around. Christopher was at the bar, ordering drinks. She spoke in an oddly inflected accent that hinted only slightly that she was of the city. 'My mother calls these sort of fellas "twerlys".'

'Twerlys?'

'As in the sort of blokes that badger bus inspectors: "Am I too early to use my bus pass?"'

Paul was momentarily perplexed, then laughed and the unease lifted. She grinned back.

She was a foundation art student, a contemporary of Christopher's twin, Helen. She was funny and vivacious and talked of art, cinema and music as easily and knowledgeably as his own friends talked about their twin passions of football and beer. Christopher leered all over her, pawing at her like a middle-aged man with a much younger mistress. She paid scant attention to her boyfriend, talking intently to Paul, seeming to revel in anybody's company other than her boyfriend's. Paul had half-expected a loose girl who exuded sexual charisma, but there was no hint of this. They looked an odd couple and he wondered what she could possibly see in his friend.

'I believe you have something of an artistic heritage,' Paul said, ignoring his friend.

Julia looked at him, momentarily confused before realising what he meant. 'Oh Mother, of course. Yes, she's a poet. She had a few collections published in the Fifties, Sixties and early Seventies.'

She drifted off, as if it were just another job, like a teacher or a nurse.

'She was quite famous,' he said.

Julia frowned at him. 'Do you know poetry?' she snapped. 'I mean, understand the world of poets.' He shook his head. 'No, why should you, I suppose?' For a second she spoke in a withering way, as if to imply: *How could you? You're just a suburban boy, a bland tax inspector's son.* But then she smiled and her eyes sparkled. 'She was renowned, I suppose, in that little world. But I think that's probably part of her past now.'

Straight away he wanted to know more: Why was it part of her past? Why was Julia so defensive? But her sharp manner deterred him. He had no wish to embarrass her by dragging out uncomfortable truths.

But then her mood shifted again and she began talking about a play put on by one of her friends in the studio space above the Playhouse Theatre and an art exhibition a student collective were hosting in an old warehouse by the river. Would Paul like to come along and join them? He could sense Christopher's rising irritation. 'Absolutely,' Paul replied.

'Listen,' Christopher said in a lowered voice, when she went to buy her round of drinks from the bar. 'After these drinks, can you do us a favour?' He arced his eyes over to the door, but Paul didn't take the hint. 'I'm hoping for a bit of hokey-pokey later, y'know.' Paul nodded, but Christopher continued, his voice suddenly sharp. 'If you could stop playing gooseberry, I'd appreciate it.'

Paul's face reddened at his friend's belittlement.

When she returned a certain awkwardness took hold. Paul and Christopher had run out of things to say, while Julia sat chain-smoking, watching the two friends and their increasingly stilted talk. But for all of Christopher's desire to get rid of him, Paul felt it was not he who impeded the conversation, but Christopher.

Through his adolescence, Christopher defined himself by his elusiveness. The notion *No one knows me*, his sense of being a wraith amongst his suburban friends, was carefully cultivated to make him attractive. But the realisation had begun to grow on Paul that this merely masked Christopher's vacuity, that he really stood for nothing and were he not so evanescent the world would see him for what he was: dull, self-serving, unpleasant.

§

Christopher's bohemian girlfriend would not leave Paul's mind. It was more what she represented: unconventional, foreign, avant-garde and her promise to shred the tedium of a never-ending summer.

'When we finished the exams, I thought there's so many things I want to do, but haven't been able to do because of studying and revising and being stuck at school,' said Fat Sam, as they sat morosely in The Swan on Friday. He was round-bellied and jowly, his red cheeks the same colour as his hair. With his plump frame and perpetual broad smile, he gave the impression of a fat, jolly old man – a butcher, or a pub landlord, perhaps. 'Well, now I'm free, I'm just bored. Bored, bored, plain bored.'

Paul waited for the call to join her at the art exhibition she had spoken of, or maybe the play, but it never came. And why would it? She was his best friend's girlfriend. He had no claim on her other than a brief meeting. But still she would not leave his thoughts, Julia and her elusive and famous mother, Nadezhda Semilinski.

Returning from a visit to the city centre a few days later, Paul entered Moorfields station, a modern palace of flickering strip lights and ugly, brown plastic panels. It smelt of piss, and as you entered Liverpool's subterranean realm you were confronted by damp and the aura of disrepair. A few years ago, when they dug the station out of the city's sandstone foundations, it was a vision of the future, but already it felt dated and decrepit.

Paul showed his ticket to a disinterested inspector and walked along the causeway that led to the escalators and platforms.

As the escalator took him down into the bowels of the city he was lost in his thoughts, amusing himself with recollections of his friends' oddities. He glanced down and through the gloom, ascending from the platform on the opposite escalator, was Julia; tall, striking, her china-white skin luminous in the dingy surroundings.

Seconds passed, not even seconds – hundredths of seconds. She glanced in Paul's direction, not at him, but upwards, to the light and the city. He opened his mouth to call her name, but as they passed he saw it was not Julia at all, but some other girl, just like her, less poised, a little taller, more awkward, perhaps, but beautiful too.

Then the escalator reached the platform and Paul, in a trance, looked back up. But the girl was already lost to the city.

∽

The riots started as a rumour. Liverpool was a city of chit-chat and tittle-tattle, but the stories of trouble – burned cars, looted shops, hundreds of riot police – seemed to spread from every direction. Phones rang in the early morning, swapping stories or checking rumours out, while local radio stations tried to make sense of a chaos of arson and burning. Dispatched to buy the *Liverpool Echo* at lunchtime, Paul met Sam's father, a taxi driver, who was at once here, there and everywhere; a wandering set of eyes who seemed to know what was happening in every part of the city.

'The trouble in L8 last night was worse than what they're saying, y'know,' he told Paul as they queued to pass over their change. L8 was the local term given to Toxteth, a once grand Victorian inner suburb, that, through years of neglect, had become something of a ghetto on the city centre's fringes. For Paul its name was a byword for danger and degeneration. You passed through it, but no one from his part of the city right-mindedly went there otherwise. 'A row of shops and buildings were burned down and all the roads were closed this morning.'

'It's normally like that, isn't it?' Paul asked, flippantly.

'It was pretty bad,' he said.

But just how bad it was he didn't fully realise, until he sat watching Richard Whitmore narrate the nine o'clock news with his parents that evening.

'More than a hundred white and coloured youths fought a pitched battle with police, some were as young as twelve, the oldest no more than twenty. It lasted more than eight hours and at the end of it Merseyside's chief constable said it was a planned attack. "We were set up," he said.

'The worst of the rioting came just after dawn when police faced a hail of stones, iron bars and petrol bombs. The missiles were hurled from barricades of burning and upturned vehicles.'

The screen cut from a line of riot police to firefighters and police officers stepped down from duty, resting on a kerb as smoke billowed from the near distance. Then a burning building, a looted shop, police and firemen tending to a stricken officer. All of the footage originated from behind lines of dome-helmeted policemen, lending the inescapable impression that the authorities were under siege.

'It began in Upper Parliament Street, one of the main roads out of the city centre, and ammunition was all around in derelict sites and empty houses. At daylight, police began a series of charges to break up the gangs massed in front of them. But as the rioters fell back they set fire to more buildings and sporadic looting that went on overnight was now widespread. Shop after shop was plundered and goods scattered around as the youths fled. And still the bricks, stones and lumps of iron were thrown and worst of all the petrol bombs.'

There was a pause for dramatic effect as footage cut to a fusillade of poorly aimed Molotov cocktails.

'And against all this riot shields and visors were not enough. At least seventy policemen were injured and twelve are in hospital tonight. Most are suffering from head injuries.'

There was an interview with a policeman in a hospital bed, his face swollen by bruising. They watched firemen extinguish a car rammed into a tree and left abandoned. Pensioners were shown being carted from their homes in wheelchairs.

'The trouble started about midnight when gangs of black youths began stoning cars in the streets. One owner said his windscreen was smashed and he was dragged from the car at gunpoint. Police had been standing by for trouble since Friday night when two officers were attacked when they tried to arrest a motorcyclist. But the rioters in Toxteth were well prepared for their battle with police. They carried with them a range of weapons including iron railings, chisels, clubs and sledgehammers.'

The makeshift arsenal was displayed before a solemn-faced senior police officer, who issued his own condemnation against the hooligans. At the end an unnamed black community leader was given his say.

'What happened last night was just the eruption, if you like. We've been saying for a long, long time now that something has got to be done in terms of jobs, in terms of economic future, in terms of giving the black community some future in society.'

Twenty-four hours later Paul's mother implored him not to go out to the Bunnymen gig, terrified that he would meet trouble, but Paul was insistent that he would be fine. 'It's a ghetto, Mum. You don't go in, but they can't come out.'

Only later did he appreciate that he spoke of the rioters as if they were foreign bandits, rather than sons and daughters of his own city.

∽

Paul had seen Echo and the Bunnymen many times before: at the Palace ballrooms and the Royal Court; at Eric's, before they closed it down. The band were obscure, or mostly unknown then, supported by legions of über-cool and in-the-know. Now they had just completed a triumphant American tour and entered the mainstream. The Bunnymen's homecoming was a one-off, a celebration with their own of their new-found recognition and fame.

The friends convened at the Grapes, an old-fashioned pub with a narrow smoky parlour, on Renshaw Street. The pub was full of activity: men in suits getting gently drunk after a day in the office; red-faced workmen rehydrating on weak warm beer; and others, students, the young, the ineffably cool starting out on a night out, many also destined for the university. Sam took charge of ordering and passed pint glasses over heads to his friends, who had formed a circle in a corner. After a few minutes Julia joined them, pushing her way through the throng. Paul introduced her to Bulsara and Sam.

'Chris has gone to find a tout,' she explained.

'We have tickets.'

'We need another one – I brought my sister.'

'I didn't know you had a sister.'

She smiled at his surprise. 'Just the one,' she said. 'Sarah. No brothers or any other shocks for you.' She peered around the room. 'I wonder where she is, actually.'

They talked about the riots; it was all anybody was talking about, and Paul grimly recalled his father's simplification of the causes. 'My Dad invoked Enoch Powell,' said Bulsara, shaking his head, and Paul started to attack the lazy stereotyping.

He became lost in his own monologue, and for a few seconds did not notice the arrival of Sarah, who stood beside them.

'Hello,' she said deliciously as he paused, recognising her presence. 'Don't let me stop you. I'm intrigued.'

It was the girl he had seen days earlier on the escalator, at the train station. Like her sister she had shiny black hair that tumbled upon narrow shoulders, luminous white skin, hazel eyes and thin lips that broke readily into a grin – at once hinting at an amusement or casual mocking. But she was tall, taller than her sister, and it brought a clumsiness to her demeanour. As she spoke, her head loped downwards, as if she were ducking under a low doorway. She wore brown jeans and a man's T-shirt, black with a Manhattan skyscraper on the front. There was frailty about her too, which Paul couldn't immediately get a handle on. Maybe it was her soft, slightly dopey voice that sounded as if she had just woken. Julia, Paul found attractive; but he felt his skin tingle with a different kind of ardour as he looked upon Sarah.

'This is my sister,' said Julia, putting her arm around her shoulder and pulling her close. 'Sarah, this is my friend, Paul.'

She offered him her hand, which he took in his. 'Very pleased to meet you,' he said, shaking it. Her fingers were long, her skin cool.

'Paul was just telling me about the riots,' said Julia. Then she whispered in a voice loud enough for him to hear: 'He's so clever, Sarah. He's the chap who's heading off for Cambridge.'

They talked about the concert, gigs they'd seen, those they wanted to. 'I've not been to that many,' Sarah confessed.

'It's not such a cool thing to do when your mum's there,' Julia explained.

Sam spluttered on his beer. 'You mean we might see yer ma' later?'

'She goes through phases,' Sarah explained. 'And there was her punk phase. I think it fascinated and appalled her. That's why she went.'

'She's friends with Roger Eagle too,' Julia added.

'No way!' said Paul. Eagle was a local legend, one of the proprietors of Eric's, the lamented home of the city's music scene. Clad in leather, and with a thick moustache dripping from his lip, he might have passed for Freddie Mercury. Everyone in the city knew who he was and he knew everyone that mattered. His role in the ascendancy of a score of local bands was already ingrained in the lore of Liverpool's music scene.

'Why not?' Julia replied, icily, suddenly affronted that he questioned the veracity of her claim. Remembering the other Nadezhda; Nadezhda the poet, the public figure, Paul simply shrugged his shoulders. 'Anyway,' she continued snappily. 'That was her thing for a while. It's not now.'

Sarah was clutching a large, bronze-coloured ten-pound note. 'Can I get some drinks for people?' she asked. There was a nervousness in her voice and suddenly she seemed much younger, less urbane than her sister – even though they were separated by scarcely a year in age. The others gave their orders and as she made for the bar she whispered something to her sister to which Julia nodded. Paul watched them, guessing that she was unsure about something, that maybe she had never ordered a round of drinks before. After a minute he followed her across the parlour.

'I thought I'd help you with those,' he said, touching the small of her back.

'Thanks,' she said. It was busy around the bar, all beer breath and anticipation. Most of the workers were gone home now and the younger crowd had taken over. The atmosphere was good humoured and lively, far removed from the epicedian prophesies of the men on television, who proclaimed the city to be doomed and in the thrall of moral degradation.

'I didn't meant to doubt you before,' he said, apologising clumsily. 'I mean about your mum. She just doesn't seem to be the type to be moshing and all that.'

Sarah laughed. 'It was one of her fads, but she's less reckless these days.' She looked to the floor, then glancing up, smiled. 'Most of the time, anyway.'

∽

Outside Mountford Hall was a scrum of the ticketless and hopeful, vying for a way in. Shaven-headed men sold bootlegged T-shirts and posters from suitcases, while others hissed the stock phrase of the local tout: 'Any spares mate?'

Inside it was hectic and sweltering, their feet stuck to spilt beer caramelised on the floor. On stage, roadies strummed guitars and patted microphones, carrying out the final parts of their sound check. Paul weaved his way to the front of the bar, re-emerging with five bottles of Newcastle Brown Ale.

The support band were all on stage now and announced themselves to the venue. No one paid much attention and most of the audience stood at the back of the hall, talking amongst themselves and drinking. Streams of people continued to enter and brows and upper lips prickled with sweat as the humidity neared saturation point.

When the first act finished they started to make their way towards the stage, meandering through the close-knit throng to gain a better view when the main event started. They were still fifteen feet from the stage, the crowd nine or ten thick, when Paul felt the back of his shirt go cold and wet. He turned and found himself facing a short man with a skinhead, his face bitter and nasty.

'What you doing, knobhead?' he snarled. 'You spilt me drink.'

'I never touched your drink,' Paul replied coolly.

'What you say, prick?' The skinhead spat the words out at him. He was all bone and gristle, his eyes narrow expressionless slits. Paul felt a horrible anxiety rise within him. He had had fights before, at school, but he was no scrapper; no match for a wizened hard nut. He glanced around: Christopher had meandered on oblivious to the rising confrontation, but Sarah and Julia were there, and Sam too.

'You being funny? Yer fuckin' wool.'

Already it had come to this: a test of local credentials. A 'wool' referenced someone from outside the confines of Liverpool's inner city; some extended it to the suburbs or the Wirral; and to others it referred to those properly out of town, like Wigan and Warrington, where the locals spoke differently and watched rugby league instead of football. It was all a big game that Paul sometimes, jokingly, played with cousins from Southport and Preston. But the closer you got to the heart of the city the more it meant. Here it was a form of inverted snobbery, a defence mechanism that meant, *I'm more Scouse than you. You don't belong here. You're nothing.*

'I'm no wool and I didn't spill your drink,' Paul answered. He made to move past, but the skinhead interposed himself between Paul and the path he sought to take.

At this point Sam leant forward and with one of his plump pink hands shoved the skinhead forcefully in the chest and barked: 'He said he never spilt your drink, now fuck off or I'll get me crew onto you.'

The skinhead stepped back and looked up at Sam towering over him. One hand clasped onto his half-empty beer glass, the other was lodged inside his trousers.

Suddenly realising he was outnumbered, his voice assumed a defensive whine: 'Don't you touch me again. I got a blade down here.'

'No you don't,' Sam guffawed, and with his laugh the tension seemed to melt away. 'You've got your hand down your pants.'

'I'll fuckin' stab you.'

'Go on then,' Sam goaded. 'But you need to do something, 'cos if you keep playing with yourself like that you'll go blind.'

'I'm warning you,' the skinhead stammered, trying to save face. Then he was gone, scurrying through the crowds like a rat in a tunnel and disappeared into the milieu.

'Thanks for that,' whispered Paul as they carried on their way. Sam just smiled.

When they reached Christopher, standing at the front barrier on his own, he was frowning, wondering where they had been.

'Some little scrote kicked off on Paul,' said Sam, then pointedly: 'You'd already flounced off to the front.'

'He said Paul had spilt his drink,' said Julia.

'He said he had a knife,' Sarah added.

'He had his hands down his pants,' Paul said, dismissively. Moments earlier he was threatened, scared; ordinarily he would have left there and then, silently and ashamed. But in the presence of the girls he felt emboldened, a bravura rising.

The lights dimmed and a hush of anticipation filled the hall. Then the raucous opening notes of 'Heaven up Here' sounded and shouts and cheers erupted as light filled the stage to reveal the four band members. The crowd surged forward, pushing towards the front, and as the band reached the chorus it rocked up and down as one throbbing, ecstatic mass. They danced and cheered and swayed and waved, sweat pouring off revellers as they partied to a state of intoxication. Fainting girls were passed over heads, like pints in a pub, to the front and over barriers and safety, while Ian McCulloch, the Bunnymen's singer, doused revellers with bottled water. Glasses and bottles occasionally came flying from the back of the auditorium, obliterating on some unfortunate's head or shoulder.

The display of light and passion and music continued for ninety minutes. Then, as triumphantly as it had started, so the concert ended. The stage darkened to black and McCulloch shouted from the gloom to a chorus of cheers: 'It's great to be back! We love yers Liverpool!'

When they got outside, their clothes were stuck to their sweaty bodies and the girls' long hair was macerated across their brows. Even on this balmy evening, compared to the broiling, airless auditorium it seemed liberatingly cool.

'That was boss,' said Sam. 'Best one yet.'

'Did you enjoy it?' Paul asked the girls.

'It was brilliant, Paul!' said Sarah, beaming at him. Her expression was enthusiastic or exultant, and possibly eager to please. She was certainly beautiful, but in an unconventional way. Every time Paul looked at her he seemed to unpick another pigment of her loveliness. And every time he did, he felt a little more enraptured by her.

2

They headed to Le Bateau, a nightclub wedged into a row of old warehouses back down towards the waterfront, by the long-disused Victorian docks. Its exterior was dingy and unprepossessing, but once inside they were assailed by sweet French pop melodies and the hum of marijuana. In a dim corner, lit only by the sparkle of a glitter ball and the distant flicker of disco lights, Paul commandeered an old sofa and sat drinking beer as his friends took turns on the dancefloor.

'I'm not a dancer,' he laughed when Sarah asked him to step up and join them. Instead she took a seat next to him and they talked about their evening, music, books, school, friends – everything. She appeared to glow in front of him, her loveliness growing as the night wore old. 'Did Julia tell you we're having a party?' she asked. This was news to Paul. How had he not come to hear about it? Had he been excluded?

'No, she didn't,' he replied. 'Maybe I'll dance with you then.' Then in a calculated show of self-deprecation, he added: 'If, of course, I'm invited.'

She laughed. 'Of course you are!' She touched his leg, barely for a moment, an unconscious, spontaneous act to reassure him, but which left him prickling with desire.

When they left the club the city was quiet and sultry, but there were hints of unrest elsewhere. Taxis drove off empty when they said they wanted to go south to the girls' home, and so they took the decision to walk them the five miles back.

'I want to see this war zone for myself anyway,' said Sam.

At Upper Parliament Street they saw the first signs of trouble. Two police cars, their lights flashing silently, were parked across the road, blocking it to other vehicles. A policeman was standing against one of the cars and as they made to walk past he stopped them and asked where they were going.

'Grassendale?' he repeated when Sarah told him. 'Well you can't come this way.'

'Why not?' Sam asked.

The policeman smiled darkly and gestured behind with his thumb. 'World War Three has just broken out down the road again,' he said.

'It looks okay to me,' said Sam.

'Looks can be deceiving,' replied the policeman. He was an unremarkable man, in his forties, of medium height and medium build with a pasty face; indeed, everything about him hinted at mediocrity, of being indistinguishable from a litany of other beat cops. But there was a lingering petulance in his manner.

'I don't see any reason why we can't go that way,' said Paul. 'Why don't you ask your boss in there?' He gestured to another officer, an older man, napping in the front seat of the panda car.

'He's asleep, isn't he?' replied the policeman sullenly.

Paul slapped his hand on the roof of the car and the other officer woke with a start. 'Oi,' cried his colleague. 'I could have you for that.'

The other policeman rubbed his face, momentarily confused,

then wound his window down. 'What's going on, Bob?' he asked.

'These kids want to get to south Liverpool,' he answered. 'They're being a nuisance, to be honest.'

The older policeman was slack-jawed and fat, his hair lank and thick with grease. He peered out from the darkened car, regarding the five friends with beady eyes. 'The niggers have gone to bed, haven't they? They'll be all right.'

'He said you can go on,' said the other policeman with a shrug. But Julia stepped forward, her face reddened with anger.

'What did you just say?' she said, stammering angrily into the car.

The fat policeman turned to her and said nonchalantly, 'I said the niggers have gone to bed, so you'll be all right. Now run along home, love, 'cos it's well past your bedtime.'

'Come on, Jules,' said Christopher, pulling her arm. But she stood firm.

'What's your number?' she said. 'I'm reporting you for racism.'

'Who you going to report me to, love?' he replied. 'The chief constable?'

'Yes,' she replied firmly, and neither he nor the other policeman could suppress their smirks.

'Well I've got news for you, love,' he said. 'I *am* the chief constable.' With his colleague he burst into peals of laughter, a cruel hectoring laugh that echoed in their ears as Christopher pulled his girlfriend away from the policemen and along Upper Parliament Street.

Julia spat threats as they walked away, and her initial rage had scarcely subsided when they saw the first hints of earlier street battles. Strewn across the centre of the derelict street was a debris of broken glass and scattered masonry. A single, upturned boot lay in perfect symmetry to the road markings. Ahead of them was a solitary parked car, a blue-grey Talbot, its windows smashed in. Two burned-out shopfronts, fresh plywood nailed over their windows, stood as evidence of previous days' battles.

They walked on the road as if the last people on earth, in silence for there was nothing to say. No one was around and the streets stood still and empty. A dog barked from a decrepit Georgian terrace that was no more than a hovel, its grandeur a long forgotten memory. Then, from the distance, came the blue flashing lights of a police van, which slowed as it neared and, as it passed, from within it came the piercing glare of a policeman. Otherwise they were uninterrupted by humanity.

As they cut due south, down Kingsley Road, the smell of smoke lingered in the air and the rubble on the street began to increase in volume. Where once there was a scattering of debris, now there were piles of rocks, shards of glass, bits of corrugated iron and wooden stacking pallets. They saw a burned-out car, then another and another. At the mouth of one side street was a medley of old vehicle carcasses, still smouldering, the carbonised remains fused into a barricade.

Another police patrol passed and a curtain flickered. A middle-aged man, black faced and broad nosed, stood watching, unsmiling as they passed, then the curtain flickered again and there was darkness. The tension in the air was palpable. When they spoke, they did so in whispers. Paul was sure they were being watched.

Then Sam cursed under his breath and they looked up. Fifty yards in the distance was the cause of the smoke: a row of shops – the remnants of a newsagents, a takeaway, a corner shop and a bookmakers – charred and smoking, the water used to extinguish the inferno dripping from its blackened remains. As they passed they saw the intensity of the rage that precipitated its destruction:

the pavement was littered with broken glass and just within the burned-out shop was some of the rioter's arsenal: a steel beer barrel; a shopping trolley; pieces of fencing; a car tyre.

They hurried on. Although the place was desolate, there seemed to be danger in the air, an unspoken, silent threat.

They turned onto Devonshire Road, along the northern fringes of Princes Park. Everything around them was still, framed in the orange street light like a flashlit photograph. Slumbered in the distance by a park bench was a vagrant, somehow shivering for warmth on this balmy evening. Christopher glowered with distaste. But as they got closer they saw that it was a boy, perhaps three or four years younger than them, his body shaking with tears. Against his head he held a rag and blood seeped through from his black skin.

The boy coughed, and with tears in his voice said, 'It was the pigs, man, it was the fuckin' bizzies.'

'What police? Where've you come from?' Sam knelt down beside him and got the boy to lift the rag from his head. It was a balled-up jumper and wet with blood. The left side of his temple was split open down to his eyelid. Sam recoiled when he saw the depth of the wound. 'Shit. You need to get to hospital, lad.'

'I can't,' he cried. 'I can't. The bizzies, man. They'll fuckin' kill me.' His accent was much thicker than their gentle inflections.

'What's your name?' Paul asked. 'What happened to you?'

He looked at them uncertainly. 'I'm not saying, lad. The bizzies, man.'

'We'll help you,' said Christopher, kneeling down too. 'Don't worry about the police. We won't grass.' He put his hand on the boy's shoulder and, after a moment, it seemed to calm him down.

'We'd gone along 'cos it was all kickin' off, but we just wanted to see for ourselves,' he said. 'We never wanted no trouble,' he told them. Nothing much had happened all afternoon, but when night came things changed. 'It was dead hot and boring till then. Then these lads, proper bad lads like, started booting this car. They were jumpin' up and down on it, kickin' the windows, then they set it on fire, then boom! The whole thing went up. It was boss.'

He was animated now, gesturing with his hands, forgetting about the scar on the front of his head as he gesticulated and recalled what had happened that day. He described how police vans came, but a barricade of burning cars and bins were put across the top of the road. 'They just stood watching us for ages, like. And these lads were goin' proper bonkers, just wreckin' everything – cars, houses, the lot. They started throwing bricks at the police, then petrol bombs. The police regrouped and brought in reinforcements. Then it all went mental. They fired this bomb thing at us and no one could see or breathe. It was choking us.' He described how the police came in with their sticks, storming past the smouldering barricades and swinging their batons and shields like centurions sacking an enemy encampment. 'I couldn't see nothin' 'cos of the gas, then BANG, something hit me. It just knocked the fuckin' air out of me. I couldn't see. I couldn't breathe. Me head was wreckin', but all I could think about was where's me brother and where's the fuckin' pigs. So I fuckin' legged it as fast I could, which wasn't very fast, and when I saw the park I hid here. I thought I'd be able to get home, but I dunno where I am now, like.' He dabbed his head with his hand again and let out a sob.

In the distance they could hear a siren, and the boy staggered to his feet.

'The fuckin' bizzies are coming for me. They're fascists, man. They done this to me just 'cos I'm black.' The siren got louder. 'I gotta go.' He started limping pathetically towards the bushes. Sam made to follow him, but the boy cried, 'Leave me alone! I gotta go!

I gotta go!' He pushed his way into the bushes and they could hear the crack of undergrowth. Sam walked back to the road holding up his hands in defeat, as if to say *what can I do?*

'We can't leave him!' Julia shouted.

'What can we do?' said Christopher sharply. 'I'm not traipsing around some park looking for him when he doesn't want our help anyway.'

'I don't believe you.' Her voice filled with irritation and disgust. 'Hello! HELLO!' But there was no reply, not even the shuffle of undergrowth and leaves.

They left the boy and carried on their way. When they reached Aigburth Road, the main thoroughfare that passed through the south of the city, normality started to return to the streets. There were no battle scars, no remains or debris of discarded missiles. Traffic passed with the usual intermittence of the early morning.

When a taxi approached from the distance, Paul beckoned it.

'Any chance you'll take us to the north side of the city?' he asked, more in hope than expectation.

'Yeah, why not?' said the driver. 'The police are knobheads, aren't they? Fuck 'em. Get in, we'll find a way through.'

They dropped the girls off at their cavernous old villa, then went back on themselves, along Aigburth Road, then through the Dingle, a panoply of sloped terraced streets running downhill towards the riverside. The driver searched for a viable route along the old backstreets and suddenly they were on Wapping, the thoroughfare that divided the centre from the old disused docks. The driver picked up speed and they raced past the Three Graces and along the potholed dock road, rattling around the back of the old cab.

Paul closed his eyes, a sudden fatigue and confusion of feelings overpowering him. Liverpool left him perplexed. He loved the vibrancy of its people, its culture of music, drink and football, but other things left him cold. He feared its insidious side: the sudden, unexpected dangers; the random, often motiveless violence; the disrepair and anarchy.

He was tired, for it was late and the end of a long, boozy evening. But he felt alive too; excited and beguiled by these strange and beautiful girls. He wanted to know everything about them. Above all, he wanted Sarah.

There was also a certain lingering fear that this elation would be short-lived. Results day, the end of summer, university all neared – would it all end there? He opened his eyes again and watched the passing warehouses, the dockers' pubs and Catholic churches, the heaps of old rubbish that faded into a blur as the taxi roared northwards. A sudden clarity washed over his mind. There was no confusion when he thought about it, just an unexpected, overwhelming joy.

3

On Tuesday Paul returned into Liverpool, crossing the tatty shopping district and making his way past the imposing neo-Grecian esplanade of St George's Hall and into the Picton Room of the city's Central Library. It was a hot day, but the reading room was cool and airy. He had with him his university reading list, a long and seemingly impenetrable inventory ordered alphabetically so that he was unsure at which point he should start. There were a few others like him; serious-looking adolescents seeking a head start when they went to university. At one desk a tramp idled, his fingernails thick with dirt. At another a man of around fifty, bespectacled and with a gleaming bald head, fingered through some Victorian ledgers. On the other side of the room, children played in amongst the stacks, the timbre of their laughs echoing in the glass domed roof.

Paul selected a couple of volumes and picked a desk. The readers' pews were arranged in large circular terraces that dipped down like an amphitheatre into the centre of the room, where more shelving and the indexing system lay. He opened *Constitutional Law: An Introduction* on its title page. It had a rich, musty smell and its pages were brittle and stained yellow. He flicked through, uncertain what he was looking for, and became lost in its dense academic prose. His mind drifted and he turned to its index and searched through, looking for a reference he might find interesting or relevant, but there was nothing and he realised he was wasting his time.

He rose from his seat and circled the room, seeking out the history section. The children were gone now and the reading room was quiet, save for the occasional rustle of pages and chairs groaning as they rubbed against the floor.

Modern history captivated him. The Twentieth Century. The age of extremes. He devoured books and documentaries on its excesses. Even though he was living through it, its complexities and savage turns fascinated and obsessed him. So many dreadful things had taken place and yet so much remained unsaid. He wanted to unravel its intricacies and hidden truths, to bear witness himself to some of the extremes of the human condition. To document it in some way.

His aspiration to somehow do so as a career remained largely unspoken. He didn't know how to articulate such an ambition. People Paul knew simply didn't do that sort of thing; they became teachers and office workers and insurance salesmen and nurses and, like his own father, tax inspectors. Who worked in the world's danger zones anyway? The military, parts of the media, human rights observers, NGOs, and charities. He had no desire to be a soldier and no idea how to enter any of these other professions. And so his dreams went unarticulated.

He picked out a photo book commemorating the thirtieth anniversary of the D-day landings and at his desk flicked through the volume. It was all men with brilliantined hair, sitting atop ruined gun emplacements and flicking victory signs. Tommies were seen relaxing in captured pillboxes. Everybody seemed to be smoking. The men's faces were framed in expressions of relief and hope, but there was little hint at their earlier ordeals.

Paul replaced it on its shelf and meandered around the room, circling its shelf-lined terraces until he descended into its centre. He had no reason to be there but felt trapped by his inertia and the sense that he should be doing something.

Then his eye caught a word that normally elicited little interest, but for once Paul felt drawn to the shelves: 'Poetry'.

He worked his way along the shelves and there, on the third one up from the floor, next to works by Stevie Smith and Stephen Spender, were three volumes bearing the name of Nadezhda Semilinski.

He returned to his desk with the books; two slim collections, *Arrival* and *Detachment*, and a larger *Collected Poems*.

He studied the dust jacket of *Arrival*. Like the other two volumes it bore a plain cover showing only her name and its title, but on the jacket's reverse was a full-page photograph: a pale-faced woman, dark haired and in early middle age, powerful and distinguished, looking wistfully into space. It was published in 1962, the same year Julia was born. There was a brief biography:

Nadezhda Semilinski was born in Austria and moved to England following the war. She contributes to Orbis, Fringe *and the* London Magazine. *This is her first collection.*

Detachment, the second volume, came five years later. It bore the same photograph, virtually the same scanty biographical details, no hint at what the volume contained, no clues as to the writer's inner life. *Collected Poems* was more recent, published in 1973. There was a new photograph and Nadezhda looked older, still beautiful, but sallow and withdrawn, her eyes cast down.

Paul opened *Arrival* and searched its contents. There were just forty poems and they possessed titles like 'Roots', 'The Weight of Absence' and 'The New Town'. They all seemed to speak of being an alien in a strange place. He turned to 'Holborn 10.03' and read of a young girl:

Roaming and alone
Disconnected in every way
from these people
With their purposeful strides
and busy lives

'The Matinee' told of witnessing at a cinema a desolate and poverty-stricken Vienna, carved up between outside powers. The city seemed alien to the place she had once known; Paul recognised the film as *The Third Man*.

To him there seemed to be an acute sadness at the city's fate and her absence from it, but gladness that she was able to see it nonetheless. She concluded:

But today,
through celluloid on canvas,
I can see Vienna from here,
The city of my birth,
from this distant shore
I washed up on

He paused over the page, contemplating the last lines over and again: *This distant shore I washed up on.* How did she get to England and what was she still doing there? If she had arrived straight from Vienna after the war, then, as a Jew, her early life must have been fraught with drama and danger? Suddenly intrigued he flicked through the pages of her books seeking more biographical information, more hints at the journey she had undertaken. But there was nothing.

He spent the next few hours reading through her work. He found her writing oddly moving, this sense of being a stranger among people and sights he considered familiar; the constant notion that she was an alien, an outsider. But there were scant hints at her past life. Austria was barely mentioned, nor even Liverpool, her present home. The war, her journey to England, her Jewishness were conspicuously absent.

Later that afternoon he approached the librarian, seeing if there was anything more recent. 'I'm sure we do,' he replied, and described to Paul a cuttings library that was maintained to chart the lives of significant locals. He walked him over to a wall on which was fixed a huge system of small indexing drawers, like a vast mahogany medicine chest. The librarian pulled open a drawer, full of narrow index cards and flicked through them until he found what he wanted.

'Here we are,' said the librarian. 'Nadezhda Semilinski, born 1925. You've seen her books, but you won't have seen her cuttings file.' He led him to a shelf-lined anteroom, and after a momentary search presented Paul with a box file bearing the poet's name. 'This should keep you going for a while,' he said.

Back in the reading room Paul tipped the contents from the box. There were several envelopes, each with different time periods handwritten across the front. Paul opened the first one, marked 1955-63, and emptied it onto the desk. It was mostly newspaper and magazine cuttings from serious-looking publications. A poem clipped from the *London Review of Books*. A short newspaper interview about being a white immigrant in

Britain. A piece of criticism she wrote for *Orbis*. More poems, some of which Paul recognised from his earlier reading. A cutting from the *Liverpool Echo* publicising a reading at the Jacaranda by 'hip and happening poet Nadezhda Semilinski.' In photographs she looked as she did on the dust jackets. Elegant, mysterious, perhaps embarrassed by the attention bestowed upon her.

There were reviews of *Arrival*, which were universally positive, some exultant. The *New Statesman* hailed 'an important new voice.' To the *Observer* she was 'one of the most powerful and lavishly gifted young poets of our time.' *Fringe* somewhat crassly prefaced its review 'Sylvia Plath is dead, long live Nadezhda Semilinski.' A month prior to *Arrival*'s publication, Plath had taken her own life.

When he finished reading the clippings Paul refilled the envelope and opened out the second one. As with the first envelope there were many poems and bits of publicity puff, but his eyes were immediately drawn to a more substantial article. Photostatted from the *Times Literary Supplement*, it was headlined: 'From Mauthausen to Merseyside: The Incredible Journey of Nadezhda Semilinski.'

It was dated April 1968 and pictured Nadezhda before the soot-stained Liver Buildings, gazing out across the River Mersey. She was tall, formidable; looking as though she would sooner be elsewhere, and when Paul read through the article he could understand why. The interviewer had tried to draw out details of her past, which she clearly had no wish to discuss. Indeed, he had jumped straight into such questioning. Tell me about life in a concentration camp? he asked. 'It was a labour and death camp,' she corrected him. 'I have no wish to discuss it.' But what horrors did you witness there? 'This is not for discussion.' How does the suffering you surely experienced set you apart from other poets?

'Poetry is poetry,' she said. 'My family were all murdered – that is something else. Poetry cannot be mentioned in the same breath.' How did you survive when others close to you perished? 'This is not something I talk about, not even to my husband.' Do you consider yourself lucky?

At this point Nadezhda had had enough and stormed off. He attributed her response to 'the unquenchable passion that exists within every great writer' rather than his own crassness.

He had completed the interview at her home – 'a grand merchant's villa that seems to belong to a different world to this crumbling port city' – and she was candid about her life in England and her work.

'I've decided to trust you,' she told the interviewer a few minutes into their second conversation and started to tell her story.

She was the younger daughter of a civil engineer – 'he built railways and the first motorways' – and a minor aristocrat. It was a privileged, bourgeoisie background, she told him. 'I suppose you could call my parents the last of Europe's intelligentsia,' she said. They loved opera, theatre, music, books, and art and travelled widely to indulge their passions. At home she and her sister were encouraged to share these loves and question everything; she recalled fierce dinner-table arguments about the meanings of novels or plays they had seen. From a young age Nadezhda felt herself divided about wanting to become a poet or concert pianist.

Austria's Anschluss with Germany came in 1938, when she was thirteen, and the Nazis took Vienna. Surely a prominent Jewish family should have been the first to escape? 'My father witnessed many things in his lifetime,' she said. 'The Great War, the fall of the Habsburgs, hyperinflation in Germany, the Depression. I think he thought that Hitler would pass like everything else. But then the war came and everything changed.'

Perhaps not wishing to revisit the earlier impasse, what followed was not revisited by her interrogator. Instead he jumped forward to her passage to England in 1946, which was sponsored by the Anglo-Jewish League. 'My life was over,' she said. 'My life had just begun.'

She studied at the London School of Economics, then found work at a small publishing house in Bloomsbury. It specialised in translating English novels into German, and German works into English. 'Everybody's preconception was that I was German, which could be a problem on the streets – I was thrown out of a few shops and restaurants in my time. People couldn't or wouldn't understand that I had suffered like they did.'

Fifties London was poor and austere, but despite this and the xenophobia she sometimes encountered she found her place amongst 'the bohemian set.' She said: 'They regarded me as a curiosity. They looked after me, welcomed me and encouraged me to write. We had some wild times! Drinking till dawn. Hanging around jazz clubs. Meeting the great and good. Francis Bacon, George Melly, Princess Margaret! I met them all.' All the while she continued to write and by her early thirties was published and renowned.

She moved to Liverpool in 1961 after marrying a German-Jewish émigré who worked in the shipping business. Motherhood and the publication of *Arrival* came two years later.

What was the greater shock, she was asked, becoming a parent or critical recognition? 'Becoming a mother, of course,' she said. 'Nothing prepares you for that! Anyway, I always felt it my destiny to be recognised a poet. Becoming a mother I never really considered until it happened.'

She enjoyed Liverpool, its vibrancy and history. The people. That it was a seaport. 'Growing up in a landlocked country can be isolating, but here you always look out to the world.' She liked the Beatles, who were at the forefront of the city's cultural revival, but disassociated herself from the Merseybeat school. 'They are like pop stars,' she said. 'In any case I am too old and not of the city. I am an outsider.'

As the interview started to draw to a close the hitherto pensive writer opened up and seemed to hit full flow. 'I realise my readers will try and psychoanalyse me through my work. It's impossible for that not to happen. It's the human condition – it's just how we all are. I do it, so why wouldn't anyone else? Of course there are little pieces of me in everything that I write, but some things are just not for public consumption. Some things are just too dark for me to go over again. But I will always be true to myself, my work. Readers will always read, and I will always write. I just want to read and write and be with my family. You know, I'm very simple.'

It seemed to Paul, as he folded the article in two and replaced it in its folder, an extraordinary life, more dramatic and full of incident than that of anyone he had previously encountered. She had known an affluent and culturally rich Vienna in the thirties; the extremities of war in the 1940s; in the 1950s a London of smoky jazz bars, artists, poets and royalty; then Liverpool at the apex of its cultural power a decade later. But that so much remained untold heightened his curiosity. Her evasiveness about the Holocaust was understandable, but surely, despite the interviewer's crude manner, it was also formative and not worth discounting. What horrors had she seen in the 'death and labour' camp? The very idea of it thrilled and appalled Paul. He felt compelled to meet her, to know her, to learn what happened.

The interview she gave in 1968 seemed to be the only substantial one she had granted in her career. There were soundbites in the local press about various poetry readings, and as the 1970s ensued she seemed to be more political, speaking in solidarity with sacked dockworkers and strikers at the Ford motor plant, protesting against South Africa playing a cricket match in the city. These interests seemed quite strange to Paul; parochial and incongruous.

The reviews for her *Collected Poems* in 1973 were polite, but less ecstatic than what had passed before. In November 1975, with the other Merseybeats, she gave a benefit at the Irish Centre for what was euphemistically called 'civil rights in Belfast' and that was the end of Nadezhda Semilisnki's file.

Paul placed the cuttings back in her folder and carried it to the information desk. The man who had helped him earlier now manned it.

'Did you find everything you wanted?' he asked as Paul passed back the folder.

'Sort of,' he replied. 'But it ended quite abruptly six years ago.'

The man pushed his glasses up the bridge of his nose and stood. 'There'll be another folder in progress, you see.'

'Can I see it?' Paul asked.

'It's not compiled here, but I can order it in for you.'

He handed Paul a slip and he filled out his details. Under the heading 'What is the purpose of your research?' his pen hovered momentarily. What was he doing? Snooping on an acquaintance's mother whom he had never even met before? He felt like a madman. Then he scribbled the word 'personal' in the box and set on his way.

4

The train crept through the steep sandstone embankments that led from Central Station, groaning along the curvature of the rails and into the dusk that enveloped the city. It took them past myriad terraced houses, then empty playing fields and concrete parades of workshops and factories. Above them gulls cawed in the early evening air. Paul watched from the grimy window as St Michael's disappeared into the distance and the train veered into another embankment shrouded by lush green leaves.

He sipped from his beer can, and Bulsara from the seat behind him said, 'Come on, Paul, it's your turn now.'

All evening they had made silly, raucous toasts – 'To John Lennon's reincarnation!', 'To the independence of Liverpool', 'To Thatcher's death' – which they greeted with silly cheers and more beer.

Roberts was sitting on a bench on the platform when they bounded off the train at Cressington. No one was sure why he had not travelled with the rest of them, but when Paul saw him rub his calf he shook his head, realising he'd walked the whole way. It was one of his eccentricities that he'd walk everywhere, even ten miles or more, to save the public transport fare.

'Did you see any trouble?' he asked him. They were walking down a tree-lined avenue to the girls' house. The others were ahead.

'Not really,' Roberts replied. 'But you could see where the rioting had happened. Lots of burned-out shops, a few wrecked cars.' He swirled his umbrella in the air. 'I brought my trusty sword, just in case.' But he had brought no beer, so they stopped at a corner shop on the way and Paul cajoled him into buying more than the two meagre cans Roberts deemed acceptable.

He had known Roberts as long as he had Christopher, but their friendship was never bound by the same intimacy. Roberts had always been the same – fusty, opinionated, outspoken, tight – and it served as a barrier. He could be wildly manipulative, Machiavellian, outrageously confrontational. But he was also loyal, principled and wise and Paul found himself drawn closer to him. There was a clear shifting from Christopher to Roberts in his order of affections.

At the house, music and the sound of voices rose from an open sash window. The front door was ajar and they let themselves in. Although it was still daylight outside, no natural light penetrated the hallway and it was dark, save for the flicker of a candlelit lantern. The smell of cannabis lingered sweetly in the air.

They went into the kitchen, from where much of the noise seemed to originate. It was lighter here, and the room was thronged with art school types. In one corner, Julia stood clutching a glass of wine in one hand, a cigarette in the other, holding court to a coterie of her classmates, immaculately uniformed in New Romantics garb. But it was she who stood out, tall and luminous skinned, effortlessly elegant. She waved at them, then arced her eyebrows in her scornful and teasing manner so that their eyes were drawn to a blue-haired girl and Paul laughed, recalling the way she mocked her fellow art students the first time they met.

Christopher was talking to two boys Paul had never seen before; Fat Sam stood apart, looking on shyly, already drunk. Bulsara was nowhere to be seen. Paul and Roberts took cans of beer and looked on at the party, slightly detached, saying nothing. 'California Dreamin'' played from a cassette player atop of the fridge.

Sarah appeared on the other side of the room, looking from side to side until she saw them and the hint of anxiousness that she seemed to exude evaporated. She mouthed 'I thought you weren't coming' and disappeared through a side door.

'Is that her, then?' Roberts asked, nodding his approval, and then seeing a girl that had just entered the room: 'There's a blast from the past.'

It was Christopher's twin, Helen, and recognising the familiar faces she walked over to join them. She was a solid – big-boned, Paul's mother would say – girl with a kindly face, wide shoulders and a broad chest accentuated by a low-cut top that hugged her cleavage. She was, in many ways, the antithesis of her brother; thoughtful, virtuous and cultured, and Paul liked her for it. But whereas he once found her alluring, to him the attraction had faded, and when he looked at her he could not help but see her brother's face.

She began to explicate her final year art project, the concept of which Paul was unable to grasp. He feigned interest and his mind wandered. He sensed Roberts slip away to join their other friends, and he searched the room for a glimpse of Sarah, but she was not there.

Finally, Helen asked him about Cambridge and Paul gave his little speech about his hopes and fears.

'You're so lucky,' she said. 'To get away from here and try

something new.' He sensed her edge nearer to him. 'You're so clever,' she whispered. 'It's amazing what you're doing.' She was a little drunk and gazed at him.

Paul laughed nervously: he had known her for fifteen years and she chose now to reciprocate some of his unrequited ardour?

'Can I come and stay with you when you go?' she purred. She was leaning in so closely that her body touched his. He could feel the cool of her breasts against his arm and smelt the tobacco on her breath. He nodded non-committally and Helen smiled. She whispered so that he could scarcely hear her voice: 'That's if having a girl in your room doesn't cause too much of a scandal at your posh college.'

Christopher watched all this unfold from across the room and like a guard dog snapped into action.

'What's all this? What's going on?'

Helen put her arm around her twin's back. 'Fancy seeing you here!' Her lips were stained crimson with red wine. 'Paul just invited me to stay with him at Cambridge.'

Christopher raised his eyebrows and looked at Paul, who shrugged his shoulders.

Helen turned to her brother and pulled on his shirtsleeves like a persistent child. 'Is Julia's mother here? I feel I should meet her. I read some of her poems. Can you introduce me to her? Please, Chris, can you?' She was irritating and very drunk; a pest. As she nagged her brother, Paul slipped away from the pair and back into the hallway, where in the near-dark he felt liberated by his anonymity.

There were more people here. A floppy-haired youth in a tweed jacket in conversation with a bespectacled boy in a skull cap; two girls, perhaps sisters, in flowery Laura Ashley dresses speaking in whispers; and a larger group that Bulsara had attached himself to.

They spoke in shouts and jeers, taking great hungry swigs from their beer cans as if every mouthful may be their last.

Paul sat on a stair, watching them through the gloom, hoping Sarah may pass. He sipped from his can, suddenly plaintive, feeling quite apart from the phalanx. Parties were never quite his thing unless ensconced in the company of his friends or cradled in the fug of too much alcohol.

Suddenly he was aware of a presence next to him, sitting a stair up, silently watching out into the near dark. A trace of perfume told him it as a woman, but who? There was the fumble of a matchbox and then the strike of a match against its side. He glanced up and as the flame ignited and flickered into life it illuminated Nadezhda's face, as milky and pale as the moon. In a wave she extinguished the match and they were consumed by shadows. The tip of her cigarette crackled and glowed red. She had appeared as if a ghost.

'Would you like one?' she asked as she exhaled.

'Thanks, but I don't smoke.' He could feel his heart beating. A sense of shame at his earlier discoveries washed over him. He felt like a peeping Tom suddenly confronted by his subject.

'You young people,' she cackled. 'Always so careful and proper! Which one are you?'

'I'm Paul.'

'Paul, Paul – the history boy, no?' He found himself nodding, but such was the dimness that she could scarcely have seen him. 'Paul this, Paul that, it's all I seem to hear from my girls these days.' He tingled at the revelation and wondered what she meant by it. 'And you had an eventful night on Thursday. Drinking, fighting, riots, arguing with the police – maybe you're not so careful after all.' She let out a hoarse laugh that echoed up the stairway. She had a strange voice, husky but precise, steeped in middle-class tones that at first scarcely hinted of her origins. But the way she asked things – by making a statement and succeeding it with a questioning 'no' – and pronounced certain words – this became *zeiss*; that *zat* – spoke of her foreignness.

His lips pursed into a crisp smile and the unease lifted. 'So you heard all about it, then?' he asked.

'Of course, my girls tell me everything – or at least I think they do.' She laughed, then asked, 'So, Paul, when you're not leading my girls astray, how have you spent your summer?' Her voice took on a mocking tone that reminded him of Julia. She cackled again and dragged on her cigarette; the smoke wafted into Paul's face and singed his throat.

'A lot of reading,' he said; then remembered: *reading about you*. 'But it's mostly been quiet and I'm looking forward to leaving.'

'A clever young man who reads,' she pronounced. 'And like all clever young men in this fine city you chose to leave. Why is that? You have everything you need here in Liverpool, no?'

'I need a change,' he replied, then repeated something Julia had told him: 'If you stand still for too long you'll disappear.'

'A good answer,' she said, and smoked her cigarette. 'Will you return?' she asked. She reminded him of Julia in every way: intent, persistent, quick.

'I don't know,' Paul said, and he really didn't.

They talked for a while about the riots and she told him about the barbarity and racism of the city's police force. She was on the boards of various community groups through the 1970s and had seen all this at first hand; had led protests against various acts of what she termed 'neo-fascist brutality'. She became more passionate and animated about the causes of Toxteth's riots; he realised that she really cared and that such things mattered.

When she finished talking about Liverpool, she turned to Paul and said, 'So, tell me about the books you have been reading. I am always keen to hear what young people are reading.' She spoke of 'young people' – *pepple* she pronounced it – as though they were a separate species to be observed with the wonderment of an anthropologist in a remote tribe.

Paul sipped the dregs of his beer and subconsciously found himself open up. 'I read some of your poems, actually,' he said. 'When Julia told me who you were. A poet, I mean. I've never met a poet before.'

'Some say: "We're all poets, actually."'

'Are we?'

'Of course not!' she said and boomed with laughter. 'It's a cliché and a lie!'

He smiled to himself but was unsure what to say next.

'Which of my poems did you read?'

He wanted to say 'most of them' but fearing that this might somehow unravel his other probing, said: 'I liked "The Matinee". Was the film *The Third Man*?'

'Yes! It was! Very good, Paul.'

She seemed pleased at this recognition and emboldened by her compliments, he asked: 'Do you still miss Vienna?'

She said nothing for a moment and in the unexpected silence the seconds seemed to tick slowly. Finally she answered: 'But Paul, who is to say that the girl in the poem is me? Who is to say that any of my poems are about me? I like to think of them as a life I could have lived had things been different. They are imaginary, but there are limits to the imagination, you see? But memory matters, so that every word I have written bears some resemblance to a life I have lived.'

'But where does the poet's persona begin and end?'

'The link is intrinsic, Paul. I can't say which parts of me are in my work and which are in my imagined life. It's a poet's privilege, and I suppose their downfall too, to use their own face as a masquerade. People will always try and psychoanalyse my work – I do it with others all the time. But it's pointless really.' She stubbed her cigarette into his now empty beer can, and thought about her next words. 'The novelist Paul Theroux said this about his own work: "The man is fiction, the mask is real." The same is true of all of my work.'

He looked out into the dark and considered his response. 'And Vienna,' he said, finally. 'Forget the poetry, as a person, do you miss it?'

He was blunt and for a second feared she may have been affronted, but she merely let out a shriek of laughter. 'Paul, Paul, Paul! So many questions! Always so many questions! Vienna is complicated, so very, very complicated.' She struck a match and lit another cigarette, pausing to ponder the lost city of her youth. 'Perhaps one day I'll tell you about it, but not tonight.'

From behind them on the stairs came a creak and the shuffling of feet. Nadezhda rose to let the person past, but recognising her daughter in the dimness, said, 'Sarah, darling Sarah, there you are.' She kissed her daughter. 'I've been talking to your friend, Paul. So very interesting, and interested in everything.' Paul also rose. His eyes had adjusted to the dark, but he could scarcely see Sarah above them. Nadezhda continued, becoming animated and melodramatic: 'He has so many questions, darling. Always questions! A clever boy!'

'Hello, Paul,' Sarah called, still a shadow, until she descended a stair and he could make out the outline of her body; the whiteness of her skin; her hair, black against black. He felt a surge in his chest, a sense of destiny overcoming him that was at once a mystery and incontrovertible – that there would be no other girl but her.

'I'd come to find you, but discovered your mother instead,' he said.

'Ha! He's tired me out!' said Nadezhda. 'Exhausted me with his questions.' She turned to Paul. 'I need some respite and my books. Enjoy the rest of the party!' As she passed Sarah on the stairs, she touched her cheek. 'Be a good girl, darling.'

They were left in the gloom of the stairs, adrift from the rest of the party.

'It's so dark here,' Sarah said. 'Come on, we'll find the light.' She took his hand and followed him down the stairs, through the hallway to a room from where music sounded. His heart bounced and his hand trembled; his breathing seemed to quicken. Soft Cell's 'Tainted Love' played from a ghetto blaster; the sound was tinny and crackly, but the dozen or so people there reverberated as one on an imagined dance floor.

He could see her now, her loveliness accentuated by the dusk. She seemed confident, exhilarated even and looked at him with adoration. It thrilled and bewildered Paul; it turned him on.

'You said you'd dance with me tonight,' she said above the music, pushing him gently with the palms of her hands.

'I don't dance when it's possible not to dance,' he answered.

'But tonight it's impossible,' she said and started to swing her hips and moved around him. Paul joined her, awkwardly at first, but when her eyes were fixed upon him, he started to ease and then lose himself to the rhythm and forget that anyone else existed.

They danced until the tape reached its end, clicking with a certain finality. Paul wiped his brow with his sleeve and she said: 'Come on, I've had my fun. Let's go and get another drink and watch the stars.'

5

The last traces of purple had gone from the sky, and above them was only the black of night and a sliver of moon. They lay stretched out together on the lawn, the earth beneath them baked hard by weeks of sun. Her toes peeked through the front of her sandals touching Paul's trouser leg. He stared into the blackness above them and she lay with her head rested on her hand, watching him.

They spoke of art and books and the never-ending summer that had erupted into conflagration, riots and turmoil; they listened to the sound of music, laughter and chatter from the house, while sipping from the syrupy bottle of red wine. And now drink and the late hour made them sombre and reflective.

'Do you think about the future?'

He smiled, and turned his head so that he could see her.

'Yes. All the time. Do you?'

She rolled onto her back, and let out a sigh. 'Constantly. Though I don't know whether it's something to fear or look forward to.'

'What do you fear?'

'This. Being here, not belonging. Being an outsider. I was born in this city, and I love it. But I feel like a tourist sometimes, longing for home.'

'Where's home then?'

'I don't know,' she said, and laughed. 'Not here.'

A low roar of laughter carried from the house. Through the dimly-lit French window Paul could see the others goading the thickset figure of Bulsara, who was drinking the contents of a glass vase. When he finished he turned it upside down over his head and a cheer erupted.

Sarah ignored the commotion and peered on into the night.

'Let's go somewhere,' he said suddenly. 'What's through there?' he asked, turning over and pointing into the darkened foot of the garden, where he could barely make out a small wooden door set into the crooked red brick perimeter wall.

'An alleyway. The outside.'

'Come on,' he said suddenly, 'let's escape! Let's go outside!' Standing up, he picked up the bottle of red wine he had brought from the kitchen and offered her his hand.

The gate was half-rotten and stiff from years of disuse and disrepair. Behind them they had trailed a path through the long dead grass and weeds. An apple tree hung heavy with fat unripe fruit. The house was now hidden by trees and darkness, the noise of the party just a distant hum of laughter and music. Otherwise it was almost possible to imagine they had arrived at the entrance of a hidden garden, secreted in the vastness of a country estate, and not in a city at all.

Sarah fiddled with the rusted catch and as Paul watched her he wanted to take her delicate wrist and hold her in his arms. But fear of rejection terrified him and he stepped back. When the gate snapped open Sarah snatched his wrist and pulled him through.

She led him down a narrow path cut between the high red-bricked villas. The orange glow of nearby street lights barely illuminated the gloom of the alley and he was conscious of the sureness of her footing as he stumbled, half-drunkenly, in the dark after her. The path turned sharply right, then switched left and then they were out, blinking, on a well-lit suburban street.

A far off police siren sounded for a few moments, then faded.

'We're back in the real world,' said Sarah. 'Come on.' She took Paul's left arm, and they started walking down the empty street, night otherwise cocooning it in stillness.

In the garden he was jokey, nervous, infuriated with himself. He wanted to escape and be free from the gaze of his friends. But now she mapped their way, confidently walking the floodlit street and he was happy to follow her lead.

'So, where did you want to go at this time of night?' she asked, looking up at him with a knowing smirk.

'Outside!' he proclaimed in mock staccato, like a plummy officer from a war movie. 'I just wanted to smell the sweet air of the outside one more time!' Sarah laughed, but Paul knew he was hiding behind the jocular façade once more. She clutched his arm tightly and they marched purposely on to nowhere.

When they reached the foot of the high street, Sarah pulled Paul's arm. 'Let's go this way,' she said, as if their midnight walk had suddenly assumed a purpose. They veered right, avoiding the ugly drag of closed and shuttered shops. The air was cool now, but the previous day's heat still throbbed from the pavement, and the first-floor windows of the houses they passed were all open as people took a collective gasp from the summer's interminable heat.

'You see that building?' She pointed to a large, red-bricked Victorian structure fifty metres down the other side of the road. It was boarded up, like so many grand old buildings in Liverpool, awaiting the demolition ball because a pile of rubble was easier to maintain for a bankrupt city. 'That used to be a registry office. My parents married there in 1960. They're going to knock it down as soon as the strike ends.' She let out a sigh, adding wistfully, 'It's as if they're destroying any evidence that my parents were ever married.'

'Why do you say that?'

'Well...' she said, and trailed off into silence.

They kept walking, arm in arm, like lovers under a blue Sorrento sky. The road swept left and uphill and was lined by old trees, their trunks a century thick. Paul recognised where he was now. It led to a small park, which overlooked the city, the expanse of the Mersey and Wirral peninsula and beyond them the Welsh hills.

They were now almost at the park. 'I think I need some of that,' she said, gesturing to the bottle of wine that Paul was cradling as if it were handpicked from a well-stocked cellar. Beside the gate, a street lamp cast its light on a sign, its glass broken and long unrepaired, warning people off after sunset. But like everything else in this crumbling city, rules meant nothing and the gate stood open.

They entered and facing them was the wall of a disused park keepers' hut covered in graffiti. Most of it mocked the aspersions of the city's rival football clubs, but one stood out ominously in the pathetic light thrown from the street: *Something's Coming.*

Through the darkness of the park they walked, still arm in arm. Paul wanted to clutch her narrow waist and hold her and kiss her, but lacked the temerity or experience to do so. Eventually the darkness dissipated and they found themselves in a grass clearing. Before them spanned the city. The majestic neo-Gothicism of the Anglican Cathedral towering over its Catholic counterpart, and beyond them the Three Graces could be distinguished above the glare of the street lights. In front of it all was the muddy mile-wide stretch of river. It was magnificent and ominous for under the shadow of the vast Anglican Cathedral, barely two miles from where they stood, was fire and the flash of police lights and ambulances. Toxteth was burning again.

'They're still at it.' He gestured at the conflagration before them.

'They're still at it,' she agreed wearily.

At the playground they sat next to each other on a roundabout. Boldly, he went to hold her hand, but she tightened her grip around his arm and tucked her head against his shoulder. Momentarily he felt rebuffed, but desire blew over him when he felt her warmth next to him.

She continued, without self-pity. 'He left. He couldn't stay. So he went back to Germany. She's never forgiven him.' Her story was sad, but lacked definition; Paul had so many questions. Sarah took the bottle from him and drank from it before passing it back.

They continued talking about family, friends, shared interests and aspirations. When she put her head back on his shoulder, Paul could not tell if it was because she was cold or tired, or because she wanted him. The black of the night was turning into an indigo and in the trees behind them birdsong rose. Morning was coming. It surprised him that the night had passed so quickly.

Sarah realised he was somehow troubled by her revelations and could feel the awkwardness permeate, so she said: 'My mother is a complicated woman. What she has seen, what she has been through, no one can begin to imagine. My father says that what she saw in her youth has made her into what she is.'

Her last words hinted at disgust rather than sympathy. Nadezhda had intrigued Paul since he had first heard her name; this exotic creature who had seen and suffered so much was the most glamorous and foreign woman he had met, but he wanted to know more. He wanted to know everything. He could not help himself.

'Has she ever talked about, well, you know?' he asked, unable to directly mention the war.

Sarah looked into the distance and then spoke, her voice almost trailing off into a whisper: 'No. Never.'

෨

In the dark blue sky of the early morning, a mist hung over Liverpool. They could see right over the river now, to Birkenhead, where ugly blocks of modern flats obscured the late-Victorian town.

She asked: 'What is Christopher's problem?'

'How do you mean?'

'You treat him with admiration when he shows you contempt.' Her voice was laced with irritation.

'He doesn't mean it,' said Paul. 'He's messing around most of the time.' But he knew she was right and he smiled inwardly at her perception and annoyance on his behalf.

'He's plausible, but I don't like him.'

'Do you resent him?'

'Oh no, I definitely don't resent him,' she replied, amused by the notion. 'And while I don't admire Julia's choice in men,' she said with a mock pomposity that reminded Paul of his mother, 'I still worship her.'

'Tell me about you and Julia.'

'What do you want to know?'

'The whole lot.'

As the sun started to rise, bringing an end to their first night together, she told him everything.

∽

As children they were inseparable. Other parents dressed their girls identically because they lacked imagination, but Sarah dressed like Julia because she wanted to be like her. She had no friends of her own, and wherever Julia played she went too. Once, when she was six, she escaped the house to follow Julia to a schoolfriend's party she was not invited to herself. Their upbringing was comfortable and happy. Neither wanted for anything. Their parents took them on overseas holidays in the summers and skiing in the winter. She could never recall an unhappy moment.

'And then Papa left.'

At first Nadezhda was distraught, then angry. She became possessive of the girls, not even letting them out of the house on their own. When the divorce was finalised they heard nothing from their father for several years. Later Sarah learned that he wrote every fortnight, but Nadezhda hid the letters.

They had a live-in nanny, Maud, a sweet old spinster from Ayrshire who Nadhezda described as a governess

'Can you imagine! A governess in Liverpool in the 1970s!' laughed Sarah. 'The city's falling down and docks and factories are closing and Nadezhda's girls have a governess!'

Nadezhda, at this time, was running free. She disappeared to London or Paris, to a poetry reading, a party, or a gig or a play, anything to escape the mundanity of home. One night she was brought back in a police car after she'd been hit by a flying bottle outside Eric's while she was waiting to see the Clash. 'The officer couldn't believe that a fifty-year-old mother was there in the first place,' said Sarah.

At the house she hosted epic parties, inviting old friends, comrades from Communist Party meetings, university students, punk rockers, squatters, Rastas, fellow poets, musicians and an entourage of other admirers and hangers-on. The girls would be heading for school and Nadezhda would be arguing about the Black Panthers with a new Rasta friend, an acned student and a washed-up squatter, while the air hung thick with marijuana smoke and the floor was a mess of discarded bottles and cans. One night half of the Liverpool football team turned up to one of her parties, and Sarah woke to find Emlyn Hughes dressed in an apron washing the dishes.

'The worst parties were the ones she invited the neighbours to. In one corner you'd have this old docker that she knew from her communist meetings, effing and blinding and cursing about the fate of the proletariat. You'd have a bunch of Rastas with their spliffs and dreadlocks. You'd have some wash-out claiming he was the fifth Beatle until Brian Epstein kicked him out. There'd be a tramp – there always seemed to be a tramp. And somewhere in the midst of this there'd be Mr and Mrs Davies from number four sipping their Blue Nun, and Mrs Jones from opposite looking for some sherry. And the look of horror was a picture, the absolute look of horror on their faces...'

The neighbours were unable to help themselves. They frowned upon Nadezhda, but couldn't pass on seeing her at play. Sometimes they stopped the girls when they were alone on the street to see if they were being looked after. The girls despised the hypocrisy and knew what they said about her.

'We lived separate lives really. Julia and I were self-contained and happy. We relied on each other. Old Maud did whatever mothering needed to be done. Mother had her meetings and her trips and her parties. She read in her room when she was home. There were always people in the house. It was different, very different. We were always seen and not heard. But we were never unhappy.'

Then came the news from Germany that their father was to remarry. Nadezhda imploded.

'I think she always thought he would return. He was an old man after all. He couldn't stay on in business forever. When she heard he was getting married again she was in a state of shock. I mean, who gets married again when they're that old? We started to speak to him on the phone quite often and he came to visit. Julia and I were delighted. We'd not seen him in years. But looking back it was quite cynical really, she was using us as bargaining chips. And it didn't work: he married that German girl half his age anyway.'

After that there were no more parties. Nadezhda stopped going out. She hid in her room with her wine and books, sometimes for days on end. Maud left. They had a cleaning lady, but she stopped coming too and the house started to fall into disrepair.

'Once a week, every Saturday, she'd get herself together, dress up like a grand lady and take us out. It was ridiculous, really. She'd always been a bohemian, a flower power girl, even a bit of a punk; now she was dressing her age. When she was ready, we'd get a black cab into town, go to George Henry Lee and Blacklers for a few things. She'd take us for tea in some grand old place and she'd sit in the window and watch people admiring her. She hardly had anything to say because she didn't go out any more and she wasn't ever really interested in what we did. We'd walk up Bold Street to Dillons to select her week's reading. Then we'd go across the road to her wine shop, she'd pick a mixed case and a cab took us home.'

'When did all this happen?'

'Five years ago, when I was twelve. We soon lost interest in the little excursions and stopped going. But she still goes on her little runs of self-glorification.'

And so their separate lives passed. Julia and Sarah thrust into premature adulthood, their eccentric mother with them in presence, but not in spirit. Money from their father kept the house going and paid for the girls to pass through the city's Jewish school. Only the lives of their schoolmates, with their bat mitzvahs and armies of cousins, made them question the normality of their existence.

'She is not a bad mother or a terrible woman. She's just unconventional. She loves us both in her way. But Julia and I have come to rely on each other for what many normal daughters would expect from a mother. That's the way it is.'

The wine was now gone and day had broken. The sky was cloudless: it was going to be hot again.

'Come on – it's late now.' She climbed off the roundabout. She stood over Paul, her china-white face lovelier with the morning.

Paul smiled. 'You mean it's early.'

'Yes, it's early!' She laughed, rocking her head back and looking at the sky. Her black hair fell onto her bare shoulders, accentuating her paleness. 'And Paul is the first lad on the playground and has bagsed himself the roundabout!' She gave it a push, and laughed again as Paul spun around. Then she grabbed its iron side and ran around with it, pushing the roundabout faster and faster. Finally she jumped on board and sat facing him, laughing as they whirled around. The imperceptible sadness which she'd always seemed to carry in her eyes was now gone. Paul let out a cheer. He'd never felt so happy. This was love, he told himself. This was true love.

∽

As they walked down the hill, tired and silent, their arms occasionally brushing as if to remind the other that they were still there, Paul tried to think of a way to kiss her before they departed. He kept glancing across and seeing those brown eyes, her stark beauty. He felt a smile of delight crease his cheeks.

Near the derelict building where her parents married a lifetime ago, they came to a stop. There seemed an unspoken realisation that their night together had reached its conclusion. The party would be long over now and the house a tangle of bodies sleeping their way into a hangover. Paul had no desire for the crude inquisition he was likely to face to be played out in front of Sarah. Her presence still exhilarated him, but he could see also the fatigue washing over her face.

'The station is at the far end of the high street,' she said. Then, politely emphasising that she wasn't asking him to go: 'Unless you'd prefer the mess and the party postmortem to your own bed.'

'I probably need my beauty sleep,' he said. But Paul had never felt so awake.

She smiled, gazing at him with wonderment and gratitude. No one had ever looked at him like that before. She wriggled her shoulders up, standing almost as tall as him, seeming to invite a kiss. But Paul didn't dare, and glanced down at his feet. When he looked up again the moment passed. Instead, he asked, 'So where do we go from here?'

She didn't reply for a few seconds, and in the cool air of the morning he realised the smell of her hair had passed onto his shirt, and he was now infused by her sweetness. He felt as if she was part of him and wanted her more than ever. Her gaze held and finally she said as if it were a formality: 'You'll call me.'

She stood motionless and he wanted again to kiss her lips. But as he tried to summon the courage the rattle of a milk float distracted him.

'Tomorrow,' she said, and bent across and kissed his cheek.

'Make sure you do.' Paul stood mesmerised, as if the caress of her mouth was indelibly marked on his face. And then they parted. He walked down the desolate shop-lined street, turning his head every few yards until she melted into the dilapidated grandeur of the streets around her.

6

The Swan was a terminal pub whose death only ever seemed to be another Friday night away. It was a place of the sociable and the wearied, of big characters and those who toiled in their anonymity; there were noxious labourers, chronic alcoholics, bored couples, underage drinkers, the workless eking out a night on their dole payment, pensioners supping towards their last rites, and those merely seeking succour in a Friday night pint. Pervasive blue smoke rinsed through the place, adding a dingy aspect in which everything seemed faded or washed out or stained: a ceiling yellowed by years of smoke; the carpet pebble-dashed with hundreds of globules of discarded gum, worn black and flat into its fabric. One of the couches was ripped and foam hung out, though on a Friday it was hidden by a gang of navvies from whom the threat of violence always seeped. Behind the bar postcards were affixed to a mirror, their edges curled, showing off patron's holidays – to Blackpool, Skegness, Weston-Super-Mare. Many of the drinkers took on the tired complexion of their surroundings: grey-faced, wan and bored. But others were full of life, wit and humour, obliging each other with their verbal jousts and dances, cracking out into periodic bursts of laughter and song that became louder as the night progressed. The pub, despite its myriad of flaws, aura of decrepitude and undercurrent of menace, maintained a liveliness, humour and vim. It seemed to offer a window into the city in which it stood, and like Liverpool it always endured. No one who visited regularly could envisage a day when it wouldn't.

For Paul and his friends, Friday in The Swan had assumed the status of a weekly ritual. Just as the glorious clang of the school bell at three o'clock once marked the end of their weeks, so a few of pints of flat beer in the evening was a ceremony all monotonously observed to see in the start of the weekend. They adhered to the fixture rigidly, even though sixth form and its strictures was now history. In a couple of months university and new starts beckoned and The Swan would be part of their pasts.

Paul had come straight from Central Library after receiving a call the previous day telling him that the other cuttings file on Nadezhda Semilinski had arrived. 'I've had a look myself,' the librarian who had helped him earlier said. 'It's fascinating stuff. Fascinating!'

He collected the folder from the information desk and dashed – he found himself break into a half-run – to the reading room. It was still early and the place was entirely empty. He opened the folder and perhaps one hundred pages spewed onto the desk. For a moment the air seemed to fill with the noise of falling paper. What secrets might he find?

Paul saw immediately that this collection was different to the one he had already seen. Where once there were essays dense with text, now there were headline-rich pages of the local and tabloid press, all pithy subheadings and pictures.

They were arranged loosely chronologically. At first it was more of the same, though more *Liverpool Echo* than the *TLS*. Here was Nadezhda at a community centre, demonstrating against its closure. There she was with some Afro-Caribbean teenagers at an anti-racism march. She was pictured at Fords, at the docks, on the steps of St George's Hall, always under a banner or placard of some sort, protesting, remonstrating.

Paul had seen it all before and finding himself ambivalent to her political proclivities flicked through the pile of papers, searching for something else. There was a poem in the *New Statesman*, an essay on existentialism and then, quite abruptly, in a June 1978 copy of the *Liverpool Echo* he found what he was looking for:

LIVERPOOL POET IN POLICE DRUGS RAID
Award-winning poet Nadezhda Semilinski cancelled a gig last night after she was detained by police in an anti-drugs raid. The Austrian-born adopted-Scouser was due to perform a reading at the Unity Theatre when police swooped on Saturday afternoon, detaining her and another woman who has not been identified.

Both were released yesterday. Emerging from the police station, Ms Semilinski protested her innocence and said the raid was nothing to do with her. She said: 'It's just some sort of mistake, that's all. I have nothing to hide, and have not been charged with anything.'

'I am just a writer and a mother, and one who is getting old at that. It's libellous to call me a drug addict or any such nonsense; it's a good job I am too poor to sue.'

A source close to Ms Semilinski said it was not surprising the raid had occurred in the light of recent publicity generated by the poet, particularly her leading role in local civil rights protests. The poet has been fiercely critical of Merseyside police and its role in breaking up strikes and its relations with the city's coloured population.

> *Merseyside police said two women had been arrested for suspected possession of a class C drug. One was released without charge and the other woman released on police bail pending further enquires and was due to return to the police station in July.*
>
> *The raid was 'intelligence-led' and involved CID and traffic officers, dog handlers and forensic investigators. A Class C drug was recovered, police said.*

It seemed completely implausible until Paul reread it, then read it a third time. A class C drug meant cannabis or some kind of tranquilliser. There was no suggestion that she was dealing it, nor had even taken the drug. The intimation was that it was a stitch-up: the police didn't like her and so went looking for her. In a city that had become notorious for its petty theft and violence, possession of weed was scarcely heinous. He recalled Julia's plea in the Caernarfon Castle: *Come to my place, I've got some weed.* It probably belonged to her mother, thought Paul.

But by the following day the story was picked up in the national press: a column inch in the *Guardian*; a paragraph in the *Daily Express*. In the tabloid press it was a big story. 'German Poet in Drugs Shame' said the *Daily Mirror*, misplacing her nationality. It made page two of the *Sun* opposite a girl baring her breasts. The *Daily Mail* used the story to initiate a debate on whether 'foreign criminals' should be kicked out of the country.

Yet there was worse to come. After this tabloid furore had dissipated, after the *Liverpool Echo* announced that there were no charges to be made, Nadezhda was in the tabloid press again. This time, however, she was front page news. It was November 1978 and emblazoned across the front page of the *News of the World* was the headline: 'Racy German Poet in Underage Sex Romps'.

Paul felt his heart skip a beat as he stared disbelievingly at the headline over a photograph of Nadezhda at her front door in south Liverpool. A smaller photograph of an adolescent with a thick fringe and wearing a Lacoste polo shirt was set next to it.

An ex-schoolboy has told the News of the World *how he romped with a notorious poet in car parks, hotels and at her home. Sean Kendall was 15 when he began the alleged fling with racy German poet Nadezhda Semilinski. The lad, now 17, claimed sex acts occurred "hundreds of times" but they did not have full intercourse until he turned 16.*

Kendall has decided to go public after Semilinski, 53, cruelly dumped him days after he decided to leave college to start working life in a Liverpool bakery.

'I was completely infatuated with her,' says Kendall. 'It wasn't a passing fancy. She's broken my heart.'

The raunchy poet began giving him English lessons in the spring last year as he studied for his O levels. Before long they were sharing kisses and cuddles under a duvet at her home. Semilinski promised there was no danger of being caught as she is estranged from her husband.

She told the boy: 'I don't think I have ever loved anyone as much as I love you.'

Scouser Kendall says: 'She's old enough to be my mum, it's true. But she's a looker all right. She's dead fit. I was a virgin when I met her, but to have an experienced woman educate me in the bedroom was something I'll never forget.'

Several times she booked posh hotel rooms for romps. The pair even had sex while the poet's two daughters Julia, now 15, and Sarah, 14, were at home. After Semilinski's daughters became aware of the scandal, Kendall tried to break up with her but she turned up several times at a supermarket where he worked and tried to win him back.

Rumours of a fling between the lad and the poet were rife at his Liverpool school, where Semilinski gave classes, and by the time he sat his O levels in May last year he was constantly being quizzed by classmates.

He told the head of the fling after he had left school. The school investigated the matter and concluded that nothing had occurred. Merseyside police are considering whether to initiate an investigation into the claims.

'Since she dumped me, I feel dirty and abused,' said Kendall. 'She took my virginity away, I'll never get that back.'

Semilinski denies charges of sexual activity with a child and abuse of trust.

There were more tawdry headlines in the following day's newspapers: 'Sex Shame of Poet', 'Frau Semilinski in Underage Sex Claims', 'The Schoolboy, the Fifty-Something Poet, their Sex Sessions', and 'The Sickening Lust of the German Poet.'

Paul felt numb as he looked through the cuttings. There was little new in these stories – they only really picked over the weekend's revelations – but each time he saw the boy's claims – 'I was completely infatuated with her. It wasn't a passing fancy. She's broken my heart.' – he was struck with a sense of utter disbelief. His story seemed completely implausible, but as a witness – from the page – the impression was that he was genuine.

On the Tuesday, two days after the story broke, Nadezhda issued a rebuttal through the pages of the *Liverpool Echo*, which was picked up by the national press the following day. 'These allegations that have been made against me are beyond the realms of fantasy,' she said. 'For some time I have gone in to give talks to students at a local school. This boy came from a poor, broken home. He had some talent, but no one helped him develop it. He was enthusiastic and so I took him under my wing. I tutored him and encouraged him to read, to develop his style. I gave him chances in life that he'd never had before. It's true that he came to my house and he visited London with me once. He had never been before and wanted to see Tower Bridge. That's the only reason. There was no scandal, nothing improper – my daughters were there too.'

The headmaster at the school also spoke in her defence. 'Sean Kendall is a troubled young man. He first made these claims more than a year ago. We launched a thorough investigation and, as a result of that inquiry, we have no reason to believe any impropriety took place.'

Nadezhda said: 'The claims that this boy has made make me a criminal. I completely deny them, but the police should investigate so that I can clear my name.'

But despite her urging, the police never became involved and the flow of mocking, jeering, angry newspaper articles continued until the stream of allegations eventually trickled dry.

ھ

He still hadn't spoken to Sarah since the party, nor thought of anything else until his excursion to the library. The brush of her lips upon his cheek remained imprinted in his mind, but it was as if she were a ghost, for each time he searched she was no longer there.

He tried calling the day after the party, but no one answered and doubt started to fill his mind. What if it had all just been ephemeral, a night together inspired by nothing more than alcohol?

At nine o'clock Paul went back into the hallway and dialled Sarah's number again. His elation had dissipated, replaced with uncertainty and stirrings of self-loathing. It was nearly dark now, the house silent except for the chatter of children playing on the street outside. Sarah's number rang and rang, but no one picked up.

One hour later he tried again, slightly more desperate to hear her voice again, to have her reassure him that last night hadn't been all some silly, wonderful dream. But again there was no reply. He knew that Nadezhda, at least, must be there: was she, were they, ignoring him?

Now it was Friday and the silence continued. One by one his friends trickled in: Roberts, Bulsara and Sam; then Christopher and holding his hand was Julia. Paul's heart leapt and his eyes darted around the huddle, but there was no Sarah.

The friends had nothing to say, their hours since the party filled with the dull routine of the never-ending summer. They barracked each other and poked fun. They spoke of football and the riots, which had dissipated over the previous few days.

Christopher, his arm clenched tightly around the waist of his girlfriend, leant in and started talking to Paul, across Julia and Roberts, about the latest football news. Roberts stood erect, looking deliberately unimpressed.

'So you've signed this new goalkeeper. Who used to be a binman.'

'That's right.' Paul was glad that it was his football team that was the source of Christopher's mocking.

'Southman?'

'Southall. Neville Southall. He's a colossus.'

Julia seemed withdrawn, out of rhythm with their verbal

jousting. She lit a cigarette and stood coolly detached from the rest of them, observing the group with a look of elegant wryness. Paul longed to speak to her, for only she could unlock the secret of her sister's evanescence. But the others knew that too, and so long as they remained in earshot it was to be untold.

Eventually the hollow clang of the bell signalling last orders sang out and Paul leant on the bar, a five-pound note curled around his fingers, waiting his turn. Through the division he could see the navvies on the other side, smoking and swearing. He caught the barmaid's attention and she stood fixed to the spot, her eyebrow lifted, indicating she was ready for an order.

As he watched her pull three fresh pint glasses from the bar and line them up, he felt a gentle push in the small of his back. It was Julia.

'Hey you.' She was wearing drainpipe jeans and a green halter-necked top that showed her white, narrow shoulders. Her thumbs were tucked in her pockets and she rocked on her heels, smiling her toothy grin.

'Hey, how are you?'

'Good.' She stood there, grinning at him for a moment, then said: 'I should ask how you are,' and gave him a playful poke in the ribs.

Paul smiled. He realised she was trying to reassure him. 'I'm fine. Grand,' and then too quickly, 'how's Sarah?'

She glanced at her feet for a moment, and then looked up mischievously. 'Lovelier by the day.'

'I tried calling a few times, but nobody seemed to be around.'

'We thought it might have been you.' For a moment it seemed as if she was toying with him, and his anxiety rose. Then she explained: 'We don't really do phones in our house.'

'Oh,' he said. He had no idea what she meant.

'I mean, Mother doesn't like using them, so we sometimes let it ring out in case it's for her.'

'I see.'

'If it's important we tend to find out sooner or later,' she said playfully. Paul was sure she was somehow trying to let him down, but she continued. 'Sarah's playing her violin in Manchester tonight, otherwise she would have come.'

From behind him the barmaid called his order, and he turned as quickly as he could to give her the money. As he held out the five-pound note he realised his hand trembled.

Julia continued speaking. 'And on Sunday I'm cooking artichoke chicken and, if anyone can bear beetroot, borscht as well.'

Paul's change was clicked onto the surface of the bar and the barmaid went to serve someone else. His anxiety distracted him.

'Paul,' she said firmly, and something in her tone made him realise that her next words would be an epiphany. 'Would you like to come over on Sunday afternoon? For lunch. If, of course, you're not doing anything else.'

He nodded emphatically and she smiled, before leaning over and whispering a warning in his ear. 'Don't tell Christopher.'

7

It had rained solidly for a day, a heavy, soaking rain that fell noisily through the fully leaved trees. It soaked the hard, once impenetrable soil and filled the gutters, forming vast puddles that stretched up the dip running through the centre of the suburban streets, while the flooded drains gurgled as if slurping on an unexpected binge. Everything smelt fresh and sweet, as if the rain had brought life back to the city. It was cooler too, the wetness exorcising the arid heat usually so foreign to Liverpool's streets.

With excitement and trepidation, Paul marched up the Semilinskis' tree-lined road, the rain bouncing from his father's golf umbrella. In his other hand he clutched a paper bag with a bottle of wine carefully chosen from Nadezhda's Bold Street wine shop a day earlier.

The house seemed so still compared to how Paul remembered it. All was silent except for the steady patter of rain outside. Julia beckoned him through, calling up to Sarah as they passed the foot of the stairs. By night the bohemian chaos of the Semilinski house excited and beguiled him and was like nowhere else he'd ever been: the mounds of books and walls covered with contemporary paintings and black and white photographs; the casually scattered wine bottles from which they were allowed to help themselves like water from a tap; the exotic throws draped over sofas. The smell of incense mingling with cigarette and marijuana smoke made him think that he was in a place far from the staid and fusty suburban world he had always known. It was new and foreign and exciting. But day cast a more unforgiving light on the home. It was shabby and musty. Paint peeled from the walls and patches of damp discoloured the ceiling. What he'd previously regarded as the cool disorder of an artist's home he could now see was a neglect that permeated everywhere Julia led him.

The kitchen was warm and orderly though, the smell of roast chicken filling the air. A glass of wine sat on the oak table next to a cutting block.

'I love cooking,' said Julia. 'I like doing something that is mundane on the one hand, but you can also bring real flair to it.'

She offered Paul a chair. 'It's been said that I do great oven chips,' he said as he sat down.

She laughed and the uneasiness and fear lifted from him. 'You don't cook?'

'Egon Ronay mentions my Findus crispy pancakes.'

She tilted her head and laughed again. 'I think it's great. I love it. It's an expression of something… I don't know…' She paused for a second, searching for the word. 'Love. It's an expression of love. Cooking for someone is a tender, intimate act.'

'Christopher's never mentioned your cooking,' Paul replied.

She shrugged her shoulders, and said with sarcasm, 'Who says I ever want to do something intimate with him?'

She seemed so relaxed and different without her boyfriend. She bounced around the kitchen, fetching Paul a wine glass as she talked and pouring him a generous measure from the bottle on the table. Even her voice seemed to have relaxed; a Liverpudlian lilt lifting over her hitherto accent-less voice. 'The best thing about cooking is all the perks of the job.' She sipped from her glass and gave him a smile. 'A glass of wine here as a reward, a quick nibble there for sustenance. And I just love artichokes. Absolutely love them. I've had, like, a jar all to myself this morning. Do you like artichokes?'

Paul tried to remember from his occasional excursions to Berni Inn carveries with his parents if he'd ever sampled this alien food. 'It's like an onion, isn't it?'

'Oh Paul! Haven't Findus discovered the artichoke yet?'

Just then Sarah came down to the kitchen. Her thick black hair seemed bedraggled, as if she had only just woken, but she radiated a freshness as she moved around the kitchen, helping herself to food and wine. Paul stood as she entered, expecting, hoping that she may lean over to kiss him. Instead she walked over to the worktop and helped herself to an artichoke.

'Hello stranger,' she said, finally, as if she'd not seen Paul when she walked in. Her mouth was full of food. 'I see you've brought the weather with you.'

'I forgot it was always sunny on the posh side of Liverpool.'

'Well that's meant to be the deal,' she said, still chewing on the artichoke. 'But they needed some rain to disperse those ghastly rioters.' She pronounced 'ghastly' *garsley* in a tone that was meant to imitate the Prime Minister.

Julia joined in: 'Oh those poor shopkeepers. They've had all their hard-earned tins of beans looted by the coloureds and the jobless scroungers. It's a disgrace! A national disgrace!'

The girls dissolved into peals of laughter and a smile stretched across Paul's face.

Sarah went about inspecting her sister's work, peering into the oven and lifting lids off heavy-bottomed pans. When she looked into the biggest pan on the hob she scrunched her nose. 'I can't believe you're making that!' A note of exaggerated disgust filled her voice.

'I like it. Mama likes it. Paul will like it.' Julia turned to him. 'As you might have guessed, borsht is not Sarah's favourite.'

'I'm sure it will be delicious,' he replied.

'It's despicable peasant food!' Sarah protested.

'It's part of our heritage!'

'Yes,' Sarah responded with mock indignation. 'And no wonder everyone hates the Jews if the best we give our guests is beetroot soup.'

Paul looked embarrassed. 'I'm sure it will be lovely,' he said lamely.

Sarah scowled at her sister and stuck out her bottom lip at Paul. She poured herself a glass of wine and picked up the *Observer* colour magazine and sat down next to him. Julia went back to the cooking. 'And how are you?' she asked, her voice suddenly free from her jovial indignation.

He looked into Sarah's eyes. 'I'm great. It's always good to be here.'

She smiled at him, delight warming her face. Then she looked outside, through the kitchen window smeared with raindrops. She said, 'It's wet, so wet.'

'It's nice outside: fresh.'

'I used to like going for walks in the rain,' she said. 'But not now. Now I like getting cosy.' She rested her head on his shoulder and Paul relaxed to the warmth of her skin against his shirtsleeve.

Julia cut into the roasted meat, and they heard the careful steps of Nadezhda descend the stairs. Paul was describing in salacious detail the cast of misfits and drunks that made up The Swan's clientele as Sarah, opposite, laughed, her elbows on the table and face cupped in the palms of her hands. But as he heard the floorboards creak, announcing Nadezhda's arrival, he became distracted, stiffening and losing the trace of his story. Finally, she entered the room and Paul stood to attention.

'Hello, Mama,' Julia called out.

'Hello, girls. Hello, Paul.' She was dressed in a two-pieced lilac outfit and carefully applied make-up brought colour to her translucent skin. Her hair was clipped up and seemed to have a new lustre. She looked ready for lunch at the Savoy, never mind her own home.

Paul offered his hand and she shook it reticently, as if no one had greeted her that way before. Her hand was cold, the skin loose like an old person's; Paul could feel her bones. She beckoned him to sit down, and filled herself a drink from the wine bottle, generously emptying what remained into her own glass. Then she lit a cigarette, fingering it languidly, like Lauren Bacall, her casual manner in stark contrast to her formal attire; as if the poetess was only playing at being proper.

'Paul brought some wine from your favourite shop on Bold Street,' Julia told her.

'Oh Paul, you shouldn't have been wasting your money on us,' she said, making a show of his generosity. 'You have enough things to spend your money on at your age. And wine is something you'll always find in our house. Wine and books and conversation. We don't have much else.' She walked over to the window and rubbed the steamed glass. 'So wet and green out there. I didn't think this heatwave would ever end.'

The dining table was covered in a fresh linen cloth and four places were set around a candelabra. Red wine was decanted into a crystal carafe and silver cutlery sparkled in its light. It was pristine, thought Paul, but incongruous to the decaying décor of the room. The carpet, like all the carpets in the house, was threadbare and wallpaper peeled off the tops of the walls. Around the floor, by the French window, were flecks of white where paint had crumbled from its frame. But Paul's eyes focused on the gleaming silver of the candleholders: to him candles on tables were the preserve of good restaurants and exotic dinner parties that existed only in the world of film or television.

She showed Paul where to sit, and Sarah sat next to him. Nadezhda remained standing, one arm rested on the mantelpiece, the other holding her cigarette. Every twenty seconds or so, she took a long drag, all the while looking silently out of the window and into the rain.

Finally Julia entered with a tray full of bowls of pink soup. Sarah scrunched her nose and asked for a smallest helping.

They ladled the pink soup silently into their mouths. To Paul it seemed unpalatably sour and he found the lurid colour off-putting, but even Sarah, for all her complaints, was eating it.

It was Nadezhda who broke the silence. 'In a manner,' she announced to the three of them. 'It is peasant food.' Julia stopped eating and cast her mother a withering look. 'It's Yiddish, farmers' food. It would be as uncommon to our table growing up as, I suppose, turnip soup, or – what's that thing with the pig's head? Brine? – yes, brine would be to Paul's family's table.' Sarah's face broke into a victorious grin, and Julia, disenamoured by her mother's pronouncement, began collecting the empty bowls. Ignoring her, Nadezhda continued: 'What do you eat at home, Paul? And if it is pigs' heads, then my apologies if I offended you.'

He paused for a moment, thinking over her question. 'We're not very adventurous in our house, I'm afraid. My mum likes an easy life in the kitchen. So we have lots of frozen things.' He realised that he wasn't painting an attractive picture, so said, 'She makes her own jam and marmalade. Her marmalade is great.' But he could see that Nadezhda's interest was already waning.

'Cooking is all about tradition,' she cut in. 'It says a lot about where you come from, about your family, about your history.' She let out an audible sigh. 'I think we are losing that now. Back in the Fifties it was a big thing that there would be no more housework in the future, no more cooking, no more domestic drudgery, that all our meals in the future would consist of a pill with all the essential nutrients, and in a way I feel we are approaching that reality.'

There was an intensity and precision about what she said, as if she had been scripting her words for weeks. She was engaging and insightful and each time she spoke Paul wanted to hear more.

'So what food do you like?' Paul asked, then realising the inanity of his question stammered: 'What style, I mean. What did you grow up with?'

'Well, not borsht anyway!' Sarah let out a laugh, but Julia, who was standing over the plates awaiting her mother's pronouncement, clattered the china crossly and walked out of the room stiffly. 'Oh, Julia, I'm teasing darling,' she called out to her, laughing. 'Darling, don't be mad.' From the kitchen they could hear the clatter of plates.

Nadezhda gave her shoulders a little shrug, as if to say: *what can I do?* And then continued: 'We ate well, but there was nothing definitively Jewish about it. We had a cook, a good cook – not a charlady as some houses did – and had a variety of things. I suppose my father strayed towards France in his tastes. He was of the generation when Paris was the centre of the universe. But the thing I will always remember, always, were the weekends when we visited Vienna. I was a young girl and when you're a young girl the only food to eat is cakes. And the cakes in Vienna, Paul! The cakes! You cannot begin to imagine how wondrous these things were to a young girl!'

She was in full flow now, as if she savouring the memory. 'Sachertorte! Linzertorte! Apfelstrudel!' She paused, for a moment tasting the sweet recollection. 'After the war, when I came to England I was so looking forward to such treats again. When I first arrived I looked through the windows of these grand hotels on Piccadilly and Hyde Park, at these rich people eating their splendid cakes. I felt such envy. The first day I had some money, I went to buy a cake. I did not have enough, of course, for somewhere grand, just a small place near where I was staying on Russell Square. So I turned up, found a seat by the window, and the waitress came with a menu. I was so excited.'

Julia was standing by the door now, drawn back by her mother's yarn watching her with the same captivation as the other two.

Nadezhda continued: 'On the menu were pictures of all these cakes, these wonderful-looking cakes that I'd not eaten for eight or nine years. But one stood out. I think as much for its name as anything. It was the Viennese Slice. All I could think of was a slice of Vienna, a taste of my past. So I ordered that…' She paused, taking a sip from her wine glass, as if she were a professional storyteller, milking her audience. 'Well, the coffee came, which wasn't really coffee at all, but I didn't mind, because all I really wanted was this cake. I could see the waitress at the counter fiddling over something. Was it my cake? Then she was coming over, and suddenly it was in front of me. My Viennese slice.' A wicked smile crossed her face as she paused again, hamming up the effect.

'Yes,' said Sarah, urgently. 'What happened next?'

'It was a nasty-looking thing. It had a thick top layer, like gloss paint, and this yellow artificial cream that was already turning to water. It was awful, absolutely disgusting.' She laughed. 'Of course there was rationing at the time, so they used whatever ingredients they could. I think the cream was made from vegetable fat.'

Julia grimaced in disgust. 'Did you eat it?' she asked.

'Of course!' Nadezhda boomed, and they all laughed. 'That was my week's money. But I never wasted another penny on an English cake.' They laughed again. Paul watched her face as she revelled in the attention. Then her eyes dropped, and she said, sadly, 'I suppose I will never taste a real Viennese cake again.'

The finality with which she spoke was extraordinarily melodramatic. 'Oh Mother,' Sarah scolded, 'You're always so morbid. Of course you'll go back to Vienna.' But it was as if Nadezhda had not heard her, for she looked blankly, lost suddenly in her own thoughts.

She took a drag from her cigarette, and the others waited for her to say something. But something about her had changed; something that was almost imperceptible – a shift in her eyes, or a heavy breath that could be mistaken for a sigh – but told them she had lost interest in talking about cake, that she wanted to move the conversation on.

Finally she said to Paul, 'So, it's Cambridge for you soon.'

It was a statement, rather than a question, but he replied: 'If the grades come through, then yes.'

Nadezhda snorted a laugh, and to the girls remarked, 'Such modesty,' before turning back to Paul. 'I have no doubt at all, no doubt whatsoever that you'll get exactly the grades that you require.' From the kitchen the tinny burr of an alarm sounded and Julia excused herself and left the room. 'I imagine you're quite the scholar,' she said, observing him through the curls of cigarette smoke. 'And what will you be reading?'

'Law,' said Sarah, answering for him.

Nadezhda nodded, her watchful face emoting a hint of surprise. 'I had you down as an historian.'

'Oh I am, I'm passionate about it,' he said, then backtracking slightly, 'but I felt at university that I should broaden out.'

'Of course,' she said, then nodded to Sarah, as if taking a mental note. 'An amateur historian, how splendid.' Paul looked at her, not sure if she was being withering. It was difficult to tell. 'Without understanding our past, we can have no conception of our future,' she muttered, recycling the old cliché.

To Paul she seemed elated, giddy with the attention – which he guessed she was no longer used to. She was beautiful, he realised, not in the awkward, kooky way of Sarah, or like Julia, so paper thin and fragile, but in a classical way. She had the bone structure of a 1940s film star, her thin lips painted crimson and eyes immaculately made up. She was intense; always watching, always listening; but with the flick of an eyebrow or nod of her chin had a way of making him seem the most important person in the world. She carried her courtliness with the same ease with which she breathed. Seeing her this way made Paul realise that the tabloid stories he'd read a week earlier were almost certainly rubbish.

'So, what's your speciality, Paul?' she asked.

'Modern history interests me most.'

'The age of extremes,' she said, sadly. 'But what interests you about it all?'

He wanted to say *You interest me. Your story. Your suffering.* But instead, he said, 'The human side. Not the politics or the endgames. But how people live through a certain period. All that tends to be lost in the grand sweep of things.'

'Art records that side of things,' said Sarah. "Guernica'. *Catch-22.*

Apocalypse Now.'

'Yes, darling, you're right,' her mother replied. 'But it tends to be subjective and without context.'

They were broken off by Julia, who brought in plates of roast chicken. As the girls fussed over the serving of the food, Nadezhda put her hand on Paul's. He felt his heart beat, but it was not an erotic charge; instead he felt a sudden kinship with her. 'This is very interesting,' she said solemnly, 'We must return to it at some other time.' She lifted her hand off his, and suddenly gleeful, exclaimed: 'Julia, you are spoiling us!'

ട

When coffee was served, Julia cleared the table and disappeared from the room. From the kitchen came the sound of dishes being washed.

Nadezhda sat smoking, impassively watching the curls of smoke rise to the high ceiling. Sarah stifled a yawn and apologised. Through the silence Paul grinned back at her.

'I suppose we should have a liquor to finish off,' Nadezhda announced. 'Then I shall leave you in peace.'

She put down her cigarette and went to the cabinet at the end of the room, its beautiful walnut and rosewood veneer incongruous to the peeling, yellowed wallpaper it backed onto. 'Sarah, go and see if your sister will join us.' Without a word she left the room.

'This is pear schnapps,' she told Paul, pouring thimble-sized portions. Then, gesturing at the crude label-less bottle: 'A friend of mine from Switzerland makes it. It's good. Potent.'

Paul looked at her and raised an eyebrow. 'I can't say I've drunk pear schnapps before.' He was suddenly embarrassed by his voice, which he thought sounded like a young boy, innocent and unworldly, that it betrayed the truth: that he had never had a schnapps of any kind before. She was watching him, he realised, and for a second held his eye. This time though, she was not scrutinising him; it was almost a gaze, a longing. There was a sexual magnetism in her eyes. He thought about her putting her cold, thin-skinned hand on his earlier and realised that he had misplaced her maternalism for wanting. But she said nothing, and moments later Sarah re-entered the room.

'Julia is going out and won't join us.'

'Very well,' said Nadezhda, sliding another glass across the table to him. 'Paul will have to have a second glass.' She caught his eye again, but this time there was a look of mischief. He smiled back at her, oblivious to Sarah, as though the challenge was a private thing between them.

'L'chaim,' she said, raising her glass. 'To life.' Paul and Sarah followed her toast, tipping the clear contents into their mouths. It scorched Paul's throat and as he felt the intoxicating liquid slide down his throat he had to stop himself from recoiling into a fit of coughs.

Sarah shouted clearing her throat. 'Mama! Good God. Was that from one of the winos at the community centre? Good grief!'

Nadezhda let out a delighted laugh. 'It's good stuff! The best! I told you it was potent!' Then to Paul, raising her now empty glass, gesturing it was time for his second shot. 'Paul,' she called; but Paul said nothing, momentarily oblivious to her attention, to everything. His head spun. When Nadezhda spoke his name a second time, he looked up but could see only a fog.

'Paul,' she said. 'Sláinte!'

'Sláinte!' he cried as if going to war and put the glass to his lips and extracted another mouthful.

'Marvellous!' shouted Nadezhda, giddy with excitement,

clapping her hands together. But Paul was barely aware of her – or anything. His head swam in an alcoholic fug. He didn't notice Nadezhda say her goodbyes to him and Sarah as she left for her rooms, her books and her wine. He wasn't really conscious of Julia's departure. A mist lay in front of him, cloying his sense of reality as the world, the girls, the ramshackle house took on a dreamlike quality.

Then Sarah was sat on his knee, her arm around his neck, her hand fingering his right ear and clarity returned.

'I like ears,' she told him. 'You have nice ears.'

He laughed at the preposterousness of her assertion. 'What can I possibly say to that?'

She shrugged her shoulders. 'What do you like?' she asked, still playing with his ear. Their noses were almost touching; he could smell the sweet fragrance of the schnapps on her breath.

'You,' he said decisively, emphatically. 'I like you.'

'Do you?' She leant in even closer, as if that were at all possible. She didn't speak, she didn't whisper, she purred seductively, the skein of their awkwardness now gone. 'What do you like about me?'

'Everything,' he said. 'I like everything about you.'

She kissed him, her lips first barely touching his. Then she leant in more, her hand pushing the back of his head into hers, kissing him harder and harder, her tongue stabbing around his mouth, nicking off the edges of his teeth.

'You're incorrigible,' she said in her lovely teasing way. 'My reputation is quite destroyed!' With her finger she stabbed his belly.

'That's just as well,' he said, poking her back. 'It will deter any rivals.'

∽

They sat with their backs to the dining room wall, watching in the half-light as the summer rain trickled down the window. It was later now, nearly dusk. Outside, masked by the rivulets of water running down the glass and the rising gloom, the chaotic, overgrown garden was lush and green. Sarah tipped the dregs of another wine bottle into his glass. Paul's lips were parched, and he was tired and drunk, but elated too. He rested his head on her shoulder and she kissed the top of it. He took a sip from the wine glass: it was bitter and cheap but he didn't care.

'I don't think I've quite recovered from the schnapps,' he said in a purposely forlorn way. 'I don't think I ever will.'

She giggled and took his wine glass off him and sipped from it. Her own glass was empty. 'I'd better help you with this then.'

Everything had felt so natural, nothing was forced. But Paul knew that their time together was drawing to a close, that there was a train to catch, a walk home and an empty bed waiting for him on the other side of the city. And yet still their togetherness lacked definition. While it did, an unease persisted within him, nagging away.

'So where do we go from here?' he asked, his tone immediately betraying his unease.

She snapped out of her contented lull and looked at him with urgency. 'What do you mean?'

'Well, y'know. Can I call you my girlfriend?'

She smiled her smile and he felt the doubt wash away. 'Only if I can call you my boyfriend.'

He kissed her lips. Everything will be all right, he told himself, everything will be just fine.

8

Outside Liverpool Central Station, a man stood in the middle of the pavement oblivious to the growing patter of rain. With a note of desperation in his voice, he exhorted passers-by to purchase the flimsy cigarette lighters standing untouched on the tray he held out in front of himself. He was small and thin, in his forties perhaps, but his face, browned and weather-beaten by countless days on the street and evenings in backstreet pubs, made him look old before his time.

'Five for a pound on your lighters,' he called, but the words all merged into one, so it sounded like a bark, the despairing yelp of a neglected dog. As crowds filed out of the station, filtering past him to the shops and offices of Church Street, no one paid any attention, no one even looked up as he let out another call:

'Fiveforapoundonyourlighters!'

From the adjacent doorway Paul surveyed the gloomy afternoon, watching the people, studying their faces as they left the station, wandering past the lone hawker and on into the city. Then a van pulled up, emblazoned with the logo of the city's newspaper, the *Liverpool Echo*, and a driver jumped out, carrying a pile of newspapers, which he tossed out towards a hitherto empty kiosk.

From behind it, a man emerged and cut open the bundle, which he laid out swiftly on his stall. As the van drove off, leaving a waft of diesel, the newsagent's voice joined the sound of the city, echoing the yelp of the lighterman.

'Five for a pound on your lighters... Echo... fiveforapoundonyourlighters... E-ho...'

Paul glanced at his watch. 1.15pm. Late.

A man stood next to him in the doorway, sheltering from the rain. He pulled out a copy of the *Echo* and Paul read it from over his shoulder. The government were setting up a task force for the city. Michael Heseltine was to be Minister for Merseyside. There will be investment, he promised, investment and salvation. Paul wondered about those poor shopkeepers.

He looked at his watch again. 1.20pm. Twenty minutes late now. His eyes surveyed the station again, but she wasn't in the latest huddle emerging up the escalators from their train. He wondered for a moment if she would come at all.

But then through the milieu of shoppers on Church Street, coming from the other direction he spotted her, her loping, bounding stride distinguishing her from hundreds of others. Despite the drizzle, her white shoulders were almost bare; she was wearing a green strappy top and narrow jeans that accentuated her long thin legs.

Spotting him she raised her hand, then flicking her wrist pointed her first finger towards him, like a child pretending she had a gun, and walked straight towards him.

'Hello, hello,' she said, finally dropping her hand as she neared him. When she reached him she put her thumbs in his trouser pockets, pulled her body against his and leant up and kissed his lips. Then, taking his wrist, she looked at his watch. 'I'm not late, am I?' she asked, knowing full well that she was.

The Café Tabac was a long narrow room at the top of Bold Street. Plastic tablecloths printed in red checks and old chipped china hinted at a decorous setting fallen on hard times; the sort of place where old ladies once congregated for their mid-morning chatter and shoppers passed by for lunchtime sustenance. But the clientele was all young. There were students on their summer breaks, making a coffee last for an hour. There was a punk with a lurid green Mohican, reading a week-old copy of the *NME*. At the far end, hidden by the half-light and a pall of cigarette smoke was an assortment of art students; their uniform long greasy hair, denim shirts were worn open over white T-shirts and big, heavy Doc Marten boots. In the corner by the windows sat a Japanese couple, backpackers, wondering what to make of it all.

'I was hungover and happy all of yesterday. I barely moved from the sofa,' said Sarah. She took his hands in hers, dipped her nearly-bare shoulders and smiled. Never will you look lovelier than now, Paul told himself. She laughed again. 'Mother likes you.'

'I know,' said Paul. 'I remember her saying so.'

She giggled. 'No, she really does. Being argumentative is all just part of the game to her. If she's not interested in you she'll leave you be. But you had her on top form: arguing and raconteuring. Like in the old days.'

A sadness, almost indistinguishable, momentarily glistened in her eyes but was sharply broken by the waitress bringing over their coffees.

Nadezhda had played heavily on his mind too. He couldn't get her out of his head: her strangeness, her foreignness, her past. He kept going back to things she had said: the hints about life in the old country; the story about the cakes; and what she'd said about him – 'A clever young man who reads!' But it was she that was watching him, and the thing that he remembered most vividly was not Sarah but the lustful way that her mother had looked at him when they were alone; the look of longing. It turned him on and appalled him.

'So what are we doing later?'

'We'll go for a walk. I want to take some pictures.' From her canvas shoulder bag she took out an SLR camera. Its casing was matt black, a short expensive lens protruded from the front. Paul took it from her and examined it. It was a Leica: he knew nothing about cameras, but it impressed him. 'I have a project for college,' she explained. 'I don't exactly know what it'll be about, but I feel I should do something about here and now.'

'What do you mean?'

'The city. What's happening to it.' He remained impassive, so her voice raised a notch. 'Don't you feel it, Paul? Don't you feel that we're part of something here?' She had become animated, her hands moving around as she spoke, and her voice rang with force and passion. He hadn't seen this side to her before; for the first time she reminded him of her mother. 'The city is dying around us Paul, it is literally falling apart. It's the basket case that it's okay for the rest of the country to kick. But there's an energy here, a spirit that says: "We don't care what you throw at us." I want to capture it: the mixture of decay and defiance.'

He contemplated her words for a moment and the realisation of what she meant became clear. Liverpool might be falling down, it might be broke and morally bankrupt, considered by many the seventh circle of a metropolitan inferno, but it would never die.

∽

At the top of Bold Street stood an old church. It was just a carcass of what it had once been: walls, arches, columns and steps; but no roof or windows, no sort of interior, just grass and rubble where pews were once bathed in the coloured light of its windows. It was bombed in the war and left as a memorial to the horrors of the Blitz. But there was no reverence bestowed upon the monument and it was as if its existence was attributable only to the fact that no one could be bothered to do the decent thing and demolish it, for it was just a ruin, and the railings that once ringed it were rusted and twisted, as impermanent and penetrable as the structure they surrounded.

Paul clambered over the remnants of the iron fence and offered his hand to Sarah, who followed him through. They climbed over the litter of broken masonry, plastic bags, old crisp packets and tin cans. Corrugated iron, its surface perforated with rust-red holes, gaping like old wounds, blocked the doorway to the old church. Sarah took out her camera and started taking pictures.

'If the black death returned tomorrow,' said Paul, 'all of England would look like this within thirty years.'

'Aye,' she said, 'but without the crisp packets.'

They drifted around the outside of the church, the click of Sarah's camera shutter interrupting the sound of nearby traffic filtering down damp streets. A brick wall separated the west of the church from Hardman Street, hiding them from the procession of traffic, although those on the smoking decks of the buses could peer over into the churchyard. A line of three of them were parked at the traffic lights: one red, one green, one cream. The passengers concentrated on their newspapers and their cigarettes, but one old man, red-skinned, bald and hunched over, spotted them and waved. Sarah returned his greeting.

'Shall we try and get inside?' he suggested, looking up uncertainly at an open window five feet above their heads, a tree branch peering out of it.

'Let's go back around the front,' she said, and he followed her back around to the steps that led up to the columned entrance. She bounded up them and pressed against the steel shutter. It creaked and bended, but wouldn't quite yield for her. When she let go it bounced back and a hail of rusty splinters rained down on her.

Paul came up alongside her and they pushed again. This time the shutter started to move and the crack of light her efforts previously yielded widened. Inside was a green and lush space, free from the litter that adulterated the rest of this so-called monument. Trees rose up from a carpet of grass and wild flowers grew from the moss-covered ruins. A crow, black and shiny and ominous, rose from one of the trees, its wings clapping above the sound of the street. They watched it fly into the flat, grey sky until it disappeared.

'What the fuck are you doing?' screamed a male voice, his harsh Scouse accent fissuring with anger. A scrawny, hollow-faced man was stood at the gap from inside the church, his neck bulging with a tangle of angry blue veins.

Paul stepped back. The man's eyes were wild, his pupils dilated; his skin the colour of chalk. He had an emaciated look.

'What are you doing?' Paul retorted.

'I fucking live here, lad.'

The man was wild-eyed and angry, jabbing the air with his fingers.

'I'm sorry, I hadn't realised this was a private address.' From behind him, Paul could hear Sarah winding on her camera.

'You being funny, lad?' His face was almost at the gap between the makeshift door and its frame. Paul noticed his arms, pockmarked with red dots and angry, pussy scabs. He had the body of a heroin addict.

'No,' said Paul blankly. 'We were just looking.'

'Well look somewhere else.' Sarah's camera shutter snapped and she was winding it on again. A moment passed before the man realised he had been photographed. 'Oi, what the fuck are you doing!' he yelled. The camera clicked a second time and the man stepped forward to make a grab for Paul. But he was too quick and jumped back. As he did the iron hoarding snapped back, trapping the man between it and the wall. He was swimming in the air, hurling threats and curses at them, but unable to get near them. But they were already gone, down the shattered steps and through the gnarled railing, running around the corner and up Hardman Street, laughing as they heard the smackhead's curses in the distance.

∽

When they came to a stop they were still laughing.

'I don't think he'll catch us now,' said Paul as he bent over and gasped for breath.

She looked back down the street. 'I wonder if he's still stuck?'

Paul laughed out loud.

'"I didn't realise this was a private address",' she said in a pompous voice, mocking his retort. 'You're such a bad Tory, Paul. I think he was madder at that than me taking his photograph.'

He laughed again as he caught his breath. 'Yes, why did you take his photograph? Was this the great Liverpool spirit you were talking about?'

They walked on along Hope Street, towards the Gothic magnificence of the Anglican Cathedral. The buildings around them were grand Georgian terraces, brownstones that rose four storeys high, but even in this part of the city decay was omnipresent.

On one side of the street were fine buildings: doctors' practices, solicitors' offices and the occasional private residence. On the other lay minicab offices, buildings with bricked-up windows and steel doors, squats and harlots' dens.

Sarah led them up a side street and the hubbub of Hope Street was silenced. The old buildings became fewer, more dilapidated as they walked uphill. Then they were in a square, a courtyard ringed with ugly red-bricked tenements. The brickwork hinted at art deco, but really they were too unattractive, too rotten to be associated with anything so lustrous.

Paul wiped his brow. Children were hacking a football around the courtyard, scrubland, muddied by the recent rain. The hulk of a burned-out car lay alongside one of the buildings. He felt awkward here, nervous. These were Liverpool's badlands.

But Sarah was undeterred. The camera came out and she started focussing on the children, flicking her wrist with every shot that she took. They moved around the scrubland in a mass, following the ball around them as one, like a swarm of swallows moving in the afternoon sky. There were around thirty of them, their ages between five and fifteen. As the tackles flew in on their chaotic game, it was clear that an undercurrent of violence bubbled near its surface. One boy, an under-grown redhead in his early teens, nudged his larger opponent off the ball who responded by volleying his elbow into the younger boy's face. He fell, clutching his nose, and when he removed his hand his face was the same colour as his hair.

Paul watched all this with the detached air of someone who would sooner be elsewhere. All the while Sarah wandered closer and closer to the action, snapping away on her black SLR.

For a few minutes the footballers were oblivious to their spectators. But one of the younger boys spotted Sarah and realising that she was alien to such parts, came striding over. She lowered the camera, so it pointed at his unwashed face and snapped. She adjusted her focus and snapped again. Finally the boy stood in front of her, barely four feet tall, hands on hips.

'What are you doing?' he asked. His voice was high pitched, his accent thick, guttural so that it came out as one word: 'Warrayerdoin?'

'I'm taking some pictures.'

'Of what?' *Of warr?*

'Of here, of you, of the boys.'

'Why would you want to do that? Me ma says this is a shit tip.' The boy wore grey flannel shorts – his school shorts, Paul suspected, even though they were deep into the summer holidays – and a green and white hooped T-shirt that was grey with dirt and sweat. His knees were scabbed by dozens of afternoons spent kicking a football around the dirt.

'I like it,' she said. 'It's interesting to me.' She had the curiosity of an American visitor making a pilgrimage around Beatles sites, he thought. A slum tourist.

An older boy spotted them and started to come over. 'Tommy,' he called, 'Worrayerdoin?'

'That's me brother,' said the younger boy. 'Bonkers.'

'Bonkers?'

'That's what we call him 'cos he's off his head.'

'Oh God,' Paul muttered.

Bonkers was about twelve, but although he was twice his brother's age, stood less than a foot taller than him. He had a hard, wizened face, not dissimilar to the man they'd seen at the church. Bad food, a bad environment – it gave all these people the same pallor, thought Paul. Bonkers marched up to Sarah, who took his picture as he came towards her. When she lowered the lens he stood no more than a yard away from her, looking up, scowling.

'This is me brother,' he said, unsmiling, pointing at Tommy. He had the same unwashed look, as if a dozen baths wouldn't remove the grime. 'You got a ciggy?'

'I don't smoke,' Paul replied and Bonkers let out a sound of disgust. He sat himself down on the grass, still looking up at them sullenly.

'He done that car over there,' Tommy squeaked, excitedly gesturing at the burnt out wreck on the far side of the wasteland.

Paul looked disbelievingly at Bonkers, who said nothing but shrugged his shoulders as if to say: *Maybe I did, maybe I didn't.*

'Is it true?' Sarah asked him.

'Well they say I'm off me head, don't they?' he replied, letting out a wicked smile.

Some of the other boys started to drift over from the game of football and were standing around, watching the four of them suspiciously from a distance. They shared the same feral appearance of Bonkers and Tommy; their hair uniformly shaved down into a close crop, so that their heads resembled dirty tennis balls, furry and grey.

'This your bird then?' Bonkers asked Paul.

'Yes.'

'Nice,' he said, eyeing her up and down. 'You shagging her, then?'

Paul spluttered in indignation, while Sarah looked to the ground smiling. The boy eyed Sarah, and taking Paul's response to be a no, smirked and said, 'Pity, I bet she's got a lovely gash.'

'Oi, come on, that's enough,' barked Paul, and then to Sarah, 'We should go.'

Bonkers raised his hands in the air, as if acknowledging that he had gone too far. 'Only messing lad. We're all friends round here, right.' It was a statement, not a question.

'Was there any trouble up here during the riots?' Paul asked.

'Not really. Some of us went to go and have a gander, but we behave ourselves here,' he cackled. 'These lads won't get a nice job, they won't have a nice house and a nice life. Some'll be smackheads, some'll end up inside. They've got nothin', nothin' at all. But you don't see them acting like savages like the blacks down the hill.'

'You stole the car and burned it out,' Sarah said.

He shrugged again. 'That's only havin' a laugh though, isn't it?'

Sarah looked down at him, her face framed in a look of bewilderment and revulsion.

'And what will you do?' asked Paul. 'If all the others are going to be smackheads and thieves, what will become of you?'

Bonkers laughed. 'I'll be all right, pal. I'll be getting off out of here. They might call me Bonkers, but I'm the only one with any brains around here. I'll be getting me exams and a nice job and a nice bird thank you very much.'

One of the older boys, standing sullen and alone ten yards from them called Bonkers. He glanced back and waved.

'Listen, girl,' he said to Sarah. 'You want to be getting on. There's some bad lads here and they'll have off with your stuff before you know it.' He pulled himself from the dirt and rubbed his hands down his shirt. 'Come on, Tommy,' he muttered. Then without saying goodbye, turned and left them.

∽

Sarah was done with slum hunting, but wanted to see the river and the docks before calling it a day. So they made their way back down the hill, through the crumbling Georgian streets, to the riverfront.

At a makeshift kiosk, set into the wall of an old brown-stoned warehouse, Sarah bought cans of Coca-Cola and they stood against the side of it, sipping the cool syrupy drink.

Above Sarah's head a poster was smeared crudely onto the brickwork, featuring the Prime Minister and the words 'Not Wanted'. Thatcher's head was tilted and her mouth was distorted so that it looked as though she had fangs protruding from her mouth. The demagogue looked demonic, like an apparition of Beelzebub.

'Take my picture,' said Sarah, handing Paul the Leica. She put the empty Coke can down and stood on tiptoes so that her shoulders were level with the Prime Minister's. Tilting her head she bared her teeth. Paul focused, snapped, and Sarah burst into peals of laughter. 'Oh those poor shopkeepers,' she laughed in a voice that mimicked Margaret Thatcher's.

When they reached Salisbury Dock there was a deadly hush in the air. There was no sign of work nor life. The quayside was crumbled into pieces, so that there were vast brown puddles everywhere. One of the docks was emptied of water, filled instead with flat, stinking mud. In the other swam a debris of plastic bags, discarded footballs, old bottles and dumped shopping trolleys. The handsome clock tower which once stood proudly over hundreds of strapping dockworkers was a solitary reminder of prouder, more prosperous times. Its four faces, however, had all stopped so that they displayed different times, none of them correct, but the long hands all pointed to the numeral IV.

'They all read nineteen past the hour,' Sarah observed. 'What are the chances of that?'

The two of them walked on, through a litter of rubbish and rubble, around the perimeter of the derelict dock. The Liver Building stood grand and impressive in the distance, its twin copper cormorants rising nobly above all around them.

By one of the empty landing berths a rabies prevention sign warned visitors in French, German and Spanish. It was the only new thing untouched by vandalism that they had seen all day, and yet it added only to the city's perpetual aura of foreboding.

Finally the docks gave way to a line of wooden sheds. Moored alongside them was a pilot boat, unoccupied though bereft of the neglect that consumed all else. They edged along the narrow quayside. The shed walls were narrow and rickety and at one point an entire wall panel had fallen in on itself, creating a makeshift doorway.

Inside was a long empty warehouse, its walls whitewashed, its floor rutted by broken concrete and yet more puddles. An intricate iron framework rose in a V shape above the building, but above that was only the dull white sky. Every scrap of roof was peeled off. Through the ironwork they could see the Liver Building again, massive and omnipresent.

'Hello!' Paul called, and his voice echoed around the empty building. But he knew no one else was there, no one except Sarah. He took her hand and they trudged across the broken floor, to an opening on the very far side.

When they merged back into the midst of the dull August afternoon, the Albert Dock was in front of them. Once this was the largest and most advanced warehouse system in the world. Now, however, it was vacant, empty and unemployed, a fitting monument to a city where work had started to become a thing of the past.

Sarah was taking photographs again, crouching down to fit the full profile of the immense red-bricked buildings. Paul kicked the edge of a warehouse wall and part of the brickwork gave way, crumbling into a puff of finely broken stone.

'You know, it could be great around here,' he said, sadly. 'These old buildings could be spruced up and you could have shops and offices and all sorts. It's on the waterfront. It's in the city centre. You just need some vision. That's all.'

She had taken the camera from her face, but still crouched and looked over the still muddied expanse of dock water. There was a sudden sadness in her.

'It's never going to get better, is it?' she asks.

Paul glanced around at the empty warehouses, towering high above them; at the decaying brickwork and empty quays; at the brown water, oozing with mud and silt.

'No,' he said sadly. 'I don't think it is.'

∽

At the Pier Head, a soulless Sixties construct of boxy low-level buildings, Sarah spotted an ice-cream van, its diesel generator noisily spluttering fumes into the warm breeze.

'Do you want a ninety-niner?' she asked, cheer and humour returned to her voice. Without awaiting his answer she skipped over to the van and came back with two ice creams topped with chocolate flakes and fluorescent raspberry sauce.

He took it from her and bit into the top; the ice cream was cool and saccharine, the raspberry acidic and exceptionally sweet.

'Shall we go on the *Royal Iris*?' she asked, gesturing over to the quayside where the ferry boat would arrive from its crossing.

'If you want,' he said, almost with a shrug.

'Come on, I've not been on it for years.'

Paul bought their tickets and they walked down to the waiting room, another ugly box with bright green plastic furniture and windows misted over by splatters of sea water, the salt fogging the glass. Some early commuters were waiting to be taken back home to Birkenhead, across the water. There were old girls with lurid self-dyed hair and cheap cigarettes, nattering about their day's work and plans for tea and the night's TV viewing. There was a couple with a young child running around their feet, and another asleep in a Silver Cross pram, its green steel frame solid and unshakeable like a First World War tank. At the bottom of the room was a photograph booth for passport pictures, but a one-legged tramp sat there, his stick balanced against the side, drinking from a bottle cloaked in a brown paper bag and muttering to himself. He was filthy, white-haired, with a thick and bedraggled beard and plump stomach, like a distorted version of Santa Claus.

Outside the ferry was docking. It bounced off the huge rubber tyres that lined the jetty, then a rope was thrown to an official and he tied it to the mooring bollard. The engine shuddered noisily to a halt and the gangway was dropped with a bang. A trickle of passengers emerged from the ferry and when they had exited the twenty or so gathered in the waiting room embarked, leaving the old tramp to his methylated spirits and photo booth.

Paul and Sarah sat on the top deck, in the open. A stiff breeze whipped across the river, blowing her sweet-smelling hair into his face. She laughed and pulled it back down, and put her head on his shoulder.

The Royal Iris's horn sounded and the engine shuddered back into life. The plastic horn-shaped speaker affixed to a flagpole crackled and spluttered and the unmistakable first notes of Gerry and the Pacemakers' 'Ferry 'Cross the Mersey' struck up.

As the boat pulled into the river, the clouds started to break over the city. Shafts of sunlight beamed down upon the Three Graces and the Albert Dock. Moments earlier they had witnessed a scene of decay and decrepitude, now it looked like God's own country.

Sarah took out her camera, wound it on and snapped. Then she held it out in front of her, so that the lens faced the two of them and snapped again. She put the camera away and kissed him.

For a minute they were lost in an embrace, their minds focussed entirely each other so that they missed the impossible irony of the approaching chorus.

9

The gloom of dusk hung like a shadow as they made their way up the front path of the Semilinski house. Sarah pushed her key into the door and twisted it left and right, momentarily grimacing with effort until the Yale lock yielded and they were inside. The house was dull, untidy and silent.

He followed her up the stairs and into a room which he'd never seen before. It was now almost dark and he stood at the door while she fumbled around with a lamp switch. A click, illumination and his first sight of her bedroom.

It was unlike anywhere else in the house. There was no ragged carpet or peeling wallpaper, no mess of unwashed crockery or empty wine bottles. Instead the walls were painted a cool cream, the floorboards stripped bare to the grain and waxed into a golden brown. In the bay window was an easel loaded up with a canvas. A music stand stood next to it. Adorning the walls were an array of pencil sketches, wood cuts and several canvas paintings. The area of the wall nearest the door was smeared from floor to ceiling in black and white photographs. It didn't seem like a bedroom; indeed the high vaulted ceilings gave it the aspect of a roomy studio flat. Paul thought of his own boxy bedroom, with its football posters and Ferrari duvet cover, and how modest and immature it seemed by comparison.

'It's amazing.' His eyes surveyed the photographs next to him, a collage of greys and blacks. Many were of Liverpool, similar sights and slums to those they had seen that afternoon. But others were of distant shores, places he had only seen on television or read about: Paris, Vienna, Berlin, Rome. There were dark, moody shots of alleyways and side streets, the underbellies of Europe's great cities. There were snaps too. A younger Julia in front of the Eiffel Tower; Sarah, aged fourteen or so, neither a girl nor a woman, her face contorted in an inscrutable pose, standing next to the *Mona Lisa*. Then there was a group shot: the two girls and an old man, white haired, his wizened face framed by horn-rimmed glasses, all hugged in heavy coats and with thick snow behind them, next to them a graffitied wall and in the distance Checkpoint Charlie.

'You've been to a lot of places,' he observed.

'Not really,' she said. 'I've never been further east than Berlin and not much further west than Wales. If you coloured all the places I've been on a world map there wouldn't be much of a mark left behind.' She beckoned him to sit down on a mauve beanbag and slid himself down to the floor and rested next to her bed. 'There's so many places I'd like to visit. New York, Chicago, Russia, Jerusalem.'

'Is that your father on the photograph up there?' He pointed to the picture taken by the Brandenburg Gate.

'The one in the snow? Yes, that's him.'

'And the paintings – you did them all as well?'

'No, just that one.' She pointed to a large canvas, depicting a plump nude splayed out on a cream sofa. It was drawn in light pastels, the skin ghostly white, darkened only by the jet black of the hair on her head and groin.

'Is that Julia?' he asked.

'Is that Julia!' she shrieked with laughter. 'I bet you wouldn't have asked that if she was here! It's a model, from school.' Paul felt his cheeks burn at his naivety. 'The other canvases are things that my father picked up when he lived in Liverpool. He used to go to all the end of term art shows at the Poly and pick things up that he liked. The one over there is a Sutcliffe.' She pointed to an oil painting, its canvas thick with angry reds and oranges, like a George Grosz portrayal of the apocalypse.

'As in Stuart Sutcliffe?'

'The one and only.'

He stood up and studied it closely for nearly a minute.

'That's incredible,' he said as he sat back down. 'It must be worth thousands.'

'Hundreds perhaps,' she said, gently correcting him. 'It's worth more as a piece of Beatles ephemera than art. But I like it. It's wild, edgy; it's a reminder of the dangerous times we live in.'

'Do we live in dangerous times?'

'I think so, yes. We saw it last week in this city. But there's a more insidious threat that could strike at any time. A button pressed and the whole world goes up in flames.'

Paul examined the painting again: it was truly apocalyptic, as the layers of oil unfolded mile upon mile of impenetrable flame. He thought of what he wanted to devote his life to: searching for the root of man's inhumanity to man. The painting did not give him any answers, but seemed a vivid reminder of man's ability to inflict catastrophe upon his enemy.

'It's almost chilling when you think what it could represent.'

They had brought wine with them and she sipped from her glass and sat watching him, smiling, her eyes filled with adoration.

A great warmth surged through his body. This was the time he'd yearned for; him and her, alone, happy, without complications.

They talked about their parents: Paul's father and his mother, a difficult woman, with her twin passions for church and the golf club; hers the Holocaust-surviving poet and the art-collecting shipping merchant. They spoke of university, exams and Paul's leaving of Liverpool.

'So, when we're old and grey Paul, do you think we'll take up golf and join the Rotarians?' Her question was only half-serious, but to Paul she spoke about their future with such clarity, in such a matter-of-fact way, that it excited him.

'I don't know about that,' he said grinning. 'They probably won't allow outsiders at the country club. No blacks, no Irish, no dogs and certainly no Jews. We'd be blackballed.'

'Ah,' she countered. 'But you discount the powers of the global Jewish cabal. We have ways and means.' They both laughed.

'So what do you think we'll be like in the future?' he asked, testing her.

'Older, happy. Away from here…' She trailed off and watched as he sat, his arms around his knees, the model of contentment. She didn't know why she loved this quiet, studious boy and wanted to be with him until the end of time. She wanted to be part of him, to be one. So she leant across the Scrabble board and kissed him, first softly, then feeling his tongue touching hers, more intensely. She crawled over to be with him and pushed his head closer to hers, kissing him harder and harder. She took his hand and placed it on her breast and helped him undress her. Then they were on the bed, he inside her and everything felt right.

She woke him gently from his doze. He murmured and blinked, then seeing her smiled.

'I've run a bath,' she whispered.

He was naked on her bed, but felt no shame in his state of undress. She wore a white bathrobe and took his hand and led him to the en suite. It was illuminated by candlelight and steam rose from the water like autumn mists over the Mersey. A smell of lavender filled the warm moist room. She held his hand as he climbed in, the water momentarily scalding his ankles. He sighed audibly as he sank into its warmth. Then Sarah dropped her robe to the floor and stepped in at the other end. He watched transfixed as her narrow slender breasts and small brown nipples slid down under the soap suds.

He sighed again and leaned back.

'Say something,' she whispered.

A sense of unreality had crept over him and his head swam in a haze of euphoria and alcohol, adding to his dreamlike state.

'I'm intoxicated by you.'

She raised her shoulders self-consciously and beamed at him.

'That was my first...' She broke off, not needing to add anything.

'Me too,' he said.

A smile stretched across her face.

'You'll be my one and only,' she whispered.

'You mine.'

He leant across the bathtub, the noise of water trickling from his naked torso filling the hitherto silent bathroom, and kissed her.

'Forever,' he whispered.

Her lips mouthed the word back, but Paul could hear only the drip of bathwater.

10

Days like this passed, then weeks; but in this long hot summer, time seemed to stand still. They had no plans or time agenda, just an elemental need to spend as much time together as they could. They visited Chester, Southport Fairground, Speke Hall; they cycled the south Lancashire foothills and sought out Strawberry Field. Some days they just spent sprawled out in Sarah's bed, making love and dozing in each other's arms. Other times they went on long, directionless walks through a city neither was quite able to call home.

August arrived and with it the dawning realisation that this time was drawing to its end. In the middle of the month Sarah had to visit her father in Hamburg, a trip that was booked long before Paul had even entered her consciousness. Shortly after her return he was set for university.

The thought of life without her, even for just a few weeks, started to obsess him, haunting his dreams and casting a pall over his daily existence. Was it all just some wonderful dream from which he was about to wake? Would they endure, despite distance and absence? Did she mean it, when she said 'forever'?

Would university change him? Would they survive such shifting circumstances?

One afternoon he woke with a start, his brow prickled with sweat and sat up in her bed: she lay next to him, naked, her arm curled around his waist.

'What's going to happen?'

She woke from her doze, and stroked his back.

'Nothing's going to happen, Paul, nothing at all. Don't worry.'

But still this lingering dread would not go.

∽

On the day before her trip to Germany he found her waiting for him in the strip-lit gloom of Moorfields station. She had with her a pale blue Raleigh bicycle and when she saw Paul disembark at the other end of the platform, waved, and, almost breaking into a run, rushed to greet him, stooping over the crossbar to kiss him. Paul had his bike too and as they pushed them through the station's dull corridors and down the escalator onto a platform cut even deeper into Liverpool's bowels, she told him about her latest concert given to the Cheshire Women's Institute.

'I don't know why I bother,' she said in her sing-song voice. 'It wasn't even a good cause, just a bunch of spoiled wives and bitter old spinsters.' They were on their train now, rattling through the tunnel, alone in their carriage. 'You know what some old bag came up and said? This miserable, grey old thing: grey hair; grey clothes; grey face. Guess what she said? Go on!'

Paul smiled and shrugged his shoulders.

'"Well that was a perfectly adequate performance." Perfectly adequate! Can you imagine!' She laughed in the face of this latest absurdity.

Through the tunnel they heard the echo of the train's horn and suddenly they were in the open and their carriage was filled with brilliant sunlight.

Paul blinked and said, 'Even Birkenhead seems lovely on a day like today.'

Sarah peered out doubtfully at the ugly embankments, its tower blocks and flyovers, an unsightly medley of concrete. 'Every day is a lovely day with you,' she said and kissed him.

Birkenhead passed now and they were in open countryside. Merseyside's urban sprawl seemed a long way away, not just a few miles from where they travelled. Small conurbations – Bidston, Meols, Moreton – came into view as the train shuddered to a halt; the doors opened, but nobody ever seemed to embark or leave the train.

They took it to the end of the line, at West Kirby, a small seaside town at the mouth of the River Dee. After pushing their bicycles through the barriers, they pedalled down to the waterfront. Families had already set themselves out on the sandy beach and in the man-made marina windsurfers sailed in the steady breeze that blew in from the Irish Sea. Wales sat just across the shallow estuary of the River Dee. Because the sea was so far out, it looked almost walkable.

Paul pointed to a small outcrop of land 500 yards into the Dee estuary. 'That's Hilbre Island,' he said.

She shaded her eyes from the sun and looked out across the sands. 'What is it?'

'Just a small island, but it's been all sorts of things. For five hundred years it was inhabited by a cell of monks and was a place of pilgrimage. Then it was a port and a customs house. Then it was home to a salt refinery and there was a brewery. Then it became a lighthouse post.'

She turned to him and asked, 'What is it now?'

'I don't think it's anything any more,' he replied.

She gazed out to sea again, a plaintive look on her face, which might have said: *like so much of this city.*

They cycled along the promenade, the sea breeze blowing in their hair and when West Kirby was behind them they turned inland, the road following a slight gradient. They were in the countryside now, traversing hedge-lined lanes and cutting through minute and prosperous hamlets. They saw a combine harvester hoovering the summer crop, a postman on his round, three children soaking each other with water pistols and a woman walking her dog. It was quiet and rural; witnessing it Paul could understand why many Liverpudlians considered the Wirral foreign to their city.

At a small stone bridge they stopped and Paul took glass bottles of lemonade from his bag and levered the tops off with his pen knife. They sat in the scrub, propped against the bridge, sipping the tepid drinks.

When he had drunk his bottle, Paul unfolded his penknife and began scraping the wall. When he finished his handiwork, he showed her.

Sarah and Paul, August 16, 1981

She smiled and asked him for the knife, then beneath it began carving.

He read the inscription and kissed her.

And Forever

'It means I love you,' she said.

'I bet you say that to all the boys.'

'Just this one.'

A little further down the lane they stopped at a stile and Paul lifted their bicycles over. It took them onto a disused railway line that was covered, it seemed, by an unending shade of foliage. The path was straight and flat and they cycled quickly along as the gravel crunched beneath their tyres. Sarah overtook Paul's bike, letting out a whoop as she passed, then slowed to let her boyfriend overtake again. They kept going until the path reached its end a couple of miles further down. At a kissing gate they stood over their bikes perspiring, breathless, elated. Paul removed a strand of hair that had stuck to her damp forehead and kissed her again. Then they pushed their bikes through the gate and stepped back into the open.

ဢ

At Parkgate they rested their bikes against the old sea wall and Paul went into Nicholls Ice Cream Emporium, emerging a few minutes later with two huge cones. In the heat ice cream dribbled down onto his hands and dripped onto the pavement, leaving a graffiti of pink and brown splodges.

They sat on the old sea wall, eating their ice cream while beneath them the wind licked the salt marsh. There was a brackish smell, of saline and methane. The River Dee was nowhere to be seen.

'What happened to the sea?' Sarah asked.

'The Dee has been silting up for centuries,' Paul said. 'When Chester's port died in the seventeenth century, this became its replacement. The packet boat to Ireland sailed from here: Handel travelled from here to Dublin before the premiere of the Messiah. It was a seaside resort in the nineteenth century. Then the sea vanished.'

She looked out at the expanse of mud and reeds. In the distance, some dark clouds had appeared over the Welsh hills. 'It's eerie,' she said and seemed to shiver.

'The sea didn't properly vanish until after the war,' he said. 'They reckon the Mersey dredgers were dumping their loads too close to the Dee Estuary and it all washed back here.'

'Is that true?' she asked, seeming surprised.

'That's what they say,' said Paul, who laughed bitterly. 'I reckon it's just a local myth.'

'Why's that?' Sarah asked.

'It's the same old thing. The prissy neighbour moaning about all of Liverpool's shit washing up on its shore.' He laughed bitterly. 'It's what they all say.'

They cycled back inland, winding a path through lanes lined by barley fields, swooping up and down inclines and flittering between sunlight and shadow. After several miles Paul pulled in off the road.

'Come this way,' he said.

She followed him down a hedge-lined lane, a car width wide, shaded by trees so that their eyes had to adjust to the unexpected darkness. Birds chattered and leaves rustled, but there was no other noise save for the tread of their feet on gravel. The overwhelming impression was of seclusion. When they reached a lamppost he chained their bikes to it and beckoned her on.

'Where are we going?' she asked in a whisper.

'You'll see,' he said, and led her through an opening in a privet hedge and into a copse. They kept walking for a minute until, quite suddenly, the tree cover above them opened out into blue skies and they stood on a vast, carefully manicured lawn the size of a couple of football pitches. Herbaceous borders and azaleas lined its edges.

'Paul,' she said, 'it's beautiful here – but where are we?'

He clasped his arms around her narrow waist. 'It's a secret garden,' he whispered.

She peered around, a hint of uncertainty framing her demeanour. There was no one else in sight.

'Should we be here, though?' Sarah asked, a sudden anxiousness permeating her voice. 'Is it okay?"

He squeezed her waist and laughed. 'Of course it's okay! This belongs to the university. It's their botanical gardens. But today, it seems to be ours.'

They explored for a while, promenading around flower beds and ancient trees, eventually coming to a rest near a large rhododendron bush. From his bag Paul unfolded a checked blanket and they sat down. Sarah lay on her stomach, pulling petals from a daisy. Paul took brown paper bags from his rucksack and unpacked a picnic.

'You brought a picnic!' she squealed. 'Oh Paul! You think of everything.'

They ate then lay dozing in the shade for an hour, their bodies contorted together so that they appeared as one. A squirrel hunting for food amidst the foliage roused Sarah and when she moved, Paul woke with a start.

She opened her eyes and looked longingly at him.

'Will it always be as good as this?' she asked.

'I hope so,' he said, and leant down and kissed the top of her head.

§

Later that evening she whispered to Paul that she wanted to tell him everything about her mother.

'I grew up in a home where anything could happen and it very often did. Because of who mother is and the way she is, after Dad and old Maud left, we went from one day to the next not really knowing where she would be or what she would do – or even what would happen to us. It was unpredictable and exciting, but it was also replete with insecurity.

'It wasn't all bad, by any stretch of the imagination. She had these fabulous highs – when she'd organise parties or take us to London or Paris. And there were her fads, like the whole punk thing, where she'd come alive with excitement at the next great fashion. There were her famous friends. Not just local people, like Roger Eagle, but from her London days – Ted Hughes and George Melly and all kinds of characters.'

But Nadezhda was always complicated, said Sarah, prone to fits of despair and introversion. 'Dad getting remarried was a real setback,' she said, 'It was hard enough that he went to Germany. She still has a lot of anger towards the country, but when he married Steffi she went to pieces. But there were other depressions that seemed to come without cause or logic. She'd lock herself in those bloody rooms of hers and we'd barely see her for weeks at a time.'

People talked about her too. The neighbours, mostly, at first. They knew about the parties, but to them, she must have seemed like a ghost, while her two young girls were always around on their own. 'They'd stop us on the street and see if we were okay, but we didn't really mind.'

But darker whispers started to plague Sarah. 'Among the other girls at school the fact that we were the children of divorcées carried a certain stigma. But that was something I could contend with. It was the other stuff that was harder. Mother as a druggy, mother as a drunk. One day some girl called her a slut and Julia just went for her. She pulled her hair and scratched her face and got sent home from school for it. After that it wasn't so bad for a while.'

126

Paul asked her how the rumours started, but Sarah just shrugged her shoulders in a poise of deliberate ambiguity.

⟋

Later that evening, he asked her straight out if the stories were true.

Sarah just laughed.

⟋

Streams of light from a low sun crept through the thin curtains, gently waking them from their post-coital slumber. She lay in his arms, his right arm hooked underneath her neck and curled down her chest, so that he cupped her breast in his hand. Birdsong rose from the garden, filtering through the half-opened window. There was the occasional rustle of wind, as if the first hint of autumn was in the air. He kissed the back of her head, raising his face slowly as he did so that he could savour the caramel-like fragrance of her shiny black hair.

Her trip to Germany had crept up on them, a speck in the distance that suddenly loomed upon them. Paul had not forgotten, but its imminence shook him. The day was to be spent packing. That night she would get a sleeper train down to Dover.

'Don't be glum,' she said when she reminded him she needed to pack. 'It's Friday, you have The Swan.'

'Is it Friday already?' He sounded surprised. 'The Swan it is. Fat Sam, Daft Bulsara, Grumpy Roberts, Christopher…'

'Creepy Christopher,' she interrupted, rectifying the lack of moniker Paul had bestowed upon him.

'You really don't like him, do you?' His question was born from curiosity: *How can you not like Christopher? What's not to like?*

'He's odious,' she said. 'He's out for himself. People like him will shaft you in the end, one way or another.'

'Has he done something to Julia?'

'No, not all.' She rolled onto her back and looked at the ceiling. 'Give it some time and you can praise my perception or damn my ignorance.'

Paul looked out into space. Maybe it was him, he thought. Perhaps he was too tolerant of Christopher's shortcomings: the flakiness, the moods, the cutting remarks, the unspoken rivalry that bubbled beneath the surface of their friendship. Did Sarah's distance illuminate their kinship for what it was?

§

Earlier that year their lifelong friendship had taken another turn over their choice of universities.

All through school Christopher was the scientist. His father was a well-liked local GP, and it was accepted that Christopher would follow him into the family business, not general practice, of course – nothing as staid and suburban as all that. He would be a surgeon, in emergency or paediatrics, maybe brains – it changed by the month. But whatever field he went into, he would be a doctor. As far as that was concerned, his destiny was mapped out before him.

Paul also knew what he wanted to do for almost as long as he could remember. History at Cambridge. Modern history. The Twentieth Century. He had no inkling which college he wanted to go to, nor which professor to seek out, but he liked Cambridge, liked the idea of the place, the prestige. He knew in his heart that that is where he was destined.

Christopher perpetually mocked this sense of vocation. History, even studied at somewhere so illustrious was worthless, he said, for no employer would be interested in the subject. History was old, he scoffed; the twentieth century was not. It was all so useless: a hobby taken too far. Paul found the scepticism objectionable, then tedious, but in his mind it cast the germ of doubt. What if there really was no value in the subject? What if it lost fashion with employers? What if events overtook him, rendering his education redundant? Paul knew as well as anybody that history was an inexorable force, that it stopped for no one.

Then at an undergraduate fair he found the third way. A young Fellow, dressed in a long overcoat and college scarf, manning the Cambridge University stall looked at Paul's grave face and answered: 'Law will open up every door for you.' It was not something he'd ever considered, but after mulling it over for months inserted it on his application form as his first choice.

When he was called for interview in January, Christopher made the long journey to Cambridge with him. They took an early train from Lime Street station, Paul's father dropping them off in what seemed like the middle of the night, and they emerged several hours later blinking in the midst of a frost-filled morning. They spent the remainder of it walking around town, cracking jokes, wandering through the light fog and crisp white meadows.

At twelve pm Paul went to his interview. He faced three men across a conference table in an oak-lined annex to one of the dining halls: an improbably old man, stooped and dressed in a black gown, his face dashed with liver spots; a tall, thin, gentle-mannered professor with an aristocratic jaw who reminded Paul of Anthony Eden; and a gruff younger fellow with a heavy Mancunian accent.

Paul should have been intimidated by what greeted him,

but he could scarcely suppress his amusement as an Oxbridge stereotype was played out in front of him. The younger man was clearly the angry young thing of the college, an aspiring revolutionary, who in his zealotry was so unremittingly hostile to Paul that the other two men qualified most of his questions with apologies or explanations. Eden's doppelgänger regarded Paul with fascination, for some reason – probably on account of his home city – regarding him as working class, a model of the comprehensive schooling system, and kept asking him startlingly inane questions – 'Is there much crime where you live?' 'Are any of your friends going to university?' 'Despite everything are people generally content with their lives "up there"?' The older man tried to keep the interview focussed, and at the end he stood up and hobbled across to the door with Paul. Then he took his hand, and said quietly: 'Well, no doubt, so long as I live long enough I'll get to know you a bit better in September.' Two weeks later a formal offer arrived in the post before school. The grades required to enter were so low that to Paul it looked like an apology for the farcical interview.

On the train home from Cambridge they drank cans of beer and talked excitedly about what the future held in Cambridge. Then Christopher announced he had some news himself. He was invited to Oxford a fortnight later for an interview.

'Oxford?' Paul asked, incredulous. This was all news to him. He hadn't even known his friend had applied there. Christopher produced a letter from his jacket pocket and Paul's eyes searched through it for details: 'University of Oxford. Monday February 2, 1981, 12pm.' Then further down: 'History Faculty.' 'Professor Theodore Eisner.'

'Is this some kind of joke?' Paul asked.

Christopher just smiled wanly and shook his head, before

elaborating his reasons. He had always admired Paul's passion for history, he said, always been secretly interested in it himself. Medicine was so dreary and safe, he wanted to do something different, something edgy. He'd seen Eisner, a historian whose fame had long transcended academia, on television, a programme about the creation of Israel and it all started to fall into place. And so he went on, but Paul wasn't really listening – to him it seemed that his friend had talked him out of doing something so that he could do it himself.

Back in Liverpool, he sought the counsel of Fat Sam and Roberts. Sam was ambivalent, but Roberts hissed with rage and concurred with Paul's darkest suspicions. One night in The Swan, as Roberts bade his farewells he ducked down and whispered in Christopher's ear: 'I think you're fucking weird.'

Christopher never spoke about Oxford again after that.

As he explicated this manoeuvring to Sarah six months later she pulled a face as if to say: *what did I just say?*

'I'm trying not to think about it all,' Paul said blandly. 'Y'know, results day and all that.' But really it was the only date he had in his mind. Indeed, suddenly the summer which had once stretched before him like a seeming eternity seemed to be concluding abruptly. Next Thursday, results day, his own fate resolved: Cambridge if things went well; if not, the dismal scramble for a place, any place, anywhere through the university clearing system. A new term, a new town lay just a fortnight beyond that.

'You won't be here for results day,' he said childishly. But what he thought was this: three weeks from now I'll be packing my old man's car ready to leave myself. We really have just days.

'You'll manage. I'll call.'

'You don't do phones.'

'I'll call.' She leant over and kissed him. 'In any case I'll practically be living wherever you end up, so I have a vested interest.' She kissed him again. 'But you'd better get in somewhere nice, like Cambridge.'

The glow of reassurance crept over him. He took her in his arms again, kissed her, then pulled her body into his until they were one again.

∽

Later, he lolled on her bed, flicking through the Everyman's edition of *Anna Karenina* she had bought him as a going away present while she pulled clothes from her drawers and made piles across her bedroom floor before stuffing them into a nylon rucksack.

'Why isn't Julia going with you?' he asked.

Sarah shrugged her shoulders and carried on packing. Finally, she said: 'They don't get on. She never forgave him for leaving.' Her bag brimmed full and she strained to close the zip. 'She can brood, can our Julia. I wouldn't want to get on the wrong side of her.'

'It was a long time ago,' Paul said.

'She has a long memory,' Sarah replied and laughed bitterly.

When her bag was ready, he followed her down the stairs and into the kitchen where she made mugs of tea. It was a grey, airless day and the house was empty and consumed by shadows.

'You asked last night about Mama,' she said, settling herself on a stool. 'If the stories about her were true.'

Paul nodded, and she said: 'I never asked you what you thought; if you reckoned they were true.'

She looked intently, in a way that reminded him of Nadezhda. Silently he gasped for air, not used to being confronted. 'I thought they were ridiculous,' he answered. 'I thought it was a stitch-up.

But then you said anything could happen in this house, and often did. So in truth I don't really know what to think.'

She sipped from her mug, considering his response. He wondered if she would elaborate on her mother's past; he wanted her to, but didn't want to ask.

She pursed her lips, as if about to say something, but then hesitated, before saying: 'You know the boy? The one who made the allegations. Sean Kendall.' Paul nodded. 'He was Julia's boyfriend.'

She sipped her tea, while Paul stared out into the overgrown garden, trying to make sense of this latest revelation.

∽

Later that afternoon, Julia returned home with fresh loaves and a box of cakes for her sister's farewell tea. Sarah was in the bath, so Paul sat in the kitchen watching Julia cut sandwiches. The room smelt of coffee and ripe tomatoes.

For weeks he had virtually lived in the house, but seldom did he see her or Christopher. There was much to catch up on, but Julia seemed distant and preoccupied. Paul asked where Christopher was, but when she answered she could not disguise her annoyance.

'He's round at Sam's,' she snapped. 'Playing computer games!'

Sam had the latest Atari console and played games on it every day for hours. Paul could not see the point, but his other friends were captivated by it.

'Boys with their toys,' Paul mused.

'I might as well not exist when that thing is on!' Her expression softened. 'Here, help me with this,' she said and rolled a hardboiled egg across the table for him to unpeel.

As he went to work on the eggshell, she said: 'I think he's

really anxious about next week, y'know.' Results day was just six days away, and while Paul's destiny was virtually fixed his friends enjoyed no such certainty. 'I think he's a little envious of your offer,' she said, but Paul knew this already and just shrugged his shoulders. Such pressure was his friend's own making, and the more he brooded on being cheated from following his own destiny, the more ambivalent he became to Christopher's fate. Part of him secretly willed him to fail.

'Do you reckon he'll get what he needs?' Julia asked.

Paul rolled the egg, now stripped of its shell, back across the table. 'I don't know what he needs to get,' he admitted.

Julia stopped preparing the food, and looked across at him, her forehead creased into a bewildered frown.

'It's not something we ever talk about,' he said, and fiddled awkwardly in his chair. How could he possibly express this strange, unspoken rivalry that had grown between them? His disillusionment with her lover? How could she understand his treachery?

'Well, he needs straight A grades,' she said. Paul blinked: that was an almost impossibly high standard and one he knew his friend surely couldn't realise. 'Do you think he'll get them?'

He shrugged his shoulders again, and said: 'Only Chris could tell you that.' But secretly he revelled in this new-found knowledge: that his friend was surely destined to failure.

Ten minutes later Sarah emerged fresh faced and steaming, her hair still damp. Nadezhda was nowhere to be seen, but Paul was now used to this reality. He could spend days in the same house, and not catch sight of her. Sometimes as he lay in her daughter's bed trying to sleep he caught snatches of Nina Simone's soulful voice seeping from her rooms. Sarah said she often stayed up through the night, reading or writing or sometimes just drinking and listening to her old jazz records. But often this was the only hint of presence in the cavernous old house.

When she arrived in the kitchen, shortly after Sarah, her face was drawn and tired as if she hadn't slept. She wore no make-up and her skin appeared so pale as to be translucent. She lit a cigarette and sucked on it hard as if it were a palliative. She glanced at Paul, but seemed preoccupied with her own thoughts and did not acknowledge him.

'All packed? All set?' she asked Sarah, who nodded. She spoke quickly and in a slightly shrill manner, as if agitated. 'You know darling, I really wish you were flying. I will worry about you.'

'We've been through this Mama,' she said with a sigh. 'Flying is so dull.'

Still it nagged at her. 'It seems so pointless and convoluted,' she said. But it was clear that her problem was not how Sarah got to Germany, but that she was going at all.

They ate in the kitchen. Nadezhda chain-smoked, picking disinterestedly at an egg and cress sandwich, but barely eating anything. She looked miserable, and her very presence sucked the life from the room, stymieing all conversation.

'Papa said we might drive down to Baden,' Sarah said. 'And Cologne, as well – but just for the day.'

'Is that so?' said Nadezhda, completely uninterested. With her fork she played with a cake, but ate nothing.

'We're not far from Denmark either, are we? I've never been to Scandinavia.'

Besides the clack of cutlery on china there was silence. Sarah pushed her plate away. Proceedings had a funeral air: Nadezhda was distant and melancholic; Julia had barely said a word, either.

'And what will you do, Paul?' Nadezhda asked, meaning when Sarah wasn't there, but unable to say the words.

'I don't know,' he said. 'The football starts next week, and then there's results day on Thursday.'

Nadezhda opened her hands, and her eyes seemed to sparkle as she came to life. 'Yes, yes! Judgement day! I had completely forgotten. And how will you fare? Very well I would expect, no?' She turned to Paul and said: 'We should do something to mark the occasion.' Addressing Julia, she said: 'We must have a gathering of all your clever friends on Thursday. To celebrate, or to drown sorrows.' She turned back to Paul and touched his hand, her skin cold and thin: 'You must come over. I will quite miss having a man around the house otherwise.'

She gave him a teasing grin and stood, mumbling about having to get something, and left the room. She returned a minute later with one of her glass medicine bottles. Sarah let out a groan as Nadezhda filled four thimble-like glasses with hooch. 'We must have a toast,' she insisted. 'We must toast your departure.' Then raising her glass to the ceiling, proclaimed: 'To safe journeys.'

The others repeated the toast then drank the fearsome liquor in a single mouthful.

∽

Later that evening, after saying farewells to her mother and sister, Sarah took a minicab to Lime Street station. Paul sat beside her in the car, holding her hand, silently savouring these last moments together. It was dark now, and as the landscape of handsome Victorian villas gave way to narrow streets of red-brick terraces, she said: 'They didn't want me to go, but you could tell that, couldn't you?'

'Yes,' Paul replied.

'It's like this every year. A mixture of resentment at Papa and hatred of Germany.' She sighed and looked out as the city flashed by. 'Do you want me to stay?' she asked. 'I'll stay if you want me to stay.'

'Of course I want you to stay,' he said with a short laugh. 'But that's for my own selfish reasons.' He squeezed her hand. 'You must go though, you really must. I'll miss you every second you're away, though.'

She sniffed, as if about to cry, and across the back seat of the car hugged him, pinning her head so tightly across his chest that she could hear the thud of his heart.

Lime Street was desolate. A bag lady wearing a Liverpool football shirt, her bare legs covered in ugly purple sores, slept on the concourse, and a Royal Mail train unloaded sacks of Monday's post onto a platform. Sarah's train lay in wait on Platform Seven, the steady burr of its diesel engine gently ticking over. A man in a navy British Rail uniform shuffled from foot to foot, awaiting its departure and his exit from the barren city.

'You for Dover or London?' he asked as they approached. He was red faced and fat and spoke in a broad Yorkshire accent.

'Dover,' Sarah replied.

'You're in the front of the train, then. Don't stray too far this end: it's getting uncoupled at Crewe and put onto the end of the Euston train. You're getting the other half of the Glasgow Express.'

'You busy tonight?' Paul asked.

The guard snorted in reply and gestured the length of the empty platform. 'Does it look busy?' he asked, and Paul blushed at the inanity of his question. 'Good news for you is that you've got the pick of the cabins. You won't be disturbed until you wake at Dover tomorrow.'

'I'm just here to say goodbye,' Paul replied.

'Oh well, you're out of luck then,' said the guard, who leered at

Sarah.

They walked the length of the platform and Paul lifted her bag into the carriage. She stood at its door, looking helplessly down upon him on the platform. 'Oh Paul, what will I do?' Her eyes moistened with tears and she stepped back down. He held her as she sobbed silently, clutching her tightly as she pulled her face into his chest, muffling her cries. Then the diesel shuddered and roared into life. She kissed him tenderly and the guard's whistle echoed in the station's glass roof. There was another couple further down the platform, also parting. Sarah climbed up the step and closed the door before pulling down the window.

She gazed down at him, and said, 'Oh Paul!' She bowed her head and kissed him through the window. The train jolted, and its wheels let out a groan as it started to move.

She leant out of the window, watching him as the train pulled away. 'I do love you, you know,' she called, but all he could hear was the din of the engine.

'What?' he shouted.

'I love you!' She waved. 'Bye!'

Paul was overcome by a sudden, terrible sense of emptiness. He stood there with his hands in his pockets, watching as the train snaked out of the station, until it was no more than an echo in the night.

11

Their former school was a mile up a main road that ran out of town and along the Lancashire coast. On one side were open fields which ran uninterrupted until they merged into sand dunes and sea; on the other a steady stream of traffic snaked its way out of the city. Vague plans to walk up and collect their results together had not materialised as the realisation dawned that they wished to learn their fates alone. In the distance, as the early morning sun shone down, Paul could see Sam shuffle ahead of him.

A girl from his form class walked the opposite way clutching a piece of paper and looked blankly in the distance. Paul muttered a hello but she continued, oblivious to his greeting, and he guessed she was disappointed with her results. At this point his stomach knotted in a sudden paroxysm of tension. What if something had gone horribly wrong? What if he had disgraced himself? What if his dreams were laid to waste?

An eerie air hung over the school, a modern functional construction that he had only known to be full of other teenagers and manned by legions of staff. His footsteps echoed along empty corridors which smelt of detergent; no one else was in sight. He paused to peer into the window of his old form room. It had once appeared so large and intimidating; not a place of learning, somewhere to be feared, slightly, where barbarous teachers and tough kids from the council estate were a perennial threat. But looking into the darkened classroom it now seemed so dingy and small, neither a place to feel fear nor be inspired. He thought: have I really spent the last seven years here?

In the drama hall was some life. Mrs Jackson the geography teacher was consoling a girl, her face red with tears. Another girl from his English class looked pleased with herself. At a side table his history teacher Mr Griffiths, his cheeks flushed, offering counsel to a forlorn-looking boy. Someone let out a whoop of delight and his eyes were drawn to the back of the hall, where the examinations officer, a middle-aged maths teacher called Mrs Speed, handed out results. He made his way over to her and she gave a cryptic smile; she was a hatchet-faced woman not normally disposed to smiling. Was she quietly revelling in his failure? A feeling of dread washed over him.

'Paul,' she said. 'Take a seat.'

His stomach turned and his heart pounded. Why was she asking him to sit? It must be bad news. He felt himself tremble, but remained standing.

'Very well then,' she said without emotion and handed him a piece of paper.

Years of work and it had come to this: a scrap of paper dictating his future.

He unfolded it and stared disbelieving at its contents, and felt himself fall back into a chair placed there by his teacher who was evidently an old hand at these times.

'Congratulations, Paul,' said Mrs Speed. 'No one else in the year got straight A grades.'

∽

At the school gate he joined Sam and Roberts, who asked him how he'd done. When Paul told them Roberts made a show of refusing to believe him and snatched the results slip from his hand.

'You clever bastard,' he said.

'Thank you,' Paul beamed. 'And how did you fellas do?'

Both had got the grades needed for their universities of choice. As they talked excitedly about their futures Paul was consumed with an overwhelming sense of relief, then joy. One chapter of his life was completed with a flourish – now what lay ahead? He thought of Sarah, Cambridge, of escape and smiled inwardly. Life had never been so good; would it always remain so?

After a while Bulsara joined them, his face beaming. No one, least of all himself, had set any great stall out on his achieving much, but he had surprised everybody and when he showed them his results slip there were cheers for he had earned three B grades – the exact same as Roberts.

'What about Christopher?' asked Sam and suddenly Paul remembered: he was the only one to get the grades his friend so desperately needed. Without being told he knew he had fallen short when everyone else had succeeded.

'Speedo said he came in first and left straight away,' said Bulsara. 'She wouldn't tell me anything else.'

'I don't think he got in,' said Paul, and he told them what he knew.

∽

Paul found him in The Swan shortly after opening time sitting up at the bar. The place was empty and smelt of stale cigarette smoke and spilt beer. Light cast long shadows through lead-framed windows, capturing fragments of dust that hung and danced in the air.

He sat down next to him. Christopher ignored him and continued to stare into the depths of his glass. Finally, he glanced up and took a sip of beer, before returning his gaze to the glass.

'Come to gloat, have you?' he said sourly.

Paul frowned. 'No. I came to see if you were okay.'

Christopher drained his glass and banged it on the counter. 'Another,' he shouted across the empty bar and turned. 'I'm fine; I'm sure you're fine. Everybody is fine. So, if it's all the same to you can you kindly fuck off and leave me alone.'

Paul recoiled at his friend's bitter dismissal and left the pub in silence.

∽

Early that evening his parents took him for a celebratory dinner at the golf club. His mother was ebullient, boasting about Paul's exam results to everyone she met. Tony, the captain, gave him a five-pound note. Another man shook his hand. A woman who he didn't know but felt he should kissed him, leaving a red splodge of lipstick on his cheek. His father beamed as he showed off, quietly proud of his son's achievements but not saying much until they went for food. Thursdays at the golf club were carvery nights and when Paul brought his plate to the counter, his father leaned across and said to the chef, 'Load his plate up man, this lad has got the best results in his year and is off to Cambridge now.' There was a choice of chicken, beef or ham. Paul got all three and his father seemed more pleased than ever.

After a celebratory round of sherries his father dropped him at the station and he took the train across the city. It was a journey that was recently alien to him; landmarks that might once have attracted his notice – the car wreckers at Litherland, the war damage further down the line at Sandhills, the black of the tunnel running through the city centre – assumed a sense of familiarity.

He thought of Sarah, as he often did. The unfolding tension of the previous days had distracted him and lessened the pain of her absence. He read *Anna Karenina* and talked to his friends about what lay ahead, the unknown, their moments of truth. Now that was settled and the elation had started to dissipate, the yawning sense of emptiness started to return.

It seemed so strange, the thought of visiting her home when she was not there. There was also a sense of unease after what had passed earlier in the day between him and Christopher. He seemed so volatile and angry, like a wounded animal. Who knew what Christopher was capable of when fuelled by a cocktail of bitterness and booze? Julia, too, at times surprised him with her belligerence. He played it over in his head again and again as the train made its way south of the city, wondering what had born it. Sarah? Jealousy? Or had she unravelled his fascination with her mother; learned of what he knew about her, her seeming disgrace?

He could hear the music and voices coming from the house as he made his way up their tree-lined road. As he walked up the broken path a clutch of teenage boys spilled out from the front door and lit cigarettes. Paul had no idea who they were. He saw the blue-haired girl from the earlier party. There was a group of sensible-looking boys with skull caps, a plump bespectacled man in a tweed jacket who he thought to be a teacher, a Rasta with two black girls who looked as incongruous to the party as the scallies bunched at the bottom of the stairs, smoking and scowling. It was busier even than the earlier party he been to the previous month. Music boomed in the kitchen and the back room. It smelt of marijuana, cigarettes and sex.

He made his way into the kitchen, where he hoped to see his friends. When he strained his ears he could hear Bulsara and Roberts' cruel laugh; but through the throngs he could not see where they were. He took a beer and stood leaning on the kitchen counter, trying to deduce who all these people were and where they were from.

There was a pat on his arm and when he turned Helen was stood next to him. 'I believe congratulations are in order,' she said and smiled, but there was none of the underlying sexual tension that underpinned their previous encounter in that same kitchen.

Paul thanked her and asked how Christopher was.

Helen smiled sadly and looked down at her feet. 'Upset. Not very happy at all, really.'

'He seemed pretty mad when I saw him this afternoon.' He told her what had happened in The Swan.

She shook her head apologetically. 'You know how competitive he is. I think you doing well just made it harder for him to take.'

Paul reached for another beer can. 'Is he here?'

She nodded and her face contorted into a grimace. 'He's fucked though.' She gestured to the back garden. 'He's out there with a bottle of whisky to keep him company.'

'Should I go and talk to him?'

She shook her head again. 'Not a good idea.'

'And what's he going to do? Will he appeal?'

She looked at him, surprised. 'Paul, this wasn't bad luck. He got BCD. Considering what he actually needed this was a total and abject failure.'

He feared seeing Christopher like this and was worried too by Julia's reaction. Would she descend into a resentful fury out of loyalty to her boyfriend or damn him with ambivalence?

But when he saw her she was bright eyed and smiling, and rushed over to greet him with a hug.

'Congratulations! I'm so pleased for you.' She took his hand. 'Come quick, Sarah's on the phone for you.'

She led him through the hall, pushing through the hordes that blocked the hallway and made her way to the foot of the stairs where the receiver rested on a windowsill.

He took it, and having to shout to make himself heard above the tumult, called her name.

'Paul, is that you?' She sounded so distant, her voice small and made meek by the crudeness of the long-distance telephone line. 'I can't speak for long: how did you do?'

He told her and she squealed with delight. He could imagine her, bouncing with glee on her heels. 'That's amazing! Well done! And the others: how they get on?'

'They did well. Christopher not so good. Anyway, tell me about your journey. How was it?' The receiver was pushed up against his ear and he shrouded the mouthpiece with his hand.

There was a delay of a couple of seconds, and she said: 'Oh Paul it was so interesting. So much better than flying! But I can't talk now I don't have much time.' There was a roar from another room, deafening her last words.

'What did you say?'

She shouted down the long-distance line to make herself clear, but still he could not hear.

'I don't have much time.'

'What did you say?'

'I don't have much time Paul,' she repeated. 'I love you.'

'I love you too,' he said, but the line was already dead.

As he passed him in the hallway the bespectacled man – the

schoolteacher – said to Paul, 'I always feel like Alice,' and laughed.

'Who is Alice?' Paul asked, but the man was too busy laughing at his own joke over the tumult to hear him.

'Of course I feel like her in all sorts of places,' and he bellowed his overloud laugh again. He had a lisp, which added to his camp demeanour. He touched Paul's arm as he spoke. 'I'm Julian by the way,' he said, 'Julian Tennant.' He was a playwright, not a teacher as Paul had thought, and a critic of Spanish and Portuguese literature.

'Do you get much call for that sort of work in Liverpool?' asked Paul, and Tennant looked at him mortified.

'Well, I rely on the kindness of my editors: Bruce Page at the *Statesman*. Anthony Howard at the *Listener*.' He listed several more editors of magazines Paul had never heard of before adding, 'Of course the dosh is atrocious!' and let out an indulgent chuckle, as if the money was totally irrelevant.

He told him he was a friend of Nadezhda's from the old days in London. He lived in Cheshire with his partner; Paul realised that this was a euphemism for his boyfriend. 'There's not a terrible amount to do in the dreary old north, so whenever Nadezhda has one of her gatherings I always jump at the chance! First to arrive last to leave!' he told Paul. Some of the other parties the girls had already recalled, about the Liverpool team turning up en masse and her neighbours aghast by the drunken old dockers. 'Lots of booze, drugs, sex,' he purred, and leant into Paul and said with a leer, 'there used to be a back room just for fucking.'

Paul's face reddened and he stood there, his mouth agape. Then Tennant rocked with laughter and barely able to speak, said, 'You should see your face!' and bellowed again. It was like the scream of a madman. 'A back room for fucking! Of course I made that bit up!'

Through a huddle Nadezhda emerged and gave a little wave before joining them. She was dressed in a white men's shirt, its sleeves rolled up, and black drainpipe jeans; her hair was tousled into an arrangement of elegant dishevelment. Her deep brown eyes, like her daughters', shone, and her white skin, which days earlier had seemed so fragile and wan, was flawless. 'Paul,' she said. 'So you've met Julian.' When she spoke her teeth, he noticed, were slightly awry making her seem a little awkward, like Sarah, and sexier. She was different to any of the other times he'd seen her; playing poetess, he realised.

'Julian, this is Sarah's beau,' she said.

'Is that so!' he exclaimed. 'A shame! I thought he was a faggot!' More laughter, and this time even Paul showed his amusement.

'You talk such rubbish Julian,' she scolded and turned towards Paul. 'Is he acting like an old queen, Paul? Or is it the village idiot routine tonight?'

Paul smiled and Julian said: 'People say appalling things about me, but you take no notice.' He told Nadezhda about his earlier little joke. 'You should have seen the look on his face, the expression of horror.'

She gave a wry smile at the recollection and said: 'Really, we're quite tame these days. Maybe it's a sign of getting older or wiser.'

'You should have been around London in the Fifties and Sixties,' he said. He cackled in anticipation of his next joke. 'We'd have been high as kites now! And of course you'd have had your back room for fucking!' He gasped for air, between laughs. 'This place would have been an orgy by now!' *Haw haw haw.*

Paul ignored him. He looked at the whole array of people different ages and backgrounds and colour and said to Nadezhda, 'Who are all these people?'

'Friends,' she said absently. 'Friends of friends. Hangers-on.

Some gatecrashers, I suppose.' She trailed off and for a moment became distracted and sad; then she saw Paul without a drink and came to life again. 'Come on, you've got no drink and you're celebrating? Are you a mad man?' She boomed with laughter and sent Paul on his way.

Bulsara and Roberts were sat on the back door step, looking out into the darkened garden. Paul handed them cans of beer he had brought from the kitchen.

'This is so strange,' he said as he sat down at their feet. He opened his can, which let out a hiss.

'What's strange?' Roberts asked. 'Being down here with us, not upstairs shagging?'

Ignoring them, Paul said: 'No, all this here. All these people. I'm sure Nadezhda and Julia don't know half of them.' Across the garden the Rasta was sitting in a huddle with three scallies, their hair shaved to the bone and all wearing tracksuits. They passed a joint around, its reddened tip glowing in the dark. 'I mean, who the fuck are they?' he whispered gesturing over to them.

'He's a poet, the black guy,' Bulsara said. 'We were talking to him earlier.'

Roberts giggled. 'And that one over there, he'll rob any car that you want. Any model! The lad next to him specialises in videos, and the other one does smack.'

Paul laughed, then Bulsara said: 'It's something else this, Paul. It's a crazy house.' He looked around back into the kitchen then out into the garden again. 'Tonight we've met a poet, artists, an actor, that playwright queer, and some of the roughest lads you'll ever see. It's mad! Could you imagine any of our folks having something like this?'

Paul told them about dinner with his parents, mocking his mother and her round of celebratory sherries that came at the end of their carvery. 'That's how one way of life has come to an end,' he said. 'A round of sherry in the golf club and suddenly I'm no longer a child, no longer stuck at home studying for exams, out in the real world.' He spoke not with sadness, but a sense of rising bewilderment.

'And this is the real world?' Bulsara asked.

Paul looked around: at the old crumbling house; the throngs of people – surely there were more than one hundred there now – a cast of eccentrics, wanderers and wannabes. He glanced up to the upper floors to Sarah's bedroom, where he spent days and nights devoted to carnal pleasure but which was now dark and empty. And then he shook his head. 'No,' he admitted, 'This isn't the real world. This is wonderland.'

ᔕ

They found Christopher with Sam and the remnants of a bottle of Jameson's towards the back of the garden. He was lying on his back, close to the spot where Paul and Sarah once lay, muttering. A pool of vomit lay nearby. When he saw his friends, Sam cast them a wearied look.

Christopher moaned: 'I am going to hell, I'm going to hell,' again and again. Drunkenness had distorted his voice, so that sounded like a growl.

'What's going on?' Paul asked.

'I'm going to hell!' Christopher yelped.

'I don't think your grades are good enough for there either,' Roberts said, laughing cruelly. But Christopher was wallowing so deeply in self-pity that he didn't recognise that he was being mocked.

'He is going to Hull,' Sam explained. 'To the university. He got in through clearing.'

Suddenly aware of the others' presence, Christopher sat up sharply. 'Is that that fucking Oxford don?' he stammered at Paul.

'No that was you,' jeered Roberts. 'Whoops! That was you but you weren't smart enough to get in.'

Christopher stood up suddenly, his face framed by belligerence. But his drunkenness made him stumble and when he shouted, 'Are you mocking me?' he looked like a fool.

They looked ready to fight each other, but while Paul and Bulsara looked on impassively, Sam stepped in and told them to calm down. Christopher sat down sadly and lifted the Jameson's bottle to his lips. 'I'm going to hell,' he moaned. 'I'm going to hell.'

∽

Inside the air was hot and filled with noise. In the kitchen a record player at full blast competed with the tape deck next door creating a confusion of sounds where the noises merged in the hall. Nadezhda moved between the two rooms, dancing like a hyperactive teenager. When the first notes of the Clash's 'London Calling' sounded across the kitchen she squealed with delight and climbed atop the counter to dance, urging her much younger guests to join in. Yet there was something frenzied and disturbing about her energy and no one joined her. Suddenly she looked sad and manic, dancing alone to this punk melody.

Julia paid no attention to her mother and moved around the house handing out beer cans and pouring wine, laughing and talking. When she saw Paul, she said with the teasing giggle, 'It's the hero of the hour' – and handed him the remaining beer. He laughed and told her about his father at the carvery earlier that evening.

She smiled and her face dropped and she asked if he had seen Christopher. He told her what had happened earlier.

She gave a wearied shake of her head. 'He was wasted when he got here. Wallowing in self-pity.' She lowered her voice again. 'I'm afraid he was calling you for everything.'

'It's not my fault!' said Paul, indignant at this contempt.

'I know it's not your fault, but jealousy can play terrible tricks on the mind.'

She left him with his beer cans and he walked into the hall. Suddenly he found the unruliness and the noise overwhelming and he wished he could be invisible or alone. The tensions and elation of the day were now tempered by a rising sense of exhaustion. He glanced at his watch but it was already half twelve and too late for the last train. He had no money for a cab, so sat on the stairs and drank alone in the shadows, looking out over this chaos, his eyes glazed with tiredness.

He could hear Julian Tennant's camp lisp and somewhere in the back of the house Christopher wailing that he was going to hell.

From his darkened vantage point, he watched as the party thinned out. The volume lowered and guests started to leave, staggering and zigzagging out of the hallway and the old house to their homes. Paul rested his head on the banister and closed his eyes. He thought of slipping upstairs and crawling into Sarah's empty bed, but cast the idea from his mind as if it may somehow violate her territory. But sleep, in the midst of so many people, would not come and as he drank the last of his beer he decided such sensibilities were absurd: Sarah wouldn't care if he spent a night alone in a bed he could almost call his own.

He was about to ascend the stairs when Julian caught sight of him. He was holding a wine glass and bottle, and in his stupor had to narrow his eyes in order to focus. When he recognised

Paul he pointed and laughed. 'I thought you were off getting laid,' and bellowed raucously. 'May I join you?' he asked and sat on the stair beneath his feet his before Paul could answer.

'This is some do,' he said and when he saw Paul without a drink offered him the wine glass. 'Don't worry. There's no germs. I've not drank from it.' He laughed his madman's laugh again: *haw haw haw.* 'I'll drink from the bottle.' *Haw haw haw.*

Paul sipped from the glass: the wine was cheap and bitter and the mere whiff of it hinted at the hangover it promised.

Julian leaned over to Paul and whispered, 'That big-boned girl. You know the one with the big boobs?' Paul frowned, not knowing who he meant. 'Not much to look at; she has the face of a man, but fabulous titties. She's a twin.'

'Helen?'

'Helen! That's the one!' he boomed, forgetting he had spoken in conspiratorial whispers a moment earlier. 'Terrible slut you know! Came on to me earlier, but I had to say "Sorry darling, you're just not my type".' He lowered his voice again. 'Anyway I was wandering from the garden just now and there she was, bent over, while one of those knuckleheads shagged her from behind.' He shook his head and said with relish: 'The filthy bitch.' He lifted the bottle to his lips and took a swig. 'Still I suppose that's the way you do it,' he giggled. 'At least then you wouldn't have to look at her ugly face.' *Haw haw haw.*

He took another heave from the bottle and let out an appreciative gasp.

'Sex, drugs, music, and plenty of booze,' he said contemplatively, then became animated again. 'This is some do. Like the old days.'

'Is it really?' asked Paul.

'Absolutely,' Julian replied. 'Back in the Fifties when we were young, though perhaps not as young as you – but then we'd had national service and the war – we were going to dos like this all the time. Then there was a hiatus when everybody got married and had children. But at heart most of us never grew up – least of all Nadezhda. After her husband left, it was like a release for her. The advent of a second youth. We had such wild times in the early Seventies. It's like that all over again tonight.'

'And what happened between the Seventies and tonight?' asked Paul.

Julian touched his knee and gave a sympathetic smile. 'Come on now, Paul, you must know.'

He meant the newspaper stories and tabloid innuendo. Nadezhda's so-called disgrace. Paul asked him if it was true.

Julian gulped some more wine and asked, 'Well, what do you think?'

'That's what everyone says when I ask them,' Paul said. He sipped on his wine, which tasted horrible. 'I don't know what to think. I thought it was a stitch-up at first.'

'Of course it was a stitch-up,' Julian exclaimed. 'But that doesn't mean to say that the stories weren't true.'

Paul blinked with surprise. 'Everything?' he asked, but Julian just smiled, a tacit admission that Nadezhda was guilty. 'Even the seductions of that boy.'

Julian smiled enigmatically. 'She's had lots of affairs,' he said, and lowered his voice again. 'They warned her – the police that is – to clean up her act or lose her daughters. And so she did.' He guffawed again. 'Until tonight, anyway.'

∽

The party was drifting to its conclusion. The music had softened to a low rumble and guests filtered out of the front door, which had remained open all evening. Now even that was closed over by Julia with a soft click. She kissed Paul on the top of the head. She made for the stairs and bed.

'Well done,' she said. 'Everyone's so pleased for you.'

'Almost everyone,' he corrected her, and gestured in the direction of Christopher, who lay splayed out on an armchair neither asleep nor awake, his eyes rheumy from exhaustion and alcohol. A trail of spittle dribbled from the side of his mouth.

'He's quite the catch, isn't he?' she said drolly and took her leave.

On an adjacent sofa, Julian Tennant and Bulsara lay end to end, Tennant snoring violently. In front of them Fat Sam curled up on the carpet like a Saint Bernard, his soft snores answering Tennant's thunderlike rumbles. From a back room he could hear Roberts arguing about politics, squabbling for the sake of squabbling until night gave way to dawn and he could head home on the train, make his way to his own bed.

Tiredness should have consumed Paul, but even in this dark hour he remained exhilarated by the events of the preceding day. He crept into the kitchen and was confronted by a chaos of empty bottles and cans, makeshift ashtrays, empty glasses, the smell of cheap alcohol and stale cigarettes. Elation subsumed any sense of drunkenness and he searched through the scores of discarded bottles for something to slake his thirst. Miraculously, he found a bottle of Valpolicella almost untouched and he cleaned a glass from a sink that was overflowing with a debris of dishes before making his way to the stairs.

He sat in the dark and contemplated what lay ahead. Within weeks he would leave this falling city and take his place among the country's elite. A Cambridge education could give him anything he wanted. Money, fame, distinction in whatever field he sought. He remembered Orwell's reasons why people became writers:

recognition; to change people politically; the love of the aesthetics of literature; or the wish to record something for posterity. He thought of his own largely unacknowledged ambitions for writing and considered, what motivated him?

He thought of the desire for recognition, but where once he sought to impress he no longer felt the need. He had Cambridge. He'd escaped the broken city. And he had Sarah. He wanted for nothing else. He didn't want to change anybody. Nor was he bothered about painting patterns on the page. No, for Paul it was all about recording the truth. He wanted to record things for eternity.

His train of thought was broken by Nadezhda, who silently sat beside him on the stair. She touched his arm and his hairs prickled.

'The cleverest man at the party,' she said. 'Top results. And you've located the last of the wine.' She held out an empty glass and he filled it for her. 'So what's going through your mind this evening, then?'

'Elation,' he answered. 'Tiredness too, now, I suppose.'

'Well, it is half three in the morning.'

'I wish Sarah was here, too,' he said.

'We all miss her,' said her mother. 'But she's much too sensible for these nights, far too grown up. All this wine and drinking and dancing is not for her.' Nadezhda took another glug of wine. Her lips and teeth, he saw through the gloaming, were rinsed red with wine. With her translucent skin and dark hair they gave her the aspect of a vampire.

From the living room her friend Julian Tennant gave an abrupt snort, as if startled from his sleep. They both giggled and in a second he returned to the steady rhythm of his snoring. Christopher stirred from his sleep and wiped his mouth. He looked neither asleep nor awake, caught in a state of semi-consciousness.

'Your friend will have a sore head tomorrow,' she remarked.

'And for a few days after,' Paul said. 'It's nothing more than he deserves.'

'And yet he blames you for his own shortcomings?' she asked, although it was more a statement of fact than a question for nobody present that evening could have escaped his cries of being sent to Hull or his angry denunciations of Paul.

'It's complicated,' he shrugged.

'Complicated how, Paul? You deal in the truth, or at least you say you do. But the truth here is simple. You both applied for Oxbridge to different colleges and universities. You got the grades you needed. He didn't. Why such vitriol your way? I can't even see how jealousy can play a part.'

Clarity emerged in Paul's mind, for she was right about Christopher. There was no basis for any grievance. His behaviour was outrageous, as it was in the very act of seeking an Oxbridge degree in history of all subjects. To Nadezhda Paul explained the saga of Christopher, the doctor's son who had forsaken his own destiny by talking his best friend out of his own. When he was done, he felt relief as if a grievous wrong had been put out in the open. But then almost immediately, he felt remorse for sharing Christopher's nefariousness to the mother of his girlfriend.

'Oh, God, I'm sorry, I should never have told you those things. Julia...'

'Don't worry about her,' Nadezhda said, taking another mouthful from her glass before taking the bottle from Paul and refilling it. 'She'll have forgotten all about him by the end of the month. He'll be gone. Easy come, easy go.'

He was taken aback by her blunt dismissal of their relationship, but before he could answer she said, 'And so you have another cause for celebration this evening.' She raised the glass and spoke loudly to the dying embers of the party. 'To success and to schadenfreude!'

And with that, she emptied the rest of her wine down her throat.

She was, he realised, very drunk by now, and from her position sat on the stairs, she swayed and gesticulating, her birdlike frame brushed against his. Yet although sodden by red wine, she spoke beautifully and expansively about politics and film and music and books.

'Books and wine and conversation, that's all I have now to keep me going,' she told him but it was not a lament, for she was full of joy and full of life.

In the near silent house, theirs was the only chatter above the grunts and snores of the other stragglers. He was enraptured by her and as the first traces of dawn crept through the lead light windows on the front door, he was reminded of his first night with her daughter, sat up talking as daylight flickered around them in the still of dawn.

'You asked me once about Vienna,' she said. 'The other week whether I missed it or whether it had made me a writer, a poet.' Paul nodded. 'And I said, "I'll tell you another time", that you were asking too many questions.' He nodded again. 'Well, you were asking too many questions, too many bloody questions.' She cackled at her own joke. 'But I'll tell you now, of course, I miss it. Not a day passes when I don't miss my old life. You spend the first years of your life wanting to escape where you came from. Well I was no different, I wanted to live in Paris or London or New York. You don't realise then that that place made you, no matter what has passed or what has happened and how many terrible things happened to me and my family. You will always belong there.

Wherever else you go, no matter for how long, you will always be a stranger, an outsider.'

She made to sip from her glass, but it was long empty. 'You don't realise it now, but you'll miss this place, too. Not a day goes by when I don't think of my youth, the years and the country I lost.'

'But did it make you want to be a writer?' Paul asked, smiling benevolently.

'No,' she said, and then laughed her smoker's laugh. 'That was my desire to show off.'

They both guffawed, their voices ringing around the sleeping house. Christopher stirred and he lay looking in their direction, neither asleep nor awake, his dead eyes focussed on nothing.

'But let me tell you this, Paul, every writer needs a helping hand. A gift, an entry into the publishing house or an agent's office. A story. It is a privilege of the giver to share that with someone who is young or hungry, but certainly talented.'

'What was your gift?'

'I was given the chance by someone powerful, as simple as that. I was no more talented than any other hopeful or aspirant. I was certainly less well connected, but someone saw something in me, believed in me, gave me space and time and money to make something of myself. And I took it. I was lucky, so, so lucky. That person was the greatest poet of his age and also the most prestigious publisher too: TS Eliot.'

Paul sat slack-jawed as she looked on into the half-light of the hallway.

'I was you once, Paul,' she said. 'I wanted to be a writer, but I didn't know who to tell or who to confide in. It was expected that I'd be a wife and mother, maybe even a cultured one, but nothing more. Then, after the war, it was just about survival, keeping sane, alive. The dream might have sustained me. I don't know. But I was given the gift of belief. Now it is my turn to pass it on.' She looked at him in the eye. Her face was pale and translucent. The whiteness, accentuated by her jet-black hair, made her eyes bright, despite the lack of sleep. Her charisma gave her a luminosity. Even after sitting up all night drinking and dancing and talking, even in her fifties, even despite all the living and all the pain, she was beautiful, like her daughters. He tried to desist from such thoughts, but she turned him on.

'Paul,' she whispered, 'I am your gift. I will make you a writer. I will bring you all the recognition that you can't admit to yourself that you crave.' She stood a little uncertainly at first and then over him. 'Please,' she said, offering her hand. 'Come to my rooms and I will explain.' And so he rose and followed her, his hand in hers leading to the upper floors of the grand old house to her domain.

12

The trill of a ringing telephone woke him from a deep sleep. His eyes widened to no more than slits and light bursting through a gap in the curtains blinded him. His temples throbbed. Confused and disorientated, he thrashed helplessly around his bed, unsure where he was before realising it was his own single bed at home. He lay down again, grabbed the pillow, and plunged his head under it to find the sanctity of darkness. A muffled silence, but still, somewhere in the depths of the hallway, the phone kept ringing.

Eventually it silenced, and he lowered himself back into a semi-sleep, but it was perforated by his nightmares. Nadezhda, pale skinned and ghostly, proclaiming 'I am your gift', and leading him up the stairs to her rooms.

A study littered with books and papers. His senses dimmed by the sharp sweet taste of a single malt. And then the moment of truth. A truth so terrible that he couldn't comprehend it, a truth that would surely destroy her if it was ever shared.

The phone rang again. There was no one else home, but he had not the energy to answer, much less converse with anyone. He ached all over. His head pounded. His legs were tired and stiff.

He tried to recall how he'd gotten home. He couldn't remember getting the train. A bus? That would have taken an eternity and he knew he had no money for a cab. He tried to summon a memory and then he recalled Sam's dad passing by in his black cab at the end of his night shift and driving the boys back to the north of the city. Down the pothole-scarred Dock Road, the boys drunk and being thrown around the back of the cab.

The phone rang out again. And now there was only silence.

Paul stepped back his recollections. He and Sam were the last to enter the cab. Roberts was sat looking impassively out of the window, while Christopher and Bulsara were barely conscious. It was dawn. Where had he been? How did he get there?

He searched the recesses of his memory. His head ached. His mouth was dry. He remembered his name being called, echoing around the house. Sam's voice. And waking. Waking at the foot of Nadezhda's bed. Falling over his own feet. His vision blurred and thinking even then in this drunkenness of the horror of it all. Searching for the door and seeing the plastic shopping bag of papers she had thrust upon him, and somehow of making it from her rooms at the top of the house without waking her, without drawing attention to himself. Down all the stairs and into the cab with his friends, the precious wad of paper clutched to his chest all the way home, until he ascended the stairs of his parents' home and into bed, still dressed.

He let out a groan and pulled the covers over his head. The phone rang for a third time, but again he let it ring out.

It was Friday. Drinks at the golf club after work. That's why his parents were absent. It must be early evening. He glanced at his bedside clock. Five thirty pm. Beside that, a Kwik Save bag thick with paper containing all manner of secrets, truths and horror.

Paul, I am your gift.

Over and over, the words came back to him. Fragments of the previous night returned. The shame, the sadness. The shock of scarred flesh. The betrayal of what everyone knew, of her daughters. The end of innocence.

Every writer needs a gift.

He hugged at his pillow as if it were the last thing on earth. His tongue had the texture of sand.

For the fourth time the phone rang. This time he pulled the covers from him and stood; his eyes blurred, and he took a moment to be sure of his balance. Then he made for the stairs, to the hallway, to the noisy ring of the phone, which he silenced by lifting the receiver.

'Hello Paul, it's me, Roberts, I've been trying for hours.' His tone was sharp, urgent.

'Hello.'

'Paul, it's Nadezhda.' His heart palpitated and his stomach lurched. 'You might want to sit down. I have something important to tell you.' Paul closed his eyes. Had the previous night come back to haunt him already? He could hear his heart pounding.

'I don't know how to say this,' said Roberts. His voice filled with sudden emotion. 'Nadezhda is dead.'

Part 2: **1989**

1

Truth always returns to haunt the betrayer, but it was the unexpected savagery of the attack that threw him and afterwards would not leave his dreams.

They followed the old white Mercedes down the narrow dirt track, observing the undulations of the hill, rocking them around the back of their vehicle. The suspension ached as they crossed potholes and crevices and loose stones rattled its undercarriage. A fog of brown dust and dull exhaust fumes obscured the path ahead, partially camouflaging the vehicle in front. Their driver reached into his breast pocket and removed a Marlboro packet. Without moving his other hand from the wheel he pulled out a single cigarette, put it in his mouth and lit it, then wordlessly offered the packet around the car, his eyes all the while fixed assiduously to the road.

They were down at the bottom of the dip in the small valley they were crossing when the stench reached them, a sickly-sweet odour of rotten food and the detritus of daily life. It seemed incongruous at first, for around them were olive groves on either side, planted in neat terraces, their shrivelled unripe fruit swaying gently in the wind. But as they travelled up the incline the twisted trees thinned out until there was nothing but rocks and dirt and shrubs. The white Mercedes came to a stop and so, after a few seconds, did they.

When they left the car, the smell in the arid air was unbelievable and they sucked hard on their cigarettes, hoping for the smoke to mask the noxious stench rising from the other side of the hill. Bits of newspaper and plastic bags blew around in the dust, littering the hillside with thousands of specks of colour. From the trunk of the car he grabbed his bag and checked his notebook hadn't slipped from the side. There was only one way up the hillside, a narrow, rutted pathway. Gulls peered at them, rising into the air and diving into the void below. One of his colleagues let out a sigh, as if to ponder what on earth they were doing there.

The driver of the Mercedes took out a cigarette and pointed up the hill. 'He's up there.'

∽

There was not one body, but two. Plastic sheeting hid the corpses and before the younger man pulled it back, he cautioned them, 'It's terrible, yeah.' When he saw his warning met blank faces he said solemnly, 'It's really bad, yeah. It's bad shit.' Slowly, almost decorously, he unpeeled the plastic sheet, then looked away. Underneath were two bodies, a female and a man entangled with each other in a bloody mess. Flies picked on the caramelised blood. In the heat they had started to decompose, merging with the rotting rubbish which was their final bed. The smell was intolerable. Nettle vomited. Those with cameras peered uneasily at the bodies, bracing themselves before they got close enough to do their work. The guide stepped back, away from the worst of the smell, and started to tell their story.

Their names were Mahmoud Mansour and Mona Islam. Without prompting he spelled their names after speaking them; it was clear he had done this tour of duty before. Mahmoud was a Fatah bodyguard, she a nurse. The photographers pointed their light meters and cameras and started shooting while he spoke. The Israelis had taken her brother, five years earlier. No one knew for sure where he was, but they had reports from human rights groups occasionally. In 1986 a letter was smuggled out bearing his name. He didn't know why he was in prison, or even where he was held. He had been tortured at first, but now he was in limbo, waiting for charges to be brought, an explanation for his imprisonment. His mother grew hysterical with fear, terrified he would never be seen again. The family made new representations to the government, the Red Crescent, local power brokers, anyone who might be able to help.

Somewhere along the line the Israelis tapped up Mona. If she helped them, they said, they would bring her brother home. At first they wanted irrelevant details. The times of public meetings, who was in, who was out, the kind of information that might be obtained painlessly. Then she became involved with Mahmoud and the stakes increased. Her Israeli handler now wanted details of his bosses, where they met, details about his working day. She tried to break it off with Mansour to no avail. It was a family match; all their honours were at stake. Then the Israelis interred him. He was innocent at that point, oblivious to Mona's indiscretions. But they warned him that they would betray not just Mona, but him too, as paid informants if he refused to cooperate. It was a lie, but he knew the consequences if it came to pass. He spoke and they betrayed him anyway.

'So who did this, then?' asked Nettle. 'The Israelis?'

'The Israelis,' the guide replied without conviction.

'The Israelis executed them?'

'No, the Israelis compromised them.'

'So who killed them, then? Fatah?'

The guide looked at his feet, but said nothing.

'Why would they do that after the story you've just told us?' the American demanded.

The Palestinian guide said nothing for a moment, then, 'They betrayed the Palestinian cause. A betrayal is a betrayal.'

'What I don't understand is why you brought us here,' said the American. His voice was tremulous with anger now. 'To show us that the Israelis compromise your people or that Fatah are a bunch of murdering thugs.'

'The Israelis did this,' snapped the Palestinian, and he gestured down at the bodies.

Mona's rotting body bore a single bullet hole to her temple, the orifice caked with a scab. Her hair was matted with blood. A single fly picked at her left eye, still open, fearful, staring accusingly at them. Mahmoud was in a worse state. There was an open wound where his nose had once been, and his mouth spewed with torn flesh. His green tracksuit was thick with blood around his waist.

Paul spoke for the first time. 'He's been tortured, hasn't he?'

The guide ignored him, although his silence was not at first an admission. The others looked on, wordlessly assessing his mutilated body. Paul repeated the question in Arabic, and the guide looked down at his feet. Suddenly it dwelled on all of them just what they were looking at.

The American jabbed the Palestinian in the chest, his face red with anger. 'You fucking tortured him, didn't you? The Israelis compromised him, but your Fatah friends did the dirty work. Isn't that right?' His face glistened with fury, his eyes bulging as he shouted. Nettle went to pull him back, but he angrily pushed him away. He was incandescent. 'You cut his nose off and then you fucking cut his dick off and then you fed it to him, you fucking savage.' He spat at his feet and stormed off, trudging back across the expanse of filth towards the car.

For a few minutes the others stood around, looking helplessly at the bloodied couple. The Palestinian guide looked on desperately, as if he were about to cry, the shoulders under his ridiculous T-shirt drooping forlornly. Paul took some photographs, wincing as the shutter of his Nikon snapped. And then the rest of them left, following the distant American back across the dump.

2

Half an hour later they were back in the ancient Mercedes, traversing the route back to Tel Aviv. The road was partially surfaced, but every few seconds they banged silently around the back as it jolted over another pothole. None of them said a word. From the front Nettle offered a box of cigarettes, but Paul ignored him, continuing to look from the window.

It was nearly three when they got back to the press club. Paul went straight for the bank of phones that stretched along the wall behind the library. He waited for the dull burr of the line, then punched in the number he knew so well. After a moment's silence it rang once, twice and then the sound of the chief subeditor's voice far away in London, in normality.

'Jim, it's Paul Davis in Tel Aviv,' he said addressing his colleague, and then, brusquely, 'Is Roy there? I've got a story from the West Bank.'

The line went quiet as the foreign editor was found, then came the thick Glaswegian brogue of Roy McEwen.

'What you got, Paul?'

'Torture and execution of Palestinian informants near Ramallah. By Fatah.'

'We've done it before.'

'This is different,' Paul told him firmly, and he described the tragedy of Mansour and Mona.

A pause and then a wearied Scottish voice. 'Who else has got it?'

'AP, some American freelance, a German radio guy, and a couple of French.'

'None of our nationals?

'No.'

'You got pictures?'

'Yes, but I'm not sure you can use them.' Paul paused trying to frame the horrors of Mansour's mutilated body in polite terms. In the end he was necessarily blunt: 'They cut off the guy's dick and fed it to him.'

There was a second's pause on the line, and Paul knew he had sold the story. 'Brilliant. Get me nine hundred words by four, London time.'

The line went dead without a goodbye, and Paul went into the library. It was a tall room with ceiling-high oak shelves and bound copies of old journals that he had never seen anyone view. Musty armchairs sat in the room's bay, overlooking the carefully manicured patch of garden in the courtyard. It was less a library than a workroom for correspondents not based, as many were, out of Jerusalem and presided over by Benoit, a Palestinian Christian full of old-worldly charm, who had worked there since the building was the Imperial and Foreign Press Club of Jaffa, and Tel Aviv was but a white concreted Jewish suburb to its north. He was nominally the librarian, but his duties extended to tea maker, translator, secretary and fax machine engineer.

'Mr Paul, tea?' he asked as Paul sat before his typewriter. Nettle, who was sitting opposite him, was already clacking away on his keyboard.

'Yes please, Benoit.'

'I have something stronger, if you prefer,' shouted the American across the room. He was sitting in one of the leather easy chairs by the window, trying, it seemed, to contextualise the day's events. Before him was a bottle of Ballantine's and a tumbler full of scotch. The idea of a long drag of whisky, something to soften the memory of Mansour's corpse, was appealing. But there was work to be done.

'Tea is fine, thank you,' he said to Benoit; and then to the American, 'Maybe later though.'

'Did you get your story in?' Nettle asked Paul, still punching away and barely looking up.

'Yes, but only because of the photos.'

'Gore sells; the first rule of the foreign correspondent. You know that.'

'I guess so,' said Paul as he sat back with his pen at the ready, thinking of his first line. He always wrote in longhand first, typing his report later, when the page was a mess of crossings out and arrows. Today he summoned the first line without effort: *The destinies of Mahmoud Mansour and Mona Islam were bonded to tragedy even before they first met.* Their story was easy to recall and the words flowed easily from his pen. Chronicling individual calamity had become his daily work and summoning adjectives to describe the plight of these people was routine.

As he neared the end of his second page, he returned to the bank of phones. First he called Amnesty International for figures on militant executions in the Occupied Territories. Then he tried his Fatah contact. In the calm of the Press Club, the cacophony from the end of the line of shouting, telephone rings, and clatter of typewriters seemed to belong to another world. Then his contact was put on the line. At first he made a show of denying everything, claiming even that there were no bodies. Paul pointed out the uselessness of his assertion; he had photographs and witnesses. His contact then blamed rival militants, his voice rising to a crescendo of accusation that he yelled down the receiver. Paul asked if he could quote him on that, and he backtracked again. It was like trying to extract information from an errant child who knew he was in the wrong. Finally he spoke over Paul in his waiter's English, 'I know nothing, nothing at all! I have nothing to say. No comment! No comment!' Then he put his phone down on him without a goodbye and Paul went back to the library and filed his report.

∽

When he finished writing he left the smoky gloom of the library and headed onto the club's veranda. The terrace was shaded by jacaranda trees and magnolia, with cast-iron white chairs and tables and a hammock, which he took for himself. Edward, the club's barman, brought him a beer and he sipped straight from the bottle.

The story was filed now, but he was still thinking about the lovers trussed with the rubbish and the insouciance with which they were murdered. Only in death had their miserable existences assumed some significance, and then merely because some misguided soul believed political capital could be made. Tomorrow the world would read of their wretched fates. But the day after there would be another story and theirs would lay forgotten in discarded newspapers, on their way to the rubbish dump to join their subjects.

He swigged from the bottle and sighed at the hopelessness of it all. He had had several years of evenings like this: pondering the futility, trying to make sense of the horrors and expunge the worst sights from his mind. He wondered how he withstood the relentlessness of it all. The relentlessness and the loneliness. Yet being here in a place where man killed man as naturally as breathing, where death met those who had barely winked at the enemy, much less compromised those they held dear, was in its way preferable to rotting in the mundanity of life in England. He had thought once when still consumed with a boyish idealism that his work would bring some sort of enlightenment. It didn't, but in a strange way it sometimes bred hope. Hope that his words mattered; hope that someone might notice. That was why he had to continue and bear witness to the daily cavalcade of torment and horror.

Edward came over and placed a ramekin of big green olives in front of him. Paul waved the empty bottle, and Edward nodded silently and turned to his small glass-fronted fridge to get him a fresh bottle. He smiled inwardly at himself and thought of Roberts back in England. Strange old Roberts who only ever bought drinks for himself, as Paul had just done himself. He tried to picture what he was doing right at that moment, in his provincial solicitor's office in an old Victorian house on the outskirts of an unremarkable northern town. Tyrannising his secretary, he imagined, or hurling abuse down the line of rival solicitors who dared hold up ongoing probate or conveyancing cases for the benefit of their own clients.

Paul had not seen Roberts for nearly a year now. That day he had called the desk in London – he always called that number, even though Paul was only at it for one day in a hundred – and seemed surprised when it wasn't directed to the department secretary. 'I'm stuck in London,' he said without greeting. 'They've sent me to some ludicrous thing at the Law Society and I'm here until tomorrow. Can you get away for a drink?' As with so many of his friends back home, London represented chaos and hostility to Roberts. To them it was an inhospitable place, expensive and replete with people who despised the very name of their home city. Roberts had spoken shrilly, as if his presence in the capital automatically put him on the defensive. Two hours later Paul took the Underground to Goodge Street and found his friend standing bolt upright, drinking alone outside a pub. He wore an ill-fitting suit with padded shoulders that made the top third of his body seem incongruously broad above his thin torso. He was sipping from a tall glass of Coca-Cola, which Paul suspected masked something more potent. On seeing him he told Paul to get him a pint of lager; Roberts could just about bear doing rounds when there were only the two of them.

'So, you're back,' he had said when Paul returned from the bar.

'For a few days, yes. Remind people I'm still alive.'

Roberts told him about his conference, complaining bitterly of the inconvenience of being away from home for the night. He mentioned a girlfriend but didn't elaborate. Instead he talked about his job. Whenever he spoke of it things were always 'hectic', 'non-stop', 'relentless.' His stock options were coming through at the end of the year, he said, and he was getting a company car, a BMW or an Audi. He never asked Paul about his work and they seldom talked of home, except when Roberts had some gossip, which he caustically regaled: Bulsara had no job, Sam weighed eighteen stone. Christopher was never mentioned. Nor were the girls. Paul, for his part, filled the conversation with banalities and football talk. As they got drunker that night, Paul suddenly changed the flow of conversation, interrupting Roberts' flow of sarcasm and self-congratulation. He asked: 'Does Christopher know where the girls are?' He blurted it out suddenly, as if he had suppressed the question all night, but just had to get it out. Roberts pondered it for a minute, then looked down into his near empty glass. 'I'll get us another round,' he said. But when he came back from the bar there was no revelation: he started talking about house prices and the moment passed. That was the thing about Roberts; he always seemed to be holding back on something, creating a sense of mystery where none may have existed.

ᔓ

Footsteps across the untidy grass of the courtyard's lawn broke his introspection.

'Hey you loner, what you doin' out here on your own?'

Paul looked up from the beer bottle he was fingering morosely, picking its moist label from its front. It was the American, smiling, clutching his brown bottle of Ballantine's and two glasses. They were together almost all day, but Paul realised he had barely even set eyes upon him. He was about forty, short, bespectacled, his blond hair dramatically receding past his temples. He wore the standard garb of all foreign press corps: khaki fatigues and a pale blue Oxford shirt. Except he had taken the time to shower and change since the afternoon. Paul suddenly felt dirty alongside him, conscious of the filth and sweat of the day's work still lingering in his pores.

The American put the whisky and the glasses on the table. 'You were right this afternoon,' he said, pouring a large measure into the first glass. 'Whisky isn't a day drink.' He held the bottle over the second glass and looked to Paul for confirmation to pour. He nodded, suddenly relieved to have company, glad for the silence and loneliness of the garden to be broken.

'Tough day?' asked the American, but continued without waiting for an answer. 'That kinda shit doesn't happen much around here.' He slurred the end of his sentence slightly and Paul wondered if he was onto his second bottle of whisky.

'It was horrible, pointless. Like you said before it showed just how divorced from reality they have become.'

'Sometimes I get too caught up in it all.'

They sipped the whisky in silence for a moment. It occurred to Paul that he had not even introduced himself, so caught up had he been in the day's events. He apologised to the American for not knowing his name and told him his.

'Larry A Mills,' the American said and held out his hand. '*Time* magazine.' Then he set off on a monologue about journalists being so tied up in their stories that niceties, like introductions, were dispensed with. He told him about a French journalist he was on assignment with in Beirut, when a sniper shot him dead. 'I was right next to him. As close to him as I am to you now. There was nothing I could do but report him dead when I got back to the bureau. Only then did I realise I didn't even know the poor bastard's name, which caused all sorts of problems. In the end I think they sent the marines in to get the body and identified him later. But the French lapped it up, this callous, ruthless American leaving the body of his colleague without even knowing his name!'

He had been in Lebanon since the start of the civil war and traversed between there and the shifting fronts of the Iran-Iraq conflict ever since. He was in Tel Aviv now on his way to follow a lead in the Israeli zone in South Lebanon. As he talked, Paul sensed that over the years Mills had become so embedded in the thrill and danger of the region as to become divorced from the life he might have once known in America. He talked of bringing tins of Saddam Hussein's favourite English chocolates when he interviewed him in Baghdad, and having an audience with Ayatollah Khomeini in Qom, as if visiting old friends. But when he spoke of his editors and readership he became animated and angry. 'They say they want blood and fire, but when you give them that they plead battle fatigue,' he said. His voice rose: 'They don't understand war, they don't want to know war unless "our boys" are involved or these people are victims.'

He fell silent and sipped hungrily from his tumbler. A tide of misery washed over Paul: this wasn't the conversation he wanted. Suddenly he yearned for his bed and the solitude of his room. Yet at the same time, something about the American both fascinated and appalled him. He represented a vision of his own future: war-weary, cynical, tired – everything Paul never wanted to be. Sometimes he saw himself on an irreversible path towards such a destiny and now he suddenly felt himself confronted by it.

'But you – we – surely have a duty to educate opinion, to change preconceptions,' said Paul in half-hearted protest.

Mills snorted. 'Do you really believe that?'

'I used to.'

'And now?'

'I've grown up. It's my work to see things, to chronicle them and let others draw their own conclusions.' He sipped his whisky and thought for a moment before continuing. 'I used to think that by bearing witness it'd help me understand the world. Actually it just confuses things even more.'

The American raised his glass. 'Amen to that!' Mills boomed. He was quite drunk, Paul could now see. But beneath the irascible boorishness Paul felt a sense of kinship and responsibility towards Mills. Maybe it was because he saw in him what he feared he might himself become.

'So how did you end up here?' asked Mills. Alternately the

whisky seemed to heighten his volatility and soften his bravura. For the moment the warmth of the liquor seemed to calm him.

'I spent a year in Cairo learning Arabic and trying to write a novel,' he said. 'Then three years ago they started a new broadsheet back home. I knew some guys involved with the paper and they needed someone cheap and who spoke Arabic so I began freelancing for them. Tel Aviv was better connected to the main stories and there were no rival hacks here so I moved. They put me on a retainer and here I am.'

His mind went back to Cambridge, as it often did these days. He had never set out to be a journalist and knew nothing of the Middle East before he left home. Despondency in his first term thrust him into his work, and involvement with the university newspaper, *Varsity*, gave him purpose outside his studies. Waking early on a Friday, he dressed without showering and walked through the dark frosty courtyards, the air condensing into small clouds before his face. At the small newsagents on the corner he purchased a slew of newspapers and the weekly magazines: the *New Statesman*, the *Spectator*, the *Economist*, and hurried back to his rooms before falling back into bed to read them, sniffing the undercurrents of the upcoming week's affairs. His Fridays were free from seminars and he filled them writing his op-ed piece for *Varsity*, filling out pages of carefully nuanced opinions in longhand, before hacking away at his work until he had condensed it into 1000 precise words. The paper went to press on Friday mornings and was on news-stands later that day. At first he had liked seeing his name in print and the light praise his words attracted: a comment from a don on an essay returned after marking; an overheard remark in a college bar from another student. But by his third year it was the process of writing he enjoyed: anticipating a story or movement, refining his own words into a manageable article.

It was the need to divorce himself from his old life in Liverpool that inadvertently thrust Paul towards the Middle East. Absence absolved him from the deadly nights in The Swan and his old friendships. He wanted to be out of reach from anyone who may hint at any impropriety. He felt shame because the imputations went unspoken; he could never voice his defence. Being away put out of mind also the summer that had defined his existence. For whatever he did and despite his other accomplishments, he felt incomplete without Sarah. Immersing himself in an existence elsewhere allowed him to forget the longing, the loneliness, the sense that his chance to love and be loved was ripped away from him.

So when the opportunity was presented to spend the summer at the end of his first year in Egypt, he took it. Peace fellowships had been set up in the name of President Anwar Sadat to fund exchanges between Egypt and the West. It provided twenty hours' language tuition each week and a stipend generous enough for him to rent his own studio and fund long nights smoking hookah and getting drunk on local beer.

Paul had thought Egypt would be hot; the memories of a school visit to Pompeii, the furthest south he had previously ventured, were all of dry heat and cloying nights which always ended with his bedclothes soaked in perspiration. But nothing prepared him for Cairo. He arrived one June lunchtime and the moment he stepped from the plane a wall of arid air hit him, the heat reflecting from the tarmac and burning through the denim of his jeans. He took a taxi to his accommodation, the window down all the way, the stench of diesel filling his lungs and tasting in his throat for hours after. Even now, seven years later, he still hadn't fully acclimatised to the searing heat and sweated profusely whenever he ventured out on a daytime assignment. But once he recovered from the shock of one-hundred-degree temperatures and began exploring the myriad of streets and alleys that connected his studio to the campus he felt a sense of belonging that eluded him in England. He avoided the other fellows and instead mixed with local students, expanding his primitive vocabulary by the day. They took him to their homes and showed him off to their extended families, as if he were a prize they had collected from the classroom. In the city's nascent nightclubs he found girls paying him attention. He found them boldly westernised, wearing clothing revealing enough to provoke blushes from his shy and religious friends.

At the end of his second year he returned to Egypt. The foundation that provided the fellowships employed him to coordinate the lives of new fellows, fresh off the plane and blinking into the extraordinary glare of a Cairo afternoon. After the initial rush of arrivals, his work consumed just a few hours each week leaving him free to renew acquaintances and resume his Arabic lessons. He became passable in the language and his aptitude for it surprised him given how wretched he was at German when at school. At night, he often became morbid and sentimental, but had no one to dissect his thoughts with. His friends were many, but they were emotionally distant and he regretted his aloofness. He tried to articulate his feelings in poetry, but found what he wrote pointless and cursory. At the summer's end he looked through what he had written and became consumed with irritation and self-loathing. The poems called attention to themselves rather than the subject. Their virtue came in their construction as if their perfect pentameter was the point rather than the sentiments they expressed. He tore them up and wanted to burn them, but desisted at the last moment and put the strips of paper into a bag, which he brought home.

'I was a terrible poet,' he told Mills. 'Somewhere at my parents' house, there's a bag of torn-up strips of paper. A summer's work! One day I might go back and recover it. Put it in the fire just to make sure no one else ever reads it.'

The American laughed. 'And the novel?'

'The novel? Oh, shit. The novel.'

Paul flicked out his fingers and mouthed the word 'Boom!' Mills laughed again. And for the first time in a terrible day, the mood lifted.

The other journalists filtered outdoors to the garden. More wine and beer was brought out. And as it flowed the conversation strayed away from the senseless slaughter in the holy lands and instead centred on home, family and lost loves. By the time Paul returned to his apartment the horrors he had witnessed were briefly forgotten in a mood of intoxicated fatigue.

3

His dreadful poetry was an outlet, he realised now, for what had become an unrequited love affair with Sarah. She was gone, gone from his life now. He had no idea where she was and his attempts to search for her never came to anything. While he clung onto fragments of their days together, his abiding memory now was of their last encounter.

Nadezhda's death had made the national news. There were fulsome tributes to her work and legacy. Fellow poets lined up to praise her and drop anecdotes about her wild days and political proclivities. Her generosity and warmth. Her sense of mischief and excess. By Monday, these were giving way to darker rumours about her. Had the shadows of her past finally overcome her? There was discourse about the war years, but nothing new, nothing revelatory, just the ruminations of pens for hire reading over old interviews and speculating. In the absence of fact, nobody knew what had happened. Suicide was the assumption underlying much of the coverage. As a female poet was that not somehow a predestined end? Sylvia Plath, Anne Sexton and Elsie Cowen were all contemporaries of Nadezhda to have taken their own lives and one pundit added the names of Virginia Woolf and Emily Dickinson, 'who also died tragically early of their own melancholia.'

As Paul, with Roberts, Sam and Bulsara, sat in The Swan, four days after her death, reflecting on the night of the party, they pondered how far removed Nadezhda was from the melancholic figure that was being portrayed.

'She was dancing on tables and moshing,' said Bulsara.

'There was something wild about her, though,' said Sam. 'That wasn't the normal behaviour of someone in their fifties.'

'She wasn't a normal person in their fifties, though, was she?' said Roberts. They murmured their agreement as they sipped from their pint glasses. Paul reflected with them on his last conversations about film and politics and books, sat alongside her on the stairs, she inebriated but full of life, full of joy. He was enraptured by her. He told his friends this, but the darker moments that transpired later, the horror of what he learned, he told no one and had already decided he never would.

'Don't you think it's strange that we were the last people to see her, but no one has asked us about the party?' asked Sam. 'If something bad had happened, we'd be the first people the police would come to.'

'It's a tragedy, but I can't see how it's worthy of all this innuendo,' said Roberts. He pushed the newspapers on the table aside as if for effect. 'If she was a schoolteacher or nurse or secretary, there'd be none of this nonsense about predestination and melancholia. No, it's a tragedy. No less, no more.'

Sarah was still out of the country, uncontactable. He waited and waited for a call from Germany, but it was still to come. He wanted to console her, to hear her sing-song voice again, to be with her, but his frustration at his own helplessness was matched by some sense of relief that he could hold onto the secrets he had learned without the burden of her presence.

The phone at their house rang out whenever he tried. He called Christopher, too, who was absent or evasive; equally uncontactable. He wondered if he was shamed or remorseful for his actions on results day, when he drank himself into a stupor of self-loathing and rage and called Paul every name under the sun. But that wouldn't have been Christopher's way. He was never one to back down.

He called to the girls' house on Sunday, making his way there on train and by foot down the elegant tree-lined streets towards the river and Nadezhda's villa. A debris of bottles and cans propped up in the back garden stood as evidence of the previous week's party. But the house was otherwise dark and silent and there was no one home.

On Monday, Christopher called him at home. His voice was sombre and to the point as he gave Paul cursory details of what had passed.

'Nobody knows for sure what happened,' he said. 'She had no record of ill health. The coroner is involved. Julia is in a bad way, as you'd expect, devastated and angry. She barely knows what day it is. She's lashing out at everyone she sees. Her father and Sarah are on their way back by road for some reason. There'll be a private funeral service. That's all I know so far.'

'And Sarah. When exactly is Sarah coming back?'

Christopher ignored him. 'Listen, mate, what happened the other night between you and Nadezhda?'

Paul's stomach lurched. 'What do you mean?'

'Well, you were with her all night. You were probably the last person to see her alive. What happened?'

'We talked, we drank. We talked some more.'

'Anything else?'

He felt the creep of nausea in his mouth and paused for a moment; a passage of time that was perhaps not even a second, but seemed to hint at some sense of responsibility. He said nothing before answering: 'We toasted the future.'

'Oh,' said Christopher, but he could tell that he didn't really believe him.

When he met the others at the pub that afternoon, he didn't relay that part of his stilted conversation to his friends. He remained fearful that they would press him further, needle him for the truth that lay within him. Of Christopher they asked nothing, for here was a friend who had finally diminished any reserves of patience or goodwill.

That night, Paul dreamed of Sarah. She felt so far away it was as if she had never been there at all. He searched his memory, seeking for a recollection of her sound, her taste; her smell. But his mind was blank. Later that night, he was haunted by nightmarish dreams of Nadhedza, vampire-like, promising, *Paul, I am your gift.*

He rose early and called the house in Grassendale, but again, it rang out. When he tried again in the afternoon, he was momentarily taken aback when it was picked up on the second ring. A male voice answered. The girl's father?

'May I speak with Sarah?'

'Now is not a good time,' said the man, in soft, lightly accented English. 'Please call back another time. Tomorrow maybe? Good day.'

With that, the line went dead. Paul found himself beset with joy and apprehension. Sarah was back, but why hadn't she called? Why was the phone not passed over to her?

He pondered these questions with Roberts later when they walked to the beach. The sun was beginning to set and it illuminated the horizon purple and orange as a breeze swept across Liverpool Bay. In the distance the Welsh hills peaked out above the sea. There were dog walkers and children riding bikes along the promenade. Otherwise they had this great expanse to themselves.

'She's in grief. She's had an exhausting journey. She's not long home. I don't think it's unusual that her father wouldn't pass the receiver over,' he said.

'But it's me!' exclaimed Paul. 'Her boyfriend, her soul mate. She said it herself.'

'Come on now, mate, you've been together, what? A few weeks.'

'Seven, actually.'

'Not everyone might understand.'

'But it's me! We're in love.'

Roberts winced at the mention of the word. 'I know that. But her father might not see it that way.'

The tide was far out, leaving a vista of compacted sand extending long into the distance.

They walked across this, heading for nowhere in particular.

'Paul,' said Roberts with sudden abruptness. 'When Sam's dad swung by to get us we looked and looked for you, but you were nowhere to be found and suddenly you were in the car. Where were you?'

He'd been asleep, passed out at the foot of Nadezhda's bed, but he wasn't going to tell anyone this. Not even Roberts, who was one of the few people he could trust to be discreet.

'I was still drunk. Very, very drunk. Passed out somewhere, I suppose.'

'Were you with Nadezhda?'

'I talked to her a lot that night,' he replied, dodging the question.

'I know that. But were you with her then? Her room was just about the only place we didn't check.'

'Jesus Roberts, what is this? An interrogation?'

'You do realise that you were the last person to see her alive. That interrogation may yet come. That could be a police car waiting when you get home. You need to be ready for that.'

'Christ, Roberts, tell me something I don't know.'

But the knock on the door never came. Not the next day nor the next week. Months and then years would pass before anybody asked him again what had happened early that morning on the day Nadezhda died.

§

The following day, after another haunted night, he rose early and resolved to see Sarah. Grassendale was lush and green, leaves shimmered in the trees. In the breeze that came in from the Mersey, the electric whine of a milk float finishing its rounds was the only hint of traffic. He felt that same mixture of trepidation and excitement as he had encountered days earlier when heading for his results. What would he find? How would Sarah be? Had the summer really all been just one long, undulating dream? A journey of fantasy and nightmare?

Outside the house was a large black Volvo with West German registration plates. His heart pounded and he felt lightheaded as he made his way up the path to the front door. Normally it was left ajar, but today he had to rap on the old brass knocker. There was a sound of voices, steps, a shuffle, and there in front of him stood Julia.

There were bags under her eyes and her white skin seemed puffy and grey. She was dishevelled, as if she hadn't slept for days.

'It's you,' she said, without greeting.

'Julia, I'm so sorry for everything that's happened. I can't even begin to imagine everything you've been through. I tried calling the other day.'

'Paul, this is not a good time,' she said, dispassionately, blinking.

'Of course, I understand.' He took a step back. 'But if I could see Sarah just for a moment. That would be...'

'Paul, I don't think it's the right time.'

'A minute.'

'Paul...'

From a back room he heard Sarah's voice.

'It's no one,' Julia called back. 'They're just leaving.'

Paul frowned, entirely perplexed at her hostility. 'Julia?'

'You really have to go right now,' she said firmly, hands on hips as if barricading the door.

Ignoring her, Paul stepped forward and called into the house.

'Sarah, it's me, Paul.' Julia's eyes ignited with rage. 'What's going on, Julia?'

'You know what this is about,' she hissed.

'I'm sorry for your loss, but I don't. I really don't.'

From inside the house, he could hear footsteps and then suddenly in the doorway stood Sarah. There was a frailty in her face, as if she was shrunken or physically diminished by what had happened over previous days. Julia stood in front of her in a pose of silent fury, acting as if a human barricade between the two lovers.

'Paul! Oh, my dear Paul. How I've missed you.' She pushed forward past her sister and he held her in his arms. But there was something different about her now, almost imperceptible. Her body stiffened slightly, not melting into his. Maybe it was that time apart. Maybe it was her grieving, but there seemed a distance between them, an indiscernible barrier as their bodies touched. He whispered words of condolence, of longing, of his love for her as they stood holding each other. Julia stood in a paroxysm of rage, looking on, grimacing. Sarah wept as he spoke, tears silently rolling down her cheeks. He smelt the sweetness of her hair, and held her slender frame in his arms, but she wouldn't relax into him.

'I'm sorry. I'm so, so sorry,' he said again and again. Eventually she stepped back and wiped her face with the back of her hand.

She seemed frail, vulnerable, but then she fixed him with the old lopsided grin.

'Paul, I have to go. It's family time now.' She leaned and kissed him on the cheek and stepped back into the house behind her scowling sister. 'I'll call you when all this is over, I promise.' He walked backwards in a state of shock at Julia's unremitting antagonism, at the brevity of their encounter. He looked at the beautiful ruins of their ramshackle old house and from an upstairs window could see the silhouette of an elderly man looking down upon him.

'I'll call,' she said and then mouthed the words, 'I love you.'

But the call never came and two weeks later he was at Cambridge.

4

An old Volvo bus took them over Allenby Bridge, a low-slung iron crossing over the Jordan River. On the other side their passports were stamped quickly and they were ushered out to a panoply of ubiquitous Mercedes taxis awaiting them.

The plan was to spend a few days in Amman and then travel down to the Dead Sea, where they could spend the weekend lying in the sun, drinking cheap beer and swimming. The Jordanian capital was a sombre arid city of low-rise buildings sprawled across hillsides and valleys in the heart of a country surrounded by bad neighbours: Israel, the Occupied Territories and the Baath dictatorships of Syria and Iraq.

It was a provincial backwater, but that was the whole point of their trip. Their very presence would attract attention and invitations from government officials and the Royal Court where British- and American-educated apparatchiks and princes gossiped freely of their lousy neighbours. If they were lucky, there would be a summons to see King Hussein, its diminutive and brilliant ruler who somehow navigated the country's survival against extreme odds.

They arrived in Amman at sunset. Mills insisted they dined at a Lebanese restaurant, a short walk from the hotel. He ordered copiously from the menu in his fluent Arabic: shawarma, a beef tartare, grilled sparrows and sheep's feet, slow cooked and gelatinous, stuffed in vine leaves. They drank beer and arak and reminisced about old reporting assignments, tyrannical editors and close shaves.

When they returned to their hotel a wave of fatigue washed over Paul and he excused himself from joining Mills for a nightcap. Instead, he returned to his room and after washing, lay on his bed with the copy of *Anna Karenina* Sarah had given him as a leaving gift.

Bound up in the now tatty volume were old photos, ticket stubs, receipts and letters. His tiredness made him contemplative and as he lay in the single bed in his Amman hotel room he rummaged through these remnants of his past.

He was drawn finally to a set of letters Roberts sent him in his first year at university. In those first, lonely days at Cambridge, Roberts was the line back to the world Paul had left behind. He wrote weekly, sometimes twice weekly informing him of the fall-out from Nadezhda's death. It was Roberts' meticulous print that informed him that Julia had dumped Christopher, and Roberts' gleeful description of Christopher's torment afterwards. He hinted that he had seen the sisters, once even that Sarah cornered him in a city centre bar with a litany of questions about Paul. But he never elaborated, and when Paul asked him about it he ignored the question as if the information was out of bounds.

In his first miserable term the missives from Roberts were all that Paul looked forward to as he plunged himself headlong into his work. Liberated for the first time from the cloying, incestuous world of his childhood, he had felt the moment that his father drove him through the gates of his college as if his life was just beginning. But when his parents left and he set out to explore his new world he felt nothing but disappointment. It was an all-male college, but everyone else seemed to have come from one of several public schools. There was a self-confidence and clubbishness amongst his fellow alumni that eluded Paul. Their plummy voices and chatter about villa holidays in France and old boys in the years above them were alien to him. To them he was a source of fascination and amusement: the state schoolboy from the condemned city. Sam had said during that long summer of upheaval that Liverpudlians were the new underclass that it was okay to kick; and now Paul knew what he meant. He was their bit of Scouse rough, their Uncle Tom; an object of their condescending fascination. When they went drinking, they plied him with beer and interrogated him about life in the urban inferno. But their questions were always indirect; their good manners, their quintessential Englishness, Paul supposed, stopped them from openly asking about his background. They assumed he was a well-bred thug, a docker's child, a street Arab made good. As Paul drank them under the table he never had the heart to tell them he was merely a tax inspector's son from a suburb.

Despondency made him introspective. He longed for Sarah. He hadn't seen her since that dreadful morning when he was barred from the house by her sister. Days passed, and then a week, but the promised call never came. The longer it was, the harder it became for him to call. Julia frightened him, her anger and unspoken assumptions. It deterred him from seeking out Sarah. He feared confrontation.

On the day he left for university, his father drove him past the old villa. There was no one home and in a mixture of melancholia and relief he pushed a letter through the door telling Sarah of his new address. Paul told himself that distance and time would bring perspective. By Christmas everything would be fixed.

At Cambridge, each morning and afternoon he rushed to his wooden mailbox and opened it, hoping for an envelope bearing her handwriting. But except for Roberts' faithfully delivered news, cheery postcards from his mother and aunts as well as the usual assortment of bank statements and junk mail, nothing else arrived.

Then, on the first Tuesday of October there was a letter from Roberts. He wrote with ineffable routine at the end of the week, and Paul would receive it on a Saturday, but this missive was unexpected. So too was its brevity and the urgency in its tone. Roberts wrote:

> *Paul,*
>
> *You must contact the girls and tell them everything that happened that night. I don't know what the Jewess said or why you can't say, but Julia and Sarah must know no matter how dreadful it is. Forget tiptoeing and sensibilities for once. The shock and mourning have passed. You have a duty to them and above all else to yourself to do this. For your silence has given rise to the whiff of impropriety that I know as well as you do is without foundation. I remain your trusted friend, Roberts.*

The letter trembled in Paul's hand as he read over the last sentence again and again. *The whiff of impropriety*; what did that mean? The whiff of impropriety. The four words went around his head again and again and again. He cursed Roberts' evasiveness, for his letter loaded with double entendres and innuendo. He was clear only on one thing, but nothing else.

Lying in an Amman hotel room eight years later a momentary shiver passed through Paul as he recalled the horror of that moment, how it suddenly dawned on him that he was in some way implicated in Nadezhda's death. He remembered running to his room for change and racing back down to the lobby of his hall to call Roberts from the payphone, then almost crying in frustration as Mrs Roberts explained he had just left for the day. He remembered running the word 'impropriety' through his head again and again, trying to summon the crimes they might have imagined he had committed. Above all else he remembered going back to the mailbox later, convinced there was a letter from Sarah in the midday post, explaining everything, making everything right, but instead finding a second letter from Roberts, longer this time, even more sombre in tone. And its words stinging the heart of Paul as he realised he had been horrifically wronged.

Even now, sipping his beer alone all those years later, the words came back to him more clearly than he could remember anything else in his entire life. Roberts had dated the letter Sunday evening. Paul kept it in his diary, for it was a seminal moment in his life, one he ruminated over, even after all these years. He wrote:

Dear Paul,

This may come in the same post as my last letter, it may have come later.

Last night – Saturday – we went to the Jacaranda, myself and some others from the university that you don't know.

It was dead and we were going to move on when Julia suddenly turned up.

She was in a bad way: very pissed, maybe on drugs. She's gone for this ridiculous new romantic-punk cross-dressing, which didn't suit her at all – all spiky hair and ripped fishnets – and has a new boyfriend, some ape who was chewing her ear, groping her, all sorts.

I kept my distance, but she spotted me and came marching over with this slightly crazed look in her eye. She wasn't right. In the space of a sentence you didn't know whether she was going to burst out laughing or into tears.

Then she went a little crazy. She starts talking about you, babbling stuff about Christopher telling her things and getting lost in this alcoholic haze. She kept talking about "the truth". She knew "the truth", Sarah knew "the truth" – even I apparently know "the truth". I told her I had no idea what she meant.

It was like dealing with a child. I told her you were at college. That set her off again. She went really mad this time.

Eventually I had enough and told her forcefully I didn't know what she was talking about. She looked at me, and her face just fell and she said, 'About my mother…' and burst into tears and started pounding her fists against my chest.

This morning, first thing, I wrote you the first note and took it to the sorting office on Brownlow Hill in the hope that you might get it on Monday. Then I went over to the girls' house to try and clear up this mess.

But they're gone, Paul. I never got the chance. They're gone to Germany, gone to live with their father. There's a young family at the house now, they'd just moved in a day earlier. Last night must have been her last hurrah. The lady at the house said that they were driving to Harwich today. They must have stayed at a hotel last night.

I'm so sorry to have to write this Paul. I think that that bastard Christopher has wronged you immensely. We need to talk, Roberts.

Paul summoned a beer from the room's minibar and took another swig from the bottle. He had read the letter so many times that he could practically recite it. In a way, recalling Roberts' letter was a coping mechanism: he had learned to use it in the teeth of all the blood, cruelty and futility of life in Palestine. For nothing he experienced in his years out there consumed Paul with the same horror that struck his heart that afternoon in Cambridge.

5

After receiving Roberts' letter, Paul took the long train journey home to Liverpool, briefly abandoning Cambridge and the unhappy life he found himself living there. He remembered the slow gallop of the cross-country train through the autumnal rolling fields and provincial towns along the way, places he'd never been to and never would. Ely, March, Oakham, Stafford, Crewe. There was the rising feeling of dread and an inability to comprehend what had happened – or was about to.

Roberts was waiting for him on a barstool at a pub adjacent to Lime Street station. When he arrived, a pint of Guinness awaited Paul on the counter alongside his friend, a touch of generosity that he took to be an ominous sign.

'What's going on?' he asked, without greeting. Roberts gestured to the empty stool next to him, and Paul removed his overcoat, sat down next to him, and took a slug from his pint glass.

'The girls have gone,' he said. 'Gone to Germany, but we don't know where.'

'Yes, I know all that. But why?'

Roberts shrugged. 'Their father, I suppose. It doesn't matter, does it?'

'Can we find them?'

He shrugged again. 'How hard can it be to find a couple of Scouse girls in northern Germany?'

'What happened the other day when you saw Julia? What did she mean with "tawdry secrets"? What did you mean about "impropriety"?'

'You better have another sip of the black stuff,' said Roberts, gesturing at his pint glass and catching the eye of the barmaid.

'Two more of these, please, and two whisky chasers, large ones,' before adding as an aside, 'you can pay for these.'

'Impropriety. Tawdry. They're strong words to use in relation to my girlfriend's mother.'

'It's a big thing that's happened. And you were the last person to see her alive. We can accept that as a fact now?'

Paul nodded meekly. 'Paul, what happened in that room that night between you and Nadezhda?'

He cast his friend a furious glance. 'Nothing. We talked. We drank. I passed out drunk and exhausted.'

'After fucking her?' Roberts asked nonchalantly.

Paul slammed the dimpled pint glass on the countertop and spluttered on his mouthful of beer. The barmaid and the gaggle of customers at the other end of the bar abruptly silenced and looked across at him and, as Paul composed himself again, resumed their low murmured conversations.

'After what?

'You heard!'

'That is not what happened.'

'I know that, but the accepted version of events is different.'

Paul's head spun; he felt as if he were captured in an unfolding nightmare. He sipped from the whisky and felt momentarily alive again.

'What,' he asked, 'is the accepted version of events?'

'That you slept with Nadezhda and Nadezhda riven with guilt took her own life.'

Paul blinked and silently mouthed the words as if trying to comprehend what had just been spoken. Chewing over the new reality the only reaction he could summon was incredulous laughter.

'But I didn't do anything with Nadezhda and Nadezhda didn't kill herself.'

'That might well be the case, Paul. But it's a version that Julia has come to accept as fact.' Roberts' manner was sombre, lawyerly as Paul's stomach lurched and his mind spun from incredulity at the absurdity of it all to utter horror.

He cast his mind back to the party, the unlikely melange of artists and students, and Rastafarians and scallies. The crazed dancing and Julian Tennant lisping, 'She's had lots of affairs.' The drinking, there was so much of that, and drugs too. He thought on to the last stages, of Tennant and Bulsara passed out asleep and on the sofa. Of sitting on the stairs drinking rough Valpolicella. Nadezhda joining him, talking about gifts passed between generations of writers. Of her, inviting him to her room. For him the night had been a victory, a victory roll, but for others it was a different experience. The drunken moans of Christopher, 'I'm going to Hull, I'm going to hell,' were an omnipresent reminder of that.

But there was something else. Another detail that had briefly eluded his recall very late on, of Christopher intoxicated in an armchair, neither asleep nor awake, watching him. Watching Nadezhda. Watching their every move. Watching Paul follow her to her room and his doom.

'It's Christopher!' he growled. 'Christopher is behind all this.'

〜

Another day, another train journey, another city. As the train rolled over the flatness of East Riding, mist rose from the River Humber and all that could be seen at the new suspension bridge that crossed the water was a single tower whose summit disappeared into the sky.

Paul was ready for confrontation and anger burned within him. But when he arrived at the student house Christopher shared in a suburb of Hull, he felt only pity and disgust. A housemate let him in and left him amid a debris of overflowing ashtrays, dirty dishes and a bin that spilled out over the floor. Mould clung to the tops of the wall and ceiling. The windows were encrusted with years of ingrained dirt. There was a smell of damp and decrepitude. It was as far removed from his ancient and comfortable halls at Cambridge as could be imagined.

It was mid-morning, but Christopher, he was told, was still asleep. He poked around the miserable house before ascending the stairs. There were four bedrooms, but only one of the doors was closed shut, the others either left ajar or open. Paul went straight for the closed door and pushed it open. There on the bed, hair greased and askance, a week of stubble on his face, was Christopher. He jumped back, hugging his sheets to his chest, shocked at the sight of an intruder.

'Paul? What the fuck? Why are you here?'

'You know exactly why I'm here,' Paul growled. 'Now get up.' He flung him a pair of jeans that lay on the floor of the fetid room. 'We're getting out of this shithole.'

They went to a nearby park. It was a dark, cold October day. The sky was grey and motionless. Paul had expected to be enraged, to be shouting and raising his fists. But this was his oldest friend, and in a public park in a provincial city far from home he cut a hopeless figure, puffy faced and unshaven, evidently depressed by the circumstances his exam results had doomed him to. Christopher lit a cigarette and hunched over it, as if warming himself into it.

'What's all this about, Paulie?' he asked.

'You know what this is about? You lied about me to your girlfriend.'

'I don't have a girlfriend any more,' he smirked. 'From what I hear, you don't seem to either.'

Paul grimaced, but didn't rise to his provocation.

'What did you tell Julia?'

'Only what I saw.'

'You were out of your mind drunk,' he said. 'You didn't see anything at all.'

'I saw you with her mother. Your girlfriend's mother. And I saw you climb up the stairs with her. And then the next morning she was dead.'

'It wasn't like that.'

'So how was it, Paul? It wouldn't be her first time seducing one of her daughter's boyfriends. But it was certainly the last.'

Paul shoved him in the chest and Christopher recoiled. His half-smoked cigarette flew into the air as he recovered his balance. He looked briefly shocked at the force with which he was struck, but regained his poise and composure, flashing a contemptuous grin in Paul's direction as he did so.

'We were supposed to be friends. Why would you do such a thing? Why would you make such assumptions?'

'But they weren't assumptions, were they Paul? You were with Nadezhda and you went to her room.'

'Nothing happened.'

'Who said it did?' He grinned and pulled another cigarette from the packet. This time he dragged heavily on it and smoke wafted into the frigid air. This was the dark side of Christopher that he remembered. Loquacious, arrogant, provocative. 'People can draw their own conclusions from those simple actions.'

'I didn't do anything. We just talked. Why have you done this? You're my oldest friend.' He could imagine the drip, drip of innuendo. The suspicions expressed to Julia, which he simultaneously passed off because of an implied loyalty to Paul, like a latter-day Iago. And then the bombshell reluctantly dropped. Shock. Tears. Comforting. Coming together over a shared hatred of Paul. A hatred based on nothing but a lie.

'Paul, you're the one always babbling on about the search for the truth being what motivates you. My girlfriend's mother died and she wanted answers and I gave her one. How did Nadezhda die? We don't know. The coroner's report is still to come. We assume it was why any emotional volatile woman in her fifties dies before her time.'

'We assume? So, nobody knows. You've put together two assumptions together to come up with some fantasy, some absolute fantasy that I shamed her into killing herself.' He held his head in his hands and paced up and down in the grass. 'I don't fucking believe you!' he said. He paced again until he faced Christopher eyeball to eyeball and shouted into his face, 'I don't fucking believe you!'

Where minutes earlier Christopher seemed shrunken, waxy faced, miserable, so he seemed to rise in stature as Paul's incomprehension gave way to shock, disbelief, misery and helplessness.

'Why have you done this?' Paul repeated again and again to which Christopher responded, 'I only said what I saw.' Around they went in circles, Christopher's delight rising as his friend's helplessness increased.

'What happened with you and Julia?' Paul eventually asked.

'She gave me the flick, didn't she? Said she didn't want a boyfriend in a different city.'

'Did you know they were going back to Germany?'

'No, I didn't. It was never mentioned.'

'And Sarah, did you see Sarah after her mother's death? Does she know about these these…' He could barely say the word 'lies'.

'About you and her mother? Yes. Although she didn't go batshit like her sister.' He paused and lit up a cigarette and smoked. 'It's funny, really. She looked a bit like you do now, as if she couldn't believe any of this was really happening.'

∽

He returned to Cambridge that afternoon and threw himself into his work. University was a place of monastic study. Paul hid himself in his books, and while others found their tribes drinking and dancing and acting and submerging themselves into campus life, he hid in his room, losing himself in study.

He avoided returning home. Liverpool had spat him out and distance inspired a certain fear. He found himself research work that occupied his holidays, searching for other people's truths, but rarely his own.

He thought of Sarah often, and the lies, the unspoken assumptions that tore them apart. The injustice left him bereft. But he had no way of challenging it. Sometimes in the library he flicked through German newspapers and magazines as if part of him expected to open a page and see his love there on the page. But it was always a forlorn hope. One time he visited the Goethe

Institute in Bloomsbury and somehow found himself looking for copies of German phone books, searching for her father's name. Charles White. But he, like his daughters, was never there.

Roberts wrote more regularly than Paul ever replied, with half-rumours about the girls, sightings of Christopher, speculation about who thought what may have happened in the days before they left the country. The letters always left him forlorn, depressed. He opened them expecting revelation, but mostly got rumour. From Roberts he heard about the coroner's inquiry, about the verdict of death by misadventure and how Paul was recorded as the last person to see Nadezhda alive. Roberts said there was only one other person there, no family. Other details were elusive.

One night, midway through his second year, in a pique of drunkenness and loneliness, Paul artlessly wrote a cryptic small ad which he filed to the *NME* in the hope that Sarah would see it. He posted a cheque for a box number and forgot about it until weeks later, when a jiffy bag filled with dozens of letters arrived at his halls of residence. A second, then a third package arrived in the following days and weeks. None were from Sarah, but, instead, girls in their teens and early twenties, seemingly enraptured by the longing in Paul's miserable prose, enclosing Polaroids, passport photographs, locks of hair, perfumed notepaper. Each told him their story, their likes and dislikes, their hopes and fears.

From these unsolicited letters from strangers written to someone searching for somebody else Paul felt the sensation lacking in his life since Sarah had gone: what it was to be wanted.

He entered into correspondence with some of these girls, sometimes blandly discussing shared interests in music or books, other times entering long discourse about his loneliness, the loss of a soulmate, the quiet desperation he felt. He found he could be open with a stranger on paper in the way he never could with someone he knew. Sarah he never directly mentioned. But the pain of loss was ever-present, and the more vulnerable he showed himself to be, the more his correspondents longed for him. Some wrote to him three times a week. Phone calls followed, and sometimes he met with his scribes. An afternoon was spent traipsing around Manchester art galleries with a public schoolgirl from Yorkshire. He went to see Madness in Camden with another before dashing for the last train home at King's Cross and never hearing from her again. An intimate correspondence with a blonde geography student at Newcastle led to an afternoon spent fucking wordlessly in a hall of residence before he made for the last train and the connection at Peterborough.

These intimate yet soulless encounters left Paul empty. He had known and experienced love and yet they were opportunistic or desperate sops, an attempt to fill a hole that could never be filled. Soon after the Newcastle excursion, Roberts wrote to him, claiming to have somehow found the music school in Hamburg Sarah was now attached to.

From a telephone cubicle in his halls of residence Paul called the number, filling the payphone with fifty-pence pieces. He was passed from administrator to administrator who sought to make sense of his broken schoolboy German, but it was too hard to make himself understood, the language too impenetrable. When the coins ran out he didn't call back. A few months later, Paul found himself on a plane to Egypt, and the path to being a Middle East correspondent was set.

6

A gift.

That was how Nadezhda described the passage of her secrets to Paul. A gift between writers.

But Paul had never considered it in such a way. To him it was always a burden, something that destroyed every notion of what people knew of her, everything her daughters held dear. It was the truth, but the enormity of that truth was so incomprehensible, so terrible, that he had buried it literally and metaphorically as far away from view as he could. He had seen it as his duty to conceal her gift, to hide it.

But after all these years something started to change and he possessed a growing recognition that people don't always choose their own destiny or that others have had more burdensome challenges thrust upon them.

He contemplated these thoughts on an empty British Airways flight back to London a week after his visit to Amman. Flying always made him ruminative and while he thought of his absent Sarah often, Nadezhda he usually banished to the back of his mind, for the scale of what he knew about her always felt like an encumbrance.

Maybe it was his return to the old country – it was nine months since he was last back – or perhaps it was because he was about to see his old friends again. Although they talked about the girls and what may have become of them, about Nadezhda they maintained an *omerta*. Was it out of respect or embarrassment?

Only once had Paul really been confronted with this part of his past.

That came in the summer of 1985, when he was staying with his parents during a brief interlude from the ferocity of the Cairo summer. His parents viewed his travels with barely suppressed bemusement; they couldn't understand why anybody would want to live anywhere other than England: the heat, the spicy food, the language. Could there be anything worse? To them their son was an enigma. They delighted at his academic accomplishments, but everything else was beyond them. They rarely asked about his time 'over there'. Instead his visits were dominated by stilted talk of the golf club, bored questions about eccentric aunts and distant cousins. They had never been close, but their lack of proximity during his Cambridge years had made them almost like strangers.

One morning his mother surprised him over breakfast.

'That young man called again last night, when you were out.'

'Which young man?'

He had been in the pub with Sam and Bulsara; Roberts she knew, and Christopher he hadn't talked to in years. Who else could it be?

'Sean somebody or other. A very intense young Liverpudlian. He calls every few months, asking for you. I don't know what it's about; he never says.'

'I don't know anybody called Sean.'

She shrugged her shoulders and went to the notepad besides the phone.

'Here we are,' she said, handing him a piece of paper with a number on it. 'Kendall – like the Everton manager.'

His momentary sense of confusion was subsumed by shock as this name from the past re-emerged. Sean Kendall, the schoolboy who had brought Nadezhda's disgrace; the schoolboy whom she had seduced – or so the newspapers claimed.

He called the number an hour later, a blizzard of confusion rinsing over as the receiver trilled in his ear. Finally, a man's voice answered.

'It's Paul Davis – you've been calling my parents. What do you want?'

'Paul, mate, sound. Thanks for calling. I've wanted to talk to you for ages lad.'

'What's this about?'

'You see, I was a friend of Nadezhda's...'

'I know what you are,' he growled, but Kendall ignored him.

'And I know who you was too. I sort of lost touch with her before she died, and I need to know what happened in her last days.'

'I don't think I can help you.'

'Ah, don't be like that. You see I know things an' you know things and we can help each other.'

'What do you know?'

'I know you was the last person to see her alive.'

'That's in the coroner's report.'

'I know – and you know how I know, Paul? I was there. Hardly anyone else was. Her friends weren't. The family abandoned her, went off their own way like she was an embarrassing secret. But I didn't. I was with her until the end.'

Reluctantly, Paul agreed to meet with Kendall the following day in the city centre.

A demonstration was disbanding when he arrived there. Schoolchildren carried banners emblazoned with images of Margaret Thatcher and hand-painted sheets with slogans like 'Fight For a Job! Fight for the Future!' and 'YTS is a Load of Shit.' One of them dragged an effigy of Thatcher along the road: a rubber mask of the Prime Minister affixed atop crudely stuffed clothing.

More so even than when he'd lived through the Toxteth Riots, Liverpool had become a city of protests: the city council, dominated by the militant faction of the Labour Party, was in open conflict with Westminster and its own party leadership; by the day there were new marches, strikes and pickets – against job losses, funding cuts, the drug epidemic, a government that had left the city on its knees. In parts of the city unemployment stood at 40 per cent. A heroin epidemic ravaged some areas. There was helplessness and anger and defiance.

He met Sean Kendall at the top of North John Street in the city's business district. He was in his mid-twenties, dressed in the casual attire of many of the city's men: white Adidas trainers, Fred Perry polo shirt, Fila tracksuit jacket, his hair cut into a wedge style. Incongruously, he carried his belongings in a supermarket bag.

'All right mate, thanks for coming,' he said.

'Shall we get a pint?'

'You'll 'ave to stand me one I'm afraid,' he said, slightly shamefaced. 'Things are a bit tight. Y'know. Work an' that.'

They went into Thomas Rigby's, an imitation medieval building, with balustrades and decorated architraves and lintels. It dated back to the Victorian era and housed a famous pub, its walls lined with oak panels. It was early afternoon and a low sun shone through the sash windows and caught the clouds of tobacco smoke and dust. The pub was empty save for a handful of middle-aged men in suits, who had abandoned their offices to drink and smoke until the landlord called time at three o'clock.

They sat up at the bar and Paul ordered them pints of bitter. He had no idea what to expect, or even why he had come.

'S'pose you want to know what all this is about?' said Kendall, before answering his own question. 'I've been trying to get hold of you for years. I've done some bad things in my past, things I'm not proud of an' I let Nadezhda down very badly.'

He told him about his troubled childhood, struggling at school and drifting into petty crime, then drugs. His dad worked long but irregular shifts at Garston Docks, his mother was from out of the area and had no network close by. One day, when Sean was eight, she just left without a word. 'Never saw her again. There was just me and me dad, who was a man's man, 'ard as nails and a drinker. A moody bastard. When he was working he'd be knackered and take it out on me. If he weren't working he'd be hungover knackered and take it out on me too.'

School was a mystery to him; he struggled to read or make sense of why he was there and it got worse the older he was. 'I'd go through periods of just not going, then the truant officer came and me dad would batter me, and I'd go back. One day there was this lady there: beautiful and elegant and glamorous, like something out of a film. I'd never seen anyone like her. It was Nadezhda, of course. Ms Semilinski.' He emphasised the 's' on her title, so it sounded like 'muzz'.

'She was volunteering at some schools and I don't think they really knew what to do with her to be honest. Poetry wouldn't be our thing in Garston. So they let her help the thick ones like me with the reading. No one had ever really bothered with me before, but it was like a light being switched on. She had me over the books and going to the library. I could barely have managed the Moomins before, but she 'ad me reading Dickens within a year or so.

'I'd go over to her house as well, and just 'ang out there. Chill out if I wanted. Sit off with her daughters. Read some of her books. It was a nice place and she always had interesting people there. I never really had a home and I s'pose looking back that's the closest I had.

'There was a bit of fooling around with Julia, as well. I was her bit of rough. I don't know whether you'd call me her boyfriend, but I think that's what she called me. I'm a few years older and she was impressionable so I'm sure it suited her.

'Although I got better at school, they never let me take me O levels and I left with nothing. Nadezhda still encouraged me to read and helped me get a job and a bedsit, 'cos I'd 'ad enough of me old man by then. I'd still go around to hers, 'ave a bit of fun with Julia – you know warra mean – but the work was 'ard. It was in a bakery, all two am starts an' that. I had trouble sleeping during the day, and didn't like being on me own, so I started 'anging around with the wrong crowd. Sitting off, 'aving a few spliffs to start off with, then amphetamines, then the smack.

'The hit 'ad a dulling effect on me. It's hard to explain how it makes you feel. Smack separates you from the world's problems and your own. It numbs pain. The feeling in my head was, "I want to feel like this for the rest of my life". It was the perfect drug.

'You think about smackheads now, hanging around in doorways like skeletons, but I never saw myself or any of the others I hung about with like that. Not at first anyway. I 'ad a job and money coming in. I'd go off and watch Liverpool all over Europe with some of the lads in the bakery. For a while the routine was great. I felt alive, really alive. Invincible. Anyone looking at me would have thought I was smashing it.

'It took a year or so for it all to unravel. I woke up one day and I was skint. They'd let me go at the bakery 'cos I was always late or skiving. You think you're ill, but you're not; you need some gear just to make yourself feel normal. Then yer start selling the bits that you own. Stuff gets pawned. You start robbing stuff, bits and pieces here and there, stuff left lying around; then burglaries, robberies. Your friends go. Julia was long gone by then, and I'd stopped going to their house. I lost all of my friends. I stopped travelling with Liverpool, stopped going the game. Parties came and went and I never went. All I was interested in was that next fix.

'People started avoiding me, because they could see what I'd become, but I didn't care.'

That's when the tabloid sting came, when he said that Nadezhda had seduced him, that he'd had underage sex with her. 'All lies, all rubbish, all complete fantasy.' Why had he done it then? 'Money. I was given two hundred pounds, and another hundred pounds a few weeks later. I never read it, not until years later. I just agreed to anything they said. "You shagged Nadezhda?" Yeah, course I did. "She seduced you?" Yeah, definitely mate, look what a catch I am with my scabby arms and Sugar Puff teeth – she was into the skeleton look, weren't she? I didn't care about nobody else, so I just went along with it. That money kept me going for two or three weeks.'

Despite all this, it was Nadezhda who saved him, he said; saved him from himself. She found him and through her connections sent him away for treatment. 'A big 'arl place in the middle of nowhere in the Scottish borders with a big lock on the door. It was 'orrible at first. The sweats and the shakes. The sleeplessness. The nightmares. The guilt. But I came through it in the end. Nadezhda never asked for nothing: not an apology, not a retraction and I was too stupid and selfish to give it.

'I went down to Bournemouth. Got my benefits, was working as a kitchen porter, life was great. Then I heard she died and I sort of went to bits again. I'd not said sorry. She was the only one who was nice to me an' I did that to her.

'I moved back up north, but the girls were gone by then, the house was sold; it was like all traces of her had gone. All that was left was the coroner's inquiry.'

He'd been talking continuously for twenty-five minutes now, and the pub was emptying ahead of its three o'clock hiatus. Paul indicated to the barmaid for another round of drinks.

'What's all this about, Sean?' he asked. 'Why are you telling me these things? How did you find me?'

He looked at him blankly. 'Atonement, I s'pose. I was never able to correct the things I'd said about her before she died. The lies. So I want to tell as many people as I can now who knew her about what I done. That I was wrong. That it was unforgiveable.'

'And why me?'

'Because you was the last person to see her alive. I sat through that inquest and it was obvious that you cared about her. I heard your statement – it was read out to the court – and you said nothin', nothin' at all about her or what she done on that night. You done what I shoulda done, which was to keep quiet when they came asking questions about her. You protected her. I shoulda protected her when they came for her.'

'Who came for her? The press?'

'She 'ad enemies. The police, but bigger forces. I dunno; she upset people – she was important, outspoken. She had a history. The press thing was a stitch-up and I was a useful idiot, but there were bigger forces behind it.'

'What do you mean "bigger forces"?'

'I dunno really. I've thought about it a lot. Maybe the government. Maybe someone from the war that wanted to discredit her. I thought you might know?'

'I don't.'

Sean told him about the coroner's inquiry. The procedural information, the doctors' reports, the autopsy, the statements – of which Paul's was one. 'She died from sleep apnoea and a combination of other factors, including heart failure,' he said.

'But it was recorded as death by misadventure,' said Paul. 'That implies some self-harm, an overdose or something.'

'There were no evidence of that. She smoked and drank heavily and took drugs, weed mostly. If you want to know what killed her, it's all of it in my opinion,' he said. 'The coroner was vague, because I don't think he knew. But she didn't self-harm or anything.' A wave of relief washed over Paul; he knew deep down that suicide or an overdose hadn't been the case, or the police or newspapers would have come looking for answers. Nadezhda hadn't committed suicide and that part of Christopher's false narrative was destroyed. After all the innuendo, Kendall's assertion seemed redemptive.

'I still don't know what you want from me,' said Paul.

Kendall was rolling up a cigarette on the bartop, as a clang for last orders came from the bell behind the bar. Paul signalled for more drinks.

'I wanna know what happened that last night,' he said.

'You've heard it in the coroner's report.'

Kendall cast him a sceptical look.

'It was my A level results day,' said Paul. 'Nadezhda threw a party and there were all sorts of people there, although not Sarah – she was my girlfriend at the time; she was in Germany. Everybody got horribly drunk and we were the last people standing. We talked and drank and that was it, really.'

Except that wasn't all, but Paul had banished the final memories to the recesses of his mind. Those last hours would remain unsaid.

'That was everything?'

'I got a phone call the following afternoon to tell me the news. It was a terrible shock. I had to write a statement for the coroner. Julia and Sarah I never really saw again. I went to university and they moved to Germany.'

'No one knows where they are,' said Kendall. 'It's as if they vanished into thin air.'

They moved onto their final pint. The pub had emptied and the barmaid was cleaning empty glasses now, waiting to end her shift. Kendall told him about his life now. He had moved to Skelmersdale, a new town wedged between the edge of the city and west Lancashire. There was nothing there and he had no work. 'They put me on a Youth Training Scheme, as a sparky. There were just twelve apprenticeships and more than three thousand applicants, so I was one of the lucky ones, but it didn't feel that way. I got twenty-three pounds fifty a week and I didn't learn nothing. I was just slave labour for this 'orrible woolyback so I ditched it.' He wasn't much worse off on the dole, he said, but the boredom was a problem; the boredom and the loneliness. 'I'm trying to keep clean,' he said, 'Keep my 'ead above water, but it's hard.' Paul cast his eye at his arms and Kendall recognised his glance. 'I'm using again, yeah, but I'm tryin' to keep it under control.'

As they left the pub soon after, Kendall told him, 'I went to a secondary modern school and there was never any discussion whatsoever about career options. I thought university was what you saw on TV. The expectation was I'd follow my dad onto the docks. He was a right twat, but he'd have got me in there. But when that came to a stop, there was nothing else. As far as life and ambitions Nadezhda was the only one who instilled any hope in me and I betrayed her. But I'm gonna make it up to her.' He showed him the inside of his carrier bag, upon which there were loose pages covered in childish scrawl. 'I'm writing a story about her life. It's gonna make good all the lies – you'll see.' And with that he was away, leaving Paul and his secrets in the heart of a city he no longer called home.

§

Four years on, he hadn't heard from Kendall again. He had expected to revile him, but instead found him oddly engaging, and even felt a little sorry for him – not that anything in his manner invited pity. He was down on his luck, but he had the wit and articulation to survive and even prosper. That was the thing about many of the sons of his city; they had tenacity and keenness to do anything that they wanted to. Nothing would stop them. He could understand, having met him, why Nadezhda had taken him on as her protégé. Occasionally he wondered what became of him and the book he had promised to write.

7

It was a happy coincidence that the biggest football game of the football season was being played when Paul was back in the country. Everton were in the semi-final of the FA Cup and it was a long time since he had enjoyed the simple pleasure of standing on a crowded terrace, swaying and chanting and shouting with his friends. Their lives had changed inexorably since leaving school – Sam was an auditor, Bulsara worked in IT; both had remained in Liverpool – but the essence of who they were remained the same. They went to the same pub, watched football and chased girls without much success. Roberts joined them sometimes; Christopher was long forgotten.

The pub was thronged with people. The chatter in the air was inflected with Scouse accents. Pint glasses were passed overhead and empties were stacked up high on the windowsills. Water condensed on the windows as pint after pint was supped. From the far side of the bar, a cry of 'Everton, oh we love Everton' went out, and the whole place seemed to shake as everyone joined in.

'Bet you miss days like this in the Middle East,' said Bulsara.

'I don't know, it's a bit like the Friday call to prayer,' laughed Paul.

On the Holte End terrace they watched in a blazing sun as the Blues took on the yellows of Norwich City. The ground was packed to capacity and as the crowd swayed up and down the terraces as one, the friends had to concentrate to maintain their footing and keep their line of vision intact. It was a closely tied match, with Everton gaining a goal advantage when their floppy-haired winger, Pat Nevin, bundled the ball over the line after a goalmouth scramble. From the other end of the stadium they could see the jubilant players jump around and they too found themselves in a melee of 12,000 celebrating bodies, hugging and kissing and shouting; fists clenched in salute.

They found themselves briefly separated, but at half-time they pushed their way towards their old spot and reconvened. Sam was clutching a transistor radio to his ear. He had a grave look on his face.

'There's trouble at Sheffield,' he said, making reference to the day's other semi-final match, where Liverpool were playing Nottingham Forest. Hooliganism was a by-product of English football, so what he said wasn't a surprise even if what he said next was shocking: 'People are on the pitch. Ambulances too. They're saying that there's been deaths.'

Others on the terrace heard what he said and as they waited through half-time Sam became a repository for information, which he disseminated among his fellow supporters. 'It's Liverpool fans. They're saying three dead, but it could be ten... More ambulances are on the pitch and lined up outside... five confirmed dead.'

The second half kicked off, but the excitement that marked the opening forty-five minutes had evaporated. An incontrovertible sombreness gripped the terraces and it seemed to transmit to the players, who were unable to raise the tempo of the game. Sam, the radio clung to his ear and the terrible updates from Sheffield were what held their attention. 'Nine dead now... they say it could be as many as fifty... twelve confirmed dead... fifteen...'

They left the stadium at full time in silence and trudged through Birmingham's terraced streets. The mood should have been ebullient, but it was funereal. 'Nothin' surprises me after Heysel,' another fan was heard saying, but he was quickly shouted down.

At Birmingham New Street station, they stood motionless around Sam's transistor radio listening to the sombre voice of Radio Two's Bryon Butler informing them that fifty-three were confirmed dead and there were more deaths expected. They listened to the harrowing stories of survivors: of a crush outside the stadium, children trampled, people pulled blue in the face from the crush.

Their journey back north to Liverpool was in near silence, the transistor radio dripping through a feed of a rising death toll and horror upon unimaginable horror.

'Nobody should go to a football match and not come out alive,' pronounced Bulsara.

'If the balls had come out differently in the draw it'd have been us there,' said Sam.

All along the train carriage that was the familiar refrain; *it could have been us.*

At Liverpool Lime Street station they were greeted by ashen-faced fans returning from the other semi-final, their grave expressions betraying the terrible things they had witnessed that afternoon. On the concourse hundreds congregated waiting for their relatives. A man in his fifties, arms bristling with tattoos, sat on a bench weeping uncontrollably. People wandered around dazed, searching for lost friends, family, survivors. A woman walked around in circles, muttering, 'Where's my James? Has anyone seen my James?' Bulsara tried to calm a woman in her thirties riven with anxiety. Bulsara called over to Paul: 'I'm helping this lady find her son, we think he's on the next train.'

Here Paul's journalistic instinct kicked in and he remembered the advice given him by his first foreign editor: 'Truth dies by the minute, record it while it's fresh in people's minds.'

He had with him the notebook he carried everywhere and people seeing him taking notes began to approach him, volunteering their dreadful recollections. There was terrible congestion outside the stadium before the match and police had opened a gate, letting thousands of spectators onto an already full terrace. The terrace was divided into pens, in which fans were caged behind iron fences. But while one area lay empty, the spectators were directed into a pen that was full. A terrible crush followed and scores were suffocated to death.

One man in his early thirties said: 'The steward put his arm on the gates and said, "Don't open it". The police said, "Open the gates, There's gonna be a crush." Then two police officers opened the gates and a crush comes through. The crush carried on right through, straight through, everyone off the barriers, crushed on the floor. I don't know. People started climbing over and all the police were doing was standing up, saying, "Get back, get back". There was already people dead. I climbed on them to get over the fence. There was nine-year-old kids, twelve-year-olds. People dying at football grounds because it's not organised properly.'

'We just got in through a side gate that was open,' said another. 'We never give our tickets in or anything like that. And as we went underneath the tunnel to go out, there was a rush behind us. I suppose people who never had tickets and we just got shunted to the front. It was just bedlam. I can't really describe what it was like. It's just something I never want to see again.'

An old lady with a blue rinse and large spectacles said: 'I'm waiting for my grandson. The number they gave us is just engaged. There's no answer. I've come to see if he's down here.'

Another man said: 'I think people were just crushing. There was a lad and his girlfriend that just screamed "Please, God help me". I believe the girl died. Her face was just blue.'

He heard tale after tale of unmitigated horror.

Another man said: 'I seen people dead. I was up against the bar right at the front. And when I was at the bar at the front, there was people dying. There was a gentleman on me arm and he said, "You're choking me, you're choking me" and he just fell. He just literally fell and that was the last of him.'

And another: 'I jumped under the barrier to get some fresh air. The next thing the police open these exit gates and make everybody, including me, go in the ground, because we weren't going to get in there otherwise. That was it really.' He added, in an almost matter of fact way: 'My dad died in the crush.'

§

Later that evening, when the last cross-Pennine train had deposited its wearied and distraught passengers at Lime Street, leaving scores of the desperate and hopeful on the concourse still without their loved ones, the friends repaired to a nearby pub. The mood was deathly and drinks were poured silently and drunk with only mutters among drinkers. There were supporters from both clubs – shocked, exhausted, crestfallen.

The friends shared stories of the previous few hours. Bulsara had calmed the lost woman and around nine pm she was finally reunited with her son – he was fourteen and had escaped with some bruises. 'I've never seen anyone hold another person so tightly,' he said. A weeping man Paul met from the same train was not so fortunate. He had lost his brother. 'He was next to me, and then he was fading and suddenly gone – the life sucked out of him, his lips blue, and then he fell,' he'd said. 'Again and again he kept saying it, "His lips went blue".'

Then a news break came up on the TV set over the bar and there was an apparition from all their pasts, speaking in front of the cameras. Christopher.

'Fucking hell,' said Sam.

The TV caption marked him out as the South Yorkshire Police's spokesman. It had been nearly eight years since Paul last saw him, on the day he confronted him in Hull. With university he had disappeared from all of their lives. He had sapped all of his friends' patience, but it was Christopher that cut the ties. He rarely ventured home, and if he did he didn't call anyone. There were no impromptu visits to The Swan, nor attempts to right all the hideous wrongs he had inflicted upon Paul. No one really knew what had become of him – until now.

And now, here he was, surreally, speaking at them from a news broadcast at a time of local and national tragedy.

The barmaid turned up the volume.

'On television and reading in the evening press there are these instant experts, doctors and a few lawyers who all seem to know more about our job than we do,' said Christopher, addressing the TV cameras. 'Telling us what we should have done. That if there'd been police officers just inside those gates that day, funnelling people into the outer areas then this wouldn't have happened. I'm saying to you that if police officers had have been in there when this mob surged through, the police officers would have been trampled to death underneath them. They just can't handle them and the vast majority of that lot had been drinking. The ones that were arriving late, and they will not be told where to go. What do you think you're trying to do? And what can they do?'

'So are you saying the fans are to blame?' asked a voice off camera.

Christopher continued: 'The police certainly aren't to blame, because if the fans will do what the police are asking them to do, there wouldn't be any problem because people would be orderly. And if people were orderly, they wouldn't have these problems. You can't push all those people if people are orderly. It's just not possible unless you know a way that I don't.'

'The fucking lying bastard,' shouted a Scouse accent from the other side of the bar.

'Police lies!' shouted another.

∽

Lying for some people was like breathing, Paul had come to realise; it was an unconscious act, essential to their existence. He had grown to accept that. It was his job to be sceptical, a purveyor of facts and the ultimate truth. But there was something particularly shocking about the unexpected savagery of Christopher's falsehoods that afterwards would not leave his mind, or those of many others.

The next day he learned from his mother that, after graduating, Christopher worked in a police response centre, dealing with 999 calls, but his ambition – his vocation – was to work on the front line. He'd been called to help the press office in the summer of 1985, a tumultuous season when the miners' strike reached its apex. 'He's done very well for himself, hasn't he? He was on the telly all last night.' But Paul could only imagine the trail of lies and distortions his former friend had left behind in places like

Orgreave, Blyth and Ashington.

Later on Sunday Paul spoke with colleagues at his desk in London and relayed the contents of his notebook to them. He liaised with colleagues on the scene in South Yorkshire, who were also taking eye witness statements and preparing to report on visits by Princess Diana and Mrs Thatcher. One of them called Paul at his parents' house.

'One of the media liaison officers was asking after you. Christopher Finlay. Says you were friends,' said his colleague.

'Were,' Paul emphasised. 'We're not now.'

'Ah... he's a strange one. I'm not sure I believe a word that comes out of his mouth. "Tanked-up mob", "boozing for hours", "arriving late", "pushing", "Fans on the pitch, urinating on the dead" – these are not descriptions that stand up when you talk to anyone else. Most of us who'd been there had stopped taking notes if I'm honest – we didn't believe him. But the tabloids had sent their own boys up from London – rotters. He says the truth will out, but I'm not so sure...'

Paul had seen Christopher on news broadcasts all through Sunday. There was something unhinged about him, he thought, something about the way Christopher gleefully described people from his own city, supporters of his own football club, that he found particularly nauseating.

'That's Christopher,' said Paul. 'But the truth will out in the end – it'll show him as a charlatan.'

ഗ

The next morning Paul bought all the newspapers. Because he lived overseas he rarely saw himself in print, but his byline was amidst dozens of others reporting of carnage, despair, confusion; a living hell. He spent the day immersing himself in them. Nobody still quite knew what had caused the tragedy, although the pattern seemed to point to the police losing control of the crowd outside the stadium. There was uncorroborated speculation of a door being broken down. Of drunkenness and fans turning up late. But none of them added up to a cogent narrative, nor did they bear any relation to anything he'd heard from any witness.

On the Tuesday after the tragedy he made his way to the newsagents again. The front pages were still consumed with stories of what had happened, but his eyes were immediately drawn to one front page that contained a headline consumed with savagery and relish and disdain for those who had died, a reality he would come to realise that only existed in his former friend's head.

THE TRUTH
SOME FANS PICKED POCKETS OF VICTIMS
SOME FANS URINATED ON BRAVE COPS
SOME FANS BEAT UP PC GIVING KISS OF LIFE

ᑫ

In his parents' living room later that morning, he sat motionless surveying the terrible headline again and again.

Truth exists in the eyes of the beholder, but when that is betrayed it burnishes the very actuality of what has passed. A lie can take hold of reality, gnawing its way into popular consciousness, inveigling into history. It eats away at those who have been wronged, subsuming a people under the myth of wrongdoing where none has actually taken place. It would take many, many years for this particular lie to be righted.

For nearly a decade Paul had existed in a world defined by Christopher's lies and a truth he himself had suppressed. Secrets and lies were at the heart of his very existence. He had learned to live with a past that was twisted by other's untruths and a present where the consequences of that lie lived on.

He reflected on his career. His was a noble undertaking, he decided, but he was a crusader for the veracity of other people's stories; he had committed his life to telling them, at times putting himself in danger to do so. But those closest to him? He had failed, he now realised. He was presented stories to tell – *a gift* was how Nadezhda had put it to him all those years earlier – but had chosen not to do so. Why had he done this? There was the preservation of Nadezhda's reputation, but it was she who had shared her story in the first place. A gift between writers, she had said. No, it was through a sense of loyalty to Sarah, who, although he'd loved her, was now absent; gone far away, somewhere beyond his ability to find her, and who self-evidently did not want to find him.

Truth exists in the eyes of the beholder, he reminded himself as he made his way into the attic of his parents' home later that day. There, encased between a loose board and some insulation lagging he found the plastic shopping bag that Nadezhda had thrust upon him the night she had died, and which he'd hidden there when he heard of her death. Now encased in dust, this collection of documents and writings had lain there for eight years, hidden like her past.

Two days later Paul returned to his home in Tel Aviv, the plastic bag enclosed in his hand luggage. In his apartment that evening, he poured himself a glass of wine, sat out on his balcony overlooking the Eastern Mediterranean and started writing Nadezhda's story.

Part 3: Nadezhda

1

It was late at night in my seventh month at Mauthausen in the summer of 1944. Nazi Germany was losing the war. France was invaded by the Allies and in the east the Soviet army were making gains across the great expanse conquered by the Germans earlier in the decade: eastern Poland, the Baltics, Romania, Finland.

These victories were relayed to us late at night in our filthy dormitories, where home-made radios crackled and fizzed with news broadcast by London. But although we knew the war was turning our way, these advances seemed far away from our prison in northern Austria.

Entering the camp was like slipping into a bad dream. The world looked the same, but the people in it had changed unalterably. On one side were those in authority, for whom cruelty was a fact of life and basic kindness and decency was an alien concept. On the other you had prisoners, whose life was sucked from them, so that they appeared hollowed out, ghoulish, even.

That night I was returning from a shift at one of the warehouses, when I saw a dozen children stood to attention in a courtyard. The oldest was no more than eleven, the youngest a toddler who grasped an older sibling's leg. Their faces were colourless. I knew they were going to be shot, and they seemed to know it too. I tried to avert their hopeless gazes, but I could not help but notice the two-year-old, who looked expectantly from his brother's leg. Maybe it was because he emitted a sense of hope in a place where there was none. Then the gate to the yard opened and the children disappeared inside. The sound of shots followed.

∽

Auslese und Ausmerze. Selection and elimination. These were the principles that governed my survival from the German death camps and the liquidation of those children and millions more, including my own family and all that I had known.

It's a German phrase that extols a part of social Darwinian dogma. It is at once cruelly appropriate while precisely describing the ordeals that I somehow lived through in the death camps. The English call the same idea 'survival of the fittest', but when applied to what we suffered you'd recognise the idea as fallacy. Picture the liberated camp survivors – brutalised, starving, emaciated, humiliated, clinging on to life by the tips of their fingernails – and you understand that their endurance was little to do with their physical fitness.

Auslese und Ausmerze: selection and elimination; a window into how I lived and everybody else that I knew died.

∽

Physically and culturally there was nothing that distinguished my family as Jews. Growing up through the second half of the 1930s I looked at these caricatures in the popular press – the hooked nose, the beady eyes, the thick burrowed brows – and searching through the crudeness of these anti-Semitic tropes saw only alien forms. I could never see any sort of resemblance to anyone I knew. Maybe it was because we never lived in a Jewish neighbourhood. Overtly our house was more demonstrably Celtic than we were Jewish, for my mother and sister each had a blaze of red hair. I was different: dark and pale, but my father was blond before his hair fell out when he was in his thirties. Perhaps he was circumcised; I never knew.

Indeed ours was a house of agnostics. I never stepped foot inside a synagogue or a church for that matter. My sister and I attended a non-denominational school. We celebrated Christmas, not Hanukkah; Easter rather than Passover, but we were to all intents and purposes non-religious. There was nothing observant in our household. We ate pork knuckle, pork schnitzels, shellfish and hams. We ate together on Friday evenings, as we did each night, but we never knew this as Shabbat. There was no challah, no blessing; it was merely supper.

Yet somewhere within the depths of our family tree there was something that marked us out as different. Our household's agnosticism masked our roots, for deep down we were this great other. We didn't look it, we didn't feel it, but I think, if only in our subconsciousness, we all knew it. The gathering storm over the German border through the 1930s alerted us to our differences with our countrymen, although maybe it was ultimately political.

Father was a socialist. If he had a creed it was that of Marx and Engels, although he was always more the ideologue than a partisan. Evenings were spent reading pamphlets about Russia's unfolding social and economic revolutions, and Marxist writers like George Bernard Shaw, Walter Benjamin and Karl Kautsky. When he expressed concerns, it was about the fate of socialists and the rise of the extreme right. He considered Hitler an idiot

– *Dummkopf von Linz*, he called him; the Fool of Linz – but was scared about the coalition of thugs, indignant middle classes and industrialist tycoons that surrounded him. He became fixated with the idea that Europe would become beholden to corporatist dictators.

I never knew my father to be an activist. We were bourgeoise, comfortable; though never nearly as rich as the family were before the Great War when it made a fortune building and operating Europe's railways. Part of our ancestry could be traced back to a Habsburg dukedom in Trieste, and growing up my father had known many of the benefits of coming from one of the Austro-Hungarian Empire's elite families. That changed after the war: the railways were nationalised, the empire dissolved, and while both he and his brother had survived the conflict, his parents were killed by the Spanish flu that inflamed Europe after the war. It left him and his brother and the small families that they bore in the 1920s. Besides that, he and his brother were left with mere fragments of the family's wealth and influence. It was enough to live comfortably: we had nice houses, independent wealth and retained some of the artefacts from our family's more prosperous past: paintings, furniture, jewellery. Father bemoaned the loss of the family fortune, while simultaneously preaching from his socialist pamphlets about the need for workers to maintain the means of production.

What did he have to fear from fascism? An unremarked religious heritage? Latent socialist beliefs? A political system in which he would be one of the haves? I don't think he had any notion of what was to follow. Instead our family sleepwalked into the abyss.

2

If there was a hesitancy or lingering sense of complacency on my father's behalf, he was rudely shaken out of it in autumn 1938. First, came a series of pogroms. Kristallnacht reminded me of an extreme version of Austria's so-called civil war; the crack of automatic gunfire, the burning of shops and synagogues, and then the next morning an endless phalanx of prisoners marched through the streets to the railway station, where they were sent to their doom.

Next, a special body, the *Vermoegensverkehrsstelle* or 'asset transfer office', was set up by the new regime and made responsible for the transfer of Jewish property to non-Jews. The sudden demand for reparation came as a shock to someone who had never really considered himself Jewish. My father was literally handed a bill for the value of our house and many of our belongings. Soon after, he was told not to come into work any more.

My father remained convinced that this was merely some passing phase in our history, but my Uncle Johannes had seen enough. Within days he and my aunt and cousins had fled Vienna, headed south to Italy, where they were to take the ship to the United States.

We learned later, much later, that they never made it that far. The Italian border had already been closed and the family were interred. Johannes' leftist past had caught up with him. Did they know about his Jewish past? I never found out. The gold, jewellery and other valuables they had sewn into the linings of their clothing and luggage were confiscated and stolen.

They became among the first inmates at the Mauthausen-Gusen concentration camp in Austria's north, where they were separated. Johannes was executed in 1940, and my aunt and cousins sent to Dachau in 1941, where they were murdered two years later.

Auslese und Ausmerze. Our family of eight had become four.

ᦕ

By then we had left our home and were living lives of itinerants. My father had access to a series of properties around the city which belonged to the railway company as worker accommodation. A sympathetic director had removed them from the books and they were shared out among families in need. We were used to a five-storey townhouse, so these two- and three-roomed apartments, which were damp and cold and in the poorest parts of the city, were a sobering reminder of the new reality we faced. We stayed for six or eight weeks at a time, before moving onto the next one, always under the cover of darkness. Our days were spent being home-schooled by our mother, while father met his connections and friends, trying to find a way out of a city that had become our prison, while searching for places to buy food.

Over the months and years that followed these excursions became shorter and more difficult as the Nazi grip over Vienna grew. They were beholden to paperwork, but we were entitled to none; or rather none that was of any practical use. As soon as my father got his hand on forgeries it seemed as if they were replaced by a new set of forms and papers that rendered the old ones obsolete. Hope of escape diminished too. There was talk of sending my sister and I to England, or emigrating to Palestine, but this dissipated as the angry knocking of war arrived.

We remained cocooned in our hiding places, tuned in to the unfolding chaos in Europe via our radio set, yet largely oblivious to what horrors were happening in the streets of our own city. Food became harder to come by, fuel too; but I think the same was true for everybody at that time. We moved between safe houses less. Had we become complacent, or did the risks of moving outweigh those of staying? It's hard to say.

Our lives were lived through books. Literature was our window to the world. We had nothing else. We couldn't really leave our apartments. We couldn't play music. We could scarcely exercise. So we filled our days reading, not just in German but English too. There seemed to be an underground book exchange and bags of books were passed between families. Sometimes the same books turned up two or three times, but we didn't mind.

The first year of the war passed. Then the second. It was interminable. Because it was censored by the Germans, the news we got was always bad: France, Poland, Denmark, Netherlands surrendering; the British humiliated and retreating from the French beaches. Even Russia's involvement seemed somehow sinister. Locally the news was seldom good: a family betrayed, someone taking their own life, another family discovered.

All along Father remained optimistic. He understood from the start that only the total defeat of Germany would set us free. He reminded us that the previous war had lasted more than four years, that we needed to be patient. I can remember him punching the air when the United States declared war, seeing it, somehow, as a turning point – as it was during the first war, when he fought against the American forces himself. By the time the British defeated the German forces in the Battle of Egypt at the end of 1942, we could get a BBC signal. He listened excitedly for days as they replayed Winston Churchill proclaiming, 'This is not the end. It is not even the beginning of the end, but it is, perhaps, the end of the beginning.'

But despite his confidence, life was getting harder by the day. There was less money, less food and less fuel. Father took optimism from these hardships – a sign that the war was being won by the allies – but it is little succour when you are cold and hungry and have lived your life indoors. I was an adult now, but a time when I should have been out dancing and chasing boys was spent entirely in hiding. It sounds selfish to describe it that way, but life was boring. But for a single air raid on Vienna there was no sign of the war even coming to Austria.

In these days and nights I resolved, when it was all over, never to leave a day half-lived, to attain something in life, to travel, to relish my freedom, to never let any group be persecuted again for their race or religion, or beliefs.

But then, late in 1943, we were betrayed.

3

There was no angry knocking, no clomp of jackboots working up the staircase to our three-roomed apartment; just the burst of the door being kicked in the early hours of the morning, the splinter of timber and the shouts of Gestapo officers. Nor were there any goodbyes. The last I ever saw of my father was a glimpse from the bed I shared with my sister, as he was dragged and kicked still in his bedclothes, terror in his voice as he expressed his innocence – from what I was never quite clear, his latent socialism or even more benign Judaism – from our little flat and into the dark and cold outside. A few minutes later, we too departed, into the back of a canvas-covered army lorry, a few possessions stuffed into suitcases that would be stolen from us. It was all so fast, so clinical.

Auslese und Ausmerze. Eight had become four had become three.

I never learned what became of my father.

~

Later that morning three became two.

We were driven around Vienna under armed guard picking up

more of the hopeless and the doomed. The cold consumed every part of my body. The feeling from my toes died and my knees knocked. I had scarcely been outside in four years and now I was plunged into the harshness of the winter elements, with scarcely a coat to keep me warm. We tried to huddle together for warmth, but the touch of cold flesh upon cold flesh did little to allay our misery. In the lorry and outside, nobody spoke, nobody said a word. There was no food, no water. When we passed pedestrians we could see them look down or into space as if we were not really there.

We were heading west, through Melk, Wieselburg and Amstetten. Soon after, we pulled off the main road and into a forest. The road was slush and ice here and the truck slid around in the frozen mud. Finally, we went up a sharp incline and pulled in next to a railway siding. Here were more soldiers. They lowered down the back of the truck and started pulling the older men and women from it.

My mother was still in her early forties then, but poor diet and years spent confined to small rooms had aged her prematurely. We were near the back of the truck and my sister and I tried to conceal her, but it was simply hopeless. When she tried to ignore the summons, one of the officers pulled her by her hair and through the back of the lorry, throwing her into the mud. My sister let out a bloodcurdling scream, and was met with the butt of a rifle. I could only gasp in silent horror as I watched from the departing lorry my mother being tossed into a cattle truck. From there she was taken straight to Dachau, where she was gassed. Murdered.

Auslese und Ausmerze.

My sister was nineteen months older than me, but to my mind was always more childish, immature, reliant upon my parents. I eschewed dolls and toys shortly after my fall, when I was eight or nine instead immersing myself in an imagined world created by my books. But for her I think it was another four or five years – when we were about to embark upon our exile – when she did the same.

In hiding we shared the same physical proximity uninterrupted for years. I'm sure, somewhere in the depths of an academic library, there is a study about the bonds that develop between cellmates, but for my sister and I, the bonds became looser. Life was interminable, boring, stolid. It revolved around mealtimes, wireless broadcasts and the books my father could get his hands on for us. We quickly ran out of things to say to each other. Our relationship became platitudinal.

Mentally I had prepared for the day that our door would be kicked in and we'd be taken away. In my recurrent dreams I heard the sound of boots rising up the staircase, the hammer on the door, the sound of it being smashed through and being dragged away like a common prisoner. In the back of that truck, heading north to a concentration camp it was a dreamlike sensation, as if I were in a stupor. It didn't occur to me then that I'd never see my parents again – separation had never been in my premonitions – but I had long anticipated that morning's epicedian turn, and I think it was easier to take because of that.

I can't say or not if my sister developed any such a sense of foreboding in our months and years of hiding. But in the back of the lorry that day she was paralysed with an almost unimaginable fear. Horror was something I learned to live with and would see many times every day. But the terror within her was unlike anything I ever encountered.

When she was struck by the rifle butt, it put her into a trancelike state. I held her on my lap, with a piece of ice wrapped in a handkerchief, trying to stem the ugly purple swelling across her face.

'This will pass,' I whispered to her. 'Be brave; we will see this out. This will all pass.'

My sister just lay in my arms, sobbing my mother's name. I knew then that she too was already lost.

$\sim$

We arrived at Mauthausen in the early afternoon. We could see that it had the aspect of a fortress as we passed beneath its vast stone entrance, an eagle emblazoned with a swastika peering ominously at us. There were walls that were two metres thick and a moat filled with frozen filth. Inside we passed row upon row of low-slung wooden prefabricated buildings, caged behind barbed wire fences. We saw inmates, grey faced and silent, emaciated in their blue striped pyjamas. One looked into the lorry as we passed and drew his finger across his throat in a slitting motion.

We had no idea what to expect from the camp. There was a notion propagated by the Nazi authorities before the war that these were mere internment camps, where 'undesirables' were kept away from the population until their resettlement, but I think war had rendered that idea entirely fanciful. On the other hand, my father had whispered wild tales he heard from the streets, of Jews being murdered and their bones turned into glue, of inmates being operated on alive and murdered, and others being worked to death.

The truck pulled up in a large asphalt courtyard. Behind it, and as far as we could see, were these identical wooden prefabs, but not a single person was around other than a pair of guards with Alsatians, that pulled and teared on their leashes, barking ferociously, as if they hadn't been fed in days.

We were ordered out of the lorry – yelled at when we tried to help anyone down from the flatbed, which was raised four foot high – and told to form a line. We had travelled for four or five hours and our joints seemed to creak as we passed down onto the freezing ground and trudged in silence the short distance to where we had been ordered.

One of the women had grown agitated through hunger and thirst on the journey and was still muttering as she crossed the courtyard. Seeing one of the officers, she approached and asked for a glass of water. Had she lost her mind? The officer said nothing, but smiled cruelly. She repeated the question. This time he raised his pistol from his holster as nonchalantly as if summoning a handkerchief from his pocket and shot her in the temple. There was a collective gasp as she crumpled to the ground and the officer replaced his gun.

'Say nothing, do nothing, this is all just a very bad dream,' I whispered to my sister.

She stood erect, next to me, her face distended by purple swelling from the earlier assault, silently weeping as we watched the blood trickle from the fallen woman's head and across the frozen ground towards us. It pooled in a small crevice and a few minutes later the puddle of crimson had frozen over.

Hours passed and we remained in line, trying not to tremble through fear or cold, trying to keep the erect posture of observance demanded by our masters. Darkness came and we were illuminated by floodlight that glared in our faces, rendering us blind to anything that emerged from the shadows.

Finally, there was some movement and a group of officers

emerged. A dog nosed ferociously around the frozen corpse of the woman murdered earlier, and was pulled on his leash by his handler. The soldiers stood ten yards in front of us, conferring in the shadows. I strained my eyes trying to see through the light, but as I did there was the crack of a pistol and the dull thud of a corpse. Two, three, four seconds passed and another shot rang out. I counted to four and there was the sound of another bullet. I counted and the soldier walked past me, raised his gun and fired again. I could feel a body fall at my feet and then off he was again.

In all, sixteen rounds were fired, killing every third person in that line.

'You are the chosen ones,' shouted the officer when the murder spree was complete. 'Your God has decreed that dying is too noble for you at this moment. You will work for the defence of the Reich and one day – who knows? – maybe your labour will set you free.'

He looked down at the corpses spread around our feet. 'Clean this filth away into the cart over there,' he said, beckoning towards a horse and cart that stood trembling on the far side of the yard. 'You will be taken to your accommodations afterwards.'

He turned on his heels and marched off into the shadows. When he was gone, his underlings set us to work. I could scarcely move from the cold, but knew that if I wanted to live I needed to set about the task in hand. And so I found the strength to bend down and begin dragging the body of my sister away.

Auslese und Ausmerze. Two had become one.

4

That night as I lay shivering on a filthy mattress, my sister's blood still not washed fully from my hands by the frozen trickle that emerged from a shared standpipe, I resolved that I would live. That whatever happened was just a passing phase. That Churchill's words spoken three months and a lifetime ago over the wireless were true and I would see 'the end of the beginning' through to its final conclusion. No matter what subjugation, ordeal, humiliation, I would do whatever it took to survive.

∽

For those first few days the cold was severe. Ice formed inside windows, and pipes froze, bulged and split. Each night snowdrifts three foot high formed outside our dormitory. We hid under the rags that passed as bedding, huddling among ourselves, strangers that we were, trying to find warmth and some comfort. There were at least a hundred of us sharing the room – cold, scared, in shock, or maybe just denial. Despite the mass of bodies it was never warm, and an eerie quiet always filled the place; never more than the low murmur of a few voices and the creak of a stove that was far too small to warm us all. It resembled a crowded railway waiting room, when the last train has been cancelled and a mass of passengers are making do for the night in a room too small and too lacking in basic comforts to accommodate them while they wait for the first locomotive of the following day to arrive. Except ours never did.

We were woken long before dawn and fed a thin gruel of oatmeal. I was issued with the hideous striped-pyjama outfits, but they had allowed me to keep my coat, which might have been the difference between life and death in those first days. My hair was cut to a short crop, but never shaved.

I was given a small metal plate with my prisoner number stamped into it and had to wear it either on my left wrist or around my neck. The male prisoners, who we were kept apart from, had patches sewn onto their uniforms, designating their reasons for being there: red was for a political prisoner; pink a homosexual; blue a foreigner, and if you were Jewish it was combined with a yellow triangle to make a star. Had I worn one, my insignia would have been a red inverted triangle over a yellow one – a particularly dangerous combination to wear in front of wildly erratic SS men.

The absurdity of my situation was that I didn't really have any notion why I was there. I still don't. I always assumed it was for my uncle or father's latent political interests. I knew about the extent of the Nazis' anti-Semitism; had lived through the purges after the Anschluss and Kristallnacht, but because I had never been brought up a Jew, never thought of myself as Jewish, couldn't imagine that that was the reason. Had someone really researched the recesses of our family tree, gone to the trouble of finding these tenuous links and hunting us down?

Death was all around us. However the Nazis had to balance their wanton cruelty with the reality that as slave labour we served a purpose in an economy that serviced their war; a war that at that stage they were losing. We did shifts in workshops making parts for guns and other weapons, or sewing uniforms or gluing the soles on boots. There was a brickworks and we stacked pallets with bricks still hot from the furnace. At the door of the brickworks we were taunted each morning by the slogan 'Work Makes Life Sweet' but we knew we were fortunate compared to many of the male inmates, the worst treated of whom were always the Russian PoWs. They were broken and demoralised. We watched them returning from the camp's quarry pale-faced and wan, exhausted and starving after a back-breaking twelve-hour shift. For them, there was no respite. They were starved and emaciated. The last reserve was always on their cheeks; when they lost that, it gave their skulls a bulbous appearance, disproportionate to the rest of their bodies. This always came in the final stages of being worked to death.

Other indignities were more overt. The SS men showed immutable cruelty. It was bred into them and came as easily as laughing did to a normal human. One day, an officer flicked an inmate's hat off his head as he walked past him, as a schoolboy might to a fellow pupil on his way to lessons. It was a small humiliation in an arena where indignity prevailed. But instead of laughing at the incident he had caused, the SS officer turned in sudden fury that the prisoner was not dressed in full uniform. The camp seemed to freeze in collective dread as he unleashed his tirade, the prisoner stood looking to the ground as his cap blew across the dirt to an area that was out of bounds.

'Go and get the rest of your uniform, or I will punish you here on the spot,' screamed the guard.

The prisoner looked pathetically as his hat blew towards the prison fence.

'Sir, my hat is in an area where I am not permitted.'

'Is that my problem?' he screamed, the spittle flying from his twisted face.

A one-foot-high wire marked the boundary of a no man's land fifteen feet wide between that and the inner perimeter fence. We watched in dread as he approached the wire, and as he stepped over it the guard raised his pistol and put two bullets into the back of the inmate's neck.

We lowered our eyes to the ground, powerless in the teeth of this perversion, but the officer hadn't finished.

'You!' he screamed to another hapless inmate. 'Recover this man's uniform. We are fighting a war! You think we can waste a good uniform like that?'

The inmate was swarthy-faced and perplexed by the tirade; he wore the blue and yellow triangle of a foreign political prisoner. Many of these men were from Spain, where they fought for the Republicans in its civil war, the losing side in another cruel conflict. He knew enough from the German officer's fury to pursue the task and so walked to the low fence where the body lay and pulled it back in from the dead zone.

But for the officer this wasn't enough.

'The hat! The hat! The uniform is not complete without the hat.'

The striped cap lay in the dirt, out of reach in the proscribed area. The prisoner regarded the hat and his task forlornly. Dead if he did, dead if he didn't.

'The hat!' implored the guard, who reached to his holster again.

I had already seen so many terrible things, enough evil and depravity to doubt the very existence of God. But sometimes, only very occasionally, we seemed to be touched by the presence of some higher being. It was a still, humid day, a white inscrutable sky high above us. The atmosphere was dead. But at that precise moment there was a rustling of leaves, of air passing through the barbed wire, and the dead man's hat rose into the air, back along the ground and past the wire demarcation. The grateful prisoner stepped forward and picked it up, before placing it at the dead man's feet.

The guard smiled grimly and replaced his gun in his holster, before going on his way as if everything that had passed over the previous couple of minutes was perfectly normal.

§

The changing of the seasons brought little respite. Winter flu was replaced by tuberculosis and diarrhoea in the summer, all of which were fatal. I felt the sickness of others touch me, but never quite settle inside. Unending cold gave way to flies and lice and a constant thirst. Inmates came and went without notice. Here one day, gone the next – dead from exhaustion or fallen at the hand of a Nazi butcher. There were the selections, where we were forced to stand in the same courtyard as when we arrived and prisoners were taken, sometimes at random, sometimes according to how distressed they looked. Sometimes they were shot on the spot. Other times they were taken and gassed. We knew all about the gassings from inmates who had come from other camps, where such murders happened on an industrial scale. Mauthausen's killing apparatus was outmoded by the vicious standards of the Third Reich.

Occasionally my thoughts were jumbled and incoherent. I'd feel consciousness slipping away, but my hands and feet must have kept moving for I never fell, never stopped working, for to do so would be to impose my own death sentence. Then my brain would re-engage with the rest of my body, through the cold or hunger or fatigue or whatever torment had imposed itself upon me, and I would come back to life, step back into my living hell.

I knew also that I needed to hold on to my desire to survive. I saw people die all the time and when they did it was as much because their minds had given up as their bodies. The rage at their situation had subsided and been replaced by fear and apathy.

Sometimes they took girls for clerical work. What should have been one of slave labour's less onerous jobs was also one of its most deadly. Every six or eight weeks they eliminated their secretarial roll, and selected a new body of office workers. The old corps were killed and discarded as easily as an office manager tossing away an old typewriter ribbon. Our German masters liked to document all their crimes, but in doing so, these girls had learned too much. It was a cruel paradox: they had willingly incriminated themselves, but feared those they colluded with. Thus their clerics were entirely expendable when that time came.

ဢ

One day I was summoned to another roll call. I had faced these life and death situations many times before. *Auslese und Ausmerze*. I wanted to live. I would do anything I could to survive. But here it was always out of my hands: a roll of a dice, a toss of a coin.

Yet this roll call seemed less indiscriminate than others I was subjected to. Normally they just pointed at their *Auslese*, not wanting or needing to converse with we vermin, but this time we were being interrogated by an SS Oberführer.

'They're selecting for the field brothel,' whispered a Czech girl who was in line next to me. 'If we're lucky they'll turn us into whores.' Lucky? 'The rest can volunteer for the offices,' she said. It was quite a choice.

When you strip it all down, it wasn't a dilemma at all. The office provided six weeks – eight maybe – before being sent to a grave with the SS's secrets. The brothel was an unknown quantity; outside the camp, perhaps near the front. There was the chance of escape; in Mauthausen, there was not. I would be brutalised, my body tossed from officer to officer like a piece of meat – but wasn't that already the case? Had I not had any physical shred of dignity torn away from me in my year at Mauthausen? Could anything worse follow?

I had also learned the ways of the SS officer corps. There was a cold savagery about them. They worshipped death. Some were psychotic. But amidst the killing and butchery they retained a need for order. The meticulous documentation of their own crimes was one manifestation of their preciseness. They followed their own protocols. There was a clear command structure that these brutes never deviated from. Things had to just be: uniform, rules, rank. They were radicalised and believed their own racial superiority. Perhaps they might lower themselves to fuck a prisoner, but would they do so with one who was diseased, starving, a living skeleton in rags? It raised the possibility of better food, clothing, shelter. It seemed a possibility better than a delayed death.

The Oberführer went from girl to girl, always starting with the same preamble: *Aber Jetzt nur die Wahrheit!* Only the truth. I smiled inwardly. One of the first and important lessons I took from Mauthausen was that truth is entirely subjective and negotiable. You use whatever form prolongs your own survival. If the will to live was strong, you gave the right answers – no matter how wrong they may ultimately have been.

Perhaps the Czech girl lacked my will to survive, but she fell in the early round of questioning. Did she wear glasses? Yes, she answered, but they were in her sleeping quarters. Female prisoners with spectacles were unsuitable for the field brothel, the Oberführer told her. He sent her to a group with the rest of the condemned girls.

He came to me: *Jetzt nur die Wahrheit!*

I nodded.

Name, date and place of birth.

I told him, adding three years to my age – as I always did.

Was I a Jew?

I shook my head.

Did I have any Aryan blood?

My father was blond, I told him. He's dead.

Did I wear glasses?

No, I did not.

Was I virgin?

Yes, I answered.

Had I been sterilised?

I cannot have children, I told him, which was true; due to hunger I had never menstruated.

He smiled. He was used to dead-eyed ambivalence, but from me he heard only eagerness, perhaps a desire to serve the Reich and provide solace to the soldiers fighting the great patriotic war. Thank you, he said. You go that way. And he sent me to the smaller group, away from the Czech girl who was by my side just minutes earlier.

5

We left Mauthausen in the same way that we had arrived a year earlier, sat in the dark on the flat bed of an open-backed lorry as the snow fell. I was more accustomed to the cold now. It never left my body from November through to April. There was always a dense throb in my shins, but I had somehow become inured to the cold that consumed my extremities.

In the back of the lorry, near the opening, a Rottenführer sat with a rifle guarding us. As Austria became Germany and we crept further over roads that were periodically riven with bomb damage and potholes we could see that there was nowhere for us to flee. The environment had become harsher and more touched by war's ugly hand the further we travelled; certainly the difference in a year was discernible. We saw damage from Allied bombing raids, some villages and towns obliterated to mere rubble. We could see from the wan faces of civilians that they were hungry too, that they were suffering. It gladdened my heart to see that here the war was being lost.

We stopped every three or four hours. At one stopping point the soldiers tossed loaves of bread into the back and we shared the meal between us. We were too wise to mistake their gesture for any deeper sense of kindness, too wily to ask where we were going, or when we were getting there.

Night came and we tried to sleep amidst the cold and the jolting, but the motion was too much to allow rest, and the lorry rolled on its seeming never-ending way. Hours passed. We saw a convoy of troop lorries heading west, the rubble of a smashed anti-aircraft gun, the ruins of many towns. As we passed through one, the Rottenführer cursed in English, 'Fucking British.'

§

At dawn, nearly twenty-four hours after leaving Mauthausen, the lorry pulled to a stop and we were ordered to disembark. In the thin light of the early morning, I could see we were at some sort of alpine hotel, not unlike those I had holidayed at in another life. There was a decrepit feel about the place. Its gardens were wildly overgrown and brambles creeped through the snow, all the way up to the hotel's pine panelling, from which paint peeled. The hotel's signage was in a different language – Polish – but the crest on the door was unmistakable: that of the SS.

Inside we were greeted by a large woman in her forties, who bossed and cajoled us into a line. She was joined by an Obersturmführer, who began to bark his instructions. We were here for a year, he said, maybe longer. To serve and provide relief for frontline soldiers was an honour. Duty to the Reich came before anything else. The hotel was run on principles of order, hygiene and obedience. We would serve twelve hours on, twelve hours off six days a week. Sundays were for rest, hygiene and medical examination.

The woman, who was introduced as Madam Gertrude, showed a list of rules, that detailed everything from the duration of congress (no more than thirty minutes), to the precautions that must be taken ('always with a sheath') to what was proscribed ('kissing, anal insertions, ejaculations on the skin or in non-vaginal orifices'). She went around, repeating many of the questions that were asked us at Mauthausen, eyeing us up and down with her beady eyes.

Then she took us to our cubicles, hotel rooms subdivided into two or three by crude walls of plywood, with a single bed and a small stove or oil radiator. They were functional but cleaner than anywhere I had been in the past year. The madam told us to rest, that we would be busy later on, and for the first time since I was dragged out of our Vienna apartment in the middle of the night I slept in a proper bed.

§

Our rest did not last long. The heft of boots, the banging on doors, the threats and admonishments of the Rottenführer; the soundtrack of life with the SS.

It was a coal-black morning and we made roll call in the snow outside the hotel. Seventeen of us had come from Mauthausen and there were another thirty or so girls there. We were still wearing the striped rags of the camps, but they wore the clothing of civilians; affluent ladies who had lunched in better times. Yet underneath it all, they were mere teenagers like me, aged beyond their years, and remained skin and bones, as underfed and miserable as anyone put to physical labour in the camps.

Madam Gertrude stood in contrast to we underfed girls. Her neck, which she wrapped in a kerchief, was made up of unctuous rolls of fat, and she had stockinged legs that looked like burned tree trunks. She repeated what we could expect and then told the new girls to strip off their clothing. There was a momentary lapse of time, as if questioning her order, for we had all seen this before; the inmate told to strip ahead of an execution so as to save the uniform for the next prisoner. But the roar of the Rottenführer's voice reminded us that this was not a request and so hesitantly we pulled off our clothes.

It was ten degrees below freezing and we stood there shivering, entirely naked, trying to hide our crotches and our breasts, as a doctor came along and observed our bodies. Then he showered us with handfuls of DDT, clouds of the white powder coating us before the Rottenführer sprayed us with a hose. Our bodies convulsed with the shock of freezing water upon our ice skin and a sadistic grin glazed the SS man's face. When he finished, icicles started to form in our hair. I wondered for a horrifying moment if they would leave us to freeze and die, but Gertrude took over and ordered us inside.

We stood, huddled and naked, dripping and freezing as the madam rifled through boxes of clothing and tossed us garments from a box. They were the dresses of the well-to-do, well-made clothes that had probably been stolen from the corpses of women like my mother. I wore a black midi dress, in the style of a flapper girl that hung from my bones. I could scarcely stop shaking with the cold as I pulled it over my head. But then Gertrude saw my wet hair dripping onto the material and became animated, warning me that I was going to ruin the fabric and so tossed me a towel lest such a catastrophe happen.

From another box, she dispensed satin and silk smalls, brassieres and slips. These were to be our uniforms, she said. They were patently too big for our emaciated bodies, but nobody questioned it.

'You are not to question anything. You are to be anything

these men want you to be,' Madam Gertrude told us. 'They have endured dreadful privations on the Eastern Front. You are here to provide them comfort and relief; it is your duty to the Reich.'

We were to go to our cubicles and light the stoves. The first consignment of officers would be with us within the hour.

6

When I took away my murdered sister's body a year earlier, pulled the clothing from her corpse and laid her cadaver on a pile with others, I gave my body to the Reich. No violation could be worse than clearing the murder scene of your own flesh and blood. Nothing was sacred any more. My body was no longer my own; it existed to serve my masters. I was stripped of all dignity, of everything except my will to see this ordeal out and survive. Nothing else was sacred. I didn't give a thought to losing my virginity, to having sex with multiple men. Could having a stranger inside me, pummelling my fragile body be worse than handling the body of my sister? Could having this happen twelve times a day, seventy-two times a week be worse than the indignities foisted on me minute by minute in Mauthausen?

These thoughts crossed my mind again as I lined up in the small draughty lobby of that alpine hotel awaiting another *auslese* with the other girls. I was dressed in a pair of white satin knickers that fell around my ankles if a large knot I had made in the waistband came undone and an oversized black chemise that tumbled down my thighs, almost to the tops of my knees. Gertrude had painted my lips with a crimson lipstick and given me a squirt of perfume.

The other girl was given similar treatment. We looked hideous; undergrown, undernourished, like children playing with the contents of their mother's wardrobe. We stepped from foot to foot trying to keep warm.

Eventually there was the sound of vehicles pulling up, and boots upon snow; a blast of cold air as the Sonderkommandos entered the building. My skin prickled with the cold, or was it fear?

Gertrude presented us whores to the soldiers. They were battle weary, the faces drawn with fatigue, their uniforms worn in with the outside elements. Some of them lingered disinterestedly by the doorway, others sneered at us in disgust; some eyed us closely, pinching folds of skin and probing our bodies with their fingers, as if we were joints of meat on a butcher's counter.

One by one the girls led away their assigned partners, until there were just a few of us left, including myself. Was there something wrong with me? Had these elite men of the Reich somehow sniffed my Jewish blood?

Madam Gertrude paraded us, speaking incessantly of our virtues like the backstreet whoremonger that she was. Eventually one of the more demure soldiers, who was smoking disinterestedly by the door, took me by the arm and I led him to the cubicle that was assigned my home.

He stood in front of the stove, warming himself, as I sat on the small bed, waiting for him to talk, to make his move. He was young, maybe even the same age as me, but there was a hardness worn onto his face.

'We have been travelling for thirty hours through the snow and the wind,' he said and hunched over the stove, before taking out a cigarette and lighting it. He looked perished.

'I can imagine how that feels,' I said. I was still cold from the hosing down we were given earlier.

He lit a cigarette and offered me the packet. I shook my head. I had never smoked before and didn't want to show my inexperience to him.

'We came from the east: Ukraine,' he said. 'We came on a civilising mission, to show these people of the virtues of the great German nation, to rid them of their communist and Jewish vermin.' He took a long drag. 'We thought we would be welcomed as liberators, but they fought and fought and fought. They didn't care if they lived or died. How can you fight an enemy who doesn't care if they live or die? They had more bodies than we had bullets.'

From his pocket, he withdrew a small metal flask. 'Schnapps?' This time I took a thimble. I had never drunk alcohol before and the clear liquid warmed my throat.

'They say that you do not become a true man until you have taken another man's life, but what is it to take hundreds of lives? Body after body obliterated by your own hand. Do you become twice a man? Ten times a man? A hundred, a thousand times?'

I didn't know whether to fear or pity him. Empathy wasn't usually part of anybody's lexicon when considering the SS, but up close, in a confined space, the soldier was vulnerable and human.

'How long have you been here?' he asked.

'Less than a day.'

'I bet all the girls say that.'

'No, it's true.'

'Did you chose to be here?'

'Yes. To serve the Reich.'

'I bet all the girls say that too.'

Time was moving quickly. From outside I could hear more vehicles. The next consignment of officers coming for their carnal pleasure? If we ran out of time and he didn't have his way with me, would I be punished, condemned?

'What do you want to do with me?' I asked. I touched the skin above my left breast, in an attempt to be alluring – it was something I had seen in the cinema a lifetime ago. 'I can be anything you want me to be.'

He contemplated my question, smiled and leaned over the stove as closely as he possibly could without touching it. 'I just want to be warm for now, *kleines mädchen.*'

From inside the lobby I could hear voices, the stomp of boots coming closer and closer. As it rose to a crescendo down the corridor from which my cubicle was on, we both looked to the door. There was a rap of knuckles, and the door burst open. A Haupsturmführer stood in the doorway and the soldier leapt to attention at the higher ranked officer. In terror, I instinctively pulled the sheet back on myself, not knowing what horror or indignity I was to be faced with now. In the commotion I lost the trace of conversation. Everybody seemed to talk at once.

Finally, the younger soldier leant down next to me and asked softly: '*Bist du die Jungfrau?*' Are you the virgin?

I nodded.

'Then you must go.'

I left the cubicle, not knowing whether I was to live or die.

7

I was taken to a larger room at the front of the hotel. Madam Gertrude and three of the other girls who travelled with me from Mauthausen stood waiting, our tiny outfits incongruous to the situation we found ourselves in. You could taste the tension in the air.

'We are greatly honoured. The Obergruppenführer will be here in a few minutes. He is on his way to business in the field,' she said. Her eyes shone with excitement. 'You know who he is? It is our link to the Führer. He has blessed us with one of his generals.'

She was like a girl about to meet her Hollywood idol, cooing and fluttering her eyelids. The significance of our visitor, I admit, passed me by at the time, but in a twisted hierarchy where military rank was deified by its believers, these men were true demigods. Some were of cabinet rank. They were the elite of a party where elitism ran through its core.

The perversion of such a character, who venerated bloodlines, stopping at a common whorehouse was part of its paradox. But then he had requested someone pure. Another *auslese*.

'What luck that we had fresh girls join us today,' squealed Madam Gertrude, her piggish eyes bulging now. She went around spraying us with her atomiser and touching up her make-up. Then there followed a rumble of boots, the door burst open and we stood to attention in our nighties and knickers and brassieres in the freezing room.

The Obergruppenführer stood in front of the four of us, eyeing us up and down. He was a small dark-haired man in his forties – all these high-ranking officers seemed to defy the Aryan prototype they so worshipped – his hair brilliantined back. His gorget patches and shoulder bars extolled his power over all of us in the room. He sniffed the waft of perfume sprayed on us a moment earlier and turned to the girl next to me.

She was pale and red-haired, not unlike my sister, and like all of us made painfully thin by lack of nutrition.

'Where are you from?'

'Prague.'

'You have been here for long?'

'We arrived earlier today. We came to serve the fatherland.'

'You speak good German.'

'My father is from the Sudetenland.'

'Is he Aryan?'

'He's dead.'

The Obergruppenführer looked at her as if she were being impertinent. 'Was he an Aryan?' he asked, emphasising *was*.

'I don't know.'

He dismissed her, and the girl on the other side of me – he simply didn't like the look of her.

'You are very pretty,' he said to me.

'Thank you.'

'You have Jewish blood?'

I shook my head.

'Not a tiny drop, even from generations back?'

'No sir.'

'But you are from Vienna? I know the accent.' There was a hint of menace in his smile when I nodded. 'You know the Führer hates Vienna; he calls it a cesspit of socialists and Jewish vermin.' He looked me in the eye. I could feel his breath on my face. 'Are you sure there is no Jewish blood running through your veins?' I shook my head again.

He turned to the next girl and carried out a similar interrogation before standing back and regarding the pair of us. There was a glint in his eye, and he said to Gertrude, as if buying a hat or a pair of shoes, 'I'll take the dark-haired girl.' He eyed the room doubtfully and said, 'Clear up this place and don't let anyone near the girl.' And with that he was gone, his officers following in his wake.

8

For two days and two nights I sat and slept in that room, waiting for him to return. With the other girls we scrubbed the place clean and Gertrude replaced the sheets and curtains. The stove was kept fuelled and food – although never more than the humble rations afforded any of the other girls, who were still confined to their work and cubicles – was brought to me twice a day. Nobody knew how to deal with me: was I slave whore, or did I command special treatment because I was now the possession of the Obergruppenführer? An officer stood guard outside the door, but didn't enter, and for those hours it was the closest I had known to normality in years.

Of course, there was nothing normal about any of my situation. I could hear everything that went on in the brothel: girls being fucked, raped, violated, battered. One was taken out and shot after biting a Rottenführer. Another was beaten by a drunk officer. Through the thin walls of the hotel I could hear Madam Gertrude pleading to spare the beaten girl, because she would be able to service officers again in a few days.

On the morning of the third day, Gertrude came to see me.

'They have radioed ahead. The Obergruppenführer will be

here in one hour.'

She brought wood for the fire. Fuel was clearly running low at the hotel and in the other rooms they were burning twigs and gnarled- up hedging, which burned quickly and gave off short bursts of heat before extinguishing. But Gertrude brought white-barked birch for the stove in my room, and stoked it while impressing upon me my obligations: duty, obedience, service.

'Madam Gertrude, why has the Obergruppenführer chosen me?' I asked. 'What does he want that the other girls can't give?'

'Your purity,' she said, and laughed at her own joke. She came and sat beside me on the edge of the bed. 'You give the man everything he wants, everything he asks for. He is leading an army that is going through hell. He has no comforts, no normality, no wife here. You are to remind him of the world he is fighting for.' I nodded, and we sat in silence for a moment.

'We are losing the war, aren't we?'

Madam Gertrude contemplated the question and for a moment I feared that she may explode into a rage when confronted with this reality. But in the end she just nodded sombrely. There was no defiance, no outrage; just an acceptance of the reality now facing the Reich.

§

One hour later there was the sound of cars pulling up outside the hotel and a low chatter. Vehicles came and went all day, but even over the short time I was there I noticed a discernible difference in the tones of those disembarking. The excited chatter of men on release about to slake their carnal needs was replaced by the low murmur of those who were shattered, fearful and facing defeat.

After a while, the Obergruppenführer came to the room.

He looked as if he hadn't slept and smiled thinly at me, as if he couldn't quite recall who I was or why I was there. I stood erect, watching him until he tried to remove his boots and went to help him. He thanked me tiredly.

He disappeared to the bathroom where on Gertrude's instructions I had filled a bath heated with water from the stove. Left alone in the room again, I was unsure what to do or how to behave in his absence, so I just stood there uselessly.

When he re-emerged, steam rose from his body, which was naked but for the towel drawn around his waist. He sat on the bed. I expected to be called into action, but he ignored me and started picking at his cuticles with a long cutter. Finally, he looked up and said sombrely, 'Things are moving fast. We are in retreat, but we will defend every scrap of this foreign soil as if it is our own. On the front they attack us from all sides: the Russian invaders and partisans in the villages and towns we liberated a few years ago. Nobody thanks you.' He laughed bitterly and silence filled the room.

'What can I do for you, Obergruppenführer?' I asked, and remembering one of Gertrude's lines: 'I can be anything you want me to be.'

He laughed bitterly again, as if I seemed ridiculous to him. I stood there in satin knickers and the chemise that was too big for me, not knowing where to look or what to do. Finally, he gestured to the desk chair and I sat on the edge of it, awaiting his orders.

'Smile at me,' he said.

I smiled at him.

'Did you always smile like that?' he said. I searched my mind. It was so long that I felt anything other than emptiness that I couldn't remember the last time I felt any sort of happiness. But then remembering the instructions of Madam Gertrude – *Tell them what they want to hear* – I nodded.

'Your smile is dead,' he said. 'Smile again.' I tried again, but he just shook his head. 'Have we really destroyed all hope in our young?' he asked. 'Think of the future, think of reasons for hope.' I thought of Germany losing the war and the terrible things he had seen on the front; I dreamed of my liberation from this hell. Then I smiled again.

'That's better,' he said.

∽

He wanted to sleep and ordered me to close all the curtains. He lay in the bed and told me to join him. I lay there awake in my ridiculous costume, waiting for him to make his move. But he just lay there with me, and within minutes his breathing slowed and gave way to a soft snore.

Later, he reached out and held me in his sleep. No one had touched me like that since I was a small child and my discomfort and fear eventually gave way to sleep in his embrace.

∽

When I woke, the sky outside had turned dark. The Obergruppenführer lay next to me, still asleep, but he too soon rose to consciousness. I waited for his touch, some movement, for his manhood to enter me, but it didn't come. Instead he just lay there next to me, contemplating the darkness and the animalistic sounds of the hotel: creaking, rutting, groaning. Eventually he told me to stoke the fire, which had run low on fuel.

As I did so, he dressed back into his uniform. I sat upon the chair not knowing what he wanted, what would happen.

From his bag, he withdrew a bottle of schnapps and poured a tot into the cap.

'A little lightness does no harm, no lightness does a lot,' he said, and necked the liquor before pouring himself another. 'I am to stay here until I am told to go elsewhere. It may be a few hours or it may be a few days. I don't think it will be much longer than that. The Russians will be here by then.'

My heart lifted and when he offered me a shot of the schnapps I drank it gladly.

'What would you like me to do?' I said, and then repeating Madam Gertrude's whore's promise, 'I can do anything you want me to do.'

'Keep the fire lit, *kleines mädchen*, I have work.'

He replaced me at the desk, while I sat atop the bed watching him. Like the little child he deemed me, I understood that I was to be seen and not heard. He worked quickly through his pile of paperwork, like an overworked clerk, crossing out and correcting, signing papers, adding notes on the end of documents. He bore a grimace that suggested he had eaten something that disgusted him and sometimes cursed beneath his breath. One day, in the future, he relayed his exasperation about his colleagues to me. 'They think their grandchildren will read about them in histories of the SS, but the only thing they will read about is their incompetence and stupidity,' he said. Now he scrutinised figures and documents that illustrated a losing war.

Finally, he finished, and reached for the schnapps bottle. He poured himself a tin cup full and passed me a tot that he dispensed into the cap.

'To life,' he said, and swigged from the mug. At that moment I was reminded of my father's toast – *L'chaim* – one of the few Hebrew expressions he ever used. To have uttered it then would be a death wish.

'We were told to make the rivers run red with the blood of Jews, Slavs, Gypsies. To fertilise the land with their corpses. But there are never enough bullets to take these people. The Jews are always too cunning. Some of them will always find a way out, a way to escape. And that was our problem. We couldn't exterminate everybody, to clear the land entirely. And so they came back at us, as partisans and saboteurs. Maybe we should have just come as conquerors. Many would have accepted us and we wouldn't have stored up problems.

'We have the Russians punching us in the face and the partisans festering in our sores. If you've seen a rotting body, it is only a matter of time before the maggots start eating the flesh.'

He sighed again and took another slurp from his cup.

'We have deluded ourselves. Some think that Hitler will solve it all, that he is developing a new weapon; a super weapon that will wipe out the eastern front! But we have nothing left. We will fall back and fall back and hope against hope that the British and Americans won't attack from the west and that we defend our own borders.'

He leaned forward and poured me another thimble of the schnapps. I was unused to alcohol, unused to the dulling effect on my mind. But I liked it. It helped me forget.

'Do you think they rinsed Vienna of the Jews?' he asked.

'I don't know.'

'They will still be there,' he said, pouring himself another schnapps. 'For how long did you hide?'

'More than four years.'

'You can double that – treble it – if you have the cunning of the Jew.'

He kept talking, about the war, mostly, for that is all that he knew. He saw the conflict not as one of conquest, but annihilation; where the enemy would be vanquished only if it was completely destroyed. Subservience was never enough. Destruction to the enemy's core was the only way of attaining mastery. He drew me into his world, but I could never give him anything of mine. I answered in monosyllables mostly. *You are not to question anything,* we were told. *You are to be anything these men want you to be.*

His rations, a grey meat in a thick gravy with dumplings, were brought, but he wasn't hungry and so he gave them to me. I crammed the food into my mouth and he laughed.

'*Kleines mädchen.* Nobody is going to take this away from you.'

ͽ

I fed the stove and we returned to bed. I awaited his touch, but that only came when he slept; an arm wrapped unthreateningly around me as if looking for mere comfort from human contact.

From the rest of the building I could hear sexual and physical violence. I wondered what awaited me. Three days had passed without incident in this place. Three more days of survival. Three less days until the war was over.

9

When I woke the next morning he was gone. The bed was cold and the stove had reduced to embers. On the desk lay two hard-boiled eggs, but despite my hunger I knew better than to touch them – I had seen people shot for less.

In the bathroom the Obergruppenführer had left his toiletries, and when I peeked out the door a soldier was still standing guard. His departure was temporary.

I retreated to the room and spent the day building the fire and staring longingly at the eggs. My hunger was permanent and something I learned to live with. But seeing food left in front of me I imagined as a test, as if I were Adam faced with the apple.

When the Obergruppenführer returned they were the first thing he looked at.

'But you haven't eaten your breakfast, *kleines mädchen*.'

'I wasn't sure the eggs were left for me.'

'You must be hungry. Eat them now and get dressed. We are leaving.'

I sat there, looking at the eggs, wearing nothing but my oversized lingerie. Going where? I wanted to ask, but knew better than to do so. *You are not to question anything.* I picked up the eggs, which were all that I owned in the world, and stood to attention.

For the first time I saw the Obergruppenführer laugh. 'But you need to get dressed.' As he said it, he realised that these were my clothes; I wasn't expected to go anywhere outside the brothel, and so why would I own anything other than my whore's costume?

Madam Gertrude was summoned with her dressing-up box and made to dress me and hand me a second outfit. As I made to leave she held me close to her, a waft of cheap perfume filling my nostrils.

'Do anything he wants you to do. He has chosen you and you are lucky. The Russians have broken through. If the Germans won't kill us, they will. Now go! You have a chance of living! Go!'

10

We drove for a day and a night in his Daimler, stopping along the way at checkpoints, taking what fuel and provisions we could. We had a driver and armed outriders. It was dangerous now, said the Obergruppenführer. Partisans were emboldened by the retreat and were attacking sporadically on the way. We were easy targets. He worked from his briefcase as we drove, but mostly we just watched the wreckage of Poland as it passed us by.

I mostly remained in the car. He didn't try and hide me, but then he didn't need to. The Obergruppenführer's power over everyone we encountered was absolute. He was to be feared. He was not for questioning.

On the morning of the second day we left the main road and after passing four or five miles, we entered a wooded area, through which a railway ran. Through the damp and the mud there was the stench of something more insidious.

The Obergruppenführer left the car, and with two of the men climbed the railway embankment and out of sight. After a few minutes they returned, scuttling down through the mud and ferns, handkerchiefs held over the faces. He beckoned me from the car, and I followed him up the muddy embankment and over the railway lines.

The smell had become more intense now, was almost overpowering. Through the mud, we came to a clearing where I was confronted by a sight that will stay with me for as long as I live. Stretched out for almost an acre was a tangle of human corpses. I had seen piles of cadavers many times before, but nothing like this. Thousands of skeletal bodies, dumped and left rotting. As a mass they seemed to move, as if the grave was expelling air like a breathing creature. But then I realised that it was rats feeding on the human wreckage, feasting in the orifices of the deceased and pulling at their lank grey flesh.

'When all this is over, and you are asked about my power, this shows you that it is not absolute,' he said. 'I wanted these people to work repairing the roads and railways. I was told there was not enough food to justify their existence. I told the Totenkopfverbände that we did not have enough bullets to justify their deaths. Mass shootings are a terrible way to kill people. They have a terrible psychological effect on the executioners; it leads to nightmares, anxieties, heavy drinking and suicides. But the Totenkopfverbände won that battle, and here we are. A waste of bodies that might have served the Reich. A waste of bullets.'

We left in silence, trying to overcome the nausea that built up in our throats.

11

Later that day, our car pulled in under an armed double gate emblazoned with the Reichsadler and swastika. Inside, the stone bluff gave way to rows of semi-permanent huts, ringed with barbed wire fencing. Around them were the same sort of hollow-faced men and women in blue striped uniforms I had left a week and a lifetime ago at Mauthausen. We were at another concentration camp.

This one seemed vaster, more highly industrialised, even more insidious; its inmates were brutalised and ground down to the bones of their humanity in such an extreme way that it transcended the memory of what I had undergone. At the centre of the camp – or perhaps I imagine its geography now – stood a huge chimney, emitting ominous plumes of black smoke into the slate-grey sky. I learned later that we were in Auschwitz, the Third Reich's heart of darkness.

Past these endless rows of dormitories and workshops we went and into another part of the camp that was separated by several layers of fence and then hidden from the inmates by row upon row of plane trees. Here, the camp took on a suburban aspect. There were detached houses and gardens divided by privet hedges. If there had been children on the street and no Waffen SS parading the perimeter of this compound, it might have passed for any normal street in Germany.

Of course, there was nothing normal about the place. There never was. The guards, unlike in the main camp, were there to keep people out rather than in for this was where the camp's elite lived, including in one of its largest residences, the Obergruppenführer.

As the Daimler pulled into the driveway, he said: 'This is where we stay.'

∽

The house was built for a family, but there was no evidence that one had ever lived there. It resembled a vacant hotel, with pristine furniture – invariably purloined from one of the Nazis' raids – and the absence of any personifying artefacts, save for a small library of books and a collection of records. There was a large garden with vegetable patches and flower beds and it was surrounded by a tall concrete wall topped with red tiles. In his office, the Obergruppenführer kept a framed photograph of him with his wife and son on holiday; unlike him, they were blond, tall and tanned – the very apotheosis of the Aryan ideal.

This was to be home for the next three months; a place of comfort, warmth and near solitude. I was under instructions to remain inside at all times, to talk to no one. Neighbours were watching and it wouldn't do for idle gossip. The house was to be lit by lamplight only when the Obergruppenführer was away; the record player was off limits. There was a maid – a girl from the camp named Hannah – who prepared meals and cleaned the house, but I was under instructions to ignore her. In the late afternoon I was to light fires in preparation for the

Obergruppenführer's return. Many times he didn't come until late at night, or not at all.

We became lovers. Perhaps lovers is the wrong word, but what happened transcended the client relationship that should have defined us. It was consensual, not transactional. The act itself was perfunctory, always with the lights off, always him atop me. Of course, it hurt the first time, but thereafter I learned to accept him. He came fumbling for me in the night. The words of Madam Gertrude played on my mind – *You are not to question anything* – but I think deep down, after everything that had happened to me I also wanted what he did, that simple primal thing: the touch of another person, even if it was that of a monster.

It was a mundane existence on the fringe of an extraordinary place where, behind the bare plane trees, industrial acts of killing were taking place; evil on an unprecedented scale. I had survived one of those camps and knew how they functioned, but in the house I may as well have been a thousand miles away from the unfolding terror. At the same time I kept a guard, as if an unspoken test was awaiting me: I kept out of the kitchen in case the rations were being counted, didn't dare tune the wireless to the BBC, and kept away from his office.

When the Obergruppenführer returned in the evenings a humdrum domesticity descended upon the house. I drew him a bath or simply sat with him as he listened to his records. We ate together. Often he was preoccupied by the direction of the war or the instructions he faced and recounted dilemmas he faced, or another military defeat. He seemed resigned to defeat, as if the question had become when not if. He had an increasing contempt for orders he received from Berlin and spoke about the place as if it belonged on a different planet.

Sometimes he asked me questions, things that seemed

extraordinarily inane but which were always loaded with deeper meaning. 'Give me two letters of the alphabet,' he asked one evening. 'B and K,' I told him. Years later, when reading a history of the camp, historians were still trying to rationalise the order to kill everyone whose surnames started with those letters – all 10,427 souls – over a forty-eight-hour period. The horror that I was somehow culpable in their selection will never leave me.

On occasions he reflected on the industrial death sprees he was undoubtedly part of. Usually, he couldn't comprehend them. Killing for the sake of killing made no sense, particularly when there were factories to man, roads and railways to be built or repaired. He spoke with a brusque Teutonic logic. There was no human emotion, just a cool rationale. The Reich needed more manpower to survive, but it was employing some of its existing human capital to destroy its untapped reserves. It made no sense, said the Obergruppenführer.

There were evenings we spent huddled under the staircase as the whine of bombers filled the night sky dropping their deadly cargo on nearby cities. The explosions always seemed to be far away, and I wondered what would happen if they landed near the camp, crashing down its fences and setting its inmates free. Would they immediately be better off in the wreckage of the outside world, or cocooned in their prisons, where death seemed the only certainty? Part of me feared that day, when I would be confronted with my past. Would I be seen by those in the main camps as a collaborator? Would history judge me as such?

Other times our evenings were extraordinarily mundane. Sometimes he talked about his world. There was a certain sanctimony about the Obergruppenführer. The Kommandant was imprisoned two decades earlier for manslaughter at a Nazi rally and he muttered about him belonging to the coterie of 'Beer

Hall' thugs who dominated the high ranks of the SS. He hated violence that wasn't prescribed by the camp rules. Many officers, he complained, were wantonly corrupt. At Belsen hundreds of SS officers were indicted for fraud after stealing valuables taken from the inmates to fund the great war effort. He hated these men, not appreciating the inescapable irony that they were stealing from the proceeds of the greatest theft in history.

There was a piety within him too. Once he told me his father brought him up to become a priest, but died before he could see this ambition through and he took a different route in life. Sometimes he wished he had chosen the Church. At night he knelt beside our bed and prayed.

Sometimes in the evenings we completed jigsaws and cipher crossword puzzles together, like an old married couple. We listened to his records and sometimes drank schnapps or wine. Most often I just sat with him while he worked or read, a wallflower on the edge of evil's abyss. At those times he looked like the loneliest man alive.

I never witnessed him raise his voice, nor inflict violence. To me, he was kind, and through that kindness there were times that I overlooked who he was. I had seen so much cruelty, suffered so much by then that my mind had narrowed on one objective and that was my own survival – and he was facilitating it. Losing empathy with other camp inmates was a coping mechanism. If you reacted as a human should do to every humiliation, every obsequity, you would break down within a week. When I was with the Obergruppenführer not only did I not consider the harm his signature on a document might wreak, I didn't care. I was immune to these sort of things.

I didn't admire or even particularly like him. But encountering his kindness in a vacuum of human decency bred an emotion within me that I didn't understand at the time, and didn't dare put a name to for many years after: love.

&

Hannah was a wraithlike presence. Some days she entered and left the house after spending half a day cleaning and preparing food and I wouldn't even have known she was there. If I met her she cast her eyes down to the floor, and shuffled off awkwardly out of sight. In the not so distant past we might have passed for sisters – young adults, pale skin, dark hair. I wasn't free and I hadn't survived the war, but now I was somehow the mistress of an elite house and she was my slave.

I ignored her because I was scared; scared at how the Obergruppenführer would react to any defiance, but also at what it might reveal of myself. I separated my recent fortune from my fate. I was focussed on my survival. If confronted with who I had been, what might my empathy reveal of me?

One morning there was the clatter of shattered crockery from the kitchen and I found her on her hands and knees trying to hide the shards under her apron. She froze when she saw me. I didn't appreciate then what she saw when she looked up at me: a death sentence for her clumsiness.

I knelt down with her and started to collect the broken crockery. 'It's okay,' I said. 'Really, it's fine; nothing is going to happen.'

She remained in the same pose as I cleaned around her and I realised then she didn't have the strength to stand. There was bread in the pantry and I brought her a half-loaf and water. She looked at it, not knowing if this was a test or an act of humanity.

'Please eat it,' I said. Her eyes were hollowed into her skull and her skin was painfully tight over her cheekbones. In my preoccupation with my own survival I had ignored this near cadaver in my midst. 'Don't be scared.'

She ate the bread as if it were the last food on earth, and then she talked. She was cautious at first and then, as her blood sugar level rose, with energy and more expansively. Conditions in the camp deteriorated in recent weeks, she said. Rations were halved, then served every other day. If starvation didn't strike, typhoid, diarrhoea, cholera were omnipresent. People were dying all around her. There were shower chambers, where inmates were gassed and then sent to the crematorium, but even the activity in the killing chambers had dropped off as they struggled to dispose of those who died through other privations.

'Sometimes I just feel like lying down in a pile of bodies and have them take me away.'

I faced an inescapable paradox: How could I try to empathise with her, without giving away my own secrets?

'Just try and see the next few weeks out,' I said. 'The end is coming.'

∽

I knew that it was all over the night the Obergruppenführer presented me with a sheaf of identification documents. All day there was movement in the camp. The sound of feet treading snow. Later I learned that they were evacuating prisoners, forcing them on what became known as the death marches.

'When the Russians come, find a ranked officer and present him with this,' he told me. 'Don't try and hide in the house; they will find you and very likely rape you or worse. Don't try and run because they will find you and rape or kill you. If an inmate finds you they will try and denounce you as a collaborator.'

I looked at the documents, an identity card, a work warrant, some sort of permit.

'It says that you are forced labour. You are not here of your own will. You are my housekeeper.'

There was a photograph of me: where it came from, when it was taken I couldn't remember. Perhaps that awful day I was first taken to Mauthausen. And there was a name – a new name – one that I had never seen before: Nadezhda Semilinski.

'Nadezhda means "hope",' he told me.

∽

That night, as I lay beside him in his bed, I dreamed of my parallel existence, as Hannah, in the camp of horrors, lying five or six to a bed of rags, the lice and the cold coruscating my skin, the hunger filling my every thought. I could hear the drone of bombers and watched as the night sky was illuminated by their lethal tonnage. This time we didn't descend into our hiding place, but watched as the sky filled with a blaze of oranges and reds before silence came. I reached out and held the Obergruppenführer for the last time.

When I woke the next morning he was gone. Hannah was permitted to stay in the house that night and she stayed with me. We waited in the house for something to happen, but nothing moved. All was quiet, all was still.

On the third day we rose to the sound of a loudspeaker and the buzz of an engine. Driving down the street at walking pace was a Russian jeep, with two officers sat in the front. We left the house for the last time, waving a white pillowcase with one hand and my papers with the other. The jeep pulled to a halt.

'I was brought here against my will to serve as a housekeeper,'

I told the officer behind the wheel. 'My name is Nadezhda Semilinksi.'

He gestured to us to climb into the back of the jeep. It was 25 January 1945 and I was liberated.

My story was over; my story had just begun.

Part 4: **1993-2021**

1

'Let's get a kid lost.'

It sounded like the initiation of a game, but it was the descent into a wickedness whose fog hung over the city for years.

A two-year-old boy had gone missing while his mother shopped in a butcher's. It was Friday morning. Most missing children's cases are closed within hours, but this one lingered on. The afternoon, evening and Saturday passed. The case was escalated. CCTV images were circulated on the news. It became a front-page story locally, then nationally.

Lurid rumours flew around the city. The mother was out shoplifting, left the child alone while stealing and he was taken. The boy was abducted by a paedophile ring and hidden on a ship that had left the port. He was taken to a local house and tortured. Street urchins stole the boy, tied him to a tree and set him alight. All seemed to be based on preconceived ideas of how people in Liverpool lived. If only the perpetuation of evil were so mundane.

It was Valentine's Day when the body was found, two days after the disappearance. Some children found him on a railway track, not far from where he vanished. The corpse was beaten, splattered with paint, covered with stones. Left on the railway tracks it was then cut apart by a passing goods train.

Over the following days, what happened unravelled. Two otherwise unremarkable ten-year-old boys spent the Friday playing truant. CCTV captured them hanging around doorways in the shopping centre, shoplifting, making nuisances of themselves. Then came the crucial moment. A camera captured them approaching the two-year-old near the doorway of the butcher's; the next image caught them leading him away out of the shopping centre and to his doom. That was the last time the boys were captured on film. These images were circulated by the press and seen globally.

The older boys then took the toddler to a nearby wasteland where they killed him. Then they returned home and rented a video like it was any other Friday night.

∽

Paul was back in England after eight years in the Middle East. Already he was agitating to go back, or to the scene of the latest conflagration. Yugoslavia had collapsed and from his desk in London he envied his colleagues reporting on misery after human misery, while he sat in the mundanity of the newspaper offices processing their stories.

'You're a bloody nuisance,' his editor, Roy McEwan, growled at him from across their bank of desks. 'Unfortunately there's not a conflict deadly enough to lose you in yet.'

But when the story of the missing boy broke, it was Paul they sent to cover it. The abduction took place three miles from where he grew up, but it belonged to a different world to the comfortable suburbs and golf club primness that surrounded his childhood.

Bootle and its hinterlands in Walton and Anfield was a

staunchly working-class part of the city, housing the thousands who had worked on the city's immense strip of docklands. These had largely closed now. Britain looked to Europe not America or the Empire in the 1990s, and Liverpool faced in the wrong direction. The containerisation of shipping fleets did away with thousands more of the remaining jobs. The working-class inner city became workless, and the poverty that followed permeated every street. Dilapidated buildings, broken paving slabs, dog shit, graffiti, abandoned houses; children buzzing around on mountain bikes, hiding under hoods, as dark and ominous as the night; women aged prematurely by decades, their faces worn by bad diet and smoking; men in their thirties ground down by the tedium and scarcity of life without work. These were the scenes that faced Paul as he made his way on foot the short journey from the New Strand – the sight of the abduction – to South Sefton Magistrates Court, where the older boys were appearing.

It was ten days after the murder and the ten-year-olds had been arrested the previous Thursday and charged over the weekend. In a city that thrived on rumours and gossip, their names spread within hours. So, too, did details of the extent of their alleged crimes, which a gaunt-faced plain-clothes officer meticulously briefed journalists about shortly after their arrests, before handing out a court order strictly forbidding them from publishing any of these details until after the trial.

A crowd several hundred strong appeared outside the court to make their anger felt. As police vans carrying the accused arrived, the crowds lurched forward and started shaking and jostling the vehicles, phlegm coating the windows of the van and the sound of fists upon metal ringing out. It was a pitiably cold morning, and as Paul watched from his vantage point across the other side of Merton Road he feared the police would be overwhelmed and the children dragged from the vehicles. The officers regained control, and dozens of them formed a human chain that guarded the accused boys as they took the few steps into the court building.

The hearing was a closed one and lasted just two minutes. The mob had scarcely subsided when another cry of rage went up as the police jostled the boys back into the police vans. They were taken to a secure unit at a secret location outside of Liverpool. That day was the last they ever set foot inside the city.

Paul approached the dissembling crowd with his notebook and went to work. The people spoke of anger and evil and revenge – it reminded him of being in a Palestinian village after an Israeli infringement. He wanted to learn about the environment these children grew up in; whether their crimes were a product of their upbringing. Yet there was no space for nuance on this frigid morning.

'They need to string these lads up,' said one man.

He went to the pub across the road to write up his notes. The place was as sombre and empty as could be expected on a Monday lunchtime. A few pensioners and office workers smoked and drank and read newspapers, and a vacant-looking woman sat alone at the end of the bar, chain-smoking. Paul ordered a pint and wrote his notes up in longhand. These would be phoned through to his desk later that afternoon. The words flowed because the story told itself. It was a crime so sensational and dreadful that it defied subtlety.

'Press?' asked the barman, as he poured a second pint for him. Paul nodded and the barman glanced to the other end of the bar, where the solitary female drinker was lighting another cigarette. 'She's one of the family,' he said in a low voice. 'The killer's family. An aunt, I think.'

'Do you reckon she'll talk to me?'

'You can only ask.'

When the drink was poured, Paul took it to the other end of the bar and sat on a stool beside the aunt. She was in her thirties, bleach blonde, with make-up applied thickly to her grey and tired skin. She had a forlorn look, as if trying to concentrate on anything other than the enormity of her nephew's crime.

'Are you all right, love?' asked Paul.

She dragged heavily on her cigarette and looked intently into the space ahead of her, but said nothing at first.

'Can I get you another drink?' he asked.

'S'pose you're press, aren't you?' she said finally. Paul nodded. 'I seen you out there with your notebook before. Conversing with the mob.' She let out a bitter cackle. 'Yes, you can buy me a drink,' she said, and gave him an inebriated grin, the inherent sadness of the mid-afternoon drinker briefly broken, and Paul gestured to the barman as she began to talk.

'He is easily led. He didn't want to hurt the toddler. He was fearful of the other boy. He was fearful, he was weak and he was provoked,' she said without prompt. 'He was – is – a normal child. Loving and fun to be with. I'm still in shock to be honest, as I was when I heard the police had taken him in.

'It is hard to take in really. We feel so sorry for him because he must be going through so much torment. You know, as a family, we just try and help him as best we can to try to come to terms with things. Our feelings haven't changed towards him. We still think the same of him as we always have. I would say he was provoked. He is one of those children that if you told him to put his hand in the fire, he would.

'All he said when his mum has said, "Why didn't you run away?" and things like that is that he was frightened. He said he was frightened of the other boy's older brother. He'd told him, "If you tell anybody I'll get my big brother to batter you up".'

She drained the vodka and tonic Paul had just paid for with the speed of a glass of water on a hot day, before slamming the empty glass down on the counter.

As she got up to leave, she said, 'There's your story. Another day in paradise. Thanks for the drink.'

2

They convened in The Swan on Friday, like in the old days. There was no Christopher, of course, but Bulsara, Roberts and Sam were there, in their old corner, pints of bitter to hand. Little had changed in the years since they left school and it remained a decrepit place. The Swan, terminal though it always first seemed, still endured – as they always expected it would.

Paul had spent the week under slate-grey skies, pounding the streets of his home city, trying to make sense of the killing. Of course, nobody knew why two otherwise ordinary boys murdered a toddler, but as he trawled the streets where they had grown up and spoke to contemporaries a picture began to build where they seemed to be products of their own environment. Poor, neglected, bullied, possibly abused, one the child of an alcoholic; this was the backdrop that bore two murderers.

Paul told his friends what he had seen – the mob outside the court, the beleaguered aunt, the days spent walking around the inner city – and in return they relayed to him the latest gossip, what people they knew were hearing and saying and feeling, which as ever in this city of rumours possessed a significant element of truth.

The conversation turned to football and, as Paul knew it would when tongues were loosened by beer, to the lost girls and their dead mother.

The previous summer he had finished his manuscript on Nadezhda's life and, after some deliberation and through want of knowing what to do with it next, sent a copy to Roberts. His response was blunt and to the point, written on a postcard that was mailed to the newspaper office: 'I think she played you.'

Paul already had many doubts about the authenticity of her claims. The night she died she told him her real name was Eleanor Hodys, but amidst the scraps of paper and pieces of documentation there was no evidence to support that.

When he researched the name he found there was an Eleanor Hodys, but he was shocked by what he saw. Like Nadezhda she was an Austrian, and like the poet she went through the camps, where she became the lover of a Nazi. But here their stories diverged: she was taken by the Auschwitz Kommandant Rudolf Hoss, who impregnated and terrorised her, threw her into solitary confinement and forced her to abort their child. After the war she was shot according to some accounts; or lived in obscurity in Vienna. Historians seemed united on one thing; that she was the Mistress of Auschwitz, even if she seemed as much a victim as anyone else.

Could she have been Nadezhda? She was recorded as being incarcerated in Auschwitz, nearly three years before Nadezhda. Perhaps crucially, all accounts seemed to agree that she was born in 1903, more than two decades before the poet. It seemed unlikely to the point of being impossible that she was Hodys.

Roberts passed the manuscript onto the other two, but Paul had seen or heard from neither of them in the intervening period – until they were face to face in The Swan. But before they passed judgement they asked how the story came into his hands.

'That night, at the party, the night she died, we talked about writing and writers; how one gets a start in life,' he told them with sudden freedom. 'She kept telling me that she had a gift for me, a gift between writers, she called it.

'She talked about how the start of her career was helped by another famous writer – TS Eliot in her case and how she was obliged to pass on the compliment to the next generation.

'It was late and we were very drunk. Most people had gone home or, like you, were passed out. She kept talking about this gift and I followed her up to her room – "her rooms" she'd call them – up at the top of that big old house. It was a study that led onto her bedroom and a dressing room and bathroom. I had never been there before.'

Paul cast his mind back and described the high vaulted ceilings, the walls lined with bookcases where papers and stacks of books were stuffed in at every angle to fit the space creating a chaos of paper and Wibalin. There were the obligatory empty wine glasses, an overflowing ashtray, wallpaper peeling from the wall. Lamps cast shadows on her ghostly, wraithlike figure as she searched the shelves. From it she pulled some books away and from beneath them was concealed a plastic carrier bag.

'It was completely inauspicious, from Kwik Save,' he said. '"What's this?" I asked her. "It's the story of a misspent youth," she told me. "Documents, photographs, memoirs – or fragments of them. What I'm about to tell you, only a few people alive know."'

'And so she began to tell me about the war and what happened to her – the story that you have read, about the camps, her family, her way of survival.

'At one stage she pulled up her sleeve and showed me the tattoo on her left arm. I winced at the scarred flesh, the number that was injected onto her skin, and she laughed that cruel cackle of hers – her smoker's laugh, if you remember it? – "You think I should get rid of it Paul? That I'd look better without it?" she asked. I didn't know what to say. "By removing my tattoo, would I remove all the tragedy that happened to me? Unfortunately, the answer is no. So why should I submit myself to further pain so that I do not have to see that tattoo? It's my badge of courage. I actually like looking at it, even though it's not very clear any more.'"

It seemed ironic, looking back more than a decade later, that at the precise moment where she neared death – having survived and accomplished so much in her past – that she had never seemed so alive as she did then. Her eyes glowed and she was full of life. As well as the war, she talked about London after the war, of making her way through austerity and in London's 1950s' jazz age, when her talent was first recognised. 'My story is your gift,' she'd told him.

At some stage he passed out. It was light when they were talking, he'd remembered that, and he was woken by the sound of voices soon after. Had she been alive when he'd left her room? He hadn't known.

The crushing hangover when he woke in his own bed hours later brought a terrible conflict of emotions. What was he supposed to do with a story that would surely bring her disgrace? The Mistress of Auschwitz. Why had she not told it herself? Or to one of her writer friends? What would her daughters think?

Then, when Roberts told him of her passing later that day, the confliction gave way to horror. This was a truth that must be hidden, a reality too far, too awful for her daughters to comprehend. He hadn't even looked at the contents of the bag when he'd climbed into his parents' loft and hidden the plastic bag beneath some lagging, where it lay untouched for the next eight years.

'But now you've written the story, what are you going to do with it?' asked Sam.

'I don't actually know,' replied Paul. 'I wanted to protect Sarah from the truth, but I don't know where she is – or Julia. It's so long ago now that I wonder if it matters any more.'

'What about your commitment to the truth?' Roberts snarked.

Paul shrugged, for he had no answer.

'You said you had doubts?' said Bulsara.

'It's a writer's duty to be sceptical and there were things that didn't add up; dates that were wrong, places where it would have been difficult or unlikely for her to have been.'

'An unreliable narrator,' Roberts proclaimed.

'Not just that,' replied Paul. 'But there's something missing. The story might be written, but it isn't complete.'

3

Julian Tennant leaned back in his armchair, like a pantomime dame, and let out the same guffaw Paul remembered from all those years earlier: *haw haw haw*. He was more jowly and plumper than the figure that resided in Paul's memory: a big belly spouted out into a checked shirt and over his belt, and he was camper too. He spoke with an exaggerated lisp and it looked as if he had lined his eyelashes with flecks of mascara, while his pink cheeks were so flushed as to give the appearance of being rouged.

They were sat in the chaos of his living room in a cottage on the edge of a Cheshire country estate ('A grace and favour place, the old squire lets me use for a peppercorn rent. You know reviewing all those books for the *Statesman* doesn't pay what it used to!'). Paul had driven there from his parents' home. It was his last weekend in Liverpool. The world had moved on from the murder of the toddler and he was heading back to London the following week. His desk job was drawing to a close and there was more talk of a posting to cover the Yugoslavia war, which was taking another dark turn.

He had spoken to Tennant on the phone when writing about Nadezhda, but the writer knew her later than the period Paul had researched. 'There was a darkness within her,' Tennant told Paul late one night as they sat talking in different countries, the phone line crackling and pausing, his recollections lubricated by whisky. 'She would sit up all night, smoking and listening to jazz records, and not speak to people for weeks. We – her friends – assumed that those black periods came because of the war, but it was never spoken about.'

Her arrival in England, the patronage of TS Eliot ('one of her fantasies'), and the time before she became known were a blank to him. But Julian Tennant had plenty of stories: poetry readings in smoky bars, hanging out in theatre pubs and travelling by boat and train to Paris to try and gain an audience with Samuel Beckett.

'When she made it, it was quite a thing. It was the mid-Fifties and she would be about thirty – but she'd done a hell of a lot of living by then. And being a poet back then, if you had made it – not like it is now – bestowed a level of credibility and minor fame. And it was a way of making a modest living too. Her books sold quite well: thirty, forty thousand copies. She was paid to do readings, reviews.'

Julian Tennant relayed these stories to Paul again. He had heard them before in their phone conversations – but he sat patiently through them, fascinated but also hoping for fresh insight.

'She was beautiful, of course – not my type though! Haw haw haw! – and men coveted her. There were lots of dalliances, lots of one-night stands, but no one pinned her down until Charles White. And although he was a nice man, he was not one of our crowd.'

'What do you mean, not one of your crowd?' Paul asked. He had rarely heard Sarah's father spoken about and was intrigued by what drew a Liverpool shipping merchant to an émigré poet in London.

'We were artists: dancers, actors, painters, writers. That was our set. London in the Fifties was an austere place, you must remember. There was rationing and smog. People and the place itself was damaged by the war. There was no "Swinging London" or "Cool Britannia" buzz about the place. We were a clique. We were the avant-garde! And Charles, dear old Charles, he was a businessman. He was older than us. He was rich, or at least affluent. He knew a lot about the arts, but he was a consumer of them – not a creator. He wasn't one of us.'

'You mean she married him for his money?' asked Paul.

Tennant pulled a face, not wanting to say yes or no. 'She did love him, she really did. He was kind – and I think that after all the upheaval in her life that's what she wanted the most by that stage. Somebody who didn't place too many demands upon her, who let her be. They had a lot in common: books, the arts, a shared faith – even if that was mostly cultural. But I think it's fair to say that for any artist, the financial freedom to do as you want and work on your own terms is attractive. But she did love him. She was never unfaithful. She was devastated when he left to live in Germany. But that wasn't the reason they separated. She would never tell me the real reason. There was a catastrophic row. It was the early Seventies, I suppose, and he just went. She never really recovered from it. She fell to pieces then and went a bit crazy; she went very political, but there was drinking and drugs. She had affairs too. It was like an extreme version of Fifties London, except she was fairly famous at this stage. And of course she had two young daughters, who turned out remarkably normal in spite of everything.

'There was a lot of drivel going around as well; innuendo; lots of tut-tutting. And that stupid tabloid story about the schoolboy.'

'Did I tell you I met him?' Paul interjected. 'Sean.'

'Ha! So did I! Says he's going to write a book about her. Sat in the same chair as you did a few years ago, then asked for his train fare home! Haw haw haw!'

Tennant slurped from his mug of tea and became momentarily muddled. Paul guessed that he was in his late sixties or early seventies, the same age Nadezhda would have been, but he seemed older. Too much time sat at home reading about the world had made him corpulent and jowly, while the world had passed him by.

'Anyway Paul, we digress! We digress! Your manuscript...' Tennant summoned a large brown envelope stuffed down some orifice between piles of books and his armchair. 'Here we are, here we are...' He unfurled the papers, and what seemed like a blizzard of Post-it notes tumbled into his lap. 'As you can see I've made detailed notes, and much of it is very good, terribly moving, horrific, but... how can I say this?... I don't see my friend here.'

'But you said that she never talked about that part of her life.'

'That's true, that's very true. But all this... being the mistress of an SS General... She was categorised as a subhuman. Do you really believe that someone given the status as the highest human being in the camp would have had her as his mistress?'

Paul had considered this for years. Wherever he had been in the world he had seen extraordinary acts not just of cruelty, but humanity too; he'd seen complexities of the human condition that he didn't think he could ever understand, much less lay down to paper. Anything was possible. That was what life had told him. What had surprised him at first was Nadezhda's lack of remorse for her affair, but over the years this had diminished. It was, he realised, a simple act of human survival.

He relayed his evolving views to Tennant, but the older man was having none of it.

'I'm sorry Paul, but do you really think that if any senior Nazi there had had an affair with a young Jewish woman, the world wouldn't know by now? These are the most investigated men on earth. By jurors, by historians, by writers. Somebody would have known, but here we are, fifty years on, and still no one has stepped forward – until Nadezhda, who isn't here to corroborate her posthumous story and – although I loved her dearly – was terrible for embellishing things.'

'Maybe because the reality is too awful to acknowledge?'

'I'm sorry, I don't buy into it, I really don't. It doesn't make sense. A racially motivated ideologue and his young Jewish prisoner mistress?'

'What if he was just a pervert?'

'Possible.'

'What if she wasn't Jewish…'

'Nonsense. She even talks about her cultural heritage in her memoir.'

'Hear me out: her number – her tattooed number – was one usually given to political prisoners. Maybe it's an anomaly, or maybe it's something else?'

'She was as Jewish as Golda Meir.'

'Was she? I didn't know her for long, but the cultural references all came from her daughters. I never heard it from her. What if that assumption was simply made about her, because the vast amount of victims were persecuted because of their faith? What if she invented that heritage to mask something else? What if…'

'I have a couple of problems with these hypotheses,' Tennant interjected, his voice booming so that it cut Paul's off in the small living room. 'And I speak as one of her oldest friends, but also a critic of many many books, thousands of them, so hear me out.

'Firstly, there's too many what ifs in the story you've sent me, too many questions unanswered. It seems like the classic unreliable narrator, and she could be bloody unreliable. Why has this never come out before? Why has no one come close to what you say is the truth? Are we expected to believe that almost everything we thought we knew about her was false?

'Second: you're a good man Paul, you're a nice fellow. You obviously loved poor Sarah – wherever she may be now! – a lot. But you were teenage lovers. It was a youthful fling. Why would your girlfriend's mother confide in you as an eighteen-year-old her secrets? She knew lots of writers. She was a writer herself. She said it was 'a gift', but I can't think of anybody – even someone as contrary and unpredictable as Nadezhda – who'd bestow such a gift upon a teenager...'

'But I have all the documents!' Paul interjected.

'You have some of the documents, some of them. None of them back up her testimony. Would you run this as a story in your paper?'

Paul paused and thought and then shook his head sadly.

'Paul. I'm sorry,' said Tennant, and repeated the mantra of his friend Roberts. 'I think she was playing with you.'

4

Paul's story about the child killers went to print the following day. A teaser went under the masthead on the front cover of his paper and it led the glossy magazine supplement. But the writer, as was usually the case, remained in a vacuum, oblivious to its existence beyond what he saw on the news-stand, unaware of any resonance it may have had. The office dealt with any letters praising or criticising his work and the occasional phone call. Little was fed back to him from there. It was a curse of the job.

'It's quite good, Paul,' his father professed, peering over the top of the Sunday magazine. 'I don't quite know if you can explain an act of evil as being bred from an environment in which a kid has been brought up, otherwise they'd be slaughtering toddlers all over the city, but there you go.'

His mother, as had always been the case when she was unsettled by the news, clutched onto the curtains and peered out the window, as if wickedness was about to confront her. 'It's terrible what the world is coming to,' she said.

Paul's mind, however, had moved on and moved back. There was the posting in Sarajevo, which he was sure he was going to take, and more immediately a return to London. And then there was Nadezhda's story, which had fallen short at the first glimmer of scrutiny.

He toyed morosely with his grey slab of roast beef at the golf club's Sunday carvery later that day, pondering his future and his past, as his mother trilled on inanely about the forthcoming nuptials of one of her friends' daughters. The greyness of February had finally broken, and there was a hint of spring in the air. Daffodil stems bulged through the earth. With the first glimpse of sunshine his parents summoned their golf clubs, dressed in their matching Pringle jumpers and were ready for their first round of the year. While they played Paul intended on spending the afternoon in the club's bar, watching football on its large- screen TV and sipping subsidised beer.

They were having coffee and lemon meringue pie when a middle-aged lady crossed the dining room and approached their table. His father was droning on about a new golf club that one of his friends had bought while on holiday in Florida – 'Brian says it's super for getting it up over the trees' – and he carried on oblivious to the stranger, until he noticed his wife looking upwards at the woman, beaming her public smile.

She was in her mid-forties and, while dressed in the standard garb of the club – the tailored trousers, the branded sweater – seemed out of place: there was a sadness that exuded from her face and eyes. She seemed ethereal, as if her soul was elsewhere.

'Excuse me, I'm terribly sorry to bother you, but are you Paul Davis, the journalist?'

'Yes!' beamed Paul's mother. 'This is my son, Paul, the famous journalist. Are you familiar with his work?'

'He had a big piece in today's paper about those child killers. Awful case,' chimed his father.

'I wondered if you remembered me?' asked the lady, ignoring

his parents. Paul squinted, trying to summon a memory of the woman, but he couldn't place her. 'On the day of the disaster,' she said. 'You were there, after Hillsborough four years ago; you were at the station afterwards. You'd come from the Everton game. Your friend Kevin – Bulsara, you call him – he helped me find my son.'

He remembered her now; how they'd found her drifting among the dazed and confused on the Lime Street concourse, weeping, looking for her teenaged son. And while he took notes and interviewed survivors, Bulsara had calmed her down and helped search for the lost boy until he was found. 'I've never seen anyone hold another person so tightly,' he told his friends when they were reunited that evening.

'Yes, I remember,' said Paul, standing and taking her by the hand. 'You found your son. It must have been a terrible evening while you didn't know what had happened. He was one of the lucky ones.'

She smiled sadly and seemed poised to say something important, but after a few moments simply said, 'I just wanted to come over and say thank you for helping that day,' and left them to their dessert.

Later that afternoon, when his parents were on the course and Paul was immersed at the clubhouse bar, sifting through the Sunday newspapers and drinking pints of Guinness, the lady sat on the stool next to him. Her name was Karen and she came to the golf club every few weeks for their carvery lunches with her brother, who was a member. 'It's lovely around here isn't it? I don't play golf, but I like to get out the house. Have a bit of lunch and a few bevvies. I live up in Walton Vale – I seen your story in the paper about it today – and as you know it's not like that around here. You got the sea breeze and the light and trees here. It's nice.'

She seemed more at ease now, less hunched, perhaps lubricated after a boozy lunch and some colour had come into her pallid face.

'You said earlier my lad – he's called Paul as well – was one of the "lucky ones". And you were right, he was. That night when your friend took me off to find him, I made a pact with God that if our Paul lived just one more day I'd never want for anything ever again.

'But although he lived, something died within him that day. He's never been the same since.'

'Seeing people his own age and younger die and suffer like that is something he'll never forget,' said Paul.

'I thought things would change as he got older, but if anything they've got worse,' she said. 'He left school. He doesn't go out. He's completely isolated.'

Paul ordered them both fresh drinks. Alcohol was lingua franca in the city, a currency that cut across class and background and differences. You shared a drink when you wanted to celebrate, you shared one when you mourned, and you shared one when you just wanted to listen.

'I don't sleep very well,' said Karen. 'I have anxiety about that day. The memories, about losing him. Although I'm very grateful for finding him, he's still lost. He's so sad, and angry – that's the worst of it, the fury. And it's an anger not at having survived, but at the narrative that has been cast around.

'That stadium was a death trap. The police were unfit to run an operation like that. They treated those fans like they were subhuman because of where they came from. And they lied and they continued to lie.

'They came around to take a statement from our Paul, and he told them what had happened. About the gates being opened and pushed into an overflowing pen while there was one empty next to it. The bizzies not opening the safety gates and letting them onto the pitch. Waiting an hour or more for an ambulance, and then them taking him off when there were others in more need than him.

'They took all this down, and it was hard, it was fucking hard for a child to do this.

'We heard nothing for a long time, and then I came in from work one day and Paul said the police had come again to take another statement from him. He was still only fifteen, still a child. He kept apologising, telling me he didn't know what to say. He said they helped him with the statement, but it wasn't really what had happened.

'I called the police in Merseyside, and then in South Yorkshire complaining about this. I was passed around from pillar to post for weeks – months – and then more than a year.

'Later I learned they were police from West Midlands, investigating wrongdoing. But they weren't doing anything of the sort, they were watering down witness statements. I get so angry just thinking about it. They still haven't shown me what our Paul supposedly told them, but they said his first statement was inadmissible. He'd told the truth and they said they couldn't use it.'

She took a sip from her glass and lit a cigarette.

'We're fighting back, you know? We're not letting them get away with it. We're documenting what happened that day. To be honest it's this fight for justice that has kept our Paul going. He's collected all the newspapers – all the good and bad – and has an archive of video tapes with all the news on. He's working on it all the time. We're going to get the police and we're going to expose their lies. We're going to get justice.

'It's why I'm very grateful to you, because you were experienced in this sort of human tragedy – not like most of the other journalists – and did the best reports. You told the truth, and not everyone did. It's why, when I seen you earlier, I wanted to say thank you.'

Paul was rarely confronted by his readers and seldom aware of the consequences of his words, nor did praise sit easily with him. He went to mutter something in response, but Karen kept talking.

'What I want to know,' she said, 'is when did the lies start?'

He thought back to that epic evening, which had begun with celebration in Birmingham and ended in stony, shocked near-silence in a pub over the road from Lime Street station. In between he had listened to shocked and devastated survivors, trying to make sense of what had happened. And then, he was confronted by his former friend, Christopher, in the most unlikely circumstances.

He attempted to relay his experiences of that day, the endless tales of unmitigated horror, both from survivors and from police; he tried to place a tragedy in a wider context – that in such circumstances there was inevitably a scramble for a version of the truth and that peoples' minds could also be scrambled by shock and disbelief. But even if Hillsborough had never quite left him, he had left Liverpool soon after and, from his vantage point in the Middle East, never really followed the legacy of what had passed; the injustices suffered by people like Karen and her son.

But the lies he knew had come from the start, from the mouth of his childhood friend. The 'tanked-up mob', the late supporters pissed up in a pub; the questioning of 'instant experts'; the inventions of police being attacked as they resuscitated victims and fans urinating on the dead – these had all come at the start and stained a human tragedy with the imprint of savagery. Paul could see from this sad-looking woman that she and others would never find peace until they had got what they termed 'justice' – in their case a version of the truth that resembled what had actually happened, rather than something that had emerged from the darkest part of Christopher's mind.

And so Paul started to talk, and he told her everything that Christopher had done.

5

The mood in Sarajevo's Holiday Inn was fatalistic and exuberant, anxious and excited. It had always been that way, but there was a heightening of these emotions whenever the fighting escalated.

Every few minutes there was the dull thud of a shell or mortar raising terror in some part of the city. Sometimes, like thunder following lightning, follow-up rounds would land closer and closer, shaking the glasses on tables. One shell, earlier that evening, brought dust and shattered plaster from the roof and moments of contemplative silence before the low bustle of conversation started again. Every few hours the French UN peacekeepers looked in to take watch before returning to their own positions behind sandbags positioned inside the hotel's lobby. Everyone was acutely aware of the dangers they faced. Just a fortnight earlier a translator was picked off in his hotel room by a sniper.

It was 1995. The war in Yugoslavia was in its fifth year and the hotel had been home for two long years. Paul had traced the war's deadly curve from the Bosnian capital, escaping every few days through a safe passage and into the ruined countryside to bear witness to the latest outrages. He had seen things that he thought existed in Europe only in history books: sieges, massacres, large-scale ethnic cleansing, fascism. The cruelty and viciousness was never-ending.

Life was hard, but he knew it could be much harsher and that he was one of the lucky ones. He had access to regular meals, shelter, warmth, running water, means of an escape – rudimentary essentials that were lacking in the daily lives of most Sarajevans. Death was indiscriminate, however, and the shells and sniper rifles carried out daily horrors across the Bosnian capital without heed to whose lives they took. In market squares people huddled around makeshift stalls, selling their pathetic wares at inflated prices, unsure when heavy artillery would raise its death rattle. He had seen the aftermath of two such massacres, where shells landed in the midst of commerce, taking scores of mothers and children.

But it was the snipers who were most feared in the debris-strewn streets. Everyone was a ballistics expert, able to distinguish the impact of a mortar from that of a tank shell, the rattle of anti-aircraft fire from that of a Kalashnikov. But the crack of the sniper's rifle was usually only distinguishable when a victim had already fallen.

In a place of terror and encirclement people were driven to madness. Children, forced to sit in shelters or their homes all day, were psychologically damaged. It eventually bred a kind of recklessness, where horror was so normalised that they became impervious to danger. He watched them playing hide and seek in bomb wreckage as bullets and shells rattled around their neighbourhood, or see games of street football resume moments after another victim was pulled from the streets by the city's overworked ambulance crews.

The evenings were spent writing or boozing in Nico's bar, for there was nothing else to do. Often there was not even electricity, but there was always a steady stream of journalists and aid workers passing through. Company, fresh faces and old ones too. Nettle and Mills had both passed through, so had many others he had seen on the beat in Palestine. The Holy Land with its dispute between Arabs and Israelis seemed binary and sane by comparison to Yugoslavia's collapse. Sometimes in the absence of other accommodations, they slept three or four to his bedroom. Or passing aid workers became instant girlfriends and they lived as a couple for a few days before passing on to another part of the war. The destruction bred a live and let live mentality, which was part of its allure.

Local girls coveted the foreigners too, offering their bodies for carnal pleasures in an attempt to ease the hardship and monotony the conflict brought. These were attempts at survival, sometimes tragically desperate, but for Paul it was a line he never crossed. It brought home the extent that people were prepared to go to ensure their survival in such difficult times; it reminded him of Nadezhda.

Few stayed as long as Paul did, who was a veteran of the conflict and, among the rotating chain of journalists, something of a legend. Other papers or TV channels pulled their reporters out every few months, but he always stayed. Sarajevo had become part of him, and like so many of its people he had become disconnected from the outside world. Everything back in England was more distant and ephemeral than it had ever been – family, friends, where he next took the story of Nadezhda.

That remained on a floppy disc, amongst the few belongings that he had with him in Sarajevo. He opened the file on his laptop from time to time, but there was nothing to be done other than tidy up and polish bits of prose. On its own it was an incredible story, but within the context of Nadezhda's complicated life there were just too many questions, too many strands that did not add up. Life in this broken city precluded further digging, more research.

There was rarely time or space for contemplation. Nearly half a lifetime had passed since he had last seen or heard from Sarah. Amidst the blizzard of transient affairs and flings – a French nurse, a freelance photographer from Berlin, a Portuguese aid worker, a Ukrainian junior diplomat – she remained the ideal against whom everyone else always fell short. His friends were increasingly settled down and married. Sam had three children, Bulsara had two; even Roberts was talking about getting married, but the idea of leaving this life behind never struck Paul.

Ironically, given their long estrangement, the one person from his old life he was able to keep tabs upon was Christopher. Through the dog-eared pages of the *New Statesman* and *Private Eye*, which turned up erratically in the Holiday Inn and were shared and devoured by hacks short of news from back home, he learned that his former friend had turned to politics and risen rapidly, first as an assistant to a Sheffield MP, then a special advisor to a shadow cabinet member. In 1994, the opposition leader died unexpectedly of a heart attack, and who should be the mastermind of his successor's campaign for the party leadership but Christopher? Now he was chief spokesman to the Leader of the Opposition and the columnists of these magazines dubbed him the second most important man outside government. On these pages he appeared as he always had done: preening, narcissistic, Machiavellian, manipulative and occasionally brilliant. There was a general election a few years away and many predicted he would play a big part.

The siege finally ended in February 1996 and Paul saw it through to its conclusion. NATO forces bombed Serb emplacements surrounding Sarajevo the previous autumn and a ceasefire had followed soon after. By Christmas, power and running water were largely restored and a peace agreement signed. But still there was discord and violence. Only weeks before the siege formally ended, a rocket-propelled grenade was fired into a tram running down Sarajevo's main street. Paul witnessed the destruction close up, and never forgot the stench of death from the burned-out tram car, the senselessness of it all.

He was in his mid-thirties now, but the restlessness remained. He was rootless. He had nowhere he called home, other than the bedroom in his ageing parents' house in Liverpool. Women were transient, and although the friendships he formed in Yugoslavia and the Holy Lands ran deep, forged as they usually were in extreme situations, they too were usually passing.

After the end of the siege his newspaper rented him a flat in London's Barbican and he returned to England to the vacuity of desk work: commissioning, editing, waiting, as Roy McEwan joked, 'for another conflict deadly enough to finally lose you in.' But it wasn't work as he knew it. He walked to his office mid-morning and was out by early evening. They gave him a four-day week, but the lack of challenge merely increased his agitation.

He used his long weekends to visit his parents and spend time with his schoolfriends and their families. The mundanity of suburban life suited him after all the carnage he had seen, but the restiveness remained. He returned to the places he had once worked. The world seemed to be perpetually shrinking and air travel was easier and more affordable than at any time in history. He watched from near and afar as a new Europe rose from the old east. Once hopeless places and countries torn apart by war were reinvigorated, energised and in some cases had started to heal.

The British capital, which he started to call home, was at the heart of what one American magazine dubbed 'Cool Britannia', the world's new centre of art, popular music and progressive politics. The notion left Paul cold. Barely a week passed without the sight of Christopher beaming at the shoulder of the Prime Minister-in-waiting, ready to give his spin ahead of his forthcoming ascent to Downing Street. There was an election due no later than May 1997. Only a fool would bet against his party.

Paul's mother would call him excitedly after seeing Christopher on the *Six O'Clock News*. 'Guess who's just been on the TV!'

But it was Karen, the mother he had first met on that terrible day in Sheffield, who grasped the nettle. With her son she had founded the Hillsborough Survivors Group, whose dual purpose was to support the victims and to fight for justice after a flawed coroner's inquest proclaimed that there would be no prosecutions for negligence.

She called Paul in the newspaper office and began mid-sentence, 'He was on the news again, your friend, spinning for the Prime Minister-in-waiting. Do you really want to see this liar spreading his poison across the country for a generation, because that's what will happen. You mark my words!'

Paul introduced her to one of his paper's feature writers, but when the story about Christopher's actions on the day of the disaster was published it lacked the zeal and anger that should have driven what was a hard-hitting article about establishment lies. Had they merely picked the wrong writer, or was Christopher simply too powerful, too close to power to be touched?

Paul called Karen to apologise for the weak article. She listened and simply said, 'It's okay, you tried, we go again,' before replacing the handset.

Four weeks later, the opposition was elected to power after a gap of eighteen years. Shortly after three am on 2 May 1997, the ecstatic and eternally youthful new prime minister appeared on the steps of the Royal Festival Hall, where hundreds of party activists cheered his arrival to a DJ playing D:Ream's 'Things Can Only Get Better'.

By his side, as always, was Christopher.

Paul switched off the TV and went to bed.

∽

The late 1990s were the last great days of Fleet Street. The internet remained in its infancy and advertising revenue filled the newspapers' bank accounts. No story was ever too far or too expensive to cover. Paul had the pick of them, and often chose weeklong assignments in the new Europe of the east, indulging himself with his expense account and writing ambitious and expansive thinkpieces. Journalists were well paid and indulged by proprietors who were made rich by their writings. Nobody worked too hard. The long lunches of legend were a weekly reality. Paul, like all his colleagues, enjoyed them regularly.

Wednesdays were usually the day anointed to memorial services for recently deceased journalists at St Bride's Church, a Wren-designed building at the end of Fleet Street, known as the 'journalists' church'.

Every month or so, a communiqué was issued advising of the latest journalists to be commemorated. Nobody really went for the church services, instead they turned up for the boozy afternoons in the pub that followed, with old-timers remembering journalistic legends of the Fifties and Sixties. Paul rarely ventured to these affairs, but one afternoon a name that he remembered leapt out at him and he added the memorial service to his diary.

Julian Tennant
8 April 1925 – 30 August 1997.

6

London was cool and bright, the sky a cloudless iridescent blue. For so much of the year a pall of grey seemed to linger over the capital, but September always brought a freshness and vitality to its streets. They were calling it an Indian summer and as Paul walked up Fleet Street, through the coolness of the late morning shadows and early sprinkling of fallen leaves, he mused to himself that the city was never as lovely as it was now.

Paul left the mild bustle and entered St Bride's, an English baroque enclave in the midst of a global city.

He was handed a booklet on his way in, a picture of Tennant adorning its cover. It was how he remembered him: corpulent and smirking, ostentatious – he was pictured wearing a mustard-coloured tweed, pink shirt and a cravat – and jowly. There were other pictures of him within the booklet, and he appeared ageless, as if he were born into middle age, never receding beyond the age of fifty, but never appearing much older either.

Inside the church was a congregation of thirty or forty, all of Tennant's generation. He recognised the jazz critic, George Melly, and the wan drawn face of the novelist Beryl Bainbridge, a birdlike figure with hair as black as onyx. There were other writers there too, who all seemed older, more tired or misshapen than their byline pictures ever projected.

'Julian,' the congregation was told by his friend, the Portuguese author, Renato Da Silva, 'lived his life through his books. He saw the world through words and worshipped their very form. Writers – or at least those worthy of his praise – were like Gods to him. Those he deemed unworthy of publication belonged to the seventh circle of hell.'

Tennant was one of life's great extroverts, said Da Silva, but the reality was that beneath that ostentatious exterior his was a life half-lived; he was a gifted writer himself, but held back from venturing beyond the critic's pages; he had many passions and admirers but no love of his life, later becoming a near recluse. A critic can be cruel, but the critic's life can seem crueller.

The writer read a poem, called 'Remember my Smile'; the mawkishness and sentimentality, Paul felt, would have made Tennant puke. But at the end of it Da Silva added his own line, 'And remember Julian's laughter too,' and he perfectly impersonated the old hack's belly laugh – *haw haw haw* and others started to mimic the unforgettable jollity of the late critic. For the first time the mood began to lift.

As they filtered out of the church and into the vestibule after the service, Paul felt a hand on his shoulder and there in front of him was a face he had not seen for more than a decade: Sean Kendall.

'Shouldn't you be in Africa or somewhere gettin' shot at?'

He was dressed in a double-breasted polyester suit, an exaggerated sheen reflecting from its cheap black patina. The wedge haircut he remembered from the mid-1980s had receded at the brow, but the addict's pallor had faded.

'You look well, Sean.'

'Good to see you alive. Warra you doing here, mate?'

'I was going to ask the same of you.'

'Got to give the fat 'arl poof a send off, didn't I?' He laughed. 'Only messin'. Julian was very nice to me. Listened to my 'arl shite. Gave me a chance. Gave me some pointers.'

They left the church entrance with the gaggle of mourners and crossed the road to the Old Bell Tavern, an ancient Tudor pub where drinks and sandwiches were being laid on. Beryl Bainbridge and George Melly hung around outside deep in conversation and smoking.

'Scouse expats,' mused Kendall as he walked past them. 'Left but never came back.'

Inside the air was full of chatter and laughter, and the handful of people in the church seemed to have multiplied. Paul took a couple of glasses of warm white wine and handed one to Sean.

'I saw Julian a few years ago at his home in Cheshire,' said Paul. 'He said that you'd been to visit him.'

'Yeah, I went a few times,' said Kendall. 'He was the only one I know from your world – writers and that – and he talked to me about books and helped me with my work. The camp old bugger was generous. He helped me get my degree.'

'You've got letters after your name?' Paul asked, but winced immediately at how condescending that seemed.

'I'll have letters before my name before too long,' he said. 'I'm getting my PhD, aren't I?'

Paul blinked with surprise. The last time he'd seen Sean, he was a recovering heroin addict without a qualification to his name, grandiosely promising to write a book about Nadezhda. But at night school he'd sat the qualifications he was denied the chance of completing when at school and done so well in them that he was given an access course in English literature at Liverpool

University. A Masters degree had followed and, he told Paul, when he was offered some part-time lecturing work a doctorate seemed the natural progression. 'I couldn't have done it without Julian, to be fair,' Kendall continued. 'He checked all my work. Gave me ideas and new ways of thinking about things. He was my biggest critic and my greatest supporter. I owe him a lot.'

A debonair woman in her late sixties turned from her small group and joined them.

'I detect an accent,' she said without introducing herself. 'You must be Sean? Julian's protégé.

'I'm Martha Bailey – I was the books editor at the *New Statesman*,' she said to the two of them, and then to Sean, 'Julian told me all about you. His bit of Scouse rough.' She laughed conspiratorially at her own joke, but Paul grimaced; he thought he'd heard the last of such inverse snobbery at Cambridge. 'Really – it's marvellous. Where you've come from to what you've done. Marvellous!' She exaggerated the 'r' when she spoke, pronouncing it 'Maarr-vellous!'. 'And you are?' she said to Paul.

'I'm Paul Davis, another bit of Scouse rough,' he replied sardonically.

'Like the war correspondent?'

'Yes,' he replied, smiling knowingly at Kendall.

'I think it's wonderful that you're doing all this research on old Nadezhda. She's really the forgotten voice of her generation of poets. I mean who would've thought when we knew her in the Fifties that she'd explode into such a phenomenon. And then disappear from view like that. Such a terrible end as well. Fifty-six is no age.'

'You knew Nadezhda Semilinski?' said Paul.

'Yes, of course I did. Knew her all the way through from when she was just a quiet pretty-faced nobody working shifts in bars and going to poetry readings in Soho, all the way through the Sixties and early Seventies when I'd publish her reviews and poems. Oh, Nadezhda was a hoot! But she was hard work too. Nobody would touch her after a while. She sort of fell out of fashion. The scandal didn't help. A tabloid poetess doesn't work for anybody: the literati don't want to know and the masses are too shocked with it all.'

'So, you were part of the Fifties Soho scene with Julian and Nadezhda?'

'Oh yes! We'd traipse around these smoky dive bars and theatre pubs. We were so serious about our art. Pretentious with it too! Smoke black market Gauloises and drink little glasses of beer in the French House. Going to readings in Notting Hill, and trying to rub together a living. It was tremendous fun.

'But Nadezhda actually made it as a poet who dented people's consciousness. She was suddenly credible and we – her friends – trailed around in her wake, enjoying her reflected glory. I mean, I suppose we all made it in little ways. But not like her. I mean she was famous: a literary star. For four or five years it was like that. And then she gave a lot of it up and got married to that fellow, Charles...'

'White?'

'Yes, that's right,' she said, helping herself to another glass of wine as a tray was passed around the room.'Julian always said she'd lived more lives than any of us put together and wanted to settle, wanted somewhere safe. But I'd see her or speak to her on the phone, and she retained that restlessness and high-spiritedness. I think she was probably bloody hard to handle, which is what drove her husband away in the end. But she retained her brilliance all the way until the end.'

'And how long did you know her for?'

'Thirty years almost to the day. September 1951. I'd come down from Oxford and got my first job at Faber, as a receptionist.'

'Was Nadezhda working there too?'

'Oh, that was always one of her fantasies darling! That she was TS Eliot's secretary. Good grief! I mean Eliot published her later on, but I don't know why she persisted with that old lie. She was so glamorous, like something out of a film. And with that foreign accent too! There were a few of us in on that scene; quite a few of us have passed away now – too much smoking and too much hard living catching up with us all. Dear old Julian was at the centre of it all, really. He'd befriended Nadezhda some months before I came to London.'

They talked about Fifties London. The evenings spent in Notting Hill bedsits sat up all night, smoking and listening to jazz records; the optimism as austerity eased and life began to return to normal after many years of hardship; the cultural changes – beat poetry, rock'n'roll, the influx of the Windrush generation, the creeping social liberalisation. She spoke too of some of the people they encountered: Eliot, Philip Larkin, Jack Kerouac on an Easter weekend sojourn to London, William Burroughs, Thom Gunn and Kingsley Amis.

But just as when he had asked Julian Tennant about her life before the 1950s the period was a void. 'It was hinted at, but not quite known why, that she had had a bad war,' she said. 'But you must understand that the war wasn't really talked about by anyone. Everyone had suffered to a greater or lesser degree, everyone knew someone that had died. The Holocaust, then at least, was just another one of these terrible things that had happened. She had her dark periods, where she went off to brood, but then don't we all?'

She called over to Beryl Bainbridge, who looked over towards them with her big sad eyes. 'Beryl! We're talking about Nadj. When did you first meet her?' The writer took a long drag on her cigarette and pondered the question. 'It was 1952 or '53. The year before I first got married.' She walked over and Martha introduced them.

'I know who you are,' Bainbridge said to Paul without greeting. 'You're like me: you escaped Liverpool.' Although they spent the next hour in each other's company, she never alluded to his work or their shared home again.

She was the city's most famous writer and like Paul had risen from its unprepossessing northern suburbs. She first tried to make her way as an actor, but found fame for her fiction. As Nadezhda disappeared from memory, so Bainbridge's career went on an upward trajectory: literary prizes, film adaptations, bestsellers. She became in many ways a national treasure.

'I was never really part of their circle of jazz fiends and poets,' she growled in her smoker's voice. 'I was much too mainstream. And then I went and kept on having children. We made the reverse journey: I left Liverpool for London and she came the other way.'

They talked about their mutual friend Julian Tennant and Paul described meeting him for the first time at a house party, but omitted mention of the evening's dreadful conclusion. Martha explained Tennant's patronage of Sean and how he was working on a PhD, a critical discourse of Nadezhda's life and work. Indeed everything seemed to return to Nadezhda; even in death, her presence seemed imprinted on every conversation.

'I always found her enigmatic,' Bainbridge declared. 'We had some common ground, but she was always aloof or unready to discuss when the war reared its head.'

A sense of drama ran through Bainbridge's presence. It was as if she was on show to the small group. She gesticulated as she spoke, a glass of lukewarm Sancerre in one hand, a smouldering fag in the other. Someone had once written about her that she played the character of 'a character' and that seemed a prescient observation. She was likeable and funny, a great talker, but there was a hard edge to her too. Maybe it was her lined face and her wide haunted eyes that lent this perception. Martha seemed to tire of her grand act as a literary dame, for she had probably seen it all before, and politely slipped away. Kendall and Paul were entranced by her though. To Paul she was more reminiscent of Nadezhda than anybody he had ever met before.

'I must go now,' she announced suddenly, before addressing Sean. 'I'd be curious to read your thesis or book when the time comes, but you can add this line from me about Nadezhda. She was my friend and rival and I liked her and loathed her sometimes. But the thing that still sits with me now, even after all these years was that she never told the whole story: in her poems, her interviews or her conversation.'

ை

The crowded pub had emptied, and it was just Paul and Sean Kendall leaning on the bar, sipping from pint glasses. The midday drinking left Paul's head in a fug. There was no way he was returning to the office. Not, of course, that there was a story to write. He was going through the motions of desk life, waiting for the next conflict to erupt.

Kendall told him that Julian Tennant had bequeathed him his estate. There was no one else: no close family; his friends had already made their way in the world and had no need for his modest legacy. There wasn't much – a cottage in Asturias where Tennant spent many of his summers, his library and some furniture, £30,000 of savings – but it would see him through until he'd finished his research, and establish himself in academia. 'Amazing, eh?' said the evidently delighted researcher.

And then came the moment of truth. 'I've seen what you wrote. Julian showed me. It's amazing. Heartbreaking. But it shows what made her. I'd like to include it in my book.'

Paul shook his head emphatically.

'Why not, Paul?'

'It was her gift to me.'

Something changed in Kendall's demeanour. The devil-may-care attitude dissipated and a fierceness rose in his eyes. 'Is that what it's about? Her closeness to you? You've still not told me about what happened that night.'

'I've not seen you for twelve years,' he replied. 'But the reply is the same now as it was then: nothing. Other than she told me her story.'

'What are you going to do with it then?'

'Nothing.'

'Yer wha?'

'Nothing.'

He told him about his doubts. The inconsistencies: the deceptions about her own identity; the wrong sequence of numbers tattooed to her arm; the questions over her Jewish heritage; the missing years. Why did no one know how she'd come to Britain? Of her first years in the new country? Then there was the lack of remorse. And the doubts about her story remaining unearthed for half a century in one of the most analysed periods in human history. Had Sean Kendall considered all these things in the pursuit of his thesis?

He had, he said.

And did he have the answers?

'I'm sorry, but I don't.'

They left the Fleet Street pub in a haze of alcohol but on good terms, agreeing that Nadezhda remained an enigma. They said they would stay in touch.

Sean Kendall returned to Liverpool where he refined and eventually submitted his thesis so that it excluded the great unknowns about his subject's life. Paul Davis returned to his Fleet Street office, where he would remain for the next four months until the next of Europe's conflagrations blew up in the little-known Yugoslav province of Kosovo.

7

His abiding memory of Pristina would always be the mud. It was a thick reddish dirt that enmeshed in his boots, coagulated on the bottoms of his trousers and splashed up onto his overcoat. Even when the winter ended, the gutters and broken pavements of this poor city in Yugoslavia's deep south seemed to be permanently oozing with puddles of filth, long into the warm dry spring until finally it dried into cakes and evaporated into clouds of dust.

Even when he covered the cruel and reckless Bosnian wars earlier in the decade, Kosovo had a reputation for lawlessness. The Serbian soldiers joked about it being bandit country, a place they never wanted to go. They were far happier in the hills overlooking Sarajevo with their artillery guns and tanks and sniper rifles than in the madness of the south.

Pristina was at the epicentre of a paranoid region in a fearful country that was blistering and falling apart under the weight of nationalism and repression. It was a city of shadows and Paul knew he was being followed, watched and listened into. There was little he could do about it, but every few weeks he drove with other journalists and human rights monitors to the Montenegrin coast and checked into the largely dormant hotels on the beautiful rugged coast to eat fish, drink raka and swim in the Adriatic. Something was coming though. Everyone knew it.

He spent another year living out of hotel rooms in this broken country when the massacre of Racak happened. It was early on a Saturday morning in January 1999, the day breaking into a monotonous grey sky when word went around that something terrible had happened. There was fighting around an Albanian village called Racak, eighteen miles south west of Pristina the previous afternoon. It was a place where small hopeless towns gave way to villages and mountain country and borderland. There was a stand-off between international monitors outside the village and Serb troops. The monitors were not permitted to pass and instead retreated to a nearby hill, where they heard gunfire and watched as artillery fire rained down on the helpless village.

At daybreak the following day carloads of journalists made their way to Racak and, when they found the roads blocked, carried on by foot, apprehensive at what they may find. The smell of cordite and death lingered in the frigid air.

Amidst the ruins they saw unspeakable things: a teenage girl shot as she tried to protect her brother; old men shot in the head, their arms spread as they died in poses of surrender, frozen with rigor mortis; whole families murdered, generations shot together at close range. There were children among the victims and a man as ancient and decrepit as the hills around him. Paul learned later that he was aged ninety-nine.

∽

He filed his story later that afternoon with grim routine at his hotel in Pristina. This was a turning point in an irregular conflict, where the motivations seemed to have crystalised: ethnic cleansing with the aim of carving a greater Serbia from Yugoslavia's remnants. The world would surely take notice now that a system of apartheid was turning into the sort of genocide it was so slow to stop in Bosnia a few years earlier.

There was a certain mundanity in his work now. Things had changed since his days in the Jaffa Press Club, where he recited his lines down the long-distance line to London. Now he had a laptop computer and so long as the phone lines were still running or his sat-phone had battery he could plug it into a wall and communicate instantly with his desk. Count the bodies, hear the stories, put it in an email, and people would be reading about it a few hours later. He didn't even need to speak to anybody back home.

Was he becoming immune to all the terrible things he had seen? Certainly he had developed a thick skin for the sake of his own sanity, but he still took as much care in documenting the lives of the dead as he did the living. He took names, ages, jobs; he heard from their families about who these people were, the lives they led as parents or sons and daughters, their faded hopes and dreams. His duty was to document the truth, but it was also to preserve the memory of the victims, to humanise them. So long as he continued to do that, his was not a passive role.

The world was taking notice though. Unlike in the past, when he seemed to write in a vacuum, cut off from the world, his laptop now brought him a few clicks away from his readers, who emailed their responses, sometimes in droves. When the story about Racak went to press, in print and then online, there were several hundred emails slowing filling his inbox as his modem hissed and buzzed the following morning. One name, however, stood out, its domain known throughout the world, even if its author wasn't.

Christopher.finlay@number-10.gov.uk Subject: Racak

Paul,

Been a while, hope that you're well. Read your article on Racak today, as did the Big Boss. He'd like to talk to you about what's going on in Kosovo before he heads to Washington later in the week. Is there a number we can get you on?

Best,

Chris

Paul smiled to himself. Yes, the world was taking notice. However he had no desire to speak to Christopher or the Prime Minister. He went to his trackpad and clicked 'delete'.

§

In the lonely nights on assignment, the internet provided a new outlet to the world, a virtual alternative to the days when propping up bars was the only alternative to work in a war zone. He was more connected to his work colleagues and events in the rest of the world than he had ever been. With his schoolfriends he was able to exchange daily emails, swapping football gossip, family news and crude memes. Sean Kendall sent him missives about his PhD thesis. And there were reader emails, sources wanting to talk, and the occasional crank.

The internet was a place of eternal possibilities where anything could exist. For his work Paul found all sorts of documentation, testimony and official reports, which usually took months – if at all – to reach him on the frontline. He worked faster than ever before, but there were different elements added to his writing, so that it was more collaborative, more informed by what was going on outside his bubble. There was the social aspect too. He was connected with his home city in ways that he had not been since he was a teenager.

On some evenings, he took to searching for Nadezhda, looking for mentions of her – no matter how oblique – that might provide some evidence for her existence before she came to England. But as the modem hissed as it opened up another page, there was always a false dawn, a dead end. The Holocaust sites dealt with those who had died, rather than survived – unless, of course, they had lived long enough to provide testimony themselves, which Nadezhda hadn't. The public archives hadn't preserved the sort of detail which might have recorded a passage to England: ship manifests, immigration documents, applications for asylum.

And what of her family? He searched for Semilinski, which was adopted, but it was as if the name didn't even exist. Was it an anglicised version of Smolinksi? But this was truly opening up a Pandora's Box of possibilities. There were thousands of Smolinskis and in the Holocaust scores of them had perished or been displaced. Eleanor Hodys, the name Nadezhda had given him on her last night, had her own corner of the web, detailing her story. She was definitely not Nadezhda.

Her daughters were equally elusive. Was there a name more English than White? There were thousands and thousands of them. A search of Sarah White brought up a soap actress, a singer from West Virginia, a cognitive neurologist, a folk singer, a plastic surgeon, a BBC producer, a clinical nurse specialist and a prostitute from Birmingham. And this was all within the first two pages of thousands of search results. And who even knew if she was still known by that name?

It all seemed so pointless, an exercise in futility. He, by contrast, was well known, famous even; his byline was read by hundreds of thousands of people each week, and accompanying it was an email address – a development by his newspaper to promote reader engagement. If Sarah or Julia wanted to be found, the most straightforward way was for them to find him.

He relayed his frustrations in emails to Sean Kendall, who he knew was investing months into standing up Nadezhda's story, searching amidst archives that remained offline for scraps and snippets of information.

'Why couldn't she just fucking tell the truth? Why did she have to be the bloody unreliable narrator to her own story?' Paul wrote him in a pique of late-night frustration one evening.

'Maybe she was and we just haven't found it yet,' came the one-line reply the following morning.

∽

In Kosovo, the phoney war went on through the winter of 1999. Neighbourhoods and villages were razed and native Kosovans began to flee for the borders with Macedonia and Albania. The province began to fill up with regular and irregular troops from Belgrade. In the cold and the omnipresent mud, Paul catalogued a looming humanitarian disaster. In Belgrade he found ethnic Albanian shops and businesses burned out. Someone threw a grenade into a mosque during Friday prayer, but it exploded harmlessly against a bluff wall. 'Now I feel like a Jew in the Second World War,' one of the Friday worshippers told him.

Down the internet line in his hotel rooms in Belgrade and Pristina he could see western moves to act before the crisis became a disaster. The British prime minister and German chancellor both spoke forcefully for the need for military intervention. There were lengthy phone calls to Washington, where their US counterpart was a reluctant participant, but air raids were eventually approved.

In March, the bombing started.

Bombs. Gunfire. Screams. Fire. Ambulance sirens. Death's soundtrack took on many forms. At first light Paul and his colleagues searched the smouldering streets assessing damage and counting bodies. Witnesses professed themselves happy to still be alive, but then spoke of their dread at the night ahead. It was dangerous in a way he couldn't remember other war zones. Journalists were considered fair game: some had their cars hijacked or burned out, others were threatened or beaten up. The death squads could come from anywhere and acted with impunity. He recorded dreadful stories of men and boys separated from the women and taken away.

This is ethnic cleansing.

Day after day he wrote that same line. Nobody tried to correct him. No editor came looking for editorial balance, or a denial from the perpetrators. Everyone could see what was happening, through their TV screens and over breakfast when they read their newspapers. Even the Serbs had stopped sending their hopeless propagandists.

Christopher he saw almost daily on international news broadcasts, dubbed into German, Serbian or Albanian, elaborating the Prime Minister's position. To a desperate people, seeking NATO's retribution he became the unlikely face of hope, the face of a Britain that was fighting the murderous regime of an ailing dictator. In his own country, he had garnered a reputation for his abrasive charm and unrelenting spin-doctoring. Nobody really liked or trusted him, but he was the man closest to a prime minister who had become wildly popular at home and abroad.

Out of the blue, Karen, whose son had survived the dreadful crush at Hillsborough, emailed him. 'I don't know how you can watch him try and justify the deaths of hundreds of people night after night,' she wrote. 'Once a liar, always a liar.' Paul responded immediately: 'Perhaps, for once, he's on the right side of history?'

That same night, NATO jets bombed the studios of Serbia's state TV channel in Belgrade. One hundred and fifty people were in the building at the time and scores were killed, including many journalists. Paul was at the border with Macedonia, following the exodus of refugees when the attack happened. There was a sense of outrage among the international journalists there, for an attack on such a facility was an attack on them all.

The following morning on the hotel room TV set, he watched as Christopher appeared before a lectern outside Downing Street and proclaimed the bombing of the TV station 'entirely justified' before claiming the TV station was used to house spy devices. 'This is a war, this is a serious conflict, untold horrors are being done. The propaganda machine is prolonging the war and it's a legitimate target.' Paul knew that wasn't true, that these people had not deserved to die. They had not worn military uniform, they had not killed people. They were innocents. Christopher, he realised, said what he needed to say. That's what made him such a success.

Paul opened his laptop after seeing the broadcast and typed a short message to Karen. 'You're right. He'll never change.'

∽

'We are the unwanted of Europe,' an old man told him. 'We are not wanted anywhere. Soon we shall all be dead.'

He was in an informal refugee encampment at the Macedonian border. The place throbbed with grief. May had arrived and the temperature started to rise, but in the hills it remained damp and fetid. Mosquitos leaped around the puddles that pooled on every track that crept from the road to the border. Above them was a railway embankment with a track now leading to nowhere.

The refugees had bribed their way across the Macedonian border, but local police had locked the train doors and sent them back. They were dumped at a railway siding, prevented from returning to their old homes and with the border closed and in agonising sight.

'People cried and screamed, but we couldn't escape,' said the old man.

The carload of international journalists filled their notebooks and photographed the pitiable scene: hundreds abandoned hungry and alone in a no man's land.

But the journalists had to go. The border had been opened to them. They were not told why, nor what to expect, but to attend a UN-run refugee camp just within Macedonia's borders, where there would be a story. In the car they speculated who or what would be there, but did not know. Normally these tip offs were a set piece for a general or mid-ranking politician – a junior defence minister, perhaps, or an EU delegation.

When they arrived they found a more ordered scene of human suffering. Families five to a sky-blue UN tent, if they were lucky; many in lean-tos made from pallets, plastic sheeting and cardboard. There were open latrines. There was the smell of shit and burning rubbish piles. The omnipresent mud flicked up with every step.

But there was no one there from the embassy, and they were left in a scene of confusion and desolation as the sun beat down. They tried as best they could to shelter from the sun while they waited, but there was nowhere – no trees, no shrubs, no buildings – and like the desperate inhabitants of the camp they sat in what little shade they could, limiting their movements so as to avoid the unrelenting spring sun.

Then came the sound of helicopters and in the sky they could pick out two RAF Chinook helicopters, their twin-blade propellers throbbing in the air. One lowered itself to the ground while the other hovered several miles in the distance. A blizzard of dirt blew into the air as the enormous machine landed and children ran forward to greet its arrival, but they were greeted by unsmiling Royal Marines bearing sub-machine guns. They chased the kids from their feet and formed a sand-swept arena. Their vehicle took off and the second helicopter landed several minutes later.

They cut the motors to a halt, a door opened and a short staircase emerged. Then came a procession of people: a man in military fatigues, bodyguards, a man in a suit, and then the Prime Minister's wife, the Prime Minister himself, and Christopher.

§

No one in the press detail anticipated such a high-profile figure to travel so near to a war zone, but here he was, the great redeemer.

Refugees chanted the Prime Minister's name and greeted him with handshakes and high fives, while his wife followed, demure and overwhelmed by the scene of desolation that greeted them. The couple listened to stories of how families were forced into exile and their hopes for a free Kosovo.

'This is a battle for humanity. It is a just cause,' said the Prime Minister. He promised to double aid and find homes for more refugees in Britain and its neighbours. The journalists were amidst a security cordon of Royal Marines, but there were some English-speaking Kosovans among them and they shouted translations back to the crowds who greeted each promise with whoops and cheers.

Amidst the holler and exultation, Christopher sidled up to his former friend. He was dressed in an expensive-looking, charcoal Italian suit, a red tie – the party colours – and a pair of black Oxford shoes, whose high polish was pebble-dashed with red mud. He was as he always had been, handsome, sly and preening.

'What a day this has been,' he said. 'Power and politics in action.'

'Is that on the record?'

'Come on Paul, do you have to piss on our parade?'

'I'm not pissing on anybody's parade, but I know these people will be here long after your photo opportunity is over.'

'You heard what our man said, we'll get these people home and those that we can't we'll find them safe refuge.'

The Prime Minister and his wife entered a refugee's tent with a pool photographer. Paul and Christopher stood outside amidst the crowds and the heat. A bead of sweat dribbled down Christopher's forehead. His shirt remained defiantly buttoned up to the collar.

'How many refugees have you taken? Two hundred? Three hundred? Look around you, there's thirty thousand people in this camp alone – and they're the ones lucky enough to have made it over the border.' Paul recounted the people in the abandoned railway embankment.

'Yes, I read your stories every day. If you want to take some credit, I can say with some certainty that they've informed the Prime Minister's thinking as well,' he said, and then as if he were caught off guard repeated his spin doctor's mantra: 'We'll get these people home and those that we can't we'll find them safe refuge.'

'Do you put any effort into the clichés and lies that leave your lips or does it come naturally, like breathing?'

Christopher looked momentarily affronted and jabbed his finger towards Paul. 'What lies?' he hissed. 'Please tell me you're not fixated with your summer fling with Sarah? It's nearly two decades ago.'

'Jesus Christ. You really are lacking any form of self-awareness, aren't you? How about the TV station that you blew up last month. What was it you called it? A "propaganda machine"? They were journalists like me doing a job.'

'It's a war we're fighting. That was a necessity.'

'The lies will catch up with you.'

'Is that a threat?'

'It's a promise. I know what you did the night of the Hillsborough disaster. I heard what was said.' The colour drained from Christopher's face. 'They're coming after you; the families,' Paul added darkly, in a low voice.

'Don't pull that stunt with me,' Christopher growled. He pulled his face level with Paul, so that there were mere inches between them now. He was rattled. He could taste his former friend's breath. 'You know what happened.'

'I do,' Paul replied calmly. 'You lied about your own people after the most invidious suffering. I watched the words leave your mouth. Don't ever forget that.'

At that moment, the folds of the refugee's tent susurrated and the Prime Minister emerged, his wife following tearfully behind him. He clasped Paul by the hand, and shot him his toothy smile – 'Good to meet you, thanks for coming' – while turning to Christopher, his hand still clasped around Paul's. 'I think we're done here, Chris.'

Christopher nodded and signalled to a marine that they were to head back to their Chinook. In a whirl, the Prime Minister let go of Paul's hand and the circus of officials and soldiers followed in his wake, the crowds lining the dirt track up to the helicopter, chanting and cheering his name. Amidst the dust and the chaos, Paul could see Christopher look back at him over his shoulder, ashen faced, as if he had seen a ghost.

8

He was back in London, working from his desk when the first of the jets hit the skyscraper in New York. Paul and his colleagues watched wordlessly as the American TV network tried to grasp the enormity of what was happening.

By the time the second jet struck the building, the terrible conflagration of airline fuel, human debris and masonry illuminating TV screens across the world, Paul knew that warfare would never be the same again. The conventional war narrative had changed unalterably. This sense heightened a few days later when the American president declared war upon a noun. This would be, he announced some days later, 'a war on terror.'

Yugoslavia's wars had been over for two years now. After a decade of bloodletting, guerrilla combat, ethnic cleansing, bitter sieges and massacres, the end was remarkably straightforward. Serb positions in Kosovo were pummelled into submission by NATO air sorties. Commandoes seized control of Pristina's airport and when reinforcements landed with supplies, the Serbian forces withdrew. Within scarcely a year the Serbian president fell under the weight of popular protests and was now in the Hague awaiting trial.

Paul returned every few months to report on the fallout, the hatreds, the new nations rebuilding, but it was as if that chapter of his life had closed. He returned to England, where his work was fêted. Other newspapers tried to poach him, but he remained loyal to his desk. He was made special correspondent, a position without a portfolio, which allowed him to traverse the world reporting on what took his interest.

He bought a loft apartment in Clerkenwell, a short distance from his office. He had lived off expenses for most of his career and was able to buy it outright from the mountain of savings accumulated in his bank account. There were girlfriends, urbane women in their thirties. They had had careers, boyfriends, money of their own, but always seemed to be looking for something Paul couldn't give them: commitment. Having been away for so long, stuck in dismal hotels in hostile environments, he savoured his new freedom and independence.

Some weekends he travelled to Liverpool to see the football. He was godfather to Bulsara's son and spent time with the boy before heading out to The Swan in the evening with his old schoolfriends. They talked about the same things they always had in the unchanging pub, the same characters flitting in and out. Afterwards he returned to his parents' house and slept in the same single bed he had filled as a boy. After a Sunday carvery at the golf club, his father drove him to Lime Street station and he returned to London and the week ahead. After years of chaos, life had taken on an unusual simplicity. For someone ordinarily so restless, he enjoyed its symmetries.

The War on Terror arrived, but Paul had no interest in following the front line in such an abstract conflict. He had done his time in the fragmenting Yugoslavia, a place where in amongst the chaos you could still draw discernible lines. The war on the noun was too conceptual, too messy, too never-ending. Instead he flitted in and out of the conflict zone, to Peshawar, Kandahar, Karachi; reporting on the fallout, for seven, ten, fourteen days at a time – never any longer. It was the same stories of misery – death, rape, hunger, homelessness – just in different colours and accents. On returning to his bachelor's apartment he would lie in a steaming bath for hours, rinsing the stench of human desolation from his pores.

Iraq was the next target. The hawks in the British and American governments had circled for more than a decade, having failed to see off its dictator after their last war. Through 2002 they lined up on the TV screens, proffering so-called knowledge about the country's weapons of mass destruction capabilities and its culpability in the 9/11 atrocities.

Paul visited Iraq later that year and found a place badly damaged by sanctions and its people fearful and desperately hungry and without basic supplies. Children died of common ailments in pitiful hospitals. Schools went without books and other learning materials. Nor did the elites go without the bite of sanctions. In the presidential palace they couldn't even service the elevators for want of special parts. How the country was supposed to be developing antiballistic chemical weapons was beyond any observer of the country.

On television and on the radio, Christopher – as the Prime Minister's spokesman – was a leading advocate for an invasion. He spoke of things he knew nothing about – an unhinged dictator, imaginary weapons capabilities, the need to bring democracy to the Middle East – with such conviction that at times Paul watched him and began to doubt even himself.

An intelligence dossier that combined unseen intelligence with allegations of human rights abuses, kleptocratic behaviour and ties to 9/11 was prepared. It swayed key cabinet members to support an invasion, but in the members' clubs of Pall Mall and the sleepy pubs off Whitehall, Foreign Office mandarins and spooks whispered their unease. 'There's no doubt that there's elements of truth in this, but the key hypothesis is built on lies,' one of them told Paul. The hand of Christopher was said to be behind the document, which its critic said bore more resemblance to a tabloid newspaper than it did a government intelligence document. When the dossier was leaked to him, Paul could not believe that something so spurious and self-evidently thrown together could throw two countries to war. It reminded him of the sort of lazily chucked together essays Christopher put together in a panic on a Sunday night before returning to school.

Nevertheless, despite the misgivings of many politicians, civil servants and public opinion, the dossier built enough political momentum to make the descent into war inexorable.

၅

Although he never held public office, Christopher was, with the Prime Minister and the American president, considered one of the architects of a war that public opinion declared abhorrent and illegal. The fighting was carried out with ruthless efficiency and the Iraqi regime crumbled within weeks. They found neither chemical weapons nor weapons of mass destruction nor evidence of complicity in the crimes of 9/11. The peace was also harder to win than anyone ever imagined. By 2006 one study said that 600,000 people had died because of the invasion.

Christopher, who became the story itself and left the Prime Minister's office, tried to reinvent himself. Private companies and foreign governments hired him in an attempt to spin dry their reputations. He wrote a fantastically bad novel. He appeared on talk shows, where he was booed by members of the audience. For wherever he went and whatever he did, he could never shake off the legacy of the illegal war.

There were the consequences of other lies too. As another of Paul's girlfriends turned up at his loft apartment to collect her belongings after another relationship had run out of steam, he wondered what life would have been like were it not for Christopher's teenage interventions. Maybe his time with Sarah would have run its course. Perhaps they would have seen through their promises to each other and instead of becoming a war correspondent they would be married, living a parochial life like his friends and parents. But whatever way, he knew that any woman he met thereafter wouldn't be compared unfavourably to his idyll.

And then there was the litany of lies that had left Christopher's mouth in the hours and days after the Hillsborough disaster. In Liverpool, those inventions stung most deeply, for they were about his own people. More than twenty years after ninety-six people had died, they were still to see justice. Christopher stood at the heart of the police cover-up, and then at the centre of a government that had done nothing to redress that.

Then one day, out of the blue, Paul received a phone call. It was Karen, the justice campaigner. Twenty-five years had now passed since the Hillsborough disaster. An entire generation. She had news. 'We're launching a private prosecution,' she said with the brusqueness that was her trademark. 'Will you give evidence?'

9

Paul sometimes wondered if Sarah was a girl lost, or a story gained. So many memories of Liverpool were wrapped up with those of her and returning to the place of his birth brought them back. The ferry trips, and excursions around the magnificence of the city's art galleries; the late night gigs and walks through the scattered ruins of Toxteth; running from the bombed-out church as an apoplectic drug addict chased them away.

Thirty years after the Toxteth Riots had brought the world's focus upon its decline, Liverpool was a city beyond recognition. The skyline was filled with giant cranes hauling into place the bricks and masonry of Liverpool's urban renewal. There was a swagger about the place, not the devil-may-care cocksureness he had grown up with, but a confidence that something very special was growing from the ruins of its past. The year 2008 brought it the European Capital of Culture, and artists, musicians, actors, curators and hundreds of thousands of tourists descended upon the city. The party never really stopped. Six years on, Liverpool was still the city everybody talked about.

Today he headed up the unreconstituted bustle of London Road and towards the red-bricked towers of the university.

It was a social call, as much as anything else, but even after all these years he still couldn't quite get his head around the letters in front of Sean Kendall's name. He remembered first meeting him nearly thirty years earlier in a city-centre pub, an unemployed drug addict in recovery who couldn't afford the price of a round. 'I'm going to write a book about Nadezhda,' was his unlikely promise then, and he almost had – but some pages remained unwritten.

Now he was considered a world expert on mid-twentieth century literature. While his volume on Nadezhda Semilinski remained incomplete, he had written a score of other books – on Stephen Spender, Thom Gunn, Graham Greene – some of which transcended academic publishing and made him famous.

As Paul knocked on his office door, he noticed a new symbol of Kendall's rising recognition: Dr Kendall was no more. Instead, his new title was affixed to the door – Professor Sean Kendall.

'Look at you – Professor Sean, who would have thought, eh?' said Paul, as he entered the office.

Kendall was leaning back in his chair behind a desk, tieless in a blue Oxford shirt and indigo jeans. The hair had thinned, but now in his fifties he still retained the litheness of a younger man. The bookshelves that surrounded the room were sparsely populated, and there was a framed Steven Gerrard shirt on the floor, waiting to be hung. The room otherwise had the aspect of a soulless middle manager's office.

'Look what the cat brought in... they haven't killed you yet then?'

Kendall stood and shook his hand warmly and asked about Paul's latest adventures. He had been in Jordan, visiting the refugee camps near the windswept border with Syria, a country ripped apart by civil insurrection and the incursion of players from other states.

'And there's me getting stressed about not finding some study on Thom Gunn at our library,' Kendall joked. 'Anyhow, what brings you to our great city? Social visit? Business?'

'Social, mostly,' Paul replied. 'Catching up with old friends.'

Improbably that is what they had become since reuniting at Julian Tennant's memorial seventeen years earlier. They had exchanged hundreds of emails and text messages in that time, conversations and bad jokes, gossiping about football and updating each other on their work. Sometimes they met in London, others Liverpool. There was a natural affinity and mutual respect that came as well as their past.

'Are you going to let me use that manuscript you knocked up?' Kendall asked him, as he always did.

'You know the answer to that,' Paul replied. 'When you prove that what she said was true then it's all yours.'

'Still waiting on that, but there's a few leads. Well, not even leads really – angles.'

'Go on…'

'So there's an old boy in London, ex-wartime spook, goes by the name of Maurice Musgrave. He's written his life story – the guy is in his nineties – and after the fall of the Third Reich he claims to have collected evidence that was used to prosecute a number of Nazi war criminals in the 1940s.'

'What does he have to do with Nadezhda?'

'Some of those that he debriefed survived the concentration camps. Now, there's a claim in his book that he brought some of these victims over to Britain in around 1947 or 1948 and set them up with new identities. That's as much as I know – as much as his publisher will tell me. Now, if we make the leap: could he have been Nadezhda's handler? Could he have set her up with a new identity?'

'Have you asked him?'

'Well, this is the hard part. He's bound by the Official Secrets Act. He fucking loves his country and is terrified he's going to prison. Believe me, I've asked his son, I've asked his publisher – I'd go and ask him, but I'm not sure how hard you should push a ninety-one-year-old.

'Now there's a seventy-year statute of limitations on this, so we either wait until 2017 or even 2018 and he's going to come out with his book with a clean conscience. Or we wait until he dies.'

'So, a few years then?'

'Looks that way. Now get this; his son reckons that there's more. He's told me this all entirely off the record, but he reckons 'arl Maurice was handling these witnesses until the 1990s.'

'What do you mean handling?'

'Keeping tabs on them. He reckons it was all benevolent: making sure they were well-adjusted to life in Britain, that they weren't going hungry or without shelter. But ask yourself this: when did MI6 become a social service?'

'You always said that you felt there were bigger forces putting pressure on Nadezhda, didn't you.'

'Exactly,' replied Kendall.

'Do you think this is why there's no proper record of her?'

'Well, we'll just have to wait and see.'

∾

At the Casa, on Hope Street, the elegant artery of Georgian townhouses that linked the city's two cathedrals, he met Karen and her son. A generation had passed since he and his friends had first encountered them in the dreadful hours after the Hillsborough disaster.

Her son Paul, after a difficult adolescence, had returned to education and qualified as a solicitor. He was in his early forties now and the pair worked as a team. She was the firebrand, but he brought legal rationale to her anger.

'You remember that time when I met you in the golf club having Sunday lunch, and I told you about the night of the disaster, and I said that I made a pact with God that if our Paul lived just one more day I'd never want for anything ever again. And he did, and I hadn't wanted for anything else, ever again,' she said.

Paul nodded his assent. She always started conversations like this, without greeting, speaking nine to the dozen.

'Well I changed my mind,' she continued. 'I want this over. And it'll be over when these twats are in prison.'

Her face was fixed with controlled anger, and her expression remained implacable even when Paul let out a small laugh.

'Well, good to see you too, Karen,' he laughed. 'I'm all in.'

Private prosecutions had been raised before. In the late 1990s two police officers were taken to court on counts of manslaughter, misconduct in public office and perverting the course of justice. The defence argued, with some success, that no fair trial was possible and after weeks of legal argument the jury found a not guilty verdict for one of the police officers and was unable to agree on a verdict on the others. At the time it was seen as a huge blow, but it raised the profile of the campaign when it was fading from public view. Now, years later, they were going for Christopher in a private prosecution in the hope that it would reignite the Crown's interest in prosecuting the police officers for manslaughter.

'Do you understand why it's so important for us?' asked her son. 'Those newspaper reports that came from his briefing paved the way for defence cases in which "drunken Liverpool hooligans" were blamed for the disaster.'

'I'm well aware of that.'

'It's important too, because he's the most high profile of those involved, even if he only had a junior role at the time. If we can get him, we think the bigger heads will eventually roll.'

'Can you tell us what happened that night, Paul?' Karen asked. 'Can you tell us again?'

He took them back to Lime Street station after they made the journey from Birmingham. He described the spectral scene, the concerned parents waiting – some hopelessly – for their children to return; the shattered men and boys returning from Sheffield having witnessed unimaginable horror. Then how later out of the shadows appeared his old schoolfriend Christopher on a TV set. 'I hadn't seen him for nearly eight years. There was a falling out. I had a notion that he worked for the police, but I didn't really know what he was doing until that point.

'He talked immediately about the drink and fans arriving late. Of course, people have a beer before the match, but not in the manner he described – "tanked-up mob". I think it was only later, when I saw him again on TV repeat the same lines that it really sank in, the effect of those few lines.

'As you know I've been in war zones and seen terrible human tragedies all over the world. The first battle afterwards is always the fight for the truth. Sometimes people say things they regret because they're out of their depth or they don't realise what they're saying because they're in shock. But this was calculated. He realised from the start that attack was the first form of defence. And I know it was no accident because he joined us later and repeated those same words and stuck by them, even when witnesses challenged him.

'In fact he went even further. I did some reporting, eyewitness accounts of those who'd returned. In the process of that I liaised with colleagues in Sheffield and they told me some of the things he'd said, things that weren't true. Fans on the pitch, urinating on the dead. A copper attacked when he tried to give CPR to a young fan. Attacking police officers. Picking pockets. It was wild. The reporters who had been there didn't even take notes because they knew it wasn't true.'

'But one of them did?' Karen asked.

Paul nodded. 'But he hadn't been at the match. He came from London afterwards.'

'The one who wrote "The Truth" headline a few days later?'

He nodded again.

'Will you put all this down in a sworn affidavit for us?'

For a third time Paul nodded his head.

10

She did not see him, but he saw her. She was walking up Harley Street, trundling a carry-on suitcase behind her, past the white-stuccoed doctors' surgeries and onto Marylebone Road. It had been more than thirty years and there was a dislocation in time and place, but he knew immediately it was her. The jet-black hair, the pearl-white complexion; she retained the slender figure of a much younger woman, but now possessed the imperious posture her mother once held. The only surprise of it all was that the sighting had taken so many years, for she was invisible in every conceivable way – physically, legally, online. But now she was resurrected, conjured back to life.

Paul, who was heading in the opposite direction to the BBC, took a few more dumbstruck steps, before turning to see her disappear around the corner and onto the cacophony of Marylebone Road.

He turned on his heels and retraced his steps, following her over Marylebone Road, past the Dickens Memorial and the Royal Academy of Music, where students were emerging for lunch, instruments to hand. Amidst the crowds waiting outside Madame Tussaud's he lost sight of her momentarily, but she re-emerged twenty yards ahead.

There was a moment of doubt. Was it really her? He had spent so many days and nights thinking about her, her sister and her mother over the years that he had almost lost sight of reality. But some scenes he could still picture vividly: her emerging into the decaying grandeur of her family's dining room, with a roast chicken on a tray in front of her, dancing to Echo and the Bunnymen, walking through the riot- strewn streets of Liverpool on the way back to her big old house.

As she cut down the steps of Baker Street station, he caught her side profile. Crows' feet crept at the corners of her eyes. Her hair had lost some of its lustre and sheen, but it was definitely Julia.

He followed her through the barriers and down the escalator into the depths of Baker Street station. It was early afternoon and the rush-hour crowds were but a memory. There was a scattering of people on the escalator. Julia was stood twenty steps beneath him and at the bottom headed onwards down a foot tunnel, towards the Jubilee Line.

Theirs had not been a long acquaintance. Ten weeks, perhaps, maybe eleven. Yet certain relationships live long in the memory and hers seemed seminal in his life. What if Christopher had not introduced her that afternoon in a city centre pub? What if she'd not brought her sister to the gig?

Three minutes. They had just missed a train. Where had she come from? Where was she going?

A school party lined up at the other end of the platform. They were six or seven years old, bedecked in dayglo vests, holding hands and chattering, a pair of teachers at each end of their line watching for any unexpected movement.

Two minutes. He glanced again along the platform at her. She wore an expensive coat, too heavy for the weather, but her face was pallid and drawn, as if she was suffering from a cold. Her carry-on case stood to attention alongside her.

One minute. He could hear the rumble of the train and the vibrations along the track. He pondered the strangeness of fate; the years spent hunting for her and her sister. The blind alleys, and there she was walking down the street, straight towards him, a vision of his past that had remained indelibly imprinted on his mind.

The train thundered into the station, enveloping the platform in cool air as it sped past and then screeched to a halt. The children giggled and were led on to a carriage adjacent to Paul and Julia, who embarked through different doors, and sat at opposite ends. Paul picked up a discarded free-sheet and flicked through its pages, the sight of Julia affixed in the corner of his eye.

He remembered the last time he saw her. The unexpected anger. The clenched lips. The unremitting hostility. Her trying to barricade him from the front door of her home. The shock of it all.

The train sped through Central London, picking up and dropping off more passengers as it stopped and started. He imagined her residing in a grand house near Green Park, or a riverside apartment at London Bridge; maybe a penthouse in Canary Wharf, or one of the townhouses beside Greenwich Park. But she remained seated until Canning Town, on the capital's eastern hinterland, near where the Olympics were hosted but not quite close enough to have been enveloped by its gentrification.

He followed her out of the carriage but instead of leaving the station into the grim milieu of cheap low-rise housing, she darted up an escalator to the Docklands Light Railway platform. Paul stood amidst the other passengers, but as it rose into the daylight he could see the warning of the platform board *** STAND BACK, TRAIN APPROACHING *** and so he stepped left and started running up the escalator, jumping into the carriage as the train doors closed behind him.

It was busier here, and he was forced to stand against a glass half-wall, his eyes searching the busy carriage for a sight of her. Eventually he saw her two doors along, looking impassively out over east London. Where was she heading?

The station names ran down: East India Dock, West Silvertown, Pontoon Dock and when the doors opened at London City airport, a phalanx of passengers disembarked, including at the last moment, Julia. Paul sidestepped a man with a huge shopping bag, and leapt out of the closing doors. Julia was away, running down the platform, her case trailing in her wake. From the adjacent runway, not one hundred metres away came the roar of a departing jet.

She had run down the left side of the escalator. Had she seen him and panicked? Or was she merely late for a flight? He scarpered chaotically down after her, pushing past a French couple and ducking past a man with a large sports bag.

He knew the layout of the airport intimately and had passed through it hundreds of times. There were barely 150 metres between the tube station and the check-in barriers. He could see her sprinting ahead and so called her name, but she ran on, impervious or ignoring him, he wasn't sure which.

He was faster than her, and stronger too, and so with each second the gap between them reduced.

And then she was before a policeman, screeching her story, and Paul was upon them. 'Julia! Julia! I just want to talk!' he shouted as he slid to a halt.

The policeman shoved him to the floor and his colleague

pointed a sub-machine gun at him, stepping back as he did so. 'Get back! Get back! Hands on the head! Stay on the floor!'

There was an unreality to the situation. This ghost of his past peering down upon him, as a gun nozzle pointed at his stricken body. He panted for breath, his heart palpitating. Sweat dribbled down his forehead. Above him, Julia explained in a panicked tone that the man had followed her, that she wanted to be left alone, that she needed to get her flight. Around them, passengers were urged to stand back by the other officer.

'I'm her friend!' Paul implored. 'Julia, it's me!'

'I don't want to speak to him,' she was saying. 'Make him go away.'

'Julia, I need to talk to you! It's been thirty years!' He felt like a madman and other passengers looked at him as if he was deranged.

'Madam, do you know this man?' the officer asked. Julia nodded her assent.

The policeman slowly lowered his sub-machine gun.

'Please,' Paul repeated. 'I'm an old friend. Please, I just want to speak to her. If she doesn't want to talk to me, let her on her way to check in and I'll go home. Please.'

He looked at Julia imploringly, who glanced at her watch.

'Ten minutes,' she said without emotion. 'I have a flight to catch.' She turned to the officer and smiled benignly at him. 'I apologise, officer. It was a misunderstanding.'

The officer stepped back, a bemused look on his face. 'Mind yourselves now.'

As he rose from the floor, Paul beckoned her to one of the compact airport's few public seating areas and she followed.

'I really don't have much time,' she said, glancing again at her watch, a silver Cartier that adorned her narrow translucent wrist.

'Fuck. So many questions. It has been thirty-five years. How have you been? And Sarah, where's Sarah?'

'Listen to me, Paul. There's a reason it was so long. We – I – don't want you in our lives. You poisoned our youth. Fucking hell; we had an eccentric upbringing and we got through that just about okay. Then you arrived and all hell broke loose. Our mother dead after her latest fling. What we knew – or thought of her – destroyed. We had to leave our home, our country! Our family broke up. And it all pivoted on you entering our lives!'

She flung her hands in the air, as if releasing the burden of three decades of pent-up anger. Paul's mind swam with a confusion of emotion, but he knew he had to deal in facts, that time was short and so his reporter's instinct kicked in.

'Wait, wait, wait! Let's reel this back. This doesn't make sense.'

'Don't patronise me!' she shrieked.

'OK, one thing at a time. Firstly, nothing – and I mean absolutely nothing – occurred between your mother and I on the night that she passed away. I went to her room, I talked to her about her time in the concentration camp. Anything that Christopher said that suggested otherwise is lies; total fantasy.'

'I'm sorry, I don't believe…'

He cut her off before she could finish. 'You have to believe me. Fucking hell, Google the pair of us. I've spent the last thirty years going around the world reporting the truth from the most difficult places imaginable. He's made a career as a professional liar. Jesus Christ – they even started a fucking war because of his lies! I'm telling you, this man will go to prison for some of what he's done or said. This is the least of his crimes.'

'But why didn't you…'

'Because I wanted to protect you and your sister. I loved your sister. I've never gotten over losing her. I would never have done anything that could hurt her; anything like that. The things your mother told me that night were so unspeakable, so detrimental to the person that we – you – knew her to be that I don't think you'd have gotten over what I learned. She told me that her story was a gift to me as a writer, but it was the most unimaginable burden. And I've tried to write it, I've tried to research it and even now I don't know what to do with it.'

She looked bereft, perplexed, and then asked solemnly, 'What was it? That she was a wartime whore? A collaborator?'

He gasped. 'You knew?'

'Not at the time, no. Later, when we were in Germany, our father told us. That is why they divorced. He learned the truth about her and couldn't live with her; couldn't even live in the same country as her. He grew to hate her for what she was, and I did too...'

'Wait, wait, wait – I can't explain it now, but I don't think the version you were told was the truth – or at least the whole truth. There were lots of things that didn't add up about her story, things that should have been documented but never were. So, for me, the war years are a mystery. She gave me her testimony and some papers, but I've never used those because I don't think it's the whole story. So many things don't add up, Julia. You shouldn't think that about her.'

'I believe what my father told me.'

'Is he still alive? Can I speak to him, or learn what he knows because a whole bunch of things don't make sense, but in short I don't think she was who she said she was.'

'He told me she was a whore, that she was the commandant's mistress...'

'That's not true. She did what she had to survive and there's some unpalatable truths there...'

She moved to leave.

'Please,' he implored. 'You said ten minutes. I have at least four left. What else? Your mother died of a heart attack. She didn't kill herself.'

'I know that,' she said. 'We didn't at the time. We thought she had overdosed.'

'Another of Christopher's lies.'

She said nothing, her lips pursed

'Sarah. What happened to Sarah? Is she well?'

Julia's eyes welled up, the harshness of the earlier visage suddenly cracking. 'I don't know; we haven't spoken for years.'

Finally, she began to talk, the earlier reticence and anxiety melting away.

Sarah had returned to Liverpool from Germany with her father immediately after Nadezhda died. The plan had been for them all to stay so that the girls might complete their education and retain a vestige of normality amidst the cataclysm. But the father brooded in the old house. It had become a hostile place, a place of bad memories. A business contact had always admired the old villa so he struck a deal to sell it quickly. They would move back to Germany.

At the same time, Paul was the source of suspicion and antipathy. Neither Julia nor her father doubted the insinuations about his supposed role on the night of her death. In fact, they believed everything – the seduction, the drunken sex, the suicide. When it was finally put to Sarah, she was in complete denial. Neither her mother nor Paul would do such a thing – until her father told them what he believed were the unspeakable truths about Nadezhda's wartime past. 'The revelation almost destroyed Sarah,' said Julia. 'You, Mother, everyone she loved were not what she thought they were.'

In Hamburg Sarah cowered in her new home, depressed, constantly weeping, not knowing what day it was. Throughout she was distant, aloof, physically and mentally frail. She rarely communicated with either her sister or her father. She rarely left her room. She even put on weight. Terrible rows followed between her, her father and Julia. Unspeakable things were said. And then she was gone.

'We thought that she would come back after a few days, and then when she didn't the police became involved. She had emptied her bank account. There was an inheritance; not a huge amount – proceeds from the house, some royalties – but she took it all and went. The police wouldn't do anything more.

'We thought she'd gone back to England, to you. She went to Cambridge, we know that because she wasn't very good at covering her tracks at first, but it's clear that you didn't see her.' She laughed bitterly. 'My father hired a private detective, but she was good at hiding. At the same time, all sorts of things go through your mind. What if she's unsafe, dead, even? For a time I even looked at my father in a different way, briefly convinced he played some part in her disappearance. Nonsense of course. But the years passed and the questions became fewer. She knew how to find me, but has never tried.

'I have no idea where she went. She had friends in America and on the hippy trail in India. She knew people in the kibbutz movement in Israel. She had the means to live for many years in these sort of places. We tried and tried to find out what happened, but she's gone.'

She looked down at her Cartier and grimaced. The accent-less harshness of her voice melted as she talked and there were hints of her Liverpool accent as she relaxed. But suddenly the businesslike visage was back.

'Please Paul, they'll shut the gate. I said ten minutes; you've had twenty-five. This is very upsetting. I'm glad you've told me what you've told me, but it's part of my past now.' She stood to leave.

'Can I have your contact, your email?'

'The past is the past. Don't you think that if I wanted to contact you I'd have done so already? The famous journalist. Of course, I've read you every day for twenty-five years – from Palestine and Yugoslavia and Iraq. I've often thought of confronting you, the way that you do Serbian war criminals or Palestinian paramilitaries. But I'm glad I didn't, because I'd have been very stupid to do so.' She smiled at him for the first time that day.

'Please, I can tell you everything. I'll email you documents. We'll find Sarah!'

'It's too late, Paul.'

They were rising on the elevator towards the security check in now. He was reminded of the first time that he'd seen her sister, mistaking her for Julia as she descended into the depths of Moorfields station three decades earlier.

'Please…'

From her handbag she pulled out a till receipt and scribbled a Gmail address on its reverse, but as she handed it to him she repeated her assertion. 'It's too late, Paul.'

'It's never too late.'

'For me it is. Please send me what you know.' She leant and kissed him on the cheek. 'Forgive me for thinking the worst. I'm glad I met you again.'

He watched dumbstruck as she left him, scanning her ticket and then melting into the crowds without looking back.

That night Paul emailed her a copy of what he had accrued from Nadezhda's notes and testimony, along with Sean Kendall's PhD thesis and a detailed explanatory note about how Kendall became the unlikely expert on her late mother's life.

She emailed straight back: 'Fucking hell! Sean Kendall; there's a blast from the past!'

As he lay in bed that night he reflected on the strangeness of their encounter. Of all the dangerous places he'd been in the world, the only time he'd had a gun pulled on him was in London's City airport. But then he reflected on the unknowns. Julia hadn't even told him what she was doing in London, how she'd filled her years, what name she had taken after marriage, where she lived. What else hadn't she told him? But for the email address she gave him, she remained one of the lost girls.

Sarah he thought of often over subsequent days. Where had she gone, and why had she begrudged her father and sister to the extent that she cut them entirely out of her life? She didn't seem the sort of person to carry a lifelong grudge: was she hiding something? If she'd followed him to Cambridge, why hadn't she found him?

Days passed, then a week. Paul sent a follow-up email, and then another and another, but Julia had gone to ground again. He even tried to elicit where she might live from the metadata in her email, but that, likewise, drew a blank.

Then, six weeks after their unlikely meeting her name appeared in his inbox.

Subject: Julia
JuliaW62Grassendale@gmail.com 10:51 10 August 2016

Dear Paul,
It's with great sadness that I report that my wife Julia

passed away ten days ago. She fought a battle against pancreatic cancer bravely, quietly and with dignity until the end. When you met her she was seeking an alternative treatment in England, a country she always believed in, but none was forthcoming. She leaves behind myself and my two sons. We are devastated.

It is my belief that after the initial shock it was of great relief that she met you and was able to read about her mother's life before she died.

As you know she remained estranged from her sister until the end and her whereabouts are a mystery.

On her mother, I can add little to your knowledge, but she specifically told me before she passed away that I must tell you that her mother remained in touch with two people from the time that she first came to England.

The first is Hannah Weinreich, who lives in Carlton Hill in St Johns Wood, London. The other is Maurice Musgrave, who lives in Northwood Heights in Highgate.

Julia believed that these two individuals were in contact with her mother until she passed away and that until very recently they were both still alive.

Good luck with your research.

JN

When Paul replied to the email with his thanks it bounced immediately back. The account had already been shut down.

Straight away he called Sean Kendall with the news.

11

Three days later Paul and Kendall found themselves walking down a street of grand, white-stuccoed Nash houses in an affluent corner of north west London. It was the height of summer, but under the shade of St John's Wood's beech trees the air was cool and fresh. They were scarcely a mile from central London, but here the avenues were wide, luxuriant and quiet. Only the distant rumble of the Edgeware Road, which lay several blocks away, impinged on the bucolic setting.

Hannah Weinreich was easy to find and when she answered his call it was as if she had expected it. Yes, she told him, Julia had been in touch in her final weeks; no, she hadn't seen the manuscript but would like to do so before they met. Paul had one biked over from his office, and she called him back a few hours later.

'We must talk,' she told him, and gave him directions to her home. 'I am around all day every day; my time is a virtue but it is not limitless,' she said and laughed a smoker's laugh. 'I am very old, and while I'm here today I might not be tomorrow.' Her accent was in clipped English, but it masked foreign origins.

'I hope you're still there tomorrow, then,' said Paul.

'God willing.'

She lived on the ground floor of a Georgian villa, set back just a few metres from the street. Through the side gate they could spot a more verdant scene in the back: mature shaded gardens, dense and cool in the August heat. Sash windows lay wide open, with shuttered blinds pulled in front of them, casting the interior into shadows.

Weinreich answered the door, a small birdlike woman in her late eighties, slightly hunched, her hair a dark grey and her skin scarred with liver spots.

She was spry and lively for her age, and had set out a plate of pastries on a coffee table, and talked as she decanted hot drinks for her guests. She had lived in the apartment for nearly sixty years, she told them, and had seen the world change around her. The area had been run down, bomb damage untended, the houses fallen into disrepair when she moved in; it was an immigrant area, which was how she came to be there, but she had stayed on in her apartment through gentrification and the neighbourhood's return to one of London's elite addresses.

'Between us we have been trying to unravel Nadezhda's early life for decades,' Paul said. 'Before she died – on the night she died, in fact – she gave me a bag full of documents; bits of writing, mostly, fragments really. I pieced them together and produced the document that you have seen. But it has never been published, and never will be as it stands, because we have never been able to verify its contents. Certain things don't add up. Names mean nothing.

'We've tried, we've researched, we've met lots of people who knew her, but we've never been able to find out if all that she says is true. We feared that she was an unreliable narrator.'

Hannah nodded her head and smiled knowingly as she sipped

from her china cup.

'We haven't found anybody who knew her before about 1950,' added Sean.

She placed her cup on the saucer and replaced it on the table.

'I knew Nadezhda for nearly thirty-seven years until her death,' she said. 'I knew her from the camps.'

'Mauthausen?'

'Auschwitz.'

'You are a survivor?'

She unbuttoned her cuff and pulled up her sleeve. Her skin was loose and wrinkled, and scarring the top of her arm was the unmistakeable six-digit tattoo, the black ink faded to a dark green. The sight of this mark, even after the passage of all these years in which the symbol of the death camps had reached a sort of public consciousness, still shocked.

She continued: 'Nadezhda was an unreliable narrator. She could be anything she wanted to be. She could invent a past or a future. A Jew or a gentile. A socialist or a collaborator. A sterile whore or a mother in waiting. In peacetime she wanted to be a poet, so she told anyone who'd listen she worked for TS Eliot. It's probably how she survived. But what is in this book, as far as I can see, is largely as it was.'

She poured herself another cup of tea and as she did so, Paul asked: 'If she was such an unreliable narrator, how do you know for sure "it is as it was"?'

She smiled, and sipped from her dainty china cup. 'Because I am in it.'

And then she began to talk.

She was born Hannah Cohn in Łódź in 1925 to a family of tailors. For most of her childhood and adolescence there was little that distinguished her upbringing from other working-class youths in her city. Her life was, in many ways, mapped out for her: training in an artisanal trade, marriage, motherhood, work in the family business. But then war came and changed everything. Hers became a familiar tale as life degraded and the war progressed: suppression, segregation, ghettoisation, separation, forced evacuation to the camps, enslavement. In some ways she was lucky. It took more than four years for her to end up in Auschwitz and when she did so she was hardened by years of hardship in the Łódź Ghetto. She knew what it was to be hungry, cold, infected with parasites; to see loved ones taken away, or killed in front of her eyes. 'You never become immune to that, but you learn to be shocked by nothing,' she told them. Only four per cent of the 223,000 who lived in the Ghetto survived life there or in the camps. None of her family made it through.

Fortune favoured her again when she was put on camp kitchen duty, where work was less strenuous and there was the opportunity to purloin food and supplement the meagre rations. 'We were watched over by our own – the Kapos – and risked our lives to do so, but we could steal bits of food. Potato peelings, cabbage leaves, rubbish; what rats lived on. The Nazis decreed us as vermin and that's how we were forced to live.

'The worst of it was always how the camps turned people inwards. Prisoners denounced and fought each other. Stole.'

While there, some time in late spring 1944, there was a selection. 'I had survived one before and those that were taken away were never seen again. You were filled with a constant terror that the end could come at any time, but lined up in front of your oppressors there was instead a strange sort of acceptance that your time had finally come. This time I was one of a dozen girls marched away.' They were taken through gate after gate and to a part of the camp she had never seen before. Convinced she was finally going to be killed, she prayed that she would be shot rather than suffocated in the gas chambers.

'We were lined up, and yelled at. It was an SS man, not a Kapo, so we knew it was a grave situation. My German was patchy, and through the shouts I could barely distinguish what was being said. I was convinced he was going to shoot us. He stepped back – I had seen this happen so many times – and I was sure he'd pull out his pistol and shoot until we were all dead. But instead we were presented with mops, buckets and brushes and led to what I can only describe as a suburban avenue.'

This was where the Kommandant and his staff lived, senior Nazis, the people running the death camps. Hannah and the other girls were added to retinue of cooks, cleaners, gardeners; slaves working in open sight of their masters and their families.

'I was put to work in the Obergruppenführer's house. It was one of the largest and nicest homes there. It reflected his status as a God among people that had decreed themselves God's chosen ones. We were led to think that these people were Aryan "masters" but very often they bore no resemblance: he was small and dark, although his wife was tall and imperious and blond.

'He was benign, polite – even. He didn't shout, he didn't avert his gaze when he saw me. He gave me direct orders, rather than going through an underling. His wife was different. She clearly hated and resented being there. He was often absent – I don't know where he went – and his wife, who hated the place, was left to brood with her children. She was vicious, cruel. She lorded over the fact that my existence lay in her hands. There were times when she beat me. She called me scum, vermin, filth, a cunt. I was deeply afraid of her.'

By the end of the summer the Obergruppenführer's wife and children left, along with many of the other families; a reflection of a war that Germany was now losing. He remained, but his visits away became more frequent. She found herself in his house with little or nothing to do. This inertia, this kind of sanctuary on the edge of humanity's abyss became a salvation at a time when privations in the camp were even more extreme than ever.

Autumn seemed to pass that year in the space of a few weeks. Summer faded and then the temperature dropped. There was snow by November. It was at this time that the Obergruppenführer returned with a young girl. Nadezhda.

'I thought at first it was a relation, but it was clear after a while that she was something else. She was his companion, shared a bed with him; was to all intents and purposes his mistress. She was shy, kept away from me – but there was nothing unusual in that. I don't think I could have imagined what she was; that we shared so many experiences and so much suffering.

'It was only when I collapsed that day through hunger and brought the plates crashing down, that I understood that she was a survivor too, was scared just like me. I thought she would be like the Obergruppenführer's wife. I feared that was the end of me.

'But she was kind. She could see I was in distress. She fed me, she gave me water, she spoke to me in Polish. I understood then that she wasn't as she seemed.'

'She spoke Polish?' asked Paul, but she waved his question away.

She continued: 'In the memoir, she underplays her role at that time. She gave me food not just for myself, but for others in the camp. She let me rest when I should have been working. She cleaned me. When I had diarrhoea she gave me a solution of water and salt and sugar, which may well have saved me.'

'Why do you think she underplayed her role?'

'Because when you do something wrong – even if it's the right thing to do – and you defy orders, you tend to vanquish it from your mind or suppress it. But her kindness and her bravery saved me – I'm sure of that – and others in the camp too while we waited for liberation.'

She smiled at the two men, and took a pastry from the plate, which splintered crumbs and icing sugar as she bit into it. As she crunched, Paul asked her again about Nadezhda speaking Polish.

'The manuscript was correct, it told her life, but she changed some significant details. There were identifying elements that even four decades later she didn't want revealed. Her name. Her home city. Her true nationality. The Obergruppenführer.'

'She told me she was Eleanor Hodys,' said Paul.

'We were all Eleanor Hodys,' replied Hannah. 'She was the mistress of the Auschwitz Kommandant. Nadezhda was the mistress of the Obergruppenführer. I was molested by a Soviet officer. We were far from alone in being sexual victims. Did it matter that one was the victim of a Kommandant, one a general and me just an ordinary soldier? I think what she meant was that we all identified with the one who became famous, notorious for what happened to her – even if she had no say in the matter.'

'So who was she?'

Nadezhda, she explained, was born as Toma Lewandowski in Lvov. She was from a well-to-do-family, educated, had Jewish blood, but the faith was latent; Lewandowski is a Polish name and didn't betray her faith. Yet it was true about her father working for the railways and in the Habsburg Empire. Were they nobility? 'I don't know – it may have just been one of her exaggerations,' said Hannah. 'They were connected and affluent though. Even after all the privations you could tell that from her: the way she was, spoke.'

She explained that her family's main sin in the eyes of both the Nazis and the Soviets – who had controlled the city for the first part of the war – was that her father and uncle were part of the Polish nationalist movement and they feared for their lives from their conquerors. Their capture in late 1943 had an aura of inevitability after four years of hiding.

'You have to understand that even if they were apolitical they would have been targeted. The Soviet secret police deported Poles to the gulags of Siberia and resettlement in Central Asia. In the west the SS sent anyone with an education or who appeared to be intellectual to the camps. There were mass round-ups of military-age men on both sides from the start.'

'The cruelties, the murders, the separations that she detailed, they all happened; they were not something you could make up if you'd not lived through them. The Obergruppenführer was real. He wasn't the Kommandant, that was Rudolph Höss, a different person.'

Sean glanced across at Paul, trying to register his thoughts. So many questions unresolved for years were now clarified. The assumed identity resolved the lack of documentation or supporting records for Nadezhda and her family and cast aside the self-perpetuated Hodys myth. The reluctance to communicate in German he understood now too; for Nadezhda it was her second or third language and she masked her imperfections by avoiding speaking it.

But other things remained unresolved, Paul thought: why persist with the nom de plume? Why lie about her nationality? What of the tattoo that was only inscribed to inmates of a camp she never occupied? What happened after the war?

'When the Obergruppenführer left, she knew that it wasn't the end. Because of her family she had reason to fear the Russians too. She also had papers that said that she was someone else, so why revert back? But it was more than that: it was a situation that she couldn't win. If she was exposed as the Obergruppenführer's mistress she would be labelled a collaborator. She was a victim, but she risked falling to a victor's justice – indiscriminate, arbitrary, unjust.

'The tattoo was my work. If she lacked something everyone else in the camp possessed it would set her apart. So, the night the Obergruppenführer left, with a needle and scalpel and a bottle of ink she was given a corresponding mark.'

Their war was not over yet. They were held in a Red Cross administered holding camp with other survivors based on the site of Belsen. Their physical condition was much better than many of the other residents and they were treated well. The Red Cross and the Soviet troops looked upon them with the embarrassment of people confronted by another man's crimes.

'They were battle-hardened soldiers and nurses, who, having fought on the Eastern Front, had seen the very worst of the fighting; the extremities of war,' said Hannah. 'But for a long time they couldn't look us in the eye. They were ashamed; ashamed that one man could do this to another.'

Nadezhda knew that her home city was lost to the Russians and had no desire to return. Vienna was an alien place, but when peace came there were moves to repatriate her to a city she had never been to.

'We had grown close by then. Both of us had lost everyone we knew. There was nothing in Poland for either of us. Lvov was annexed by the USSR and I – who came from an observant family – had seen the wickedness of anti-Semitism in Łódź. The place scared me. I didn't want to return.

'Nadezhda had a way of bluffing and persuading, and at the point of repatriation she got me on a train south to Austria, away from the Russians, away from Poland into the British occupied part of Austria. Here we were held at a converted alpine hotel and waited. We didn't know what'd happen next. It was late 1945 and Europe was still in turmoil. Austria was in ruins. People were hungry. It was rumoured that the Russians would take control. We didn't want that.

'Between us we resolved that we wanted to go to England or America. There was nothing for us on the continent and Nadezhda felt constantly under threat: from the Russians, from the Germans, from the other survivors.

'But she was clever. Cunning. And the British were more methodical than the Russians. We were debriefed, quite extensively. And here she met Maurice Musgrave.'

∽

Later that afternoon they made the short journey across north London to Musgrave's home on the edge of Hampstead Heath. He had rejected and then ignored any advances since Sean first came across a possible connection. But when Paul first spoke to Hannah and asked if she knew him, she let out a laugh and replied: 'I've been trying to get rid of Maurice for the last seventy years! He won't speak to you? Come with me, you'll struggle to get away from him.'

He lived in a 1930s mansion block and when he opened his door to them, Paul could imagine him living there since the block was first built. He was in his tenth decade, but stood erect in a brass-buttoned navy blazer, a blue striped corner protruding from his left breast pocket. A thin moustache smeared his upper lip, and his thin hair was brilliantined back. He had the aspect of a retired major, for that, it emerged, was precisely what he was.

'I don't know why you've brought these young men, Hannah,' he complained as he sat back down in a winged armchair. 'There's nothing I can tell them. I'm bound by the Official Secrets Act – you know that.'

'Come off it, Maurice, you've spilled the beans in your own book,' she scolded. 'You just want to keep all the best stories for yourself.'

'Ah yes, but the publisher has promised not to publish until seventy years after the event, which will put me in the clear with the Act, you see.' He turned to Paul, and said as an aside, 'She doesn't understand that I might end up in Wandsworth jail for spilling the beans.'

Hannah was fiddling in one of his cupboards and retrieving whisky glasses and, eventually, a bottle of Glenmorangie, from which she began pouring stiff measures for the four of them. 'Work away! Help yourself!' said Musgrave, as if a prisoner in his own sitting room.

The parquet floors of his apartment were furnished as if he lived in a sixty-year-long time warp. There was a Formica table, dusty velvet- covered sofa, a Span sideboard and an old wood-veneered television set. There were framed prints, depicting St Paul's and Westminster in the Blitz, and framed mementoes from his military career. He was very old, but alert and bright eyed.

'Now, Maurice,' the old lady scolded, as she handed him his drink, 'half of London has read this book in manuscript form, so you've broken your precious act many times over. There are no secrets, and they're not going to incarcerate an old fool like you anyway. Anyway, it's 2017: the seventy years are for the most part up. Now tell these boys what happened in Austria at the end of 1945.'

The old soldier grimaced and took a sip from his glass, and tutted to himself as if he had been defeated. 'Okay, okay,' he said, and then wagged his finger towards Paul. 'I don't want to be reading this in my Sunday paper, you understand. At least not until my book is out and you get me my publicity.' He cackled to himself, and began to talk.

At the end of the war he found himself in Aden where he expected to be shipped straight home. He had fought all over the Middle East, mostly in North Africa; so when he was told en route to Britain that he was to be dropped off to join another regiment in Palermo, it was a surprise and disappointment. Here he was placed in counter-intelligence and charged with the task of hunting down Nazis in Italy. 'The Italians weren't bloody interested,' he said. 'Their war had ended a year earlier. They'd already moved on. Half of the people we were hunting were in government within a decade.' Instead they sent him north to Austria, where he was dispatched to the hotel in Carinthia, that was now home to Nadezhda.

'One war had ended and another had just begun: the Cold War,' he explained. 'We were there to debrief the evacuees as much to find out what the Russians were up to than what the Nazis had done.

'Nadezhda was obviously someone very different to many of the others there. She spoke several languages and while others were broken by the war, she was very much alive. She wanted to move on. I also had a suspicion she wasn't exactly who she said she was. We spoke in German as well as English, and she wasn't a natural in either.

'One day, to catch her out, I greeted her in Polish – *Jak się masz?* – How are you – and she responded – *Tak sobie* – I'm so-so – before elaborating on her life awaiting repatriation in Polish. The mask had slipped, and it took her a few seconds to realise it. Her face fell, it was a look of terror at first, as she tried to pass it off as a language she had picked up in the camps. But she knew and I knew.

'I took her in to interrogate her, and she suddenly became quite open. She had it mapped out in her head. She'd help me if I could help her and Hannah get to England. I said I'd try, and she told me that she'd give evidence that'd prosecute a top Nazi – the Obergruppenführer. My ears pricked up: I was five months into the job. I'd not had a sniff of a Nazi in all that time, and here she was handing me a top one on a plate.

'The Obergruppenführer was a chap called Fedor Hargiman. He wasn't an ideologue, he was a functionary with a great eye for detail and organisation. Hundreds of thousands of people died as a result of his instructions. He was probably a very nice chap, as Nadezhda describes, and may never have laid hands on a person in his life. There was a banality in many of these men's evil. In a different world he might have organised shipments of cargo on the railways or steam lines. But here it was human cargo.'

'Here,' he said to Paul, gesturing across to the pile of papers, 'pass me that.' The old man shuffled through the wad of papers. 'This is my book,' he explained without looking up. 'Here!' he exclaimed and began reading from his own text:

'His character is that of an amoral psychopath, which in itself, and correlated with his personal development history, indicates a dearth of parental love and unconscious hostility toward the father. Secondly, there is the influence of National Socialism, which enabled this sadistic psychopath to commit unprecedented

inhumanities in a framework of apparent social and political
respectability. In summary, this man has no moral or ethical
standards; his reaction to the mass murders of which he is
charged is apathetic.'

'The memoir that you sent me only had half the information in
it. She was deliberately vague in her writing, but she had an eye
for dates, places, numbers, names. She spent some of her time
in his office going through his plans, and even purloined some
documents and hid them on her body as she fled. We were soon
able to corroborate lots of the information. In fact, one of the
biggest bits of information she gave us was of one of the sites of
the Wola massacre – where she described seeing a mass grave –
which, ironically, exonerated Hargiman from involvement. But
everything she gave us we were able to follow up on and find
something. There was enough there to prosecute him.

'When we interrogated him, there was no remorse, just this
bureaucratic obtuseness. He spoke about planning, building and
running a concentration camp so that it ran smoothly. I'll always
remember the German word he used: *reibungslos* – without
friction.

'She did not attend his trial – we felt it would be too much and
her role misconstrued. Make no mistake she was a true heroine:
a survivor, a brave and extraordinary witness whose evidence
brought a monster to justice. She provided sworn affidavits under
her "real" name – Toma Lewandowski – and Hargiman hung for
his crimes.

'When it was all over, in late 1947, we decided on a plan:
she would remain Nadezhda Semilinski and her history was
transported from metropolitan Poland to Vienna; her father
would be a socialist, not a Polish nationalist, but everything else

remained the same.

'We had some concerns too. The Russians were upset that we had not just their star witness, but someone linked to Polish statehood and there was a risk they would do something to her. They were killing lots of Polish war heroes at that time. The Israelis and some American Jews were vengeful and there was a danger that they'd see her as a mistress and a traitor – and track her down. So she would remain Nadezhda, she would move to England with the Anglo-Jewish League, who would help set her up in a new life – with the assistance of the service – and she would keep quiet about her past.'

He took a sip from his whisky, and gestured to Sean to top it up with water.

'I'm at the limit of the seventy-year rule now, aren't I chaps?' he said, and laughed. 'L'chaim!' he toasted, and took another sip. 'Can you imagine Nadezhda keeping quiet about anything?' he asked. 'I think in keeping with her spirit I'll keep spilling the beans.' Musgrave had returned to England at the same time as his protégés and his success in Austria saw him taken on by MI5. One of his duties was to keep tabs on Nadezhda, Hannah, and others who had given evidence and found sanctuary in Britain.

'For the most part it was straightforward work. Maintaining files, having a cup of tea with them every now and again, keeping your ear to the ground. These people had suffered so much that they just wanted peace, to lead ordinary lives. But Nadezhda was different. She became famous. She wouldn't keep quiet. She was evasive about her origins, but that only seemed to inspire more curiosity.

'Then there was this stupid bloody interview she did in the late Sixties when she was asked about Mauthausen. I remember going around all the newsagents near the embassies and buying up all the stocks of their TLSs hoping that they wouldn't pick up on it. I don't think they did at first, but it caused a lot of disruption.

'She began to question herself and the past that she had walked away from. She told her husband and he couldn't deal with it; he didn't see the good that she had done, the justice she had served; he only saw her as the lover of a monster, and I fear a lot of people at that time would have seen it the same way. He left her, as you know, and she ended up going a bit crazy.

'But the craziness wasn't without provocation. She had come under the notice of the KGB in the 1970s and they started manipulating her, pushing her towards certain causes. Race relations, trade unions – that sort of thing. Things she believed in anyway. It was benign for the most part and I don't think she was aware of who was ultimately pulling the strings, but it took a darker turn. They wanted her to take more extreme views – calls for the obliteration of Israel, nuclear disarmament, leftist uprising, that sort of thing – and when she wouldn't they were quite explicit about who they were and what they knew, and who would find out if she didn't cooperate.'

'Is this where I come in?' asked Sean.

'Exactly,' said Maurice. 'They used you in the seductress story as a warning to her. It was meant to be a prelude to "Nazi whore" revelations if she didn't do as they asked. There was a big industrial dispute at the Ford plant in Halewood at the time. The KGB were all over it and they wanted her to use her voice in favour of militant action. There were other things too: the drugs bust, which was a ludicrous stitch-up to scare her into compliance.

'It was at this stage that I became seriously involved, pulling strings with the Soviet embassy and telling them to bugger off and leave her alone, which they did after a fashion.'

He sighed; he was tired and the whisky was dulling his eyes.

For someone who had refused to entertain the notion of speaking with Paul and Sean hours earlier, he had spoken continuously for ninety minutes now.

'And then she died, quite unexpectedly,' he said. 'We feared for a short time foul play, that the Israelis had caught up with her or the Russians had done something, but the autopsy said otherwise. She was just someone who was out of time after leading many lives.'

∽

In the pub later that day, after they had said their goodbyes to Maurice and taken Hannah home in the taxi, the two friends reflected on the unravelling of Nadezhda's secrets and mysteries. There was a quiet wonderment that so many questions were finally answered after all those years. Something momentous had happened that afternoon, the closing of a chapter. But so long had passed that there was a sense of unreality that their questions were resolved.

'There's nothing left to know, is there?' asked Paul, and Sean shook his head.

'Does that mean I can use the manuscript you've been taunting me with for twenty-five years?'

Paul smiled. 'Of course. But it was better to wait, wasn't it?'

Sean nodded his assent, and passed Paul another glass of beer.

'Old Maurice gave us a title as well,' said Sean. 'The Many Lives of Nadezhda Semilinski.'

'I like it a lot,' said Paul and, raising his glass, the friends toasted Nadezhda's many lives.

12

The private prosecution of Christopher was over almost before it had even begun. He was too well integrated into the establishment to be allowed such a fall from grace. The party he had served had been out of power for almost a decade, but its friends remained integral parts of the law, business and the media. From his own office on the executive floor of a national newspaper, Paul was better placed than most to see the drip drip of favours to the spin doctor, even when they were oblique.

Public discourse about Christopher's alleged crimes remained focused on his right to a fair trial, which, after two decades as a polarising political figure was not without some rationale.

One day, Paul was summoned to his editor's office. She was the first female editor in the paper's history, a suave and unrelentingly ambitious woman a decade younger than Paul, who seemed more acutely attuned to the ear of the leaders of the two main political parties than her readers, who fell away in their thousands month after month. She had never done a day's reporting in her life.

'Tell me about this private prosecution, Paul. It's not really going to see the light of day, is it?'

He shrugged his shoulders. He felt as if he was fifteen again and hauled into the headmistress's office.

She continued: 'Christopher is sort of, how should I put it… a friend of a friend of a friend. I knew him a little bit when he was at Downing Street…'

'He was my best friend for fifteen years. We grew up together…'

'Yes, well, this is the thing. It's kind of awkward. He's putting it around that it's some youthful vendetta. Over a – how I should I put it? – a girl…'

Paul burst into laughter. 'You're kidding me? Your friend of a friend of a friend put this to you? The guy's lies helped send this country to war! Does he honestly think he's going to prison over an argument we had when we were eighteen?' His editor folded her arms across her chest defensively. Paul continued: 'He lied from a position of power. It's all captured on tape. I gave a sworn affidavit as an eyewitness. It's part of a prosecution brought by victims of one of the worst tragedies in this country's modern history, but this mendacious fuckwit thinks it's because we fell out over a girl nearly forty years ago!

'He lied then as well, you know,' Paul added.

'Do you think it will go to trial in the end?'

He shook his head. 'It's a stab in the dark. It might bring focus back to the real issues, which is the prosecution of police officers. He's just an unpleasant footnote. But we should be ready to go after them all as soon as the prosecution collapses.'

Three weeks later the judge threw out the case at a preliminary hearing, saying a fair trial was impossible. That same night the BBC broadcast a new documentary about police conduct while Paul's newspaper published an eight-page special report. Paul was interviewed as part of the documentary. 'He lied then, he lied about the war, the lies were never-ending,' he said. The clip became a social media meme and by the end of the week it was seen nearly

4 million times. Another clip of a youthful Christopher, repeating the lies on the ten o'clock news about the 'tanked-up mob' was seen by more than twice that many people.

Having been almost impervious to the 'dodgy dossier', this had finally shredded what remained of Christopher's reputation. Within days of the shaming he began to lose his many board positions: a PR company, a financial advisory, a private healthcare company. He deleted his social media profile and seemed to withdraw from public life. Several months later, Christopher re-emerged in Kyrgyzstan, working as an advisor to one of its corrupt president's sons. His reputation in Britain had finally been destroyed.

∽

Paul approached publication of Kendall's book as if it were his own. He spent days poring over drafts and galleys, making incisions to the text and adding words here and there, bringing extra nuance and complexity.

Sean repeatedly offered him a co-author's credit, but Paul always declined, joking that it was his gift to Kendall 'as a writer'. But although the book ultimately challenged Nadezhda's own notions of herself – notions that had in death also formed her family's view of her – he retained same of the old reticence he had four decades earlier in challenging in print what had previously been known about her by her friends and public. Were these secrets better taken to the grave? Or was it better that the narrative was controlled; that the story was told sensitively and in full?

The ultimate question for Paul was whether Sarah would see the book, and if she did, would she step out of the shadows? That had always been his biggest hope and his greatest fear.

The Many Lives of Nadezhda Semilinski was published in March 2019. Thirty-eight years had passed since her death and although most of her work had been out of print for decades, Faber published an accompanying anthology and there were retrospectives in several Sunday newspaper supplements.

At the launch reception at the London Library, they drank wine, ate canapés and toasted a person who had touched their lives in different ways. All of Nadezhda's contemporaries were dead now. Maurice Musgrave didn't live to see his own book published and Hannah Weinreich died just two months after Paul and Sean visited. There was a scattering of familiar faces. Roberts travelled with Bulsara and Sam to be there, and they looked across the room of journalists and critics and publishers with a mixture of scorn and bemusement.

'You choose to live in London with these lah-di-dah literati when you could be with real people like us every week,' Roberts snarked. They still visited The Swan every Friday, a routine they had unfailingly kept up through marriages and careers, children and divorces. They'd never even liked the place, and Paul wondered at times if they even liked each other.

'I'll take my chances being shot at or maimed by ISIS,' Paul joked, pulling another glass from a tray as it was passed around.

'Was it worth it, Paul?' asked Bulsara. 'All the waiting, I mean?'

Four decades spent searching for confirmation, for verification of her words, confirmation that she was not, as he often feared, an unreliable narrator.

'I think getting any story right is always worth the wait,' he said.

Paul looked at his friends. Roberts had barely a hair on his head; Sam's red mop had turned to grey and lines extended from the corners of his eyes. Bulsara was retiring in the summer so that he and his wife could look after their first grandchild on weekdays. They were all middle-aged if not old. Paul had led a full and interesting life, much of it on the edge. But a part of his existence had been on hold ever since Nadezhda passed on her story. It was at once a gift and a curse. He had seen out wars and seemingly unending conflicts, but unravelling her mystery preoccupied him for far longer.

Life certainly hadn't passed Paul by, but elements of it remained unfulfilled. He had never settled. He had no children. His parents were in their eighties now, but when they died he would have no family at all. He had many friends, but those closest to him were all in that room – the three schoolfriends and Sean Kendall. Could he pin those shortcomings on Nadezhda? Certainly his search for the truth about her bred an unrelenting restlessness. And his destiny as a foreign correspondent – which was so disruptive to a normal life – was born partly from his desire to escape the shame that Christopher thrust upon him after her death.

The book was a critical success. At first assumed to be a literary biography, it soon transcended that genre and attracted the notice of war historians. When the book turned to paperback its initial modest success was soon outstripped. It became an airport bestseller, a widely downloaded audiobook and film rights were sold. During the strange year of 2020 when much of the world was locked down because of the coronavirus pandemic, its success became international as readers took inspiration from its messages about human endurance. Paul once feared that revealing Nadezhda's secrets would expose her to ruination, now people saw her as a heroine.

One subplot remained unravelled, however, and that was the whereabouts of Sarah. She remained the lost girl. Maybe, as Julia had once suggested, something dreadful had happened to her; that she, like the rest of her family, was now dead and forgotten. It seemed in many respects the only logical conclusion, for the world was such a hyperconnected place that it was inconceivable that she couldn't not now know the truth about her mother. And if she knew that then surely she would step out of the shadows.

But even as the book sold more and more copies – 100,000, 500,000, and finally a million – Sarah's silence remained constant.

13

They drove through a city transformed. It was a notion that went through Paul's head whenever he returned to Liverpool, but just how far it had changed only seemed to strike him forty years after his departure.

It was late summer in 2021 and he was driving into the city centre, through the low-rise interwar suburbs of the northside and along the Dock Road. His father sat beside him in the passenger seat, pointing out buildings and businesses that had gone, offering a commentary on what had risen in their place.

A mile from the city centre, the late Victorian industrial colossus of the city's tobacco warehouse, the biggest brick building in the world, now turned into luxury apartments, rose thirteen storeys high on one side of the road; on the other, at Bramley Moor Dock, Everton's new stadium, a vision of concrete and glass was being built on the banks of the Mersey.

'You know we used to do raids over the other side of the Tobacco Warehouse where they had the Sunday markets?' his father said as they drove over the dock bridge and towards the city centre.

'No, Dad, you never told me that.'

'You know the old Heritage Market? It was a haven for knocked- off goods from the docks. They never even had to transport it very far. We'd go off with the coppers and customs and excise men, a couple of Sundays a year, about eleven o'clock – straight after Mass, it was. We'd round all the scallies up, go through their takings and have them in court the following week.' He let out a chuckle. 'We'd be done by two o'clock. I'd join your mum at the golf club. I'd get a full day's pay at triple time. Never make the blindest bit of difference, mind you. The same fellas would be back the following week.'

Paul's mother had died earlier in the year, and arthritis had seen an end to his father's golfing days. Paul increased the frequency of his visits from London, keeping the old man company and making sure he looked after himself. Many of his father's old friends, as well as his sisters, had passed away. He called Paul during the week to complain there was no one else left.

'Old age is cruel,' he lamented. 'Never grow old.'

Paul was never especially close to his parents. They were socially conservative and parochial, and he was neither. He found his mother excruciatingly overbearing and grandiose. After the initial pride at seeing her son's name in print, she had long stopped reading his newspaper – 'Full of lefty nonsense' – and became exasperated when he made the link between the wars that he covered and the influx of destitute refugees – 'scroungers' – that she claimed were 'clogging up our streets'. She unashamedly voted for Brexit, taunting him when the results came in that the country was going to be reset along the lines that favoured 'true Britons'. If his career had been about telling the truth about the worst of humanity, it had been a failure insofar as it failed to dent his mother's consciousness.

When she died of heart failure, after the initial mourning it seemed as if a burden had lifted from his father. He became more engaging, more open to the world. He started taking an interest in Paul's work, and he read through his back catalogue on his iPad as if opening his eyes to four decades of history. He'd call him about reports on Yugoslavia or Iraq or Palestine from decades earlier and profess, 'Well I never knew that!' or, 'That's bloody outrageous!'

The pace of Paul's work had eased. The world slowed down after 2020's great pandemic. There was still human misery and suffering at every turn, but there seemed less of a compunction to follow it himself. In any case, the economic catastrophe unleashed after the pandemic had decimated the travel industry, while shearing budgets across the media. The world had become a bigger, more difficult place to travel and the days of picking and choosing his own stories were at an end.

He took his father to major golf tournaments and to the Formula One Grand Prix at Silverstone. There were day trips to the Lake District and York. Sometimes he even joined Paul and his friends at The Swan, crossing the last great divide between their generations.

Today they were heading to a preview of a major new exhibition in the crypt of the Anglican Cathedral, *1981: A City in Turmoil.* It was a major retrospective of the Toxteth Riots and their legacy. The law company of which Roberts was now a senior partner were sponsoring the event and putting on a lunch afterwards. Bulsara and Sam were going and Paul was bringing his father and Sean Kendall too.

'Do you remember your mother, when the riots happened?' his father asked with a chuckle. 'She saw Upper Parliament Street burning, and thought the darkies were going to come and ransack our little cul-de-sac at the other end of the city!'

'Dad! You can't say that word,' Paul scolded.

'Sorry, coloureds.'

'Dad!'

'It's a different world, isn't it? There's so many words you can't say any more.'

It was a glorious summer's day, the sun shone from a cloudless sky and the air was fresh and cool. They were driving along The Strand now, past the Liver Buildings and the Albert Dock. In 1981 there was talk about filling in the dock and making it into a car park; now thousands visited it daily, and as they stopped at the traffic lights Paul and his father got a glimpse of that day's clientele: Chinese, Koreans, gigantic American pensioners with their belongings stuffed into bumbags, Spanish students and a Dutch cycle tour.

Further along, as they headed to Upper Parliament Street and through the Baltic Quarter, the people on the streets took on a younger, hipper complexion. When these streets hadn't been torn apart by rioters, it was the city's red light district, a place of drug-addled prostitutes desperately turning tricks for a hit. Now it was a place of clothing boutiques, cafes, micro-breweries and media companies.

At the cathedral they parked up and showed their invitations. They were waved into the vast vaulted hall, where the low chatter of other guests rumbled up into the eaves. The exhibition took place down a staircase in the crypt, and Paul took his father's arm as they took a slow path down into the cool depths of the cathedral. Here, the chatter was louder, and Roberts – standing erect in the formal suit that had, over the years, become his uniform – marched over and took Paul's father by the hand.

He led Paul's father off towards the start of the exhibition, boards with photographs and glass cases with artefacts; there were mannequins of policemen with original riot shields, charred and battered by debris, and on a plinth was the carcass of an Austin Allegro, which had formed part of a barricade. The room was filled with several hundred people, although as Paul couldn't help but notice, few of the faces were black. Everything had changed and yet nothing at all.

He helped himself to a glass of champagne, and started to follow his father and Roberts, when he bumped into Bulsara and Sam.

'Your dad's enjoying himself,' Bulsara observed.

'Well, a whole new world has opened up since Mum died,' Paul laughed. 'It gets him out the house anyway.'

They talked of their recollections of the summer of 1981. The eternal wait for the exam results, the long nights in the pub, the riots that at once seemed so far away and then so near, Paul's summer of romance. At some point they were joined by Sean Kendall and these middle-aged men swapped stories in the easy bustle of the cathedral's vault.

'You know, it's funny we're here looking back at 1981,' Kendall reflected. 'For me that year will always be about Nadezhda Semilinski passing away, and this is where she was finally laid to rest.'

Paul looked at him surprised.

'Here? In the cathedral?'

'In St James' Cemetery, yes.'

The cemetery sat below the rock outcrop on which the vast sandstone cathedral was built. The cathedral and ancient oak trees cast it into cool shadows, and catacombs were built into the walls. There was an oratory and a lodge and a memorial to William Huskisson, a Georgian-era MP who was killed on the maiden journey of the Rocket, the world's first passenger rail locomotive.

Kendall explained that while the cemetery had closed in the

1930s, there was a small writers' garden where literary figures from the city could be interred. It was seldom used – there were scarcely a dozen burials there in half a century – but at the end of 1981 Nadezhda's ashes were placed there and a small plaque dedicated to her.

'I never knew any of this!' said Paul. 'It's not in your book, is it?'

'It is!' said Bulsara.

'None of you told me this!' laughed Paul.

'It's there in the book, soft lad,' said Kendall.

'Can you take me to see it while we're here?'

'Sure, let's go now.'

∽

They left the cathedral and descended a pathway into the gardens of St James' Cemetery. The blue skies had now filled with clouds and there was a sudden humidity in the air. Puddles under foot were left by a brief downpour and there was a sense in the air that another shower was imminent.

The cemetery was an oasis in the middle of the city. Gravestones had been cleared and fixed to the walls and park benches invited visitors to sit and relax. Magnolia and rose bushes grew from beds. A family with young children splashed in the puddles beneath the Huskisson memorial.

The writers' garden was at the far side of the cemetery, beneath a fifty-foot wall of sheer sandstone that rose up to street level. There was less order here; they had to trample through long grass, and an iron gate gnarled with rust stood in their way. Kendall forced the gate open and they stepped into a small walled garden, no more than forty foot in each direction. It was allowed to overgrow, as if it were at once out of sight and out of mind.

Before them lay a sea of broken masonry; bracken; mud; brambles and dark puddles. Immediately in front of him a wild rose bush trawled out of control, snaking across what remained of the footpath and over decaying headstones. Wilting petals hung off it and lay strewn across white masonry, gravel and into puddles.

'It's over there,' said Kendall, pointing towards a darkened corner.

'Do you mind if I have a moment to myself?' Paul asked.

'Take as long as you want.'

He walked around the rosebush and back onto the path, his pace slow as he sought to avoid the obstacles spewed randomly across. All was quiet, all was still except for the distant hum of an aircraft 10,000 feet overhead and the light breeze rustling among the trees. In this corner of the graveyard the trees shot up from every free space of dirt they could find, regardless of the carnage they may wreak. One grave-bed was uprooted by a tree, the roots pushing the headstone out of its resting place.

Finally, he came to the corner where Nadezhda's ashes were interred. A small white headstone bore her name, along with the inscription 'Poet, Mother, Survivor.'

He stood there for several minutes, thinking about all that he had lost and gained from ever knowing her.

§

Lunch was being served on long tables bedecked in white cloths laid out in the nave when Paul and Sean returned to the cathedral.

'Where've you lads been?' asked Paul's father.

'Just visiting an old friend,' Kendall deadpanned, as he placed a linen jacket on the back of his chair.

Roberts was playing host, passing hither and thither between tables, addressing guests and ensuring wine glasses were filled. He leaned over their table and asked how they were enjoying the hospitality.

'It's a fine spread, David,' said Paul's father, addressing Roberts by his first name. 'But we could have done with some soup to start off with; warm the bones up.' He took a sip from his wine glass, his third that afternoon, and Roberts gave a small frown at the rebuke from the old man, who was now demolishing a bread roll.

'It's an interesting exhibition, Roberts; I'm going to go and have a proper look when lunch is finished and the place has emptied out a bit,' said Paul.

'You'll see yourself up there,' said his father.

Paul laughed uncertainly.

'What do you mean, Dad?'

'There's a big photo of you up there.'

'Dad, I think you're getting confused.'

'Excuse me young man...' He looked around at Paul's friends with a gesture of comic offence. 'I may be eighty-seven years old, but I know my own mind and I know my own son. There was a little exhibition in an anteroom of black and white photography and there was a picture of you there, aged about eighteen.'

'Roberts, you organised this event – is this some sort of trick?'

Roberts stood back and raised his hands defensively. 'I don't know anything; I just write the cheques.'

Paul's father put down his bread roll. 'I'm telling you what I saw; there was a picture of you.'

Paul laughed and stood up, taking his jacket from his back and putting it on his chair. 'Right then! I'm not going to be able to eat my lunch without proving the old man wrong.'

With that he marched off, down the marble stairs and back

into the depths of the crypt. It was silent here, and empty too, but for a couple of gallery attendants who stood bored behind the desk.

They directed him to an opening at the end of the hall, and Paul set on his way, hungry and muttering about his father, but he was immediately brought to a silence, for in front of him, magnified on huge boards, in grainy black and white, were the scenes of forty summers ago.

These pictures were not the backdrop to his summer, they were scenes that he had actually lived. The bombed-out church. An outraged drug addict, cursing as he and Sarah fled. The dilapidated grandeur of Hope Street. Bonkers and Tommy, the street urchin brothers playing football. The broken clock at Salisbury Dock, its faces all fixed at nineteen past the hour. The gigantic voids of an abandoned warehouse. And there he was, as his father had said, a young, eager-faced vision of himself; a teenager, stood beside the decaying Albert Dock.

And suddenly there she was too, Sarah, posing next to a fly poster caricaturing Margaret Thatcher in a photograph he had taken himself at the Pier Head, beneath it the slogan 'Not Wanted'. He had never owned a photograph of her, only what rested in his memory; and here she was, suddenly in front of him, perfectly preserved after all these passing decades, the lost girl, her porcelain skin, lopsided grin and black hair luminous in the grain of a black and white poster. His heart pounded. There she was again, a ghost resurrected, kissing Paul on the *Royal Iris*, the Liver Buildings in the background separated by the muddy expanse of the Mersey. He was looking at the title poster now. *1981: My Summer of Love*. Photographs by Sarah Weisz.

'Excuse me!' yelled Paul into the empty gallery. 'Excuse me!' He could hear the footsteps of the gallery attendant, who within seconds was beside him as he stood open-mouthed reading the captions, muttering as if a madman, 'It's me. It's me.'

Sarah Weisz is a contemporary artist who was born in Liverpool in 1963.

'What is it, sir? Are you okay?'

After living in Germany she settled near Eilat, Israel, where she has lived and worked for many years.

'It's me, I'm on these pictures, a long time ago – can you see?'

Her work is in many collections including the Pompidou Centre, Tate Modern, Walker Art Center, Dallas Art Museum, Sprengel Museum and Reina Sofia Museum, amongst others.

'Are you okay, sir?'

'I knew the artist. I took one of the pictures!' he stammered. The attendant looked at him as if he were crazy. 'But the name is wrong: it's Sarah White, not Weisz. Why is the name wrong? It's Sarah White. Why is it wrong?'

They stood staring at the biography for a few seconds before the attendant broke the silence. 'Maybe she didn't want her name to be anglicised when she moved to Germany. Weisz is German for White, you see?'

And in an instant, forty years of elusiveness dissolved.

Part 5: Sarah

1

It was the ceaseless trilling of the telephone that she always remembered about the day her mother died. She was in the garden, dozing under a canopy of apple trees, when she heard its distant ring. In reality it probably rang for no more than thirty seconds, but at the time it seemed like an eternity and she always recalled her rising irritation that her father hadn't answered. Why wasn't he answering? Would she have to go and get it? He knew she didn't like speaking in her second language.

They were such silly considerations. Perhaps somewhere in her subconscious she knew that that call would change everything.

It came to a silence, and for a few seconds there was nothing but the chatter of birdsong. Then from the house she could hear the low tone of her father's heavily accented English, which rose quickly to a point of exasperation. 'Julia, will you please calm down!'

She sat up then, alert; knowing that something was wrong.

A couple of minutes later her father emerged into the garden, a bucolic scene of rambling trees, wildflower and meadowgrass. His face was sombre, inscrutable. She knew at that moment that something terrible had happened to her mother.

⏀

They drove to Liverpool in silence, a twenty-hour journey broken up by an overnight ferry from the Hook of Holland to Harwich. Her father puffed on his pipe, filling the car with sweet blue smoke as she looked out at the passing country.

This hadn't been a death foretold. Her mother had no ailments. She could be morose and suffered crippling depressions that left her bed-bound, but she was rarely physically ill. She wasn't old and set against her father – who always lent the perception of a spry old man – she was positively youthful. And yet in being volatile, constantly living on edge, her passing carried a certain inevitability. 'Your mother's lived many lives,' her friend Julian would tell her on his visits to the house. 'She's got many miles on the clock.'

Sarah took the news with a sort of stunned silence. Her father wasn't one for consolation. He was not a man to throw his arms around her.

'I'll go and pack,' she told him, and left him standing alone in the hallway.

⏀

Julia used to say that any joy in her father disappeared the day that he left the family home a decade before Nadezhda died. There was no gathering storm of marital discord, no rising crescendo of arguments. While their mother was passionate and emotional, their father was a placid man, someone of impeccable routine and habit. He arrived home at exactly the same time each evening to join the family meal, then spent his evenings listening to jazz and reading. He seemed in awe of his wife, of her fame and recognition and although they belonged in different professions she retained a deep respect for his learnedness and knowledge of everything from Weimar-era jazz musicians to modern playwrights; classical music to her fellow poets.

They went out several nights a week, to the Playhouse or Everyman, and for weekends away in London. They were a sociable couple and their home was always open to an array of artists and writers who they called their friends. These were decorous occasions, far removed from the wild nights Nadezhda hosted after their marriage broke down. They sipped their wine and chattered. Theirs was a comfortable bourgeois bohemian idyll. They had their daughters, who were loved. They were respected. They wanted for nothing. It was content, secure, perhaps a touch dull at times in comparison to the other lives Nadezhda had lived, but culturally rich and full of interesting interludes and people. Why then had it broken down?

The fights started like an explosion, without warning; it was a volcanic eruption, completely unexpected. Their father, who never raised his voice, shouting in German and English; Nadezhda screeching and wailing. Tears. The sound of objects being thrown around her study. Slammed doors. The girls curled up together in bed, holding each other tearfully until the unexpected storm passed.

When it did, there was the low but indistinguishable murmur of their father's voice; businesslike, as if on the phone to his work colleagues. Their mother was acquiescent, agreeable, and at some stage the girls fell asleep, convinced that the ruckus had simply been one of those things that passed between parents.

Except this didn't pass. The following day their father didn't return home on the 17:08 from Moorfields, as he did every day, or any service after that. They discovered later that he was staying in the art deco splendour of the Adelphi Hotel and commuting on foot to his offices. He returned briefly the following weekend to collect some belongings, and explained that he was going to Germany for work. There was no timescale put on the trip. In fact he never returned. He had spent the intervening days delegating management of the business to one of his associates, while transferring the holding company back to Hamburg, where it retained offices. England had been his home since he was a young man, forced to flee Germany, but now he was escaping the place he had found sanctuary for four decades. He fled his home and his marriage and never came back.

The girls always assumed it was one of their mother's infidelities that caused the marital breakdown. Later, when they were older, she always denied that was the case. 'I never looked at another man when I was with your father. I swear that is the truth.' For his part, he remained inscrutable, distant – both physically and emotionally – and tightlipped, not just about Nadezhda, but most things. In Germany he worked longer hours and at home lost himself in his books and records. His daughters visited him every summer, and each February went skiing with him in the Swiss Alps. But he never said much about anything, with each passing year growing more distant from the girls. His second marriage to a much younger woman heightened the gap. When she was sixteen, Julia stopped visiting altogether, leaving Sarah to see him on her own and spend weeks amidst a silent house while he worked, or sitting among his brooding silences.

It wasn't sadness that permeated her father's life, it ran deeper than that. There was a resentment, a sort of controlled anger about whatever unspoken dispute had ended their marriage. He was joyless, utterly mirthless, and never was Sarah reminded more of this than as she sat with him as they drove through the Fens and across England to the city her father had once called home.

ᔕ

In the gloaming, they found Julia in the kitchen, smoking silently, alone, brooding over a mounting pile of ash and cigarette butts. Sarah went and hugged her, but her sister's body remained erect, refusing to fall into her embrace. It was as if everything they once had between them was lost in the days since she left for Germany. Their father stood uselessly at the door, not venturing towards either girl.

'I'll take your mother's room,' he said solemnly, by way of greeting and left them alone.

Over the following days they passed silently, like ghosts in this big old house. Their mother's death made national news. There were fulsome obituaries and fellow writers and activists lined up to heap praise and tell stories about her. Journalists turned up at the house and the phone rang so much that in the end her father pulled the cord from the wall and they were again enclosed by silence. The door was left unanswered as they retreated to their bedrooms and soon the knocking retreated too.

Christopher appeared from time to time and his presence afforded some relief from the gloom that beset a home that was once so vibrant and full of life. But where was Paul? Christopher was evasive when she asked, and Julia remained entirely aloof, remaining in her room and maintaining long silences when spoken to. When Sarah went to the hallway to reconnect the phone, her father stopped her.

'What are you doing? Now is family time. Tomorrow we lay your mother to rest. The boyfriend can wait.'

Sarah tried to argue against the unfairness of it, that

Christopher was omnipresent, but her father merely shrugged his shoulders as if to say that Julia was no longer under his control.

The funeral was a brief austere affair at the city's crematorium, but their father had insisted on a private non-denominational ceremony. 'There will be time for a memorial when the dust is settled,' he insisted. There were no guests, no song, no wake afterwards; just a civil celebrant who uttered a page of words that her father put together. Sarah could not stop crying. She couldn't imagine anything Nadezhda would have wanted less.

In the silence that palled over her home, an unreality rinsed over her life. She could not comprehend the permanence of her mother's absence. Having experienced her depressions and absences in the past, part of her expected her to just appear in the kitchen one morning and life to carry on as it always did. But it never happened, of course.

In the loneliness that accompanied her grieving, she longed for her lover. She wanted Paul, she needed him. It was as if she had stopped existing in the absence of human contact. Yet for reasons she could never quite comprehend, she remained fixed in the house. It was as if the family time that her father decreed became an unspoken curfew to which she would unquestioningly adhere. Years later she looked back at these days of solemn inertia with regret. Had it really only been weeks earlier that they had taken long rambling walks and bike rides around the city, or lay in her bed, making love? There were times that this serious, studious boy, to whom she had given her heart and her body, seemed like a dream, an apparition who had filled a void in an unending summer.

Julia was silent and emotionless throughout these terrible days, an inelegant dishevelment taking hold of her. Sarah would head to her room for succour, but find her sister buried under her duvet in a half-sleep, or be so unrelentingly focussed on a book that her gaze never lifted and Sarah would leave. There were bags under her eyes, as if she hadn't slept for a week; her skin grey and lifeless, hair matted with grease. It was as if she had become a complete stranger in the few weeks they were apart. After a while, Christopher stopped coming too and although she never mourned his absence, it added to the ethereal mood.

Her father, too, remained enigmatic, spending hour upon hour in Nadezhda's study, pulling books from walls and searching through boxes of documents and manuscripts, searching for something he couldn't describe to her. He waved away offers of assistance. 'It's something your mother worked on; very special, very personal. She described it to me once; I don't know what it is, but when I see it I will do so...' At night he sat in the garden, puffing his pipe, enigmatic and ruminative; monosyllabic whenever his daughters tried to engage with him.

A house once full of life and creativity became a place of shadows and silence. And then one morning, entirely unexpectedly, Paul turned up at their front door.

ᕤ

But for the fact that Sarah was passing down the stairs at the time, she wouldn't have known anyone was there. From the front step she could hear voices spoken in a forced hush, the shrillness of Julia's tone, the rumblings of an argument about to break out. Who could it be? There had been no journalists for a week. Was it one of Nadezhda's more unpredictable friends? Jehovah's Witnesses or an unwanted salesman? She ventured down the hallway and pulled open the front door. It was none of those people. Her heart leapt. It was Paul.

'Paul! Oh, my dear Paul. How I've missed you,' she cried as she rushed past her sister. He opened his arms and cradled her, whispering words of condolence and longing, of his enduring love. She wept. He held her tightly. She had waited for weeks for that moment, but amidst the sweet sorrow something seemed to have changed. It was imperceptible and even though she reflected on the moment many times in the weeks and years that followed, she could never quite understand it. Even as their bodies embraced it seemed different; as if they could no longer just melt into one. He kept saying, 'I'm sorry. I'm so, so sorry,' while from behind them she could feel her sister's eyes burning holes through her. She remembered her father's mantra of 'family time', this undefined period of mourning in which life had seemed to stop.

Eventually she stepped back and, wiping her face, fixed him with a grin.

'Paul, I have to go. It's family time now.'

She kissed him on the cheek and stepped back into the house. Julia remained on the step, arms folded, glaring at her boyfriend.

'I'll call you when all this is over, I promise,' she said. But it was a vow she did not keep.

§

The fighting started almost as soon as the front door closed.

'What was all that about?' Julia hissed.

'What?' Sarah replied, perplexed and blinking, as she stepped back into the hallway.

'He has no place here after what's happened.' She barged past her sister and headed to the stairs.

'What? Since when are you my keeper?'

Julia turned and growled. 'Stay away from him!'

'What the hell are you talking about?' Her sister was marching up the stairs now, the sound of her feet stomping carrying through the empty house. 'Julia!'

She turned around at the top of the stairs. 'You heard! Stay away!'

Sarah ran up after her. 'Are you insane? Have you taken leave of your senses?' As she reached the top, Julia's bedroom door slammed. Sarah tried to push the door open, but her sister had sat behind it. She pounded the door with her fists. 'What are you talking about?' She beat the door again. 'Julia! What do you mean?' But Julia would not budge and remained defiantly silent.

Sarah made her way back downstairs for the front door and out into the street. She looked up the treelined road, but Paul was long gone and the whine of the local train in the near distance told her that he was already heading back north and away from their elegant riverside suburb at the south of the city.

'Sarah! Come back here!' Her sister was stood at the front door again, screaming instructions like a mad woman. Sarah stood looking at her as if some demon had taken hold of her. From a neighbour's house she could see the twitch of a curtain, as Julia, near hysterical, called her again. Sarah marched back up the path.

'What is this about?' she demanded, as Julia slammed the front door again. She glared at her sister, eyeball to eyeball in a way that she could never remember doing, even as a young child.

'We need to talk,' she replied.

'Talk to me then. You're behaving like you're insane.'

'Come and sit down.'

'No,' said Sarah. 'We talk here.'

'OK, we'll talk here,' said Julia. 'Paul isn't everything that you thought that he is.'

And so she began to recount the events of the night their

mother died – the wild partying; Paul drunk on his own success; her mother and boyfriend seen talking and drinking late into the night, and then walking hand in hand up the stairs. Sarah let out a low terrible moan, a repetitive howl of 'no', that became more terrible and more distended as the tears flowed down her face. It was a narrative that was framed by Christopher's recollections, but concluded with Julia finding their mother's body the following afternoon. It was intoxicated, she said, by a cocktail of prescription drugs, alcohol and guilt.

Sarah slid to the floor sobbing, as if she had been struck in the stomach. Her sister towered over her.

'This isn't true,' she said. 'It can't be true.'

'How can't it be true?' Julia demanded. 'It's not as if she didn't have form in this sort of thing.'

'Oh shut up Julia, you know the Kendall story was a lie.'

'Was it? And this wasn't a lie too?'

'She was our mother! She wouldn't do that sort of thing.'

'She was capable of anything.'

'She loved us, she wouldn't.'

'Go and ask your boyfriend, then. Why was he sobbing that he's sorry, he's so sorry? What's he got to be sorry about.'

Sarah let out another sob. 'He was sorry for our loss!'

'Was he? I don't believe a word that comes out of his mouth.' She glowered down and taunted. 'Go and phone him. Go on! Or even better, wait and see if he tries to come back. He knows he's been sussed. That's the last we've seen of him.'

'It's not true.' She cast Julia a look of defiance.

'You brought a cancer into our home. It swallowed poor Mama. Don't let it do the same to you.'

The silence over the following days cast a deathly pall over Sarah. She clung to the duvet, waiting for the phone to ring; for the doorbell to go. Strewn across the wooden floorboards of her bedroom were images of the summer. A cousin in Hamburg had access to a darkroom and she had spent a long afternoon bringing to life the cartridges of film taken with Paul, walking the beautiful ruins of their home city. Had this all just been illusory? Had it all just been an impossible wonderful dream?

She pondered why she loved him, what made their embrace so quick, so binding, so all-consuming, so right. It was a question she asked herself many times over the following decades. Was it just a youthful passion, something that was driven by hormones and inexperience and seemed more real and intense because of it? Or did something unique bind them? In the loneliness and quiet of these days she was reminded that she had always felt an outsider, a tourist in her own city, as if she didn't belong. Even here in her own home she had begun to feel like a stranger. In Paul she found someone who shared that remoteness and incongruity in his surroundings; they were both outsiders but when they came together they finally belonged. That was at the heart of their love, she told herself, and that is why it would endure.

But the call never came. Paul remained silent on the other side of the city. Over these days she passed her sister on the stairs or in the kitchen, ignoring her, but seeing the glint in her eyes that asked: *and he's still silent?*

Days, a week, a fortnight passed, but the phone did not ring. She wondered in darker moments whether Julia was manipulating his absence, creating a barrier, diverting calls or hiding letters. At others it was as if Paul's ongoing silence was an admittance of his guilt. There was nothing to physically stop Sarah making the call herself, but Julia's challenge – *wait and see if he tries to come back* – cast a psychological barrier. She willed him to call, to break the silence, to prove her sister wrong. But every hour that passed when he didn't increased her belief that he had committed a grievous wrong.

§

Her father in these days and weeks existed in the shadows, prowling the house and immersing himself in the detritus of his ex-wife's affairs. There were so many books, so many papers to sort through that it seemed at times as if he might be overwhelmed. He was permanently preoccupied, distracted, consumed by the minutiae of Nadezhda's affairs, but unwilling to share the burden with his daughters.

In Sarah's room he appeared several times a day, bringing her coffee or food, or simply to say hello. He was detached from her life beyond her education and knew little about Paul other than his existence. He never asked about him, never mentioned him; his assumption was that her depression was a form of grieving for her mother, not at the loss of her boyfriend.

September came and with it the realisation that Paul had left for Cambridge. Her melancholy took on a physical complexion. She felt nauseous all the time. She lay alone and listless in bed at night, unable to sleep and when dawn came vomited what little she had eaten the previous day. Julia, whom she hadn't spoken to in weeks, appeared at her bedroom door and looked in at her with a mixture of anguish and concern. She was faded and weak.

One evening her father came to her room and told her they were moving to Germany. There was no discussion, no debate. It was presented as a fait accompli. She was too weak to argue. It was as if she had given up on life.

'I have a place for you at the conservatory, near my home there,' he told her. 'You can board during the week and spend weekends with us. Julia starts at art school in ten days.

'The house is being sold. The proceeds will be split between you and Julia. It will set you up in life.'

He looked around the room, with its double-height ceilings and views out towards the river. Amidst the dishevelment, it was a handsome house, in many ways the perfect place to bring a family up. But that life had passed them by. It was a disruptive childhood, full of schisms and hidden truths and lived in the shadow of a character as big, brilliant and flawed as her mother.

'This place has too many memories, there's too much history,' said her father. 'I fear a time when your mother's past will catch up with you. I think it's best for everyone that we leave.'

She didn't ask what he meant, didn't even think about it at the time, although for years those words would haunt her. A few days later they were on the road again.

2

It was the magic hour when the sun started to set and the date palms filled with the chatter of thousands of starlings. Coolness had started to fill the Jordan Valley and a southerly breeze from the Red Sea grazed the trees. At the top of an eighty-foot high palm, Shlomo was fixed with a harness to the tree, like an engineer installing telephone lines. He had a large hooked knife, and with his left hand he cut at the tops of bunches of date kernels. They were big bunches of arid husks, some weighing twenty kilos, and he tore at the sinews of the branches, trying not to graze himself on the sharp scales on the tree trunk. Sarah and Marie stood at the bottom trying to catch them before they hit the ground before placing the harvest into a wheelbarrow.

'Where do you think you'll go after the harvest is complete?' Sarah asked as they waited for the next bunch to fall from the tree.

Marie was a transient, passing through as she made her way around the world with her backpack, although Samar was a dead end. Ten miles south lay the port of Eilat, but the borders on each side with Jordan and Egypt had been stubbornly shut for years. Few of the passing ships took passengers, least of all single Irish girls on the hippy trail.

'I'll take a boat to wherever it'll take me,' she replied in a north Dublin drawl that immediately reminded Sarah of the Scouse accent. She grinned to herself: that's what they all said. 'And you?' she asked. 'Where will you go next?'

Sarah smiled. 'Nowhere,' she answered. 'This is home now.'

She had come a long way in a short period of time. Life here was unrecognisable to the one she had led as a schoolgirl in Liverpool. Two years had passed since she left the city, almost silently in the night. She said no goodbyes; indeed could scarcely even remember packing her things. The removal men came in the morning after they had left in her father's Volvo, bound for Harwich and a new life in Germany, and packed the remainder in tea chests and followed their journey the following day.

She remembered sitting in the back of the car and watching as they passed out of the grandiosity of Grassendale, along Aigburth Road and then Booker Avenue, past Strawberry Field and Netherly and out onto the M62 and away from Liverpool to their new life, and thinking of it as a surrender to other people's preconceptions. She thought of her father's warning – *I fear a time when your mother's past will catch up with you* – and wondered what he meant and who really cared. Part of her wanted him to stop the car and to say to hell with it. But she had lost all her old defiance, all her willingness to fight. The reality was that she didn't care any more where she went or where she lived. Other than its familiarity, Liverpool at that time held no more allure than Hamburg or anywhere else she could think of.

Julia still seeped with resentment. She seethed and snarled and spoke in monosyllables to her sister and father. How she had acquiesced with her father's desire to move them to Germany Sarah did not know. In the weeks since Nadezhda's death Julia had cropped her hair and brushed it into a dark quiff, layering her already ghostly white face with white powder and smears of rouge to adopt the garb of the New Romantic. Christopher was dispensed with and a new boyfriend, a young beefcake with a thuggish demeanour, briefly replaced him. It seemed to be a provocation to her father, who she openly resented. But her full fury was reserved for her sister.

She blamed Sarah wholly for everything that had happened: Nadezhda's death, the grieving, the disruption and dislocation and now the move to another country. She had this slightly crazed look in her eye, as if it wasn't clear what she would do or say next. Throughout this ordeal, Sarah was largely passive, forlorn, sick. But the tension that suffused the two sisters was palpable.

It was a long, miserable journey to Hamburg. Throughout the North Sea crossing Sarah was violently sick. Their father sat on his bunk impassively reading a Graham Greene novel and puffing on his pipe, Julia lay down listening to her Walkman, while Sarah hugged the toilet willing the journey to be over. When they arrived at her father's home she was grey from nausea and exhaustion.

He lived in a three-storey detached house in Blankenese, overlooking the Elbe. In many ways it was similar to the home they had left in Grassendale, a merchant's villa overlooking the stretch of water that made the family wealthy. But whereas Nadezhda presided over a scene of decaying chaos, in Hamburg, Steffi, her stepmother, presided over order. The house was impeccably decorated, the walls lined with Charles' art collection. There was rare Italian furniture, acquired on their summer holidays to Lake Como, and a Steinway sat in the bay window at the front of the house, overlooking mature gardens. The kitchen in Grassendale was a place of congregation and meeting, but here it assumed Teutonic functionality; all sharp edges and gleaming surfaces, as if a show house. Sarah, on her summer visits, never felt comfortable touching anything.

§

There was something to admire in her father's ability for attracting younger and more glamorous women. He was a sombre businessman – elderly now, although his upright and energetic demeanour gave him a vitality that belied his seven decades – without a hair on his head and a wardrobe that fitted his age and profession. He was a man of few words, businesslike but highly cultured and when he wasn't working seemed lost in his passions for classical or jazz music and with his head buried in a book. Like her mother, he knew and held opinions across a vast swathe of literature that seemed to range from Dante through to Martin Amis. He was wealthy; the art of making money seeming to come effortlessly and at times she wondered whether that was what attracted first her mother, and then Steffi. But that would be to sell both he and his women short, because beneath the initial impression of a rather dull businessman was someone more complex, more nuanced: urbane, generous, wise.

Steffi was thirty years his junior and in her mid-thirties when they married. She was blond, lean, tanned, with an athletic physique from long afternoons spent pounding the courts of the local tennis club. She owned an art dealership that catered for the city's elites and met Charles through her work, shortly after he returned to Germany. Julia, perhaps more attuned to Nadezhda's decline, despised her from the outset as a money-grabber, but she was affluent in her own right and, in her straightforward way, had always tried to treat the girls as grown-ups. There was no attempt to be a surrogate mother or big sister figure, no bending to their adolescent tastes.

While Julia remained in Liverpool in protest, Sarah on her biannual visits had grown fond of her. There was a candour and forthrightness in Steffi that was lacking in her own mother. After months facing Nadezhda's complexities and crises, dealing with someone so undemanding came as a relief.

She knew that Steffi, who was now in her forties, was desperate for children of her own, despite her father's age and despite the apparent lack of maternal instinct. Her father, in one of his brief moments of forthrightness, had told Sarah that they were seeking fertility treatment in Switzerland and of the toll it took upon both of them. But ostensibly she remained the same as ever: strident, businesslike, always emerging from her gallery in the late afternoon for an early dinner before returning back into the city for a concert or play.

Sarah's melancholy went largely ignored until they arrived in Hamburg, but Steffi was immediately alarmed by her appearance.

'You look like shit. What the hell happened?' she asked, taking her stepdaughter by the arm and leading her up the stairs to her room. Besides clothes, Sarah brought few of her possessions with her – her violin, a sketchpad, camera, a book – and had wrapped her Stuart Sutcliffe painting in brown paper, deeming it too valuable to be left in the hands of the removal men.

Amidst the sharp white lines and antiseptic atmosphere of her new bedroom, she rested and took long baths. After a few days her skin started to lose some of its greyness, but in the mornings she still felt dreadful, vomiting and unable to eat. Steffi brought tea and water to her room and offered to call a doctor. Despite her brusqueness, she was kind and tried to rationalise the vast changes that had happened over the previous weeks: her mother's death, changing countries, the loss of a boyfriend. She scratched the surface of Sarah's feelings, each day going a touch further than the previous day, trying to eke out more.

Julia, on the other hand, continued to ignore her, and had already escaped, renting a studio on the same block as the art school and moving out of her father's home without even unpacking her belongings.

On the second weekend, their second cousin Angela visited. She was the youngest daughter of her father's first cousin, a permanently resting actor, who had dropped out of each of a succession of increasingly expensive educational establishments before launching her theatre career in a provocative fringe ensemble five years earlier. Thereafter she went to a kibbutz to find herself, but wound up on the Silk Road trail and after traversing a path through Afghanistan and India ended up in Goa, where she seemed to have spent a couple of years doing no more, by her own admission, than smoking weed and partying. Angela was charming, brilliant and funny and her father, like the rest of the family, regarded her with their sombre, indulgent bemusement.

'We finally have you in the fatherland for good!' she greeted her. 'God, you look like shit.'

'Thanks,' said Sarah.

'I mean it. I realise that your life has been ruined, but you've really let yourself go!'

'It's been quite a few months.'

'So what do you want to tell your big cousin about first: the dead mother, the forsaken homeland, the vanquished boyfriend, or the war with the wicked sister?'

Angela shared the raven hair and pale complexion of the sisters, but retained the unkemptness of someone recently returned from the hippy tail. She wore a flowery dress over a pair of tight bootcut jeans and strappy sandals. Her nose was pierced and a dragon tattoo decorated her left ankle. At one stage she wore dreadlocks, but then declared that level of bedragglement required too much effort to maintain before lopping them off. She was warm and funny and had a perpetual bewilderment with the state of the world, as if everything that she faced was patently absurd. After weeks of existential crisis, she seemed the perfect antidote. For the first time in what seemed like an eternity, Sarah smiled.

'I don't think the reality has set in about Mother, just yet,' said Sarah. 'She lived life on the edge and had done a lot of living. I suppose you could look at her and say that it wasn't a surprise.'

'But she killed herself, right?' Angela asked with characteristic bluntness.

'They don't know until the coroner sits. There was no note and the toxicology report was inconclusive other than the fact that she drank shitloads of alcohol. I've thought about it lots. She had her bad periods, when she was very depressed, but I don't think of her as capable of this.'

She found herself talking about Paul, about what was seen the night of Nadezhda's death, the mystery and elusiveness that passed in its wake.

'And you didn't confront him?' Angela asked.

'Did I need to?'

Her cousin shrugged her shoulders. 'Do you believe he did anything wrong?'

'Julia said that he would slope away and not call; that it would be admission of guilt. And that's what happened.'

'Forget what Julia said. Do you think he'd do a thing like that? There's a narrative that your mother killed herself in a pique of guilt, but you don't seem to believe that; why do you believe this?'

Sarah paused and contemplated her cousin's cool rationale. Paul was chivalrous and shy; he wasn't opportunistic or predatory, it simply wasn't in his nature. It would be utterly out of character for him to behave in such a way. She thought of his vows and commitment to her. Why would he behave like that with her own mother? But instead of answering, Sarah burst into tears.

Angela held her as she sobbed. It was Sarah's first human contact since before all this had started, and she lay in her cousin's arms unburdening weeks of anxiety. She stayed there for ten minutes or more, as Angela shushed and stroked her hair.

When she had regained her composure, she said: 'I think it's Julia's sense of certainty that convinced me. She blames me for loving Paul, blames me for bringing him into the house and everything that followed. I'm at the root of all her anger. I think that's what has made it all so hard. Julia was everything to me, and now she's a stranger. It's not Mother that I'm missing or Paul; it's her.'

That evening she and Angela headed into Hamburg. 'There's nothing that alcohol and weed won't cure,' her cousin pronounced on their way into the city. Oktoberfest had just begun, and they drank and danced and partied their way around the heart of the city, returning to the house by the Elbe late into the night. For a few hours all of Sarah's problems seemed to have gone away. But the following morning, she found herself clutching the toilet basin throwing up her guts again.

Angela followed her into the bathroom and held her hair, as Sarah retched again.

When she was finished, with tears and saliva still spilling down her face, Angela held her by the shoulders and looked her in the eye. 'Darling,' she said. 'Do you think you might be pregnant?'

That evening, when Angela was gone, her father summoned her to his study. He was sat behind a floating art deco style desk; a great slab of walnut suspended on stainless steel legs. A pullover was drawn over his shoulders and he sat smoking his pipe pensively. Wisps of blue smoke circled in the light cast by his desk lamp. Her heart fluttered as Sarah wondered briefly if Angela had raised her earlier question with him.

'I need to talk to you about your mother's affairs.' There seemed deliberate ambiguity in his words, for it could mean one of so many things: the affairs of her heart, her literary estate, the dispersal of her assets. She sat in front of his desk, rapt like a patient at a doctor's surgery.

He puffed his pipe and continued: 'The sale of the house went through the day after we left, the money less a few costs has been divided between yourself and your sister and placed in accounts held by Coutts.' He handed her an account book. 'There's about thirty-seven thousand pounds in there. The sums from her literary estate will be passed through a limited company I set up to handle your mother's affairs years ago. I have made Julia and yourself directors and any earnings will pass through to a joint Swiss account to minimise the tax liability.' He passed over two forms and told her where to sign her name. 'Her belongings are held in storage. I will have her papers and her library properly archived and in the fullness of time yourself and Julia can decide what to do with them; I suspect they will have some value. As for her other things, I suggest you take whatever you like – you can keep it in storage for as long as you wish – and we will arrange for the rest to be dispersed. A lot of it has no monetary value, but I'm sure you and your sister would like some mementoes.'

He leaned back on his chair and puffed from his pipe. *Is that it?* she wanted to say, *The affairs of my extraordinary mother finalised between two puffs of a pipe.* But she knew her father's ways; he was always so impassive and businesslike, unsentimental to his core. Having lived through so much himself, she guessed that was how he conditioned himself to the world. He rubbed his temples and removed his glasses.

'Sarah, I don't believe your mother killed herself,' he said. 'I know Julia is very angry right now and believes that she did. But I knew and loved your mother very much and for a long time. It simply wouldn't have been in her nature.

'But equally there are some things, about your mother and I, that you should know.' He took a long puff of his pipe and for a second seemed to lose himself deep in thought. Finally, he said: 'Your mother wasn't the person that you thought she was.'

In the near dark of his elegant office, Charles Weisz began to tell the story of how he and Nadezhda had come to be.

∽

It was 1955, a decade after the end of the war. Austerity had ended, but many lives were grey and pallid. People still mourned their dead. Daily life could be a grind, even for the privileged. There were few material pleasures. His family were lucky, most escaping Germany for Britain and the US in the mid-thirties before the harshest of the Nazi policies had taken hold and long before the outbreak of fighting. Being in the shipping business had advantages in these times, he said, and they were able to facilitate the escape of many Jewish families in the years leading up to the war.

He led the family's Liverpool office, overseeing shipping and logistics from what was still Europe's greatest port. His brother ran operations from Glasgow. When fighting broke out, the War

Office requisitioned their fleet and the brothers worked with civil servants operating the Atlantic Fleet, bringing food and munitions in from North America. These were perilous convoys and many ships and lives were lost in the cold waters of the North Atlantic, but they played a central role in keeping Britain fed and the Allied forces supplied. 'The sacrifices made on the waters saved millions of lives in the long run,' he said.

Although he was part of the British war effort, turning over the resources of his business to the Allies and giving a monastic devotion to his war work he was still considered with suspicion, an outsider, a potential spy. He had anglicised his name as a young man – for nearly four decades, until he returned to Germany, Charles Weisz was Charles White and his daughters adopted that name – tried in everything he did to integrate into local society, but friendships and relationships did not come easily for he was still ultimately considered 'the Kraut' – even by members of the synagogue he briefly attended. 'Religion was never for me; it was a cultural badge for which our family suffered, but the lack of acceptance by our own tribe hurt the most,' he said. 'I was always an outsider.'

Only at the football, where he was part of a vast, sometimes unwieldy crowd did he feel a sense of belonging. 'We had sixty, seventy thousand people at Goodison Park each week, and our heroes – names that will mean nothing to you – Dean, Lawton, Jones, Mercer didn't care that I was an exiled German – maybe even a spy! But football on its own is not enough to sustain a man.'

When peace came he found his solace in London, where he would spend a weekend every few weeks losing himself in rooms of the National Gallery, the bookshops of Charing Cross Road, or at concerts or plays in theatre land. 'I was in my early forties. I was quite alone in the world, but I retained a hunger for culture and knowledge and acceptance and here I found it,' he told her. 'There was a jazz club on Carnaby Street, the Sunset Club, where the city seemed to come together. There were American GIs, Africans, Caribbean immigrants, Londoners, Jewish exiles; nobody cared what you looked like or where you'd come from. The music united everybody.'

Here he befriended a couple of editors and they formed a circle that got together every few weeks and spent the weekend traversing not only London's jazz clubs, theatres and art galleries, but also dining and drinking with writers, attending poetry recitals and readings. 'Spoken word had become a "scene" by the mid-Fifties,' he told her. 'And it was here that I met your mother.'

There was a myth, he said, that he was Nadezhda's patron and benefactor, that his money had given her the freedom and impetus to launch a career. But that wasn't true. She was published and critically appreciated, was making a living and held minor fame when they met. 'The only thing my money did was to bring me into contact with people in her extended circle; I was considering buying into a publishing house at that time and was friends with some editors and agents and so I came into contact with more writers, but that was it.' She had her circle, he had his, and there was an intersection that afforded them some common ground.

She was beautiful, passionate, wild, brilliant, avant garde and coveted. 'I was quite staid and quiet; I was also nearly a generation older than her. It was an improbable romance, but we clicked straight away. I can't begin to articulate how excited I was just to be with her, but also to be able to call her my girlfriend and then fiancée. It was invigorating.'

They married a few years after meeting. She moved to Liverpool and they bought their big house near the river. For several years they divided their time between the city where he worked and cultural life in London, but then family life began. Julia was born in 1962, Sarah the following year. 'And we were always happy, Sarah; you must remember that – they were good years when you were a young child. We had a rich cultural life and both I and your mother were professionally successful. We had many friends. Even Everton were the best team in the country and there was talk that I might join their board – can you imagine! We wanted for nothing.'

'So why did it change, Papa? Why did you walk away?'

He gave a grimace, as if the memory still pained him.

'Sometimes a situation causes you such intense pain, such turmoil, that you have to take radical action to remove yourself from it – even if it is the cause of even more suffering in the short term. As a family we left Germany in the 1930s because it wasn't possible to stay any longer and forty years later I felt the same with your mother.'

'What was it Papa? Why did you leave?'

'Because I couldn't stay. I shouldn't have left you and your sister like that, but I wasn't able to stay.' She thought for a moment that his implacable face would give in to tears, for even more than a decade later the recollection of his departure still pained him.

'You have to understand that the war and what those of my generation lived through changed everything. There were a lot of secrets and a lot of things that just weren't talked about. It was implicit, understood. Your mother never really asked me about what I did during the war – it was important, but mostly logistical, nothing dangerous or dramatic on the frontline – and while I had an understanding of what she had been through I never really asked her.

'I knew she had no family left. She alluded to a childhood in Vienna, but never talked about it in any detail. But what she had experienced during the 1940s or even how she came to live in Britain, that went almost completely unspoken. You try and join up the dots and make assumptions and I know I did, and I'm sure she did about me.

'She told me things over the years, fragments really. Then there was an interview she gave in 1968. I'll always remember it – "From Mauthausen to Merseyside" – and there was a vivid black and white portrait of her before the Liver Buildings. She was beautiful, brooding; like a film star. But I remember that she was very distressed after giving it. She had actually walked out on the journalist at one stage before resuming it and then when it came out she was very depressed. She had these depressions all the time that I knew her, and she simply disappeared for days at a time.

'You would have been five years old when the interview happened and it seemed to set something off within her. She had always looked forward, but suddenly she started to regress into her past. The hints at what happened became more frequent, but when I look back they didn't always add up. Dates overlapped. Details differed. Her father was a civil engineer, Jewish and part of the Habsburg family. Really? Her parents, her sister – she was always clear that she had a sister – were all murdered, but sometimes out of nowhere she mentioned a brother. Had she forgotten him, I started to wonder, or had he actually been an invention? She said she studied at LSE, but there was never anything to support this.

'I have to be honest, that at times I started to doubt her. She had this thing – this idea – that TS Eliot was her patron, had given her a job in the forties, but it was absolute nonsense. I knew it to be a lie. I did not call her out on it – perhaps I should have done – but there were more and more things that didn't seem right.

'She came to London with the Anglo-Jewish League in 1946, and then it was 1949 but she was granted asylum. Then it was somewhere in 1947. It seemed to me that she was becoming the unreliable narrator of her own narrative.

'This fixation with the past became more and more pronounced. She said she was working on a memoir of her war years. I was glad, in a way, because I thought that maybe she would get it out of her system. As a reader – not just her husband – I would have wanted to read it too. The lies – inaccuracies is how I considered them – I didn't really care about. All of our generation experienced things that I would never wish upon anybody else and we had our ways of dealing with things and I thought that this was hers. But I was concerned that it was unleashing a new volatility within her.

'It was a couple of years later that she showed me what she was working on, this so-called memoir.' He took off his glasses and rubbed his face. 'We sat in her study, she watching over me as I read it. It was only short, fragments of her past really. I imagine if you watch over somebody having a stroke it would be a similar experience to how she saw me. It was as if an explosion had gone off inside me and after it I was numb to my core.

'It was less a memoir than a confession. The years where we thought she was in the camp, she was on the other side of the fence.'

'How do you mean, Father?'

His pipe had extinguished and in the half-light, he fiddled around with his tobacco pouch before filling the chamber, lighting and taking a long comforting drag. The tobacco crackled and fizzed and glowed in the dark.

'She was the commandant's lover,' he finally said. 'She lived out the war as his plaything, in luxury and safety. Everything I thought I knew about her was wrong.'

Sarah sat wordlessly, trying to comprehend what he had told her.

'Until that day your mother and I rarely had a cross word. But I told her that she must never publish it, for it would ruin us all. We shouted and argued long into the night. She threw things at me, vases and glasses. It was a terrible row. Terrible. Eventually we stopped fighting. We tired ourselves out. By then I had already decided that I couldn't stay, couldn't even live in the same country as her. It was over.

'The consensus we reached was that she must never publish these words, must never even mention the manuscript's existence again. In return she wouldn't lose you and Julia. Maybe I'm old-fashioned, but I believed that children should be with their mother in these cases. And so that's what happened.'

They sat in stunned silence, Sarah feeling as if she had been struck across the temple. Everything she thought she knew about her mother's past was obliterated. There was no place in her mind for denial, no place for anger, just sheer and utter incredulity.

Finally she asked: 'But Papa, was the story true?' Sarah asked.

He shrugged his shoulders as if to say: maybe it was, maybe it wasn't.

'I'd like to think not. But over the years I have done some hunting, some tracking down. It obsessed me for a period. I think it's true that your mother wasn't who she said she was. There is no record of anyone of her name – or anything resembling it – passing through the camps in the way you would expect. And why lie about something so awful, so monumental?'

They sat in a silence marked by their mutual disbelief. Her father had had more than a decade to get used to this reality, but for Sarah it was all new, a fresh horror cast upon her.

'And this memoir you talk about, what happened to it?'

'Maybe it was destroyed,' he said. 'Maybe she gave it away. But I spent a long week carefully sorting through her belongings searching for it.'

'Did you find it?'

'No. It was no longer there.'

∽

Sarah lay awake all night contemplating the new world that she lived in. All the certainties she had grown up with were eviscerated. Her mother was dead, Julia had abandoned her in blind rage; her home and country were abandoned; what she knew of her past lay in shreds; and Paul, the boy who had briefly brought her such happiness, was gone. She felt naked, as if new to this world.

The following morning the nausea returned and she hugged the toilet basin, pleading for the sickness to end. She thought of Angela's question, something so ridiculous and throwaway that she hadn't given it a second thought at the time. But then she cast through her exhausted mind trying to think of the last time she had bled, trying to summon a memory of physical truth that would render her cousin's probing absurd. But the recollection would not come, and Sarah crept back under her duvet and fell into a deep nightmare-filled sleep.

While passing a row of shops on an afternoon walk, her eye was drawn to a display in a pharmacy window. 'Easy to Read Colour Result Advance Home Pregnancy Test: Results in Two Hours', the display read in English and German. She stared at the display for a minute, before heading inside and buying a test set.

In the en suite, Sarah unwrapped what seemed like a high school chemistry kit: a clear plastic tray, two test tubes, a test tube holder, an eye dropper, and a white plastic stir-stick. She had to urinate in the tray, then mix her urine with two clear liquids and stir the solution with the white plastic stick. The wait was painful. She lay on her bed, smiling at the absurdity of the situation and how she'd joke about it when she saw Angela at the weekend. But when she returned to the bathroom after what seemed like an eternity, there was nothing to laugh at. The water had turned a shade of turquoise, as clear and blue as the Mediterranean on a summer's day: she was carrying Paul's child.

ග

For the first time in weeks she felt a sense of calm, as if the act of confirmation – even of something so unexpected and disruptive – brought normality where none had existed. The nausea eased and she started to sleep normally.

At the weekend Angela visited and as they sat on Sarah's bedroom floor, listening to Yazoo and drinking tea she told her everything. Although she was colourful and non-conformist, at heart her cousin retained her Germanic pragmatism. She listened to Sarah unfurl her new realities and tackled them one by one.

'Nothing has changed about your mother other than there are now known unknowables,' she said. 'Does her war history change anything? It might change how people perceive her because she was a public figure, but she was still your mother, she still loved you. When we talk about the war in this country, we know that no one was blameless. People did unimaginable things simply in order to survive, or because they believed them to be right at the time. The guilty have been punished, but we can't be puritanical about the sins of an entire people. The past is the past; you can't change it, and any shame your mother might have can't reflect on you.'

She rolled a joint in her fingers, forming a roach with a piece of her cigarette packet and adding tobacco from a torn up Marlboro Light.

'I won't be joining you,' Sarah joked as Angela struck a match.

'And the boyfriend,' said Angela. 'Does this change anything with what might not have happened?'

'No,' Sarah replied. 'It's just another known unknowable.'

'And you won't ask him?'

'He had his chance to come forward.'

'So you believe your sister?'

Sarah shrugged. 'He knew where I was.'

'And now?'

She shrugged again. She had thought about this over the previous forty-eight hours; how Paul might react at the news of her pregnancy. She knew him to be noble, valiant – despite what was claimed – and could imagine him walking away from university to take a job and support his new family. She could see him being banished by his mother or marched up the church aisle to remove the stigma of an illegitimate child. This wasn't what she wanted: a resentful teenaged husband, stuck in a dead-end job, harangued by his suburban parents. It was the sort of fate he had worked so hard to escape; it wasn't one she intended to impose upon him.

'So you will get rid of the baby? There are ways. Discreet, safe, legal. No one else needs to know,' said her cousin. 'I can help you.'

The thought hadn't even crossed Sarah's mind. From the minute that she learned of her pregnancy she knew that she wanted the child more than anything she had ever wanted. She articulated this to her cousin, who gave an understanding smile.

'But Sarah, your life is just beginning. You're so talented. You have so much ahead of you. A baby – a little human – just stands in the way of what you can achieve. It changes everything.'

'It will give my life definition.'

'Darling Sarah. You've been through so many shocks the last while. Please think this through. You're committing your life, your future, your prospects to this child.'

But Sarah had already made up her mind. She would bring the baby up inside her father's house. Steffi would help. She had money of her own. Her father would support her. They would work through it.

Later that day, when Angela had returned home and her father's house was quiet and full of shadows, she approached her father in his study. He was sat on an Eames chair, his slippered feet rested on the ottoman. A single lamplight illuminated the novel he was reading. Steffi was out, dining with some friends. The soft lilt of Miles Davis's saxophone filled his study.

If the mood was cerebral, it soon turned into a kind of mayhem as she told her father what she learned earlier in the week. At first, he took the news in silent contemplation, puffing on his pipe. But then he erupted, in a way she had only been witness to once before, and launched his book at her, before reeling off a string of curses and obscenities in German and English.

'You fool! You fool! You utter fool! Why have you brought this upon yourself?' He hurled his pipe towards her and it hit a wall, a shower of orange sparks fizzing in the dark. 'You've ruined your life before it has even started! And with this stupid boy! You don't think your sister hasn't told me about him? You're an imbecile! You're just like your mother! You can't control yourself! Get out! Get out of my sight!'

She rushed up the stairs in tears. But when she had locked the door and calmed herself, her resolve had only increased. She would see this through with or without her father.

434

∽

The following day she remained exiled in her bedroom, as she had for so much of her time in Germany.

In mid-morning Julia, visiting from her studio flat in the city, knocked at her door.

'Is it true?' she asked brusquely, as she walked in without greeting. Her visage was still harsh and she bristled with hostility.

Sarah nodded.

'Are you keeping it?'

She nodded again.

'You fucking idiot,' she said and with that she left the room.

Scarcely could Sarah have imagined then that they were the last words she would ever speak to her.

∽

Steffi, by contrast, was more conciliatory, bringing her over the next few days a flow of cups of tea, cake, sandwiches, fresh bedding, towels and jugs of water. She was an impish, infectious presence; darting around the room, collecting used cups and discarded laundry, relaying snippets about her father's evolving moods; trying to summon clues as to her stepdaughter's ultimate intentions. Sarah pitied her, because she knew how badly she had wanted children of her own and some of what she had suffered physically and emotionally in her efforts to do so. Here she was now, readying herself to become an unlikely grandmother at scarcely the age of forty.

During the day when her father and stepmother were at work, Sarah mooched around the immaculately curated house, admiring the artwork, flicking through the books and moving from one piece of expensive furniture to the next. She rarely gave consideration to school, or continuing her education. She felt as if she was still on one of her summer visits, a tourist, an outsider. There was no sense of belonging or home.

Her father summoned her to his study one evening. She was keeping a low profile, confining herself to her bedroom in the evenings and mornings, until he and Steffi were gone for the day. Sometimes she passed him on the landing and he muttered a greeting, but Sarah cast her eyes down to avoid the confrontation that she so feared. All the while she could feel herself becoming physically and mentally stronger, and her body begin to change. There was a sudden plumpness to her breasts and her belly had begun to distend. It was too early to feel it move, but she could sense over those few days something different, something primal existing inside her.

Nearly a week of this uneasy truce with her father passed. He sat behind his vast walnut desk, while Steffi posited herself on the Eames chair. Sarah sat between them like a naughty schoolgirl about to be chastened.

'Your stepmother and I have discussed your situation and how we see it playing out,' he said. 'We are worried about you and your education and the repercussions this will have both for your career and whatever reputation you might have.' Sarah gave a grim smile. Her father was demonstrating his concern by talking down to her; it was, she realised, the only way he knew how.

'This is what we think should happen,' he said, before elaborating his plan. Sarah was to give birth in secret; nobody outside the house need know; she was new to Germany and the remainder of her schooling could be delayed by a year. The child would then be adopted by her father and Steffi. All the financial and emotional responsibility would lay with them. Sarah could remain at the house for as long as she liked; she could enjoy as many or as few of the privileges and burdens of parenthood as she wished. She would be considered a 'special' big sister, but be able to continue her life as she wanted.

'What do you think, Sarah?' Steffi asked. There was a manic glint in her eye and for a moment Sarah felt unsafe, as if her next utterance could spark some sort of violence against her. A feeling of defiance such as she had never known rose within her. She would protect this child with everything that she had.

She smiled thinly at her father and stepmother.

'I'll give it my consideration,' she said. 'There's such a lot to think about.'

The next morning when the house was empty for the day, she made her way down the stairs and called her cousin.

'Angela,' she said. 'You have to get me away from this place.'

∽

As Sarah and Marie made their way down the dirt track to the kibbutz two years later, pushing wheelbarrows full of date kernels and talking in the near dark, she described her disappearance from the Hamburg suburbs to this distant corner of Israel.

'I wanted to be away from anywhere that I knew to have the child. I feared my father and stepmother, feared that they would take the baby away from me. They were rich and powerful and I was just a girl in a foreign country. Would they use legal means to separate me from my baby?

'At the same time I was finished with England. I couldn't see a life for me there. It was part of my past and I was looking to the future. I was also scared that they might come after me. I wanted to disappear from the face of the earth.

'I had financial means to do what I wanted for a few years. I was naive and idealistic. I had in my mind California, Australia, the new world.'

Angela, however, had curtailed some of Sarah's more excessive ideas. 'You're not going backpacking, darling. You need somewhere safe, with good people who can support you when the baby comes. You can't just go to some of these places and expect to start afresh with a child and no one around you.' There was a musicians' commune in Asturias, a convent in Tuscany, a cooperative school over the border in Austria, but Angela put them all out of Sarah's mind. 'I know a place,' she said. 'I have lived there. I know the people. They have a supportive network. They will take care of you. You will be safe.'

The place was Kibbutz Samar in Israel's deep south. It had been founded on social-anarchist foundations in the mid-Seventies. Angela had lived there as a volunteer for six months. 'There are committees and rules, but it puts the individual at the heart of the experience,' she said. 'If you have a community of satisfied individuals, you are going to have a much stronger community. It is very secular. It is revolutionary in terms of the kibbutz movement.' In the confines of Sarah's bedroom, she showed her photographs of her stay: of the wild oranges of the desert nights, the lush groves of date palms, and the modest but immaculately clean living quarters; she sold her the ideal and promised to join when she had the child. Together they plotted Sarah's escape to this new world.

The logistics of the plan were simple. Sarah would make a chain of travel reservations going in a predictable direction one way – Hamburg, London, Cambridge, Liverpool – while travelling in the opposite direction – Amsterdam, Tel Aviv, Eilat. Here Ariel, one of Angela's friends, would collect her and take her to the kibbutz. Sarah could teach music, English and art in the commune's small school. They had had a vote on it already. She would join as a volunteer and after two years they would have another vote on whether she would become a fully fledged member: a kibbutznik. By the time her father had realised he'd been duped, Sarah would be far out of sight. Angela would follow in the new year and pledged to stay for six months until, at least, the baby was born.

And so, one late October morning, an hour after Steffi and her father left for work, a taxi took Sarah to Hamburg Hauptbahnhof for her train to Schiphol airport. By nightfall she was in Tel Aviv, spending the night in the arrivals hall of Ben Gurion airport. First thing the next morning she took an internal flight to Eilat. As promised, Ariel was waiting for her at the small airfield with his flatbed truck; he was a tanned gregarious man in his early fifties.

'So you're our fugitive?' he laughed and put her case in the back of his flatbed truck.

He drove her north through the desert, a harsh and jagged landscape, where Bedouin appeared from time to time, herding goats in the bare vegetation. The ground was mostly beige and white- coloured rocks and stones.

'This is wild country,' Ariel said. 'Jordan ten miles that way; Egypt twenty miles that way. We are wedged in between.'

Ariel explained how the strictures of Kibbutz Samar worked. They placed great impetus on the individual's role at the heart of the community, instead of dictating rules and jobs as other kibbutzim did. 'Normally in a kibbutz there is a ranking system that affords status to those who live in a community,' he explained and screwed up his nose. 'I imagine it is the same with prisoners in a jail. Volunteers have the least amount of status in a kibbutz; new volunteers considerably less than that. But here we treat everyone the same. If you like it and decide to stay, we will have a vote on whether you become a full kibbutznik.' She must have given a look of apprehension, for he chimed: 'But it's okay. You'll like us, and we'll like you. You'll love it here, and it's a wonderful place for a child to grow up.'

Twenty-four hours after leaving the Hamburg suburb she arrived at the kibbutz, and was driven up the palm-lined road. As they drove, Ariel pointed out features of the small commune: swimming pool, dining hall, laundry, nursery, school. Her living quarters were a small chalet-type accommodation. She shared for the first few months with Andrea, an American volunteer who was returning to New York for Rosh Hashanah. 'She's a JAP,' laughed Ariel. Sarah blinked in confusion. 'Jewish American Princess – it's okay, you'll like her.'

For the first time in months she relaxed. It all felt so fresh, so new. There was a freedom about the place. Here there was no past, no history – only the present as if everyone was starting afresh. That also bred a lack of inhibition; people spoke with freedom and clarity. She was among strangers and there was no shared narrative; instead they were all working to define the future. They looked to what lay ahead and in making new memories rather than reliving old ones.

The work for most of those who lived there was, for the most part, arduous and monotonous. Sarah taught music, art and English at the school, but until she was heavily pregnant also helped with the farming. There was a seriousness about the work. Talk and general chitchat was frowned upon. But after they returned to the communal dining hall the place filled with laughter and talk and eating. There was plenty of free time too, and Sarah read and painted and played her violin. Fridays and the Shabbat meal were the highlight of the week. People dressed up for dinner.

Andrea was highly politicised and her rhetoric was filled with how frequently Jewry had suffered, and would continue to do so. She probed about Sarah's parents and their fate in the war. But she was also funny and gregarious and a good host to the intricacies and absurdities of life in Israel's deep south.

The kibbutzniks were an eclectic bunch. Everyone was from somewhere else: all over Europe, the USSR, North Africa, South America. Most spoke several languages, but at the school and for the children Hebrew was the first language.

The first few days passed slowly, but as she settled into the gentle routines of life in the desert the weeks and months flew by. Andrea returned to the US and early in the new year her cousin Angela joined her as she had promised to do so.

As well as belongings Sarah had stashed with her, she brought with her news of her cousin's discarded past. Her father had raged at Sarah's disappearance and then retreated in on himself. He hired a private detective, who followed Sarah's dummy route through England but invariably uncovered nothing before giving up. Julia was rarely seen or heard from. It was as if the family had imploded in the space of a few months. And yet by Christmas he was staging a grand drinks party, smoking cigars and sipping champagne as if none of it had happened. 'You know what he's like,' mused Angela. 'Business as usual.'

The days were short and the nights cold in the desert winter. Sarah was excused from kitchen and farming duties and spent her days at the school as her belly swelled and the baby's arrival neared.

He was born the day after Passover, a time of spring and optimism. He had Sarah's dark hair and pale skin, but had inherited the sky blue eyes of his father. She named the child

Simon Paul Weisz.

Ariel visited on the first night, with a blanket his wife had knitted for the new arrival. 'The responsibility to raise the child is for all of the kibbutz,' he explained. 'For the kibbutz, the children are at the heart of everything.'

3

Sarah had never been fearful of being alone as a mother, and any lingering concerns left her the day that she arrived at Kibbutz Samar. She saw in her first moments there the nurseries and schooling facilities, the sense of collectivism that imbued everything. There were many strong figures in Simon's childhood and soon after he was born they were afforded the full status of kibbutznik.

The years of Simon's childhood were quiet and happy, with a revolving cast of interesting and caring friends. Sarah continued to teach, but nourished her soul with painting and music. She had many suitors. The transient nature of the kibbutz community brought with it both an alternating array of arrivals as well as a live and let live mentality. But they came and they went and few lasted longer than six or seven months. Her single status attracted wry comments from her friends. 'Tied to a child at eighteen and with a roving eye for life,' Ariel joked. Yet the reality was that she liked no one's company as much as her own; the freedom to mother on her own terms, and to paint and photograph and indulge her own passions when she wasn't laden with the work of the kibbutz. She was self-dependent. There wasn't a maternal instinct to slake.

The other truth was that no one filled the void left by Paul. She told herself that you held the first love in your heart until your last rites. No one made her as happy as she was that summer; it was an ideal that had been nurtured but never lived up to.

She thought of him sometimes and wondered if he still thought of her, whether he had tried to look for her or had any notion that he had a son. She had long stopped believing the conspiracy theories about Paul and her mother; they were too fanciful, too extreme, and she regretted her adolescent mind for giving them any credence. She was too emotionally immature, she realised now, and looking back she just wished she had taken the time to call and find out the truth, but she wasn't sure if it would have changed anything. She would still have moved to Germany, she would still have given birth to Simon – but under what circumstances she couldn't imagine. Life in the kibbutz made her happy and gave her a sense of belonging that she hadn't encountered before and so she regretted nothing about what transpired.

She didn't miss her father, for she hardly knew him, but the schism with Julia played on her mind. For her, it was the ending of the one certainty of her childhood. But the hostility and anger revealed a side of her sister previously alien to her. Maybe she would have softened when the grieving ended. Maybe nothing would have changed. But with the passage of time, the yearning for her lost sister diminished, for she existed in a new world.

Simon knew about his famous grandmother and the complicated and fractured family Sarah had walked away from. The communal nature of his upbringing gave Simon many strong male figures, but periodically the questions arose about Paul. He knew that his father was a good man, that his mother had loved him very much. But he didn't know his identity. For many of these passing years Sarah herself had no conception of where

Paul was or what he was doing. She tried to imagine identities for him: novelist, crusading lawyer, diplomat; scarcely could she have imagined that for many years he lived a few hours' drive away, chronicling the affairs of her adopted country.

It was early in the new century that she stumbled across Paul's whereabouts. The internet had connected her to the outside world in ways that she hadn't thought possible. For so long she was remote from everything, even from the news agenda and the ruptures in her adopted country Israel. Simon was undertaking his national service and was stationed near Jerusalem. The second intifada was underway and she checked for news, emails and instant messages every few hours, hoping upon hope that he was safe amidst the unfolding carnage. And there, like a bolt from the blue, was Paul, reporting from the frontline of a conflict their son was fighting in.

She clicked on the byline image. His face had filled out, and his hair thinned, but it was definitely him. A Google search revealed he had been based in the Occupied Territories in the past, but was returning as a special correspondent. At the click of a mouse she found him in Yugoslavia, Rwanda, Iraq, Chechnya: a litany of the late twentieth century's hellholes. His email address was incorporated into the byline. Two clicks and they would be reconnected. She pondered the approach, not sleeping for days as she cast around the implications of emerging from the shadows. The painful parting, the secrets and lies about her mother's legacy, the clandestine son – who was now, most improbably of all, a soldier yards away from where he stood with his notebook and laptop.

But she desisted. She always did. There were too many known unknowns. What if he was married, had other children? What were the consequences of her letting off the human hand grenade of a secret child in their midst? In the unfolding intifada Paul stood behind Palestinian lines; what were the ethics of revealing to him now that he stood face to face with an unknown son?

For years she followed Paul around the world, reading his reporting assignments as soon as they hit the web. He was brilliant, articulate, forensic; but he gave so little away of his inner life. She was scared of disrupting any personal life he had; fearful also that he would not forgive her for abandoning him, for giving in to the lies and innuendo; terrified, ultimately, of his rejection.

Her logic changed as the Noughties progressed and she gained fame and recognition of her own. She had started to exhibit in the mid-1990s, desert-scapes and a small exhibition of black and white photography of a Bedouin tribe. The kibbutz displayed her work in the visitor centre it built to cater for the small stream of curious visitors and tourists, and continued to do so when she left the community and moved into a small villa a few kilometres down the road. At the time of the move, Simon was just about to enter national service and would progress straight to university and, while Sarah retained close bonds with the community, she had decided the time was right for some distance.

One afternoon she received a call from Ariel. An American tourist from a cruise ship had visited and liked her work: did she have any more for sale? Could they come and visit her now? 'Now?' asked Sarah, casting her eye around her home studio and trying to count the number of passable canvases that were stacked up against her walls.

'Now!' said Ariel. 'I think you need to meet this lady, Sarah. She's bought everything!'

The lady was June Hirschfeld, a gallery owner from New York's Upper East Side. She made straight for the little exhibition at the kibbutz, marvelling at Sarah's use of the two mediums. 'It's very rare to see such an accomplished brand of abstract expressionism in a young artist,' she said. 'It shows great maturity. At once liberated and deeply considered. These paintings are ablaze with kinetic energy, powerful symbolism and brooding colour combinations; they're simply wonderful.' When she was told Sarah's story, she licked her lips and said, 'Every artist needs a narrative and what a story this is!'

At first, Sarah was reticent and shy; it wasn't often that she met anyone from outside her community, least of all New York art dealers. She told her, expressly, that she wanted no mention of her mother in connection with her work; if she was to make a name for herself it would be on her own merits. June muttered her disinterested agreement as she leafed through the piles of canvases stacked against the wall of her small home studio.

'First time around, we split everything fifty-fifty,' she said. 'First time around you never know how people will react, but I'm sure my clients will adore your work.' She had a Louis Vuitton clutchbag, which seemed incongruous to their desert surroundings, and from it she produced a roll of hundred-dollar bills. 'There's five thousand dollars down payment. I'll send you the rest of your proceeds in a few months.' Ariel and one of his sons started removing the canvases from the studio and putting them with the rest in the back of his pick-up truck.

The two women talked as they left the studio, but as they exited June's eye was drawn to another painting that hung in the hallway of Sarah's home. It was the Stuart Sutcliffe painting – the angry melange of reds and oranges – she had hung in her bedroom as a teenager. Sarah told the art dealer about him and how it came into her possession. It was, she realised as she spoke, her last link to Liverpool.

'The fifth Beatle?' June said smiling.

'The fourth really. Before Pete and Ringo. He died when he was twenty-one. They said John never got over his death.'

'It's wonderful.'

Four months later an envelope with a cheque arrived at Sarah's home bearing a New York postmark. She always remembered the amount, for it was the same in dollars as what she had received for her share of the house in Grassendale: $37,000. And so her career as an artist began.

∽

Later, when individual paintings sold for that amount and more, and the Tate and the Pompidou began to acquire her work, she used her burgeoning fame and recognition to justify her withdrawal from her old world. 'Anyone who wants to find me can do so now,' she told Angela on her visits, or, as the new century ensued, video calls. Angela warned that she was becoming idiosyncratic and difficult in middle age, qualities she despaired of in her own parents. 'You're absurd! You Germanised your name! Nobody knows you as Sarah Weisz!' She stubbornly resisted Angela's attempts to bring a reconciliation with her family; she didn't need them, she insisted, she was happy without them and didn't need the complexities they might unleash.

Her father, she learned in the midst of one of these visits, died in 2000. He worked in his shipping company until his nineties, estranged from not only Sarah, but Julia too. Angela was unable to elaborate on this new schism; nobody had seen nor heard of Julia for years. Like Sarah she had just taken off one day and become lost to the world. In more reflective moments, Sarah reflected on the sadness of her family; the ruptures and disputes that could all be linked to that one tragic night in Liverpool. Years later she would be told of Julia's early death from pancreatic cancer. She wept then, mourned for months for all that she had lost.

Her career and the money it brought afforded Sarah opportunities to travel, often to the American east coast, but later to the Far East and China in particular, where her work became wildly popular. The influx of new wealth brought a frenzy of bidding, for the Chinese market considered her trademark red and orange palettes to be lucky. She became wealthy beyond her imagination, but knew not what to do with her money for she had everything she needed in the humble life she lived in Eilat, a place she always gladly returned to after her trips.

Simon, on leaving the army, pursued a career in corporate law that brought him placements all over the world: Singapore, Hong Kong, London. Sarah visited him in all of these cities and stayed for weeks on end, immersing herself in museums, art galleries, restaurants. Hers was an increasingly solitary existence, but she had almost everything she wanted. She was fulfilled with work, had money, travelled, had a home she loved and friends there. Simon had his father's seriousness, his grandfather's businesslike demeanour, but also retained his mother's ability to laugh in the face of life's absurdities. He was gay; she met and befriended all of his boyfriends and they travelled each year to Tel Aviv, or Ibiza, or the Mardi Gras in Sydney. Hanging out in gay clubs and partying long into the night kept her young.

Simon had an intermittent curiosity in his heritage. Sarah told him about Nadezhda often, her extraordinary life and the contradictions and complexities of her character, also the challenges of growing up in a house where chaos often reigned. He knew about his grandfather and Julia too, but the source of the schism she remained elusive about. Paul was something unspoken, a topic that had become unbroachable between mother and son.

They were holidaying in Sydney in early 2018 when she decided to tell him about Paul. Mardi Gras had ended and they were walking out of the city, up Broadway, and towards the city's elegant inner suburbs when there was a clap of thunder and the skies opened and they ran for cover into the nearest pub, the Australian Youth Hotel. It was like a throwback to the old country, with its antique screens and coloured glasswork around the bar. The room was lined with oak. It immediately reminded Sarah of the pubs she frequented in Liverpool a lifetime before.

'Your father would like it in here,' she said, and she asked Simon to order her a pint of Guinness, as if her nostalgia for the dark, thick, stout would summon her lost lover. But the drink did stir something inside her, for she suddenly felt unencumbered enough to talk expansively and at length about Paul, their summer-long romance and the intensity of feelings it still summoned nearly four decades later. She talked too about the rifts and disputes, the broken family that that whirlwind summer left in its wake.

When she finished talking, her glass and several more were drained.

'Any questions?' she asked, smiling and clapping her hands together.

Simon was approaching his late thirties now and his once dark hair was flecked into a salt and pepper combination. He had never settled, moving from one city to another, from one lucrative job to the next, boyfriends left in his wake. He was a high flyer, loved by his scores of friends from all different walks of life, but there was always a restlessness about him, as if his mind was always focussed on the next move, the next break. Sarah considered this often, and wondered if solving the mystery of his parentage might ease this restiveness.

'What I don't understand is how this went unresolved for so long,' he said. 'A phone call is all it would have taken. He could have told you the truth and everything would have changed.'

'It was more complicated than that,' she replied.

'Mother, it really wasn't.'

'Sometimes in life we put barriers up where they don't need to exist and it sets us on paths that we don't ever expect.

'I miss my sister; we separated over something that we should never have fallen out about and maintained a rift until it was too late. I regret losing touch with your father. But then maybe we weren't meant to be. You and I wouldn't have lived the life that we lived had I returned to Liverpool and made your father give up on university so that he could take on a dreary job to support us. Maybe it would have been better, maybe it would have been worse.'

She took her son by the hand. 'I'm a great believer in fate, and I think that fate has dealt us a good hand so far.'

4

Life and fate. It became Sarah's stock answer whenever her son ruminated on the mistakes of the past. She invited him to contact his father, knowing that he never would without her lead. He became irritated by her stubbornness, this streak that would rather leave destiny to the Gods rather than her own hand. Simon knew that a couple of clicks on his laptop would resolve so many questions, but without his mother's blessing he knew he never would.

He learned about Christopher and how his lies far transcended those in his circle. He relayed to his mother stories of his spin-doctoring for British politicians: his dodgy dossier and lies that led to the outbreak of an illegal war; he emailed her his father's evisceration of his former friend, when his lies about the Hillsborough tragedy reached full public consciousness. His entreaties met no response, as if they served as confirmation of the folly of years of silence.

What are you hiding from, Mother? he emailed her one afternoon.

Life and fate has a funny habit of working things out, she pronounced in her reply.

Later that year, Sean Kendall's biography of Nadezhda was published and what Simon assumed was a literary biography of a hitherto obscure figure became a phenomenon. His mother bristled at the mention of the book, said that she knew Sean Kendall and that it could only mean bad things. Why hadn't she been consulted about the book? she asked. She stopped considering herself an anonymous figure when she found recognition as an artist, but couldn't recognise that the world was a bigger place than she imagined. Dropping from the face of the earth for two decades, exorcising her past and changing her name made her anonymous to those who knew her in her old life.

Simon relayed to her the parts about his father and his role on the night of Nadezhda's death, how it finally exonerated him from the lies that Christopher allowed to pass. 'Can't you see that he tried to protect you? He thought that concealing your mother's story was the right thing to do; he felt it was so ominous that he'd sacrifice everything to save you from the truth.' Simon's earnestness and sense of conviction reminded her of Paul when he was half his son's age. She burst into tears and hung up the video call. She mourned for her lost love and for her own foolishness.

∽

It took a long time for Sarah to summon the courage to read her mother's biography. She knew there would be uncomfortable truths; realities about her mother's life that she hadn't been fully confronted with before. Most of all she was scared of what she might find about herself.

It was in the long spring of 2020, when most of the world seemed to have closed down over the spread of a flu virus. Simon was in Melbourne and she was stuck in Eilat, alone with her paints and her camera, plans to fly to Australia and the US laid to waste by the pandemic. In the end she found herself not even able to drive down the road to her friends at the kibbutz. Was this a vision of the future she faced, alone and cut off from the world?

As a long and empty evening stretched ahead, she summoned Sean Kendall's book from one of her shelves, where it had lain untouched and ominous since Simon brought it on one of his visits eighteen months earlier. She remembered Kendall as a rough teenager, whom her mother spent an inordinate amount of time trying to give a start in life, only to be repaid by lurid headlines and lies. It dented Sarah's trust in human nature, and she long wondered what sort of book he would write – even if he was now a professor.

The parts about what happened on the night Nadezhda died were as Simon had described. But there was a lot there that she hadn't known, particularly about the war years, that altered her perception of who her mother had actually been. Her mother tormented herself as a villain, and her father had seen her in such terms as well. But the reality was that she was as much a victim as anyone else in the camps, and in acting towards her own survival had saved many lives. Kendall had reclaimed her mother's reputation and legacy in a way that she couldn't have thought imaginable.

She sat reading the book from cover to cover and at dawn called her son. It was late afternoon in Melbourne, and he was finishing work for the day when he answered.

'We'll go and find Paul,' she said. 'I promise you: before you turn forty, we will meet your father. If life and fate doesn't set him upon us before then, we'll go and find him. But first there's one thing I need to do.'

5

She had left Liverpool forty years earlier, but the city had never really left her. Her final memories were defined by tragedy, but she retained many good recollections of her home city: the fallen grandeur of its architecture, scarred as it was then by pollution and war damage; the spirit and the devil-may-care attitude of its people; the defiance in the teeth of a hostile government that actively considered a policy of 'managed decline' for it. She had never gone back, never really considered going back – despite Simon's occasional entreaties – until the day the mayor invited her to do so.

It was almost a throwaway remark at the end of a long video call with one of June Hirschfeld's assistants, Norah. She was at the start of their day in New York, Sarah nearing the end of hers in Israel. Even after all these years, June still managed her affairs, handling sales, invitations – of which there were many – and all other inquiries. They were nearing the end of their bimonthly call, when Norah said they'd had an email from a British mayor's office asking if she wanted to partake in a citywide exhibition.

'Which city?' Sarah asked.

'Let me search my inbox,' Norah replied. 'I don't think there was much money involved – something to do with an anniversary of some riots.'

Sarah's heart skipped a beat. 'Was it Liverpool?'

From the end of the long-distance line, Norah read out the email. 'The mayor of Liverpool is hosting a citywide retrospective to commemorate the fortieth anniversary of the riots in Liverpool 8 and the epoch-changing summer. We would like to invite you to submit your work…'

'I'll do it,' said Sarah.

'Wait, there's no mention of a fee,' Norah drawled in her thick New York accent.

'I don't care. It's something I want to do.'

∽

One of the few things Sarah salvaged from her former life was a box of photographs and negatives taken while studying for the A levels she never completed. They were hidden at Angela's house while they planned her escape, and subsequently brought to her. It was a catalogue of a lost summer, and when she opened it up for the first time in years the memories all came back. The cathedrals. The anarchic Bullring. The bombed-out church. An outraged drug addict. Street urchin brothers they found playing football. An abandoned warehouse. And there was Paul, her lost love, her son's father: stood beside the decaying Albert Dock, on the Mersey ferry, in front of the broken clock at Salisbury Dock. She had a critic's eye now and knew the photographs were good, technically and aesthetically; they retained the energy of youth, but were at the same time deeply considered. She was proud of them.

And now, fifteen months after that first invitation, they were to be exhibited at the Anglican Cathedral, the vast construct of post-Victorian Gothic that towered over her home city. She was making the long journey across Europe to be there for the opening of the exhibition and a gala lunch, attended by the great and good of Liverpool. The thought of it made her smile wryly, for it was the sort of event her mother would have both loved and hated.

Her work was in an annex titled 'My Summer of Love'. She had chosen thirty of her photographs, which were printed on huge display boards, the grain of the old film accentuating a city that she remembered being defined by its dirt and decay. It was August 2021. Forty years had passed since her anguished departure from her home city. She was now older than Nadezhda was when she died. She wondered how the city might have changed – they said that it was a city transformed – and how she would feel about it all. She expected everything to be different and yet nothing at all. She had always been an instinctive person. What would be her first thought on returning? Would there be, after all these years, a sense of belonging, or would she remain an outsider?

Her connecting flight at Heathrow was late and she was fearful that she would miss everything, but Tony, the driver who was waiting for her at Manchester airport, told her that everything would be just fine. As they sped down the M62 he talked to her about left-wing politics, football, music – passions that she recalled fed the city, but for so long had been absent from her world.

At the Hope Street Hotel, an elegant Georgian-fronted building that stood midway between the two cathedrals she left her bags at the front desk and left immediately for the Anglican Cathedral. She was fifteen minutes late – 'fashionably so', her mother would have joked – and there was a freshness in the air after a recent deluge of rain, which ran in rivulets down the

Yorkstone gullies and splashed on the cobbles of the cathedral's approach.

It was a stunning building – Britain's largest church and the world's largest Anglican cathedral – managing at once to inspire awe at its size, while providing in its vestibules and side chapels a sense of intimacy and seclusion from the madness of the world. She stood in its narthex, taking in the bewildering scale of the building as the distant burr of the diners rose from the other end of the building.

'Sarah Weisz?' A young female attendant was waiting for her. 'We were told you were running late. It's fine, you haven't missed much. Will I take you through to the lunch?'

'Would you mind if I took a quick look at the exhibition first? Just so I know my way around.'

'Of course, let me take you through.'

She followed her through the cathedral and down a marble flight of stairs and down into the depths of the crypt. It was quiet here, and empty but for a gallery attendant who stood bored behind a desk. From an anteroom towards the end of the crypt she could hear animated voices. She remembered the Liverpool way; everything was a little drama.

'It's this way,' said the attendant, and she followed her towards an opening with a large display bearing the title of her exhibition. Sarah's heart gladdened as she saw her name and the familiar grain of a photograph taken a lifetime ago.

'The name is wrong,' said the voice from the anteroom. It was animated and confused, not aggressive, but almost pleading. 'Why is the name wrong? Why is it wrong?'

'Oh dear!' blushed the attendant. 'Someone's not happy.'

Sarah followed her into the room. A man was in deep conversation with another attendant on the other side of the room, in front of a photograph taken from the fore of the *Royal Iris* forty years earlier, blown up in size so that it filled an entire wall.

The couple didn't look up at first and Sarah paid no notice to her old work, for another image was emerging in front of her. A light was shining, extinguishing all the years of shadows, saturating her in blinding light.

She trembled.

The man looked up.

Paul.

She was paralysed by what she had seen.

Paul walked towards her, but she remained rooted to the spot, frozen by the sight of this ghost.

My father reached for my mother and embraced her, the long lost years and loneliness vanishing as she melted into his arms.

The outsiders finally belonged.

Note on historical sources
& acknowledgements

Some of the historical matter dealt with in *The Outsiders* – the Holocaust, the Hillsborough tragedy, Palestine's intifada, the Yugoslavian wars and Liverpool race riots – arguably transcends fiction. To maintain historical accuracy, where possible I have tried to incorporate the words of actual eyewitnesses to an event. In particular, the lies spoken in the wake of the Hillsborough disaster were not something a reasonable person could make up: they are quoted in the novel as they were said at the time – by police officers and newspapermen – and treated with the contempt with which they deserve.

I must confess to one liberty with Liverpool's geography: there is no writer's garden at St James' Cemetery, where no one has been buried since before World War Two.

Although it is fiction, lots of life experience and plenty of reading informs these pages. In particular I would like to acknowledge the works of the great Czech novelist and survivor, Arnošt Lustig, as well as the French historian, Christian Bernadac, whose early histories of the Holocaust, now out of print, maintain the freshness and anger of eyewitness accounts. In particular, *The 186 Steps* is a breathtaking account of the horrors of the Mauthausen camp. I worked with my former colleague, Simon Hughes, closely on his definitive history of Liverpool in the 1980s, *There She Goes*, which was a vital reference point. I've spoken to many war correspondents over the years, but Lindsay Hilsum's *In Extremis: The Life of Marie Colvin* was a vital work when checking the plausibility of Paul's career.

I would like to thank my first readers: Mary Corbett, John Corbett, Veronica Miller, Helen Johnson and Simon Hart. Ceylan Hussein provided sage advice on the use of German within the text. Sarah Hughes has provided endless wisdom and support marketing and publicising the book. The former Liverpool footballer Howard Gayle always makes me think twice and think differently about my home city. I have wanted to work with Lightning Books editor Scott Pack for a number of years and was glad that the opportunity to do so lived up to expectations. Thank you to Kat Stephen for her exemplary copy-editing. The photographer Ant Clausen captured the essence of my home city in his evocative cover photo.

More than two decades ago as a precocious student I showed off a very early and very rough draft of what forms the prologue to this book to a young Irish girl in my student residence. Somehow impressed by my prose and aspirations as a novelist, she agreed to go out with me and, after more than twenty years of hanging around, Catherine – long since my wife – has finally seen it become part of my first novel. She didn't have to wait as long as Sarah and Paul for a happy ending, but I hope the wait was worth it. This book is dedicated to her.

If you have enjoyed *The Outsiders*, do please help us spread the word – by putting a review on Amazon (you don't need to have bought the book there) or Goodreads; by posting something on social media; or in the old-fashioned way by simply telling your friends or family about it.

Book publishing is a very competitive business these days, in a saturated market, and small independent publishers such as ourselves are often crowded out by the big houses. Support from readers like you can make all the difference to a book's success.

Many thanks.
Dan Hiscocks
Publisher
Lightning Books

Also from Lightning Books

The Mating Habits of Stags
Ray Robinson

Shortlisted for the Portico Prize 2019

Midwinter. As former farmhand Jake, a widower in his seventies, wanders the beautiful, austere moors of North Yorkshire trying to evade capture, we learn of the events of his past: the wife he loved and lost, their child he knows cannot be his, and the deep-seated need for revenge that manifests itself in a moment of violence.

On the coast, Jake's friend, Sheila, receives the devastating news. The aftermath of Jake's actions, and what it brings to the surface, will change her life forever. But how will she react when he turns up at her door?

The Mating Habits of Stags is a journey through a life of guilt and things unsaid. As beauty and tenderness blend with violence, Robinson subtly explores love and loss in a language that both bruises and heals.'

Poetic and powerfully brutal...a one-off
The Times

A wonderfully empathetic account...full of candour, lyricism and compassion
The Spectator

A taut, spare story of survival that turns on its heel to become something altogether braver, rarer and more precious
Melissa Harrison